T

COME HELL OR HIGH WATER

A DCI LOGAN NOVEL

JD KIRK

COME HELL OR HIGH WATER
ISBN: 978-1-912767-59-5

Published worldwide by Zertex Media Ltd.
This edition published in 2021.

1

www.jdkirk.com
www.zertexmedia.com

BOOKS BY J.D. KIRK

A Litter of Bones

Thicker Than Water

The Killing Code

Blood & Treachery

The Last Bloody Straw

A Whisper of Sorrows

The Big Man Upstairs

A Death Most Monumental

A Snowball's Chance in Hell

Ahead of the Game

An Isolated Incident

Colder Than the Grave

Northwind: A Robert Hoon Thriller

WRITING AS BARRY J. HUTCHISON

Space Team

Dan Deadman: Space Detective

The Sidekicks Initiative

CHAPTER ONE

HERBERT GIBSON WAS A JOKE. And he knew it.

Truth be told, he always had been.

It had started in Primary One, when he'd come waddling into the classroom with his drawers around his ankles, asking the teacher to wipe his arse for him, because his mum wasn't currently available to handle the task.

He could still remember the look of horror on her face. The stares of his classmates. The whispers. The giggles. The rising prickly heat that told him he'd made a mistake. That he'd messed up. That this whole school thing he'd been so excited about might not be everything he'd hoped for.

It had just sort of snowballed from there.

Being sick on Elizabeth Wilson on the school trip to Blair Drummond Safari Park in Primary Seven.

Being caught tugging himself off under the desk in Miss Bartholomew's Maths class in the first year of high school.

Being convinced to run for School Captain in Sixth Year, only to receive just one vote. His own.

His whole life, he'd been laughed at. Teased. Ridiculed.

Today, though, things changed. Today, he was going to show them. He was going to show them all. They might have laughed at him before, but no one would be laughing after what he was about to do.

He might have spent the first nineteen years of his life as a nobody, but in a few hours, everyone would know his name. Everyone would be talking about what he'd done.

He just needed to figure out where he was first.

His phone had no signal out here. Luckily, he'd anticipated that, and had gone old school with a fold-out paper map. What he hadn't been prepared for was just how large the map unfolded to. Nor did he have any idea how to refold it so that it fit back in the plastic holder it originally came in.

As a result, it was sort of bunched together in his hand so that it might spring open at any given moment. A rain shower earlier had helped take some of the fight out of it, but it now felt heavy and limp, like it might rip apart if he tried to spread it out again.

Fortunately, he was reasonably confident that he wouldn't have to. His target was somewhere on the section of the map he was studying. He was sure of it.

Herbert raised his eyes from the drawing of the terrain and looked out over the real deal. He could see the coast from where he was standing. Water. Rocks. That sort of thing.

"So that's... what? North?" he muttered, then he shook his head. "No, can't be north. North's up. That's west."

He was right. It was west. It was very west, in fact, given that he was currently less than a twenty-minute hike from the most westerly point of the United Kingdom. As *west* went, you didn't get much wester.

"So, I'm..."

He glanced around at his surroundings, then back at the

map, searching for some identifying feature with which to triangulate his position.

"...somewhere here," he decided, narrowing it down to an area of some nine square miles. "And I want to go..."

His head rose and fell as it tick-tocked between the map and the real world. He raised a hand and made a vague sort of chopping motion towards where he could see water in the middle distance. If he was going to find a lighthouse, that seemed as good a place as any to start.

"That way," he concluded, then he forcibly gave the map another fold, stuffed it into his backpack, and went trampling through the heather and bracken.

There was an argument to be made, of course, that he should've stuck to the road. It would've made finding the place considerably easier, and saved him several nettle stings, two panicky tick removals, and a six-minute chase with a demented cleg pursuing him like it was the fucking *Terminator*.

Not to mention the six billion midge bites.

But taking the road meant being seen. And being seen meant risking being caught. And he couldn't chance that. Not now. Not yet. Not until the deed was done.

After today, they wouldn't laugh at him.

After today, he'd be *immortal*.

The idea had first come to him a few months back, like a vision from the Lord Himself. He'd resisted at first, and tried to push the thought away. It was too risky. Too extreme.

It had proven too enticing, though. Try as he might, his thoughts kept returning to it, driven there by every rejection from the lassies at the pub. Every sniggered comment about the events of his past. Every regurgitated nickname from his childhood. They had all driven him to here. To now. To this.

They were the ones responsible for what he was about to do. Not him. They'd left him no choice in the matter.

The canisters *clunked* together in his backpack, and he felt a little shiver of anticipation. He could only be ten, maybe fifteen minutes away from the target. Quarter of an hour until his fortunes started to change, and he cemented his place in history.

The plan was elegant in its simplicity. He would head to the Ardnamurchan Lighthouse, one of the most popular tourist spots in this part of the country.

He would set the camera on his phone rolling, and clearly identify himself for the benefit of those watching. Ideally, this would be a live stream, but assuming he didn't get a signal, he'd upload it to his *YouTube* channel later.

Then, when the coast was clear, he'd spray paint the biggest dick he could on the side of the lighthouse, and run like fuck before anyone caught him.

Herbert laughed out loud at the thought of it. Spray painting a reasonably well-loved tourist attraction so it resembled an enormous penis? That was gold. If that didn't go viral, nothing would.

Twenty-four hours from now, he'd be up there with the best-known names on the internet. Rebecca Black. Charlie Bit My Finger. That fat lad who thought he was in *Star Wars*. He'd be bigger than them all!

And all it would take was a couple of cans of paint, a steady hand, and an extendable ladder.

Herbert stopped and drew in a breath so sharp he inhaled a score of midges. Even as he coughed them back out, he realised his error.

The ladder.

He'd forgotten the bloody ladder.

Herbert turned to look back the way he'd come, but the prospect of hiking all that way back to where he'd parked the van would've been a daunting one even if he'd known how to get there. Given that he had no idea of the van's whereabouts beyond *somewhere roughly in that direction*, going back for it wasn't an option.

"Fuck it," he grunted, trudging on before the cleg from earlier had a chance to catch up with him.

How tall was the lighthouse? About thirty-five metres.

What was that in feet?

God knew. Ninety? A hundred? Something like that.

And what was he? Five-eight or five-nine, depending on footwear. At full stretch, with his arms up, maybe seven feet.

A seven-foot-long schlong on the side of a lighthouse was still funny, obviously, but was it viral video material? Maybe. If it was detailed enough. Veins, and ball hairs, and all that. Maybe some flying droplets of spunk.

It would all be in the selling of it. He knew, despite all the many comments on his channel to the contrary, that he could be funny and charming on camera. That was half the battle. Win them round with the banter, then seal the deal by spray painting a seven-foot penis on a relatively popular landmark.

This wasn't a disaster. This could still be a success. He could still make this work, ladder or no ladder.

It was thirty seconds later when Herbert fell in the hole. It was quite a large hole, as holes went—more of a sudden dip in the ground several metres wide than a narrow drop into a confined space—and he really should've seen it coming.

He slid and rolled down one of the steep sides, wet mud soaking through the back of his trousers until he looked like he'd suffered an explosive bout of diarrhoea.

He landed at the bottom with a *squelch* and a *splat*, and the world came alive with insects. Even more so than it already had been, which was saying something.

Herbert spent a terrifying few seconds batting them away and shaking them off, then he jumped to his feet, made a mad dash for freedom, and fell once again.

He landed in darkness. Soot. Ash. His sudden arrival woke the smell of fire, and of smoke, as he struggled to push himself back, away, up.

But there was something beneath him. Something hideous. Something wrong.

A face grinned up from the remains of the fire. A skull, the skin and flesh charred away, the eye sockets hollow. Mostly.

Lost, alone, and miles from home, Herbert Gibson scrambled backwards through the mud, and the heather, and the bugs.

And then, he wiped his tears on his blackened hands, vomited down his front, and screamed.

CHAPTER TWO

DETECTIVE CHIEF INSPECTOR Jack Logan of Police Scotland was suspicious. This was not entirely unusual—most of his days were spent being suspicious of one thing or another—but right now his finely-tuned polis instincts were making their presence felt even more so than usual.

It was the suddenness of it that had first set him wondering. His girlfriend—a word he was only just getting used to using—Shona Maguire, had sprung it on him at eleven o'clock the night before. They both had a day off—him from the polis, her from the mortuary—so they should take a wee day trip to Largs, she'd said. They should go and eat ice cream at *Nardini's*, she'd said.

In all the time Logan had known the pathologist, she'd never once mentioned Largs before. Granted, she was a big fan of ice cream, and *Nardini's* was widely recognised as one of the best places in Scotland to secure some Class-A Mint Choc Chip.

Still, it was suspicious. She was up to something. He just couldn't quite figure out what.

They sat at a slightly shoogly table beneath a red and white striped awning, the cafe's *no dogs* policy preventing them from venturing inside with Taggart.

Logan had owned the dog for just over three months, and had spent that time hoping the wee bastard might start behaving more sensibly any day now.

So far, this train of thought had only led to disappointment.

On the plus side, Taggart was now toilet trained, and Logan no longer had to be ready with a bottle of disinfectant spray and an apology whenever he entered a building with the animal. Other than that, though, he had demonstrated a disappointing lack of maturity. He must be coming on for five or six months old now, too. High time the bugger started to grow up.

"How's your ice cream?" Shona asked. She was sitting with her back to the cafe doors, so she was looking out across the road, past the car park and the giant metal statue of a Viking, to where the water gobbled up the beach.

Logan jabbed at the contents of his bowl. In sunnier climes, the ice cream would have melted by now. In Scotland in late September, it would stay mostly solid for a good hour yet.

"It's good, aye," he confirmed.

"Can't believe you went for vanilla," Shona said, with a suggestion of a reprimand. "All those flavours, and you choose vanilla."

Logan looked down at his bowl again. Taggart was partially visible beneath the table, staring up in the hope of being fed. Considering he'd already had half Logan's fish and chips, he was on a hiding to nothing.

"I like vanilla," Logan remarked. "Anyway, you went for

literally all the other flavours, so I thought I'd better balance it up."

Shona grinned and plunged her spoon into the rainbow of colours, chips, and sprinkles that filled her bowl. "You've got to take these chances when you can," she said, then she gestured at the cafe, and the area immediately surrounding it. "Like today. How often do we both get the same day off?"

Logan blew out his cheeks. "About once a week."

"OK, yes, things have been pretty quiet recently," Shona conceded. "But you don't know when a case is going to come up, and we end up working all hours. That's why I thought, sunny day, why not take a trip to Largs for some ice cream?"

"Sunny-ish day," Logan corrected, indicating the layer of light grey cloud cover overhead. "And because it's a four-hour drive each way."

"But it's nice, though, isn't it? To get away for a bit. It's lovely."

"Aye. It is," Logan admitted. His eyes narrowed. "What aren't you telling me?"

Shona shoved an enormous spoonful of ice cream into her mouth, but somehow managed to say, "How do you mean?" without letting it touch her teeth.

"This. Here. You're up to something."

Across the table, Shona shook her head. "No 'mnot," she said, moving the ice-cold dessert around in her mouth in a way that maximised flavour and minimised the risk of brain freeze.

"You bloody are."

Shona shook her head. "No. 'm not up to anything!"

A voice spoke from the steps on Logan's right. It was harsh, and sharp, and achingly familiar. "You have got to be bloody kidding me."

Shona swallowed. "OK, I am up to something," she conceded, then she turned and smiled at the couple standing on the steps of the cafe, and at the furious looking young woman, in particular. "Hello!" she said. "You must be Maddie." Her gaze flitted across the table to Logan. "Your dad's told me so much about you!"

There had been raised voices. Accusations slung, most of them in Logan's direction. Maddie had accused him of masterminding the whole meeting. Of luring her here when he knew damn well that she had no interest in seeing him.

His protests had been drowned out by the shouting, and by the barking as Taggart tried to get in on the drama. It was the man that Maddie was with who eventually calmed things down. He was her husband, Logan knew, although only from stalking her social media profiles, his wedding invitation having failed to materialise in the post earlier in the year.

"What are you saying, Anderson?" Maddie had demanded when he'd started to explain. "*You* set this up?"

"Um, yes. Sort of," Anderson admitted. He plastered on a nervous smile and gestured to the empty chairs beside Shona and Logan. "Should we take a seat? People are staring."

"Let them bloody stare!" Maddie snapped, but then she sighed, pulled out the chair next to Shona, and placed it at the end of the table as far from Logan as it was possible to be.

"Drinks!" Shona exclaimed, rocketing up onto her feet. She met Anderson's eye and they both nodded enthusiastically. "We should get drinks!"

"Good idea," Anderson said. "I'll just... We'll just..."

Hesitantly, he bent and placed a kiss on Maddie's cheek, then went scurrying into the cafe, hot on Shona's heels.

The double doors swung closed. Logan regarded them in silence for a few moments, before finally giving his verdict.

"What a pair of conniving bastards."

His daughter scowled. "Don't pretend you didn't know."

"I didn't," Logan insisted. "First I heard about coming to Largs was last night. First I knew you were going to be here was when you came up the steps."

Along the table, Maddie folded her arms and gave the briefest roll of her eyes. She didn't believe him. She didn't trust him.

And who could blame her, after everything he'd done?

"I mean, don't get me wrong, it's great to see you," he ventured. "You're looking well."

"You've got fatter," Maddie replied, and there was a real sting to it, like the words had been meant to hurt.

"Aye. Well. You should've seen me a year ago." He picked up his spoon, swirled his ice cream around in the bowl for a few moments, then set it back down again with a *clink*. "Congratulations, by the way. On the wedding. I sent texts, but I don't know if you got them."

"I got them fine."

"Right. Right, aye. Good." He tapped his fingers on the tabletop. "Anderson Crawford."

"What about it?"

"Nothing. Just, you know, that last name as a first name thing. Never been a fan of that."

"Jack can be a surname, and Logan can be a first name, too," Maddie pointed out.

"Aye, fair enough," Logan conceded, but he couldn't just leave it there. "It's no' the same though, is it? I mean,

Anderson Crawford. Anderson. Who calls their child 'Anderson'?"

"His parents. And you know what else they did?" Maddie asked, spitting the words out like they were poisonous. "Supported him. Were there for him. Didn't let him down."

"Right..."

"And not once—not *once*—did they use him as bait to lure out a serial killer. Nice of them, eh?"

"You weren't bait," Logan said, though there was no conviction to it. "I mean, not exactly."

She shimmied her chair back even further from the table. "You're unbelievable," she muttered.

"Look, last name for a first name or not, he seems..." Logan gestured at the door that Anderson and Shona had gone through, grasping for the perfect descriptor.

"What?" Maddie asked. "He seems what?"

"Nice enough," was what Logan settled on, which didn't impress his daughter one bit.

"He's not 'nice enough.' He's lovely. He's kind. He's thoughtful. He's there when he says he'll be there. He doesn't lie, or keep secrets—"

"Apart from this one," Logan pointed out, and he looked pleased with his little victory. "He kept this one from you."

Maddie crossed her arms and sat back so hard the chair gave a little squeal of complaint. "What do you want?" she demanded.

"This wasn't me," Logan insisted. "I had no idea. About this. Any of it. I thought you were in London. Your, eh, your mum says that's where you're living now."

Maddie gave a sulky shrug of her shoulders, neither confirming nor denying this.

"What's that like?" Logan asked. "Is it no' full of, you know, Londoners?"

"We're outside London," Maddie said. She shifted in her seat. "But yes."

"Yes, what?"

"It's full of twats."

"I didn't say 'twats.' I said 'Londoners.'"

Maddie shrugged again. "Same thing."

Logan chuckled. Down on the ground, Taggart raised a paw and put it on his knee, reminding him he was under there, and that the ice cream appeared to be going spare.

"You got a dog," Maddie stated.

"Aye. I mean, no. I mean, sort of," Logan said. "Not by choice."

"You never let me get a dog," his daughter reminded him. "No matter how much I asked. Too much hassle, you always said."

"And I was right. He's a bloody nightmare." An idea struck him and he perked up in his seat. "You want him? You can take him home with you, if you like. All his stuff's in the car."

"No. You're alright."

"When I say he's a nightmare, that's an exaggeration, he's actually very easy to care for. He'd fit right in. You'd get on like a house on fire," Logan said, really trying to close the deal. "He's very low maintenance."

"We live in a flat, and we're both out all day," Maddie said. "It wouldn't be fair." She glanced under the table. "Anyway, he looks a bit daft."

"Everyone keeps saying that," Logan said, leaning back so he could get a better look at the animal. "I just think he looks like a dug. They all look daft."

"Lassie didn't look daft," Maddie pointed out.

"True," Logan conceded. He looked down at the dog's lolling tongue and uneven ears. "Not sure I'd trust this bugger to get me out of a well, right enough."

"What's his name?" Maddie asked.

"Taggart."

She laughed at that—a dry noise at the back of the throat. "Aye," she said. "Of course it is."

"One of the guys I work with—Ben, you remember Ben?"

"Of course."

"He reckons he's gay."

Maddie frowned. "Ben reckons he's gay?"

"Aye."

The lines on Maddie's brow deepened as she thought this through. "But he was married to Alice for years."

"What? No, not... Ben's no' gay. He thinks the dug's gay."

"Ben thinks the dog's gay?" Maddie said, incredulously.

"Aye."

"And is it?"

"That's no' really any of my business," Logan reasoned.

"I suppose not," Maddie agreed. She reached under the table and patted Taggart on the back of his head. He turned immediately, tail wagging, and scrambled gracelessly up into her lap, making a meal of trying to lick her face.

"He likes you," Logan said.

"I'm not bloody taking him. You can get that idea right out of your head," Maddie replied.

Logan watched her with the dog for a while, then voiced the thought that had been in his head since he'd found out she was married.

"I would have come."

Maddie looked up from Taggart. "Sorry?"

"To the wedding. I wouldn't have let you down. If you'd invited me, I would've been there."

"You think I didn't invite you because I thought you might not turn up?"

Logan nodded. "Aye. Because I know that in the past I've—"

"That's not why I didn't invite you," Maddie said.

Logan blinked. "Oh. Isn't it?"

"No!"

"Right. I see." He tried to recalibrate his thinking on the matter, but couldn't. "Why didn't you invite me, then?"

"Because I don't like you," Maddie said, then she flinched and shook her head. "Don't. Didn't. I don't know." She sighed and looked down at Taggart, who seized the opportunity to lick her on the chin. "I was angry."

"About what happened in Inverness?"

"About everything! About two-and-a-bit decades," Maddie retorted. "But yes, you almost getting me raped and murdered didn't exactly help matters, let's put it that way."

"I wouldn't have let anything happen to you. I'd never let anything happen to you."

"But that's just it! You did. You let *that* happen," Maddie said, the pitch of her voice rising an octave or more. "You think because you stopped him—you think because you swung in just in the nick of time—that everything's fine. That all's well that ends well. That *I'm* fine. But I'm not. Because it doesn't work like that, Dad."

She ran a hand through her hair. Logan recognised the movement as a mirror of one he made himself. Usually when he was frustrated.

"You might be able to just reset everything after every case," Maddie continued, her volume dropping again. "You can just move on to your next big adventure and forget everything that happened before, but that's because you're... you. I'm not. No one is. You get to move on with your life—eat ice cream in Largs—and I'm stuck reliving it. Everything that happened. All of it, again, and again, and again. How is that fair?"

"It isn't," Logan admitted.

"You want to know why I didn't want you at the wedding?" Maddie asked. "Because, when I look at you, I see him. I see Owen Petrie. I see what he was going to do to me. To Mum. To everyone. I look at your face, and I see his."

Logan looked away, across the road, past the big metal Viking, to where the water met the shore. He nodded, his throat tight, his eyes prickling.

"Right. I see," he said, then he shrugged. "I mean, if you'd told me that, I could maybe have worn a balaclava."

It was a gamble. A big one. Her stifled snort of laughter told him it had paid off.

"You're a dick," she said.

He turned back to her. "You know, one of them full-face IRA ones. No' the ones with the big hole in the middle. That'd just have made me look like a fanny."

"You are a fanny," Maddie told him. A smile tugged at the corner of her mouth. "Imagine the photos."

"What, if I was done up in paramilitary gear? Aye, they'd be belters, right enough. Love to see one of them on your mum's fireplace."

She laughed at that. A proper laugh, albeit a brief one. "She'd be raging."

Logan reached a hand across the table—across the divide—and placed it on her arm. She regarded it like it was something bordering on offensive, but didn't pull away.

"I'm sorry," he told her. "I didn't know."

"But that's the point. You should've known. You should've understood."

Logan conceded the point with a nod and a squeeze of her arm. "Aye. I should've," he said. "Although, there is one thing I did do right. One thing I'm proud of."

"What's that?"

"I never gave you a last name for a first name," he said, with absolute sincerity.

Maddie sniffed. Smiled. "Madison *is* a last name," she said.

Logan sat back in surprise. "Is it?" He stared at her for several seconds, his eyebrows slowly creeping back down his forehead until they met as a shallow V above his nose. "Fuck."

Shona stood back from the counter in *Nardini's* while Anderson ordered up two teas, one coffee, a jumbo chocolate milkshake, and a bowl of water for the dog. She could see Logan and Maddie through the little square windows in the door, but was trying very hard not to look. Looking felt intrusive. Best to leave them to it for a few minutes.

There was a small TV on the back wall, showing a news report on a missing ten-year-old girl. She tuned her ear to it, listening to the details. North of England somewhere. Not Jack's turf.

She was watching the tearful pleas of the girl's parents—a well-dressed black couple that the on-screen text revealed both had 'Dr' before their names—when Anderson arrived, tucking a receipt into his slim carbon fibre wallet.

"They said they'd take it out to us," he told her.

"Oh. Right," Shona said. She chewed her lip for a moment, then indicated an empty table. "Or we could sit and wait for it? Give them a chance to chat."

"And delay us getting shouted at," Anderson added.

Shona smiled, clicked her fingers, and pointed at him. "Bingo. That, too."

They took a seat. Anderson, like Shona, was avoiding looking out at the veranda where Logan and Madison sat. He picked up a salt cellar, studied it like it was some rare antique treasure, then set it down again.

"How do you think it's going?" he asked.

"Not a clue," Shona admitted. "But I haven't heard anything breaking, so that's positive."

Anderson smiled. It wasn't a particularly noteworthy smile. He wasn't the 'slick, slimy bastard' that Logan had described, based on nothing but a few Facebook photographs and his own worst fears. He was a fairly unassuming-looking guy. No fancy watches. No red corduroy trousers and fancy shirt. No braying laugh. None of the things, in fact, that Logan had theorised he'd have.

He'd been friendly enough on Messenger, too, once he'd got over the initial shock of Shona getting in touch, and been persuaded that arranging the meet-up was a good idea. Maddie did speak about her dad, he'd told her. Not in a particularly flattering way, but she spoke about him. She regretted the state of their relationship and wished it could be better.

Granted, she had never actually said as much, but Anderson had read between the lines.

Which was the main reason he didn't want to look outside, in case it turned out that he'd completely *mis*read between the lines, and they were now trying to kill each other with dessert spoons.

He and Shona filled a few minutes with idle chat. Anderson asked how the drive down had been, what the weather was like in Inverness, and what time they were planning to set back off up the road.

Shona asked if Anderson had ever seen the Richard Donner cut of *Superman II*.

He hadn't.

A waiter passed then, carrying a tray of drinks towards the front door. Shona leapt to her feet and intercepted him before he could make it all the way.

"Wait! Hold on! Those are ours," she said.

The waiter regarded her with suspicion until Anderson produced the receipt and held it up as evidence.

"We'll take it," Shona said, grasping the edge of the tray. "It'll be safer that way. Probably."

The waiter, who had absolutely no idea what she was on about, and no desire to find out, happily let her take the tray, then headed back to the kitchen. Shona took a deep breath and met Anderson's eye.

"You ready?"

He drew in a deep breath, then nodded. "Ready."

"Right, then!" she said, backing up to the door. "Let's do this!"

She bumped the door open with her bum, stepped out onto the veranda, then turned with the tray. She hadn't known what to expect, but had braced herself for a range of possibilities that went from 'stony silence' to 'wanton destruction.'

Instead, she found them sitting there, side by side. Not smiling, exactly, but not *not* smiling, either. They both turned as she and Anderson stepped out of *Nardini's*, and the similarity of their matching expressions proved their blood-relative status better than any DNA test ever would.

"Well, well, well," Logan said. "Here's the very bastards now."

Shona side-eyed Anderson. "I don't see any blood," she said in a stage whisper.

"You owe me five quid," Anderson told her.

"No blood," Maddie said. She glowered at her husband. "Well, not until I get you home, anyway."

"Oh. Promises, promises," Anderson said, then he wilted like a dying flower as both Logan and Maddie glowered at him.

"The fuck's that meant to mean?" Maddie asked, beating her dad to the punch. Possibly literally.

"Nothing. I just... I panicked," her husband admitted.

Shona placed the tray on the table and divvied up the drinks—tea for Logan, coffee for the youngsters, and the milkshake for herself.

Taggart slid off Maddie's lap when the bowl was placed on the ground, and then failed to hide his disappointment when it turned out to contain water and not food. He lapped at it forlornly, then lay down in the shade beneath the table.

Once the drinks were deployed and the tray stashed under the table beside the dog, Shona took her seat. She looked from Logan to Maddie and back again. "So, you're not going to kill us, then?"

"Not out in the open like this, no," Logan said. "Too many witnesses." He took a sip of his tea, looked over the rim of the mug at his daughter, then went for it. "We... Shona and I... We were thinking of maybe hanging around for the rest of the day. Maybe going for dinner somewhere. If, you know… I mean, I'm not sure what your plans are, but if you wanted to join us, you'd be…" He sighed, shook his head, then set his mug down. "I'd like you to come to dinner. Both of you."

Anderson's hand slipped over Maddie's. He gave her a nod of encouragement.

"Is it somewhere nice?" she asked. "Last time you took me out to dinner it was to Pizza Hut."

"You liked Pizza Hut!" Logan protested.

"I liked Pizza Express."

Logan rolled his eyes. "Same thing."

"It's not remotely the same," Maddie countered.

"I mean, they both do pizza, so they definitely share some similarities."

"Jack." Shona tried to squeeze the word into a gap in the argument.

"So do McDonald's and Burger King, but you wouldn't get them mixed up."

"I do!" Logan insisted. "I have! That birthday party you were invited to, mind? We just thought we were there early. Turned out we were at the wrong place."

Maddie gasped. "You told me they phoned to say it had been called off!"

Logan bit his lip. "Did I?"

"Jack."

"Yes! You said they phoned to cancel!"

"Maybe they did. My memory's not—"

"*Jack!*"

This time, there was no ignoring it. Logan and Maddie both turned to Shona, then followed her gaze to the table, where the screen of Logan's silenced phone was illuminated, indicating an incoming call.

The name 'Det Supt Mitchell' filled most of the display.

They all stared at the mobile, saying nothing. It was Maddie who eventually broke the silence.

"You'd better answer it."

Logan shook his head. "It's probably nothing."

The theme to *The A-Team* suddenly blared from somewhere in Shona's direction, making everyone at the table jump.

"Jesus!" Logan muttered.

"Sorry, that's mine," Shona said, getting to her feet. She took her phone from her pocket, and her face fell when she saw the name on the screen. "I have to take this."

She stepped away, tapped the icon to answer the call, and placed the phone to her ear. "Shona Maguire," she said.

On the table, Logan's phone continued ringing in silence.

"Right. Yes," Shona said, listening to the voice on the other end of the line. She looked back over her shoulder at the gathering. "I'll be there as soon as I can."

Logan closed his eyes and groaned.

"It's fine," Maddie told him, pushing her chair back. "We should probably get going, anyway. Beat the traffic."

Anderson looked from the phone, to Logan, and then up to where his wife stood over them. "What? Aren't we going for dinner?"

"No," Maddie said, and her smile was a thing made of plaster and stone. "We aren't."

CHAPTER THREE

"CHEER UP, boss. It might never happen!"

Logan stopped. Turned. Looked straight into the beaming face of DC Tyler Neish, who had jumped out of his car at the first sight of the DCI and was now hurrying over to intercept.

Tyler's year had been a mixed bag of fortunes, from the high of his wedding to DC Sinead Bell, to the low of having one of his goolies removed due to testicular cancer.

His recovery had gone well, though, and what he insisted on referring to as his 'near-death experience' had only served to make him even more annoyingly chirpy.

"I'm sorry?" Logan asked, almost daring the DC to repeat what he'd said.

Anyone with any sense would've picked up on the tone of the question. Anyone with any sense would've swapped their glaikit grin for a more suitably sombre expression.

Tyler did neither of those things.

"I said, 'Cheer up, boss. It might never happen!'" he clarified. "You've got a face like a bulldog licking pish off a nettle."

Logan made a sound like a bough of some ancient oak tree shifting on the wind. He turned from Tyler, and looked across the low hills of heather and bracken that lined either side of the narrow road.

"What's that over there?" he asked, pointing to a random spot in the distance.

"What's what, boss?" Tyler asked, following the finger.

"There. About a mile that way."

Tyler squinted, his eyes narrowing, his nose wrinkling up. "I'm not seeing anything."

"Aye, well, go and have a look."

Tyler's gaze shifted left and right between Logan and the utterly unremarkable stretch of scrub a mile off on the left.

"Go and have a look? But it's all boggy, boss."

"Aye," Logan said, patting the younger officer on the shoulder. "I know. Chop-chop."

Tyler opened his mouth to object, but some deeply buried sense of self-preservation alerted him to the fact that anything he might say would only make matters worse. Instead, he zipped up his jacket, groaned inwardly, and set off in the direction the DCI had indicated.

Logan allowed himself a little nod of satisfaction, then continued on to where DI Ben Forde—the elder statesman of the team—stood gathered with a group of Uniforms and a few guys in sturdy boots and bright jackets. Some of the local Mountain Rescue Team, Logan guessed. He could hear the helicopter hovering somewhere beyond the hills.

"Jack. There you are," Ben said when Logan reached the group. "Thought you weren't coming."

"Aye, well, I'm here now," Logan said flatly, and Ben,

unlike Tyler, immediately picked up on the tone and adjusted accordingly.

"Young lad out hiking came across a body. Burned down to the bones, he reckons. Bits of a metal frame around, too, suggesting he might've been in a tent. Silly bugger didn't take a note of the exact location, though, so we've got the helicopter searching."

"What? So, we don't actually have a body?" Logan asked. "You called me in on my day off, and we don't even know for sure there's a body?"

"Well, it was Mitchell who called you in," Ben said, his internal dashboard lighting up with warning signs. "I said to leave you be, but she wanted you brought in. To be honest, I think it was more Shona, since they've still not got a replacement for—"

"Jesus Christ," Logan seethed. He held up a finger and thumb an inch apart. "I was this close to..."

Ben gave the rest of the sentence a moment to arrive, then pressed for more information when it didn't. "To what?"

Logan sighed and let his arm fall back to his side. "Forget it. Doesn't matter." He looked around at the Uniforms and Mountain Rescue Team, finally acknowledged their presence with a nod, then searched the sky for the helicopter he could hear buzzing around. "No sign of anything yet?"

"Not yet, no," one of the rescue team said. He had a walkie-talkie style radio in his hand, and was presumably the one in contact with the chopper. "Going to start getting dark in a couple of hours, so we might have to pack up then and try again in the morning."

"In the morning?" Logan asked, his eyebrows forming a single straight line across his forehead.

"I told her not to call you in," Ben said, interjecting

before the unsuspecting Mountain Rescue man got both barrels. He looked along the row of parked polis and unmarked vehicles to where Logan's BMW stood way at the back. "Is Shona with you?"

"She's keeping the dog company," Logan replied. He looked around at the wilderness, his gaze briefly lingering on DC Neish trudging forlornly across the boggy bracken. "Is there any point in me being here right now? Anything you need me for right this minute?"

"Not really," Ben said. "Not until we've found the body."

"If there even is one," Logan added.

"Aye. Even then, that's more Shona and Palmer's team."

"Christ. Palmer's not here, is he?"

"Not yet," Ben said, and Logan's shoulders sunk back from where they'd risen up around his ears, like a cat getting ready to hiss. "But they'll be on their way."

"All the more reason for me to clear off, then," the DCI said. "This lad who found the body. Where is he?"

"He's at the local station with Sinead and Hamza."

"What, up in Fort William?"

Ben shook his head. "No," he said, a little ominously. "Nothing as grand as that..."

Logan and Shona had driven right past the police station in the village of Strontian on the way to the scene, but had both mistaken it for a toilet block.

It was a small, grey building with a triangular roof that came to a point on all four sides, so it vaguely resembled a hat.

The building sat at a junction leading to what the

signage declared as 'Strontian Village Centre,' which comprised a shop, a small cafe, and quite a lot of grass.

Despite his mood, Logan had to admit that the drive over had been something spectacular. From the moment the BMW had driven up the ramp and onto the Corran Ferry for the short hop across Loch Linnhe, through the winding narrow roads through tiny, blink-and-you'll-miss-it hamlets, Logan felt like he had finally found the Highlands he'd always imagined.

They'd had to stop twice to shoo sheep from the road, which had excited Taggart no end. Their phone signals had dipped in and out, before giving up the ghost completely some ten miles back.

Some whining from Taggart had forced them to stop for a pee break at somewhere Google Maps identified as Sallachan stone beach. There, standing at the edge of the loch, with a breeze wafting across the water, and the mountains rising from the opposite shore, you could be forgiven for thinking you'd travelled back in time.

Logan half-expected some blue-faced bastard with a sword to turn up and try to recruit them to go fight for '*Freeeeedom!*' And, whether it was the way the landscape stirred some ancient pride or patriotism, or the fact that his current mood meant he was itching for a scrap, he was pretty confident he'd have said yes.

It was there on that rocky beach that Logan had finally given voice to the thoughts that had been rattling around in his head the whole way up the road.

"You were completely out of line arranging that—with Maddie, I mean—without telling me," he'd said. Then, before Shona could reply, he'd added, "Thank you," and squeezed her hand as they'd stood watching the dog go bounding along the water's edge, his ears and tail and eyes and tongue all alive with the sheer bloody joy of it.

"Getting called in like this, it's not great," Shona said, as they'd stood there. "But you know what I always say? You've got to make the best of a bad situation."

"You never say that," Logan told her.

"No. But I'm going to start."

And they had made the best of it, even if only then, for those few stolen moments on the shore, with the dog running wild and free.

It was good that they had time. It had taken the edge off Logan's anger, and very probably saved Tyler's life when he'd tried his, "Cheer up, boss," nonsense some twenty minutes later.

Now, the BMW *thunked* into a pothole in the Strontian Police Station car park, and Taggart's tail wagged excitedly when he realised they were stopping again. It was clear that he liked the stopping part. Then again, he liked the moving part, too. He appeared to like most things in general, in fact. The wee bastard was nothing if not consistent.

Hamza's car was parked outside the building, alongside a battered 2002 Vauxhall Astra van with an extendable ladder strapped to the roof rack. There were no marked polis cars present. They'd be up at the scene with Ben and Tyler.

That was assuming, of course, that a station this size was big enough to merit a car. For all Logan knew, the officers stationed here might ride around on horseback.

"You coming in?" Logan asked, as the BMW rolled to a stop next to Hamza's car.

"In a bit. I'll take the dog for a wee walk first. Maybe scope out the shop. I've been craving a *Twix* since we passed that bus outside Glasgow."

"What bus?" Logan asked.

"The one with the big *Twix* advert on it. The one where I said, 'Imagine that bus is just full of *Twixes*,' then we tried to figure out how many *Twixes* you could fit inside it." Her eyes narrowed. "Well, I mean, it was mostly me who tried to... Were you even listening?"

Logan blinked. "Hmm? Sorry, did you say something?"

Shona laughed, punching him playfully on the arm. "Well, guess who's just blown their chance of getting a *Twix*. I'll bring *Twixes* for everyone, but not you. I'll be dishing them out like the *Milkybar Kid*. Except, you know, with *Twixes*." She stopped talking, blinked slowly, and frowned. "I've said '*Twixes*' so often I'm no longer convinced it's a real word."

Logan regarded her in silence for several seconds, then patted her leg. "Aye, well," he said, opening the door. "Good luck with all that."

CHAPTER FOUR

LOGAN WOULD HAVE THOUGHT it impossible, but the inside of the station was even less grandiose than the outside. It was made up of four rooms, one of which was a bathroom, and another a small kitchen.

The remaining two rooms, while larger than the others, seemed to have been put there with no real purpose in mind.

They each contained a table or two, some chairs, a filing cabinet, and various posters on the walls proclaiming the perils of drinking and driving, and other traffic-related offences.

One of the rooms also contained DS Hamza Khaled, DC Sinead Bell, and a manic-looking young man who wasn't so much in need of a shower as a high-powered jet wash. He was caked in mud, black with ash, and had what appeared to be dried vomit down his front.

The red rings around his eyes suggested that either he'd been crying, or he suffered badly from hay fever. Given the look on his face, Logan was going to go with the former.

"Detective Sergeant. Detective Constable," Logan said, nodding to the officers in turn.

"Sir," they both replied, Hamza in his dulcet Aberdonian tones, and Sinead with her local Lochaber twang.

She insisted she didn't have an accent, and while it was nowhere near as strong as Hamza's, or even his own guttural Glasgow growl, it was there if you knew how to listen.

Logan laser-targeted his gaze on the man sitting at the scuffed and mug-ringed table. "And who do we have here?"

"This is Mr Herbert Gibson," Sinead said.

"Herbert? There's a name you don't hear very often," Logan said. "Fortunately for all involved."

"Mr Gibson is the one who phoned in the report about the body," Hamza explained.

"Is he? Is he, indeed?" Logan said. He adjusted his mouth into something almost smile-shaped. "So you're the reason I got called in on my day off."

Herbert blinked, frowned, and swallowed all at the same time. He was not a tall man, so even standing he'd have been dwarfed by Logan. Sitting, he could only tilt his head all the way back so he could look up at the towering detective.

"We haven't found the body yet, I understand," Logan continued. "You definitely saw it, though, Herbert? You're not pulling our leg, are you?"

Herbert shook his head. "N-no, no. I saw it. I definitely saw it. It was there. He was dead."

Logan raised an eyebrow. "He?"

"What?"

"I understood from one of my colleagues that you said the body was burned beyond all recognition."

Herbert pressed his blackened hands together, like he

was getting ready to pray or beg for mercy. If the bastard was lying, though, neither one would do him any good.

"It. I mean... *it* was dead."

"But you don't know where."

"Not... not exactly. But roughly. I told them roughly where to find it."

"And yet, they have not," Logan said.

He pulled out the chair directly across from Herbert and lowered himself onto it. It lost him some of his height advantage, but made it much easier to eyeball the man sitting opposite.

"It's there. It's definitely there. I saw it. I'm not lying," Herbert insisted.

"Who said you were lying?" Logan asked. He turned and looked back at Hamza and Sinead. "Did you say he was lying?"

"No, sir."

"Not us, sir."

"Nobody's said you're lying, son," Logan said, fixing Herbert with that glare again. "Because you look like you're brighter than that. You look like you're smart enough not to waste police time like that. I mean, clever-looking lad like you, you'd know just what an absolute shitshow that would be for you, were you to have made something like that up. On my day off, of all days."

He let that sink in for a moment, then leaned forward a little and lowered his voice, like he was sharing a secret. "But now would be the time to say, if you were lying. Before any more damage was done, and taxpayers' money spent. Now would be the time to tell us if you were making it all up."

Herbert shook his head. "I wasn't. I'm not. Honest. It was there. I saw it."

Logan sucked in his bottom lip, scraped his teeth across the stubble, then nodded. "Fine. Good. So, mind telling us what you were doing out there in the arse end of nowhere then, Herbert?"

"I was just... I was hillwalking."

"In them shoes?" Logan asked, rocking himself onto the back legs of his chair so he could look under the table at Herbert's mud-slicked footwear. "Who goes hiking in a pair of *Converse* trainers?"

"Mr Gibson was happy to let us look in his bag, sir," Hamza said.

Herbert's head snapped up, his eyes widening. "I didn't know I had a choice!"

"We expressly asked for your permission," Sinead reminded him.

"Well, yeah, but I thought you were just being polite! I didn't realise I could say no."

"Why would you say no?" Logan asked. "Unless you've got something to hide."

Herbert's eyes somehow found it in them to widen further. "What? No. No, I just..."

"Did we get a look at Mr Gibson's phone?" Logan asked.

"No, sir," Sinead replied. "He claims he's forgotten the PIN to access it."

"It's... it's the stress," Herbert said, shrinking a couple of inches under Logan's withering gaze. "It'll come back to me."

"We did find some interesting items inside the bag though, sir," Hamza said.

"Did we now?" Logan rubbed his hands together as the bag was placed on the table before him. "This is exciting," he said, lifting the flap. "I wonder what I'll find."

First out of the bag were two cans of red spray paint.

Logan turned the canisters over in his hands, gave them a shake until they rattled, then set them down, lined up, between himself and Herbert.

"Interesting hillwalking equipment you've got there, Herbert."

"That's not all, sir," Sinead said. She indicated the bag with a nod. "It gets better. Or worse, depending on how you look at it."

Logan lifted the flap again, and peered into the bag. He frowned for a moment as he tried to figure out what he was looking at, then he raised his gaze to meet Herbert's.

"Curiouser and curiouser," he said, pulling a crumpled sheet of A4 paper from the backpack. He regarded it for several seconds, before voicing his thoughts. "Correct me if I'm wrong, Herbert, but this appears to be a lot of drawings of dicks."

"Fifty-seven dicks, sir," Sinead said.

"Fifty-seven?" Logan whistled through his teeth. "That is a significant number of dicks." He tapped the bottom of the page, where two phrases had been written. "Hashtag Herby Goes Bananas, hashtag Big Dick Energy. Mind explaining this?"

"Hashtags," Herbert said. "They're like, on *Twitter*, you use them to make it easier to find—"

"I know what a hashtag is, son." Logan waved a hand over the paper. "I meant *all* this. Explain all of it."

Across the table, Herbert sniffed, wiped his eyes on his filthy sleeve, then swallowed. "Where do you want me to start?"

"Maybe start with the fifty-seven dicks and go from there," Logan suggested.

Herbert shifted in his seat, glanced at all three detectives without meeting their eyes, then shrugged. "It was just... It was a prank."

"I bloody *knew it!*" Logan barked, and the flat of his hand slammed down on the table like a thunderclap. "I knew from the moment I walked in you were a lying wee bastard!"

"N-no! Not the body, the body's real! The paint. The dicks. That was the prank. It was going to be, I mean, then I found him." He jumped in his chair. "*It*. The body, I mean."

"Oh," Logan said, relaxing back into the chair. "Right. I see. And what was this prank going to be?"

"It was just... It was... It seems stupid now."

"I'm almost certain it does," Logan said. "What was it?"

Herbert took a breath, held it, then let the words tumble out as he exhaled. "I was going to make the lighthouse into a big willy."

Logan sat there. Mute. Motionless.

Several seconds passed before he said a word.

"Excuse me?"

"You know the lighthouse? Ardnamurchan Lighthouse? I was going to... I thought it'd be funny to paint it like... like..."

"A big willy," Logan concluded.

"Exactly. Yeah."

"And what would be the point in that?" Logan asked.

Herbert glanced furtively across the faces of the detectives. "Just, you know, it'd be funny."

"Would that be funny, do we think?" Logan asked the others, and he was relieved that DC Neish wasn't there.

"Not at all, sir."

"Not to me."

"No. Not to me, either," Logan said. "And I'm sure not to the people responsible for managing the lighthouse, either. Or, you know, anyone over the age of eight."

"No, but... I was going to make it look like a big dick. Like a big penis," Herbert said, assuming the detectives had surely just failed to grasp the hilarity inherent in the idea.

"No, we got that. That came across loud and clear. We just didn't find it funny," Logan said.

"How?" Herbert asked, seemingly genuinely perplexed. "I was going to film it. It was going to go viral. I was going to be famous."

"So that's what this is about," Logan said, the penny dropping. "Attention. You want to be noticed, Herbert. Is that it? You want your fifteen minutes of fame?"

"No, that's not... I mean, yes. But that's why I was going to the lighthouse. That's why I was doing the big willy."

"And you just happened to stumble upon a corpse on the way?" Logan asked, clearly not buying a word of it.

"Yes!"

"That your van out front?" the DCI demanded, throwing a thumb back over his shoulder.

Herbert followed the direction of the digit, but the sudden shift in the direction of questioning had thrown him off. "What?"

"The van. Out front," Logan said, making a show of simplifying the sentence structure. "That yours?"

"Um, yes. Yes, that's mine."

"Then why not drive? To the lighthouse. There's a road. Correct?"

"Well, yes. Yes, but... I didn't want anyone to see me."

Logan paused and sat back. He rolled his tongue around inside his mouth while he mulled over this answer. "You didn't want anyone to see you," he muttered, then he turned to the other detectives. "Hear that? He didn't want anyone to see him."

"Strange, sir," Hamza said.

"Why's...?" Herbert's gaze flitted from face to face. "Why's that strange?"

"Well, you can't go viral if no bugger knows it was you," Logan pointed out. "I mean, if it was fame you were after, I assume you were going to show your face in the video?"

"Well, yeah, but—"

"So, why not drive? If everyone was going to know you did it, why not just take your van and be done with it?"

Herbert sat in the chair with his mouth hanging open. "I mean... I mean... I suppose that would've made sense," he admitted. "I didn't really think about that."

"Or—and here's what I think, Herbert—this whole vandalism thing is a cover story. You weren't going to do anything to the lighthouse. It was a cover to explain why you were out there. Weird choice, though. I mean, I'd have just said I was out for a walk."

"I did say I was out for a walk!" Herbert protested. "You didn't believe me."

Logan leaned sharply forward, and the younger man instinctively drew back, his eyes widening once more in fear.

"Because I think you're a liar, Herbert. I believe that you wanted your moment in the spotlight—that bit I buy—but I think that's what all this is about. I think that's why you're wasting our time with this whole dead body nonsense."

"It's not nonsense! I saw it!"

"I don't believe you, Herbert. I think you're wasting our time in the hopes you might get on the telly. A wee bit of publicity on the STV evening news. That's what this is about."

"It isn't!" Herbert cried. He fumbled a hand into a trouser pocket, fighting back tears.

Hamza and Sinead moved as if to tackle him to the ground, but Logan held out a hand to stop them. They all watched as Herbert produced his phone, hurriedly tapped in a sequence of digits, then brought up a photograph of something that had once been a person.

"See! I'm not lying! It was there, I saw it!"

He yelped when the phone was snatched from his hand by the Detective Chief Inspector. Logan studied the picture, swiped through a couple of others and a video showing the remains from a variety of angles, then passed the mobile back over his shoulder to Hamza.

"DS Khaled, see if you can get a GPS position off these pictures, will you? Fortunately for Mr Gibson, it seems he's telling the truth about the body," Logan said.

"Um, see?" Herbert said, his conviction rapidly fading as he watched his phone being handed over. "Like I said, I'm not—"

Logan cut him off. "*Un*fortunately for Mr Gibson," he said, and the very air itself seemed to crackle around him. "I take a very dim view of people taking photographs of a potential murder scene."

Before he could continue, the door behind him opened. Taggart burst into the room, ran laps around the table, then attempted to launch himself at Logan, Sinead, and Hamza all at the same time, with predictably mixed results.

"Sorry, I let him off the lead," said Shona, leaning in through the open doorway. She smiled awkwardly and held out a thin plastic carrier bag weighted with bars of chocolate. "*Twix?*"

CHAPTER FIVE

THE PHOTOGRAPHS ON THE PHONE, and the location geotags in particular, were the missing piece of the puzzle. Forty minutes after Logan had handed the mobile to Hamza, he was trudging across a rugged Highland landscape towards where the top of a white tent rose from a dip in the ground.

Throughout his career, he'd come to resent the sight of those tents, knowing full well what waited inside them. Although, it wasn't the *knowing* bit that was the worst, it was the *not* knowing. Those tents, with their cordon tapes and their uniformed guards, were like the worst lucky dips in the world. You rarely knew what you were going to get, but could be reasonably confident that you were going to hate it.

These days, of course, he didn't just resent the sight of those tents, he despised them. These days, those tents didn't just contain something terrible, they drew something terrible to them, like a fly to shite.

Namely, Geoff Palmer, chief SOCO of the Scene of Crime team.

Logan and Palmer had never seen eye to eye. Partly, it was the height difference—Palmer was a stubby wee man with rounded shoulders, a potbelly, and a head like a partly deflated basketball. Despite his physical shortcomings, he considered himself quite the catch—which was a real testament to the power of the human imagination, Logan thought —and he had been angling for a date with Shona for as long as Logan had known him.

Even now, when Logan and Shona's relationship was public knowledge, the cheeky bastard still chanced his arm.

Sure enough, as Logan and Shona picked their way through the heather, bogs, and bracken, they heard a cry of greeting from over by the tent, and an arm clad in a white paper suit raised to wave at them.

"Shona!" Geoff called, completely ignoring the DCI. "There you are. Glad you could make it. Watch yourself down here, it's slippy."

He wheezed halfway up the incline and held a hand out to guide her down. Logan took it firmly, used it as an anchor point to descend the slope, then gave the Scene of Crime man a nod.

"Cheers for that, Geoffrey," he said, holding a hand out for Shona. She took it and he all-but lifted her down to stand between them.

"Eh, aye. No bother," Palmer said, wiping his sleeve like it had been contaminated in some way.

"What've we got today, then?" asked Shona.

"Body. Male, we think, though there's not a lot of him left to identify."

"Burned, I hear," Logan said.

"And the rest. Think animals have been at him," Palmer said. "He's not fresh. Probably been here for weeks."

"And they have to find him today of all bloody days," Logan muttered.

Palmer frowned up at him. As usual, he had his full SOC paper suit on, complete with elasticated hood. The way the elastic formed a near-perfect circle made Palmer's whole face look like a giant zit crying out to be popped.

"What? Why, what's today?"

"Our day off," Shona said. "We were away."

"Oh. Well, I'm sorry to hear that had to be cancelled," Palmer said, though his face said something entirely different. "There's a tent, by the way."

Logan and Shona both looked at the large tarpaulin construction beside them.

"Well spotted," Logan said, which drew a tut from the SOCO.

"Not that one. Inside. The body. It was in a tent. That got burned, too." Palmer waggled his eyebrows—you could tell by the way the hood moved—and grinned. "So, you could say that this one is going to be *intense*."

He clapped his gloved hands together and then held them apart like he was bracing himself for their applause.

He'd have a long bloody wait.

"*Intense, in tents*. Because he's in... There's two tents. Plural."

"No explanation necessary, Geoff," Logan said, stony-faced. "We got it. I mean, I got it. Did you get it?"

"I got it," Shona confirmed, remaining equally as impassive as the DCI.

"The comedy thing still not going well, then?" Logan asked.

Palmer puffed up with outrage. "It's going brilliantly," he said, though his insistence didn't last long. "I mean, it's early days. I'm still finding my feet, but it's building momentum. And you know what I always say—'Even Tommy Cooper didn't become Tommy Cooper overnight.'"

"Aye, you do always say that, right enough," Logan agreed, despite the fact he'd never once heard the SOCO utter those words before today.

"I'm up for Scottish Comedian of the Year," Palmer crowed. "It's a big national award."

"What?" Shona spluttered. "How?"

"Did everyone else pull out?" Logan asked.

The lower half of Palmer's face smiled, but the top half just looked a bit confused. "What? No. You just... you put yourself forward for it."

"Aah," Logan and Shona both said in unison.

That made sense. Only Geoff Palmer, after a single—and by all accounts disastrous—five-minute spot at a local open mic night, would nominate himself as the best comedian in the country.

"I do this great bit now—really funny stuff—about squirrels," Palmer said.

"Squirrels?" Shona asked, but Logan was already a step ahead.

"Nuts," he said, clicking his fingers and pointing at the Scene of Crime man. "It's something about nuts. It is, isn't it? Like... you both like fiddling with your nuts. It's something like that."

"What? No!" Palmer scowled, folding his arms. This made his whole suit ride up, so for a moment, it looked like he was shrinking down out of the hood. "It's nothing that obvious."

"What is it, then?" Shona asked.

Palmer sniffed, shook his head, then indicated the tent

behind him. "Can we just crack on and declare him dead, do we think? Some of us have lives, you know? We can't all stand around here gossiping all day."

It took Shona no time and zero medical training to conclude that the person under the tarpaulin was dead. He was as dead as anyone she had ever seen, in fact, and possibly even deader.

The fire had consumed all of his skin and most of his flesh. What little it had left behind, the heat had scorched into leathery knots that clung like tumours to his charred and blackened bones.

There were teeth marks here and there. Small and sharp. Pine Martens, maybe. They'd had a go at what was left of him, but it must've been slim pickings.

There was no smell to him. Not the stench of death that generally hung around bodies, anyway. Instead, the tent was thick with the smell of ash. It hung in the air, sharp and bitter, and with a note of an accelerant to it. Petrol, maybe, or something alcoholic.

She made her assessment, noted the time, then backed out of the tent and breathed in the fresh air.

"Yep, he's dead alright," she confirmed. "Usually I jab them with a pencil and see if they react, but I didn't even need to bother this time."

"Cause?" Logan asked.

"Dunno yet. Going to be hard to determine. He's been burned, but no saying if that was before or after he died. Problem is, there's not a lot left of him to tell us much. The way he's lying there, I don't think he was alive when he was burned. Or not conscious, at least. Doesn't look like he made any attempt to get away from the flames, or put them out in any way."

"You think someone burned the body so we couldn't identify it?"

Shona shrugged. "Maybe. But, they left the teeth intact."

Palmer snorted. "Amateur. That's the first thing I'd have done, knocked out the teeth. Smash the teeth, cut off the fingers, carve out any identifying tattoos, *then* burn. That's how I'd do it."

Logan regarded him solemnly for a moment. "Aye, well, we'll keep that in mind, Geoff," he said, then he turned back to Shona. "Could he just have been smoking in his tent, and set himself alight?"

"Theoretically," the pathologist conceded.

Geoff snorted for a second time. "Aye, if he was smoking while doused in petrol. Could you not smell the accelerant?"

"Could've been alcohol," Shona said.

Palmer rolled his eyes so hard they almost went all the way around. "In that case, where's the bottle?"

Shona shrugged. "I don't know. Have you looked for it yet? An animal could've carried it off a bit."

Palmer glanced back at the tent, then around at the dense thickets of heather and brush around them. "I don't... I'd have to check."

"How about you do that, then?" Logan suggested. "Since you've come all this way, you might as well make yourself useful."

Ten minutes later, Logan stood at the side of the single-track road with DI Forde and a ludicrously mud-slicked DC Neish, who had fallen no less than six times while on Logan's wild goose chase.

The midges were out in force. They formed clouds around the detectives, whose hands moved in a constant cycle of scratching and swatting at the bloody things.

The Mountain Rescue helicopter had touched down on one of the wider areas of the road a few hundred yards in the direction of the coast. Shona stood at it surrounded by the rescue team, discussing how they could retrieve the body without causing it any further damage. She already had her work cut out for her, and having the corpse fall to bits while being winched into the air would not make it any easier.

"So, turns out that lad was telling the truth, right enough," Ben said, slapping himself on the cheek to squash a midge mid-munch. "Just as well Mitchell called you in, I suppose."

Logan gave a low grunt, but said nothing.

"Was the body a mess, boss?" Tyler asked. He gestured pointedly down at himself. "Because, you know, it gets fairly muddy out there."

"I'm sure he's had more glamorous days, aye."

"Any sign of an ID?" Ben asked. "Or is that too much to hope for?"

Logan shook his head. "Anything he might've had on him would have been burned away. Might need to go on dental records."

"I could take a look through the Missing Persons register, boss," Tyler suggested. "See if we can narrow down the search a bit."

"Nice try, son," Logan told him. He pointed over in the

direction of the SOC tent—a several hundred-yard yomp away through the boggy bracken. "I want you over there helping the Mountain Rescue boys."

Tyler glanced furtively at the knot of men standing by the helicopter with Shona. They had the wiry frames and weathered faces of experienced Highland climbers, and the air of authority that came with knowing exactly what they were doing.

"What, me, boss? With that lot?" the DC asked. "Won't I just, you know, get in the way?"

"Probably, aye."

"Well, that's not great, is it? What if I mess everything up?" Tyler asked. "What if I make an arse of it?"

"Oh, don't worry, son," Logan said, laying a hand on the younger man's shoulder. "We'd expect nothing less."

He held up a finger to thwart any further protest from Tyler, then flicked the same digit towards the tent. With a sigh of resignation, Tyler set off back across the heather, dragging his muddy feet behind him.

"You think maybe you're being a wee bit hard on him?" asked Ben, once Tyler was out of earshot.

Logan mulled this over while he watched the DC go plodding away. "Aye, maybe," he conceded, then he cupped a hand at the side of his mouth and shouted, "Tyler!"

Tyler waved his arms in panic as he almost lost his footing, then turned back to the older detectives. "Boss?"

"Cheer up, son," Logan told him. "It might never happen."

Tyler's lips moved, but whatever he was saying he had the good sense to say quietly. He gave a double thumbs-up, and set off on his way again.

"There," Logan said, giving Ben a nod. "That should perk him up no end."

"Bad day?" Ben asked. He knew the signs. For a man who tried so hard to be private, it was often possible to read Jack Logan like a book.

Logan breathed out slowly, then shook his head. "I was with Maddie."

"Your Maddie? How did you manage that?"

"Shona," Logan said. "She arranged it. I didn't know a thing about it until today."

Ben looked approvingly over to where Shona seemed to be wrapping up with the Mountain Rescue boys.

"And? How did it go?" he asked. "I don't see any obvious stab wounds, so that's encouraging."

"We were talking," Logan said. "It was nice. And then some bastard had to go and interrupt and—"

"Eh, is one of you Detective Chief Inspector Logan?"

It was only the near-perfect comedy timing that saved the new arrival from a colossal ear-bashing. Instead, Logan simply muttered something indecipherable below his breath then turned to find a female constable looking up at him.

She sounded... not local exactly. Somewhere near Edinburgh, maybe, or a little further south. She looked to be of Asian origin—Chinese or Japanese, probably. Logan didn't have a trained enough eye to be able to spot the difference. She wore a high-vis jacket and a questioning expression, and stood with her hands on her hips in a way that suggested she wasn't planning on taking any shit from anyone.

"You DCI Logan?" she asked again, clearly impatient for an answer.

"Depends who's asking," Logan said, and there was an automatic downturn at the corners of the constable's mouth, like she'd heard too many similar answers from arseholes in the past, and was quite frankly sick of it. So filled with disdain was the expression, in fact, that Logan followed it up with a somewhat more professional response. "I mean, aye. That's me. What do you need?"

"I don't need anything," the constable said, apparently none-too-happy with the suggestion. "I might have something you need, though."

Logan shot Ben a sideways look and raised an eyebrow, silently questioning who the hell this woman was.

"And what might that be?" he asked.

"The body. Your man out there," the constable said. "I think I might know who he is."

CHAPTER SIX

HAMZA WATCHED Herbert Gibson driving off in his van, his wheels finding every available pothole as he crawled away from the station at a sedate and definitely legal pace. He had a long drive ahead of him to get back to his parents' house in Mallaig, given that the investigation had shut the road on the route he'd usually have taken, forcing him to take the long way around.

He had been told to report into the Mallaig Police Station on the way home. There was no way of forcing him to, of course, and no real point in sending him there. Still, he'd agreed, and if he thought the local constabulary was keeping an eye on him, then he'd be less inclined to flap his trap about everything that had happened.

Word didn't just travel fast in small communities, it grew arms and legs. An accidental death became a murder, became a massacre, and soon tensions and suspicions were running high, and accusations were being thrown around like monkey shite.

Turning back to the station, Hamza spotted Sinead

walking sideways into the car park, her arms stretched wide to accommodate the enormous corkboard she was carrying.

"That shop's amazing," she remarked, peeking out around the side of the board. "They've got everything."

The station at Strontian was unlikely to be their permanent base of operations, but they'd be using it for the rest of the day, at least, and—depending on the direction the case took—possibly longer.

The room they'd claimed wasn't really designed with detective work in mind and was instead mostly used for storing traffic cones, archived paperwork, and a single riot shield that had been propped across two chairs and now served as a makeshift coffee table.

It was lacking many of their usual resources—a window, for one—but the one Sinead could not tolerate them living without was a Big Board.

Up in Inverness, and even in the smaller station at Fort William, they had their pick of Big Boards. Sinead usually settled on a big rolling whiteboard, as she could both stick things to it, and write directly on the surface itself.

She'd gone to the Strontian village shop in the hope of maybe finding some large sheets of paper to stick to the wall in their newly-claimed Incident Room, but had instead found a corkboard so large she could barely carry it.

"I managed to get an artist's easel, as well," she said, as she dragged the board past Hamza. "To stand it on."

"Nice one," Hamza said. He looked her up and down. "Where is it?"

"I'm not a bloody octopus," Sinead pointed out. She raised her head over the top of the board and smiled at him. "I said you'd come and collect it."

"Oh, you did, did you?" Hamza said, drawing back his

shoulders. "Are you forgetting which of us gives the orders around here, Detective Con—"

"Aye. Jog on and get it," Sinead replied, and Hamza smirked.

"Fair enough," he said, slipping his hands into his pockets and strolling out of the car park. "But it had better be bloody paid for!"

"This is it."

The officer who had eventually identified herself as Constable Suzi Tanaka pointed up a slope to where a dilapidated old touring caravan stood half-hidden by weeds and tall grass. It was a filthy, crumbling midden of a thing, propped at the front with bricks and broken planks, and blackened with what Logan first thought was fire damage, but realised upon further inspection was just years of weathering left unchecked.

Curtains were closed in all the windows. At least, he thought so, but the green moss and yellow scum staining the acrylic made it almost impossible to see for sure.

The caravan, Constable Tanaka had explained, belonged to a local 'character' who went by the name Bernie the Beacon. He had moved to the area eight to ten years earlier—nobody could quite remember when he showed up or where he came from—and he was notable for two reasons.

Firstly, he was a forager who never spent a penny on food, and existed solely on what he could find in nature, in other people's bins, or splattered on the road. He'd often be found in the bar of the Salen Hotel—he did spend money on drink, it seemed—crowing about his favourite roadkill recipes.

The second notable thing about him was that he was a lunatic.

That was how the locals described him, at least, and while Constable Tanaka didn't feel qualified enough to put a label on the man, she had to admit that he was an odd one.

His oddness manifested itself in some quite particular ways—beyond the eating dead animals from the side of the road thing, that is.

The simplest way to describe him, if not perhaps the most accurate, was a conspiracy theorist. He believed the government was out to get not just him, but everyone, and that they were poisoning the water, the food supply, and the air itself with 'microagitators' designed to cause brain cancers and birth deformities.

He did not, as his tab at the Salen Hotel would testify, believe they had done anything untoward to the alcohol supplies.

He believed Wi-Fi was causing sterility in children and senility in the elderly.

He believed the Earth wasn't just flat, it was a box, inside which lived an Illuminati-style cabal of lizard people who were secretly running the whole show.

He believed an awful lot of things, it seemed, most of which anyone in their right mind would dismiss as a load of old shite.

Despite the natural scepticism of both locals and any visitors to the area who made the mistake of getting into conversation with him, for the past few years, Bernie had been producing a quarterly newsletter he called 'The Beacon,' which he claimed shone a light on the everyday deceptions of the government, the machinations of the evil lizard race living beneath our feet, and the dangers of high speed internet access.

It also usually contained a recipe for pheasant, venison, or—depending on what recent pickings had been like on the B roads around Acharacle—badger.

The publication was generally well-received in the area, though not for the reasons Bernie may have hoped. It was routinely mocked and derided, and occasionally spoofed with counterfeit editions that were no more or less ludicrous than the real thing, and so completely pointless as an attempt at satire.

"And he hasn't been seen since when?" Logan asked, regarding the caravan like it was something toxic. Which, given the state of it, it probably was.

"Ten days. Two weeks. Thereabouts," the constable said. "It's hard to be sure with Bernie. Your mind sort of shuts him out when you see him. Pretends he's not there, sort of thing. It's a form of self-preservation, I think. If you make eye contact, you're basically inviting him to come and talk to you, so most people round here just instinctively try not to see him. Easier all round."

He had a tent, she'd told him. A small, one-man pop-up number whose description fit the remains of the one they'd found with the body. He spent much of the year wild camping, telling locals that the caravan was his office, while the wilderness was his home.

"Want me to break the door down?" the constable asked, the look on her face suggesting she was dying for the opportunity. "Always wanted to see what he's got going on in there. Bet it's mental."

Logan considered the offer for a moment, then shook his

head. "Give me a minute while I check something first," he said, taking out his phone. He swiped to his contacts, grimaced at the very sight of Geoff Palmer's name, then tapped to call.

Nothing happened.

"Who are you with?" Constable Tanaka asked, indicating the phone.

"Vodafone."

The PC shook her head. "Won't get a signal with Vodafone. Won't get a signal with Three, either. Or EE." She shrugged. "In fact, any of them, really. It's a bit of a blackspot." She tapped the radio on her shoulder. "We're old school here."

"Right. Aye. Fair enough," Logan said, returning the phone to his pocket. "Are you able to call over to someone at the scene?"

"Yeah, one of the local lads is up there. Why?"

This, in many ways, was better, as it would save him the task of having to talk to Geoff Palmer himself. Once was bad enough. Twice in a single day? He wouldn't wish that on anyone.

Well, maybe Tyler.

"Get him to talk to the Scene of Crime team. See if they found anything on the remains."

"Like what?"

"Just anything," Logan said.

While she made the call, he picked his way up the slope and through the jungle of grass that surrounded the caravan. It definitely felt empty. It felt abandoned, in fact, with the weeds and moss combining to give the impression that Mother Nature herself was claiming squatter's rights on the place.

Up close, he could confirm that the windows were blocked on the other side, although not with curtains as he'd originally thought. Cardboard had been taped over the already barely semi-transparent acrylic, fully shutting off the inside of the caravan from the world beyond its flimsy walls.

If they had to break into the place, it wasn't going to take much effort. With a bit of huffing and puffing, Logan was convinced he could blow this house down.

"Copy that, Chris, ta."

Logan turned away from the caravan as Constable Tanaka ended her conversation. "Well?" he asked.

"Not much on the body, sir. Almost everything's burned away."

"But?"

"But I think you already know what I'm going to say," Suzi replied.

"They found a key," Logan said.

"They did," the PC confirmed. "Chris, the new guy, is bringing it over."

Logan nodded. "Good stuff."

"I was to pass on a message to you, too. When you hear the helicopter in a minute, you've to look up."

"Look up? Why? Did Palmer say that?"

"No idea. I was just told to pass it on. It is now passed on, so my work is done." The constable tapped a finger to her ear. "Although... that sounds like the chopper starting up now."

Clearly, the younger PC's hearing was better than Logan's. He tilted his head, angling an ear in the direction they'd driven from, but didn't hear anything.

Then, just as he was about to say as much, he picked up the faint *whumming* of helicopter blades firing up.

Just a minute or two later, and the sound was unmistakable. They must've driven four or five miles from the site to get to the caravan, but the helicopter sounded like it was just a couple of hundred yards away.

Mind you, the way that bloody road twisted and turned, maybe it *was* that close if you were to draw a straight line between there and where they stood.

The way the sound bounced off the surrounding hills made it difficult to pinpoint where it was coming from, and had Logan not remembered the vague direction they'd driven from, he'd have no idea of which way to look.

Even then, when the helicopter did finally rise high enough to come into view, it was further over on the right than he'd been expecting, and the sight of it took him by surprise.

Although, not as much as the sight of the woman dangling from a harness beneath it.

Even at that distance, and over the sound of the rotors, Logan could've sworn he heard her laughing. She waved both hands—not directly at him, exactly, but at the world in general in the hope that he saw, and Logan raised a hand to wave back.

"Who's that?" Constable Tanaka asked.

"That," Logan said, as both helicopter and winch raised higher into the air. "Is someone making the best of a bad situation."

CHAPTER SEVEN

THE KEY, blackened and charred as it was, fit the lock of the caravan door perfectly. Given the smell that rolled out when Logan pulled the door open, though, he almost wished that it hadn't.

"Jesus Christ," he uttered, burying his nose in the crook of his elbow to stop himself boaking.

He was no stranger to the scent of death, and identified it right away. There was something different about this version, though. It was *gamier*.

The partially eviscerated remains of a pheasant hung from a hook that had been screwed into the caravan ceiling, like the world's most gruesome light fitting. Its feet were attached to the hook with a bent length of wire, and its bloodied wings had fallen open so they were pointing almost directly to the floor.

A bucket had been placed beneath it, though judging by the dried brown stain at the bottom of it, there hadn't been much blood left in the bird to catch. No bloody wonder, given the mangled mess of its torso, which had exploded under the pressure of a motor vehicle driving straight over the top of it.

The pheasant seemed to move as the sunlight from the open door hit it, then Logan saw the maggots wriggling around in its rotting carcass.

"Aw, you manky bastard," Logan said, then he stepped back out of the caravan, coughed, and spat onto the grass.

"You alright?" asked the constable who had turned up with the key. He was a young lad. So young, in fact, that he'd make Tyler seem like an elder statesman, and Ben look like some sort of reanimated cadaver.

He was good-looking, too, with blond curly hair, skin as smooth as marble, and eyes of such a deep, rich brown you could almost fall right into them.

Logan had taken an instant disliking to the bastard. Judging by the way Constable Tanaka stared at him, though, she held him in much higher regard.

"I'm fine," Logan said, not wishing to show even a suggestion of weakness in front of this younger, fitter, significantly more attractive man. "Just needed to take a couple of big breaths."

Constable Chris Miller nodded sagely. "Swimming."

Logan blinked. "What?"

"Swimming. That's what you do. You take big breaths."

He took a big breath to demonstrate, and held it, held it, *held it...*

Logan watched the younger man going red, then purple.

"Aye. I suppose so," he said, calling an end to the demonstration before the silly bugger passed out.

Chris exhaled sharply, like his lungs had gone into full

reverse thrust. "I'm good at swimming," he announced out of nowhere.

"He's *really* good at swimming," Constable Tanaka said. "He's being modest."

"No, *you're* good at swimming," Chris told her.

"Not as good as you, though," Suzi replied. "You're way better than I am."

"I'm not *way* better. You're really good. Anyway, I've got bigger feet. And you know what they say about guys with big feet?" Chris said.

Constable Tanaka smirked. "I do."

"Dead good at swimming," Chris concluded. He pointed to Logan's feet. "Are you any good at swimming, sir?"

Logan looked from one constable to the other, then glanced around to see if any hidden cameras were watching on. There was a real danger, he thought, that this whole conversation was another of Herbert Gibson's internet pranks. Otherwise, the Police Scotland recruitment crisis was much worse than he thought.

"I'm going back in," he said.

"To the caravan?" asked Suzi.

"Aye, to the... Where else would I be talking about?"

"Aye. No. Just..." Chris shrugged. "You were talking about going swimming, an' that. We weren't clear on what... But, aye. The caravan. Good call. Want us to come with you?"

"Be a bit of a squeeze," Constable Tanaka said. She smirked at the younger officer. "But I'm game if you are."

"No. Just wait here," Logan said, then he pointed to Chris. "In fact, better still, you wait somewhere else. Go back to the scene. Ask for DC Tyler Neish. Tell him you've been given direct orders to assist him."

If the constable answered, Logan didn't hear it, preferring to take his chances with whatever waited in the caravan than listen to that pair of cretins for a moment longer. PC Tanaka had struck him as promising when he'd first met her, but something about the other constable's presence appeared to have pruned her IQ.

The smell in the caravan wasn't as bad, now that he was prepared for it, and it had a bit of time to waft out through the open door. It was still a long way from pleasant—it was still a considerable distance from neutral, in fact—but it would be tolerable enough in short bursts to let him have a poke around.

It was not a big living space, but then if what he'd been told was correct, Bernie only used it for what could, if you were feeling generous, be described as 'work purposes.' And, if you were feeling less generous, 'his demented ramblings.'

The walls were covered in old newspaper cuttings, Polaroids, and handwritten notes in fastidiously neat block capitals. There were hundreds of separate pieces of paper, pinned up with no clearly discernible pattern, then joined up with sagging lengths of string.

An article about sewerage in a local river had a string connecting it to a printout of an internet page about the possibility of water on the planet Mars, which in turn was linked to a list of the months of the year, with all the months ending in the letter 'Y' heavily circled and underlined with a red pen.

One whole wall and a boarded-up window were decorated with adverts for something called 'The Westerly Wellness Retreat'. The name rang a bell somewhere at the back of Logan's brain, but he couldn't quite place where he'd seen or heard the name before.

Bernie seemed to hold some deep fascination for the place, though, and had torn out or printed off thirty or more advertisements for the place, before haphazardly pinning them up. Judging by the colour of some of the paper, and the way its edges curled, some of the cuttings were a year or more old.

Another wall held mostly Polaroids. The subject of many of them was a grey-haired man who never seemed to be aware that someone was taking his picture. Strings ran from several of the images, linking them to everything from a medical negligence case in Yorkshire to mass bird deaths in Arizona.

The man, too, was familiar, but the smell of the rotting pheasant carcass was starting to take its toll, and Logan couldn't face standing around while he rifled through his memory banks. Instead, he plucked one of the photographs free, lumbered down the caravan's fold-out metal steps, and blew the stench of decay out through his nostrils with what little air was left in his lungs.

"That's ripe in there," he remarked, then he held up the photograph. "Who's this?"

"That? He's a local politician. Well, a politician who lives locally, anyway. MSP. Forget his name, but I can look it up. Bernie had a bit of an axe to grind with him."

"Oh? How come?"

The PC blew out her cheeks. "I think he was doing the bidding of a race of lizard men or something. That was the gist of it."

"Aye, well, I suppose that's as good a reason to hold a grudge as any," Logan conceded.

He looked down at the photograph, realising now why the man had looked so familiar. He was the Scottish Parliament member for the local constituency, and no doubt popped up on the news from time to time. He wasn't one of the big hitters, though, and things generally had to be pretty desperate before the media turned to him for a quote.

The photograph was taken from behind a bush, judging by the foliage in the foreground, and showed the politician putting a black bag into his green wheelie bin. To the casual observer, it was a late-middle-aged man taking the rubbish out, but there was no saying what Bernie saw in the photo, or why he felt the need to pin it to his wall.

"Was he aware of this grudge?" Logan asked. "The MSP, I mean. Did he know Bernie was spying on him?"

"Oh, yeah. He's put in umpteen complaints. Got really angry a couple of times, when Bernie accosted him while he was out with his daughters. He's got a non-harassment order out on him at the moment."

"And did that put a stop to it?"

Tanaka shrugged. "I mean, he hasn't put in any more complaints lately, so presumably, yes."

Logan studied the man in the photo, and wondered how recently it had been taken. "Is he around at the moment? Is he here or in Edinburgh?"

"Why would I know that? I don't have his diary," the constable sniped, before she remembered the seniority of the man she was talking to, and worked quickly to salvage the situation. "I could find out, though, sir."

"Aye. You do that," Logan told her, shooting her a look that made it clear he'd picked up on the insubordination, but was choosing to overlook it just this once. "Is there anyone else Bernie was rubbing up the wrong way round here?"

"Pretty much everyone at one point or another,"

Constable Tanaka said. "He could be an annoying bastard when he wanted to be."

Great. That narrowed it down.

"You think it's murder, sir?" the PC asked.

"We're not sure yet," Logan replied. "Could've been an accident."

"But you don't think so."

Logan considered the photo in his hand, then the caravan behind him. "No," he admitted. "I don't think so. But fingers crossed that I'm wrong."

Forty minutes later, Logan stood in the makeshift Incident Room, taking it all in. It had changed quite a bit since he'd had his little chat with Herbert.

Space-wise, there wasn't much taking in required. The room was about a quarter of the size of the Incident Room in Fort William station, which in turn, was significantly smaller than the one in Inverness.

Two mismatched desks—one a flat-packed laminate thing, the other made of scuffed black metal—stood against the wall across from the door, facing one another. A long extension socket trailed from a plug on the opposite side of the room so those using the desks could plug their laptops in, and Sinead was in the process of taping the cable down so nobody tripped over it.

There was a single chair, which Ben had already claimed, despite the fact that it was a hard plastic thing with no wheels, and a few inches too short to make sitting at either desk in any way comfortable.

Various bags and boxes had been shoved into a corner, then an attempt had been made to hide them with a piece of bright blue tarp that only served to draw attention to them.

Perhaps most notable of all was the six-foot-tall squirrel that stood propped in the corner on Logan's right, and which had caused him to eject a hissed, "Jesus!" when he'd first entered the room and clapped eyes on the bloody thing.

After the initial moment of fist-clenching alarm, Logan had recognised the outfit as 'Dinny the Drink-Driving Squirrel'—the mascot of a public awareness campaign that had been run across Scotland eight or nine years ago.

Logan had never quite understood the need to have a talking cartoon squirrel fronting the TV adverts and rocking up at gala days. Very few eight-year-olds drank to excess, and fewer still took to the roads afterwards, so quite why the campaign seemed targeted at them, he had no idea.

"Is this...? What's this?" Logan asked, taking in the whole of the room. This involved moving his eye just a fraction of a millimetre in each direction. "Is this it? This can't be it."

"This is it," Ben confirmed.

"This can't be it," Logan insisted, but Ben once again confirmed that it was.

"Sinead managed to find us a Big Board, sir," Hamza said, indicating the rectangle of cork that now sat precariously balanced on a three-legged wooden artist's easel.

"Is that what that is?" Logan asked. "Could she no' have maybe found us a window at the same time?"

"We've been in worst places, Jack," said Ben.

"Aye," Logan conceded. "But no' on purpose. Speaking of worst places, mind you, where's Tyler? I've got a caravan I want him to check out."

The mention of Tyler's name brought an explosion of

movement from the corner of the room, as Dinny the Drink-Driving Squirrel suddenly came to life, raised his arms above his head, and let out a decidedly Tyler-sounding roar.

He lurched forwards, arms still flailing, then the weight of the outfit caught him off guard, and Logan stepped aside as Dinny went stumbling across the room.

Tyler ejected a muffled, "Shite!" as he tripped on the extension cable, lost his balance, then landed face down on the tarp, partially collapsing the boxes beneath it.

Silence hung over the room for several seconds, then Logan sighed and turned back to the others. "So, aye, if you happen to see DC Neish anywhere, tell him I've got a job for him, will you?"

"Will do, Jack," Ben said. "I'm sure he'll turn up in the fullness of time."

There was a knock at the door behind him, and Constable Tanaka poked her head into the room. "Just so you know, sir, that MSP we discussed? He's at home at the moment."

"Good. Thanks for checking up on that," Logan said.

"I've written down his address," the constable said. She handed over a piece of paper with an address scrawled on it, then looked down at the mascot lying sprawled on the floor. "What happened to Dinny?"

"Help!" came a muffled voice from inside the fallen squirrel. "I can't get out."

"Hm? Oh. He's back on the bevvy. Sad state of affairs," Logan said, then he tapped the piece of paper she'd handed him. "Glenuig. That far from here?"

"Not really. It's this side of Roshven," the constable replied. Then, when Logan continued to stare blankly, she clarified. "About forty-five minutes' drive."

"I know where it is, sir," Sinead said, looking up from where she was reapplying the tape that had been ripped up by Dinny's giant squirrel feet.

"Good. Then get your coat," Logan told her. "You and I are going to pay this fine upstanding politician a wee visit."

CHAPTER EIGHT

IT WAS JUST over twenty miles from the station in Strontian to the croft where the MSP lived. On a normal road—one that didn't wind like a pile of dropped string—the journey would've taken half an hour, tops. On this narrow, twisting, pot-holed monstrosity, though, it was going to take substantially longer.

For a number of reasons, Logan was relieved he hadn't brought Tyler. Not only was DC Neish an annoying bastard, but he had a hair-trigger stomach that would've ejected most of its contents at the first downhill S-bend.

Besides, it was going to take him ages to get out of that squirrel costume, and as amusing as that would be to watch, Logan didn't have that sort of time to waste.

Not that there was any great urgency, of course. The Golden Hour—that period immediately after a murder had been committed when the chances of making an arrest were at their highest—had passed days, maybe weeks ago. Statistically, their chances of making a collar on this one were slim.

The victim—if, indeed, he was a victim of anything other

than his own stupidity—was a bit of an unknown quantity. Constable Tanaka didn't know his last name, and had her doubts that anyone else would, either. She also didn't know where he'd come from, or what had brought him to the area in the first place.

If what she'd said was right, and he'd made himself a pain in the arse to the local population in general, then—given the likely lack of forensic evidence—pinning down the killer was going to be a tall order.

The one positive with a case like this was that media interest was likely to be low. At least, it was likely to be low unless they got wind that a vaguely prominent political figure might be tied to it in some way, at which point it would become a circus.

That was why they were driving out to see the MSP now, so they could dismiss any involvement before the press had a chance to hear about it.

It was approaching dinner time, and Logan realised he hadn't eaten anything since that ice cream at *Nardini's*, which now seemed like a lifetime ago. He'd tried to text Maddie to apologise for having to run off, but his phone remained steadfastly signal free, and every attempt ended with a big red *message failed* error.

The sun was on a downward trajectory, painting the sky in shades of orange and purple, and silhouetting the handful of grey clouds into dark bottomless voids.

A glance in the driver's side wing mirror showed that Taggart's head was still hanging out of the back window, his stupidly long tongue trailing out behind him and flapping in the wind.

The road rose, then dipped sharply, and both detectives made a sort of *hurp* noise as their stomachs smooshed upwards. That one had made even Logan feel queasy. It would likely have killed Tyler altogether.

"Rough road, but pretty nice around here," Sinead remarked, as they turned a bend and saw a stretch of beach lining a body of water on the left. "I think that's Loch Moidart. Maybe Loch Sunart. Something like that, anyway. We used to come out here when I was younger. Before Harris was born. He's nearly as bad as Tyler on windy roads."

"Aye. It's nice," Logan agreed, but he barely glanced at the scenery unfolding beside them. Instead, he stretched out his fingers, wriggled in his seat, then exhaled. "How are you doing?"

Sinead turned away from the view to look over at him. "Fine, sir. Aye. You?"

"Fine. But, I mean... How are you really doing?"

Sinead frowned. "Still fine."

Logan kept his eyes on the road ahead. Sinead waited for him to say something more, then went back to looking out of the window.

"It's just..."

She turned back again. Waited.

"Just what?"

"After, you know. Everything that happened. To you. Recently."

"Oh. That." She rubbed a hand across her mouth like she was checking how dry her lips were. "I'm fine. Not like it's the first time something like that happened." She smiled, but it was a poor attempt. "I seem to have a bit of a knack for being taken hostage."

It was more than that, though. They both knew it. What had happened... The things that had been done to her... And the things, worse still, that had *almost* been done...

"I was talking to Maddie today," he said.

Sinead sat up at that. "Your daughter? Wow. That's... that's great news! I didn't think she was speaking to you."

"Just barely," Logan replied. "But she was talking. About things from before. About Owen Petrie."

"Oh."

"And something she said, it got me thinking," Logan continued, slowing to let a car coming in the opposite direction squeeze past on a rare straight section of road. "I, eh, I have this tendency to assume things are fine."

"Things *are* fine, sir," Sinead insisted, but Logan pressed on, regardless.

"I think that because the immediate danger has passed, then that's it. Trauma over. Everything back to normal." He turned to look at her, and the look on her face told him everything he needed to know. "But that's not how it works, is it? Not for most people."

"I mean..." Sinead began, then she sighed. "No. That's not how it works."

"No," Logan said, nodding. "Which brings me back to my earlier question. How are you really doing?"

Sinead pulled the strap of her seatbelt away from her shoulder, then replaced it in more or less the same position. She crossed her feet, decided she didn't like it, then crossed them again the other way.

Eventually, when she had finished footering, she gave the tiniest of shrugs. "Good days and bad."

Logan said nothing, just left the silence waiting there to be filled.

"I've been getting a lot of sleep paralysis," she told him.

"Wake up frozen, and think I'm back there. Think it's happening again."

"Have you spoken to a doctor?" Logan asked. "Could be some lingering effect of the drugs."

"They ran tests. Reckon it's psychological."

"I see. Well, I mean, that's no' really a surprise, given everything." He flexed his fingers on the wheel. "Still can't believe that bastard of a constable. I wish you'd said something earlier about him. We could've..."

"I know. I should've told you," Sinead admitted. "Although, I've thought about it a lot. What he did. Tried to do, anyway. And, the fact of it is, if he hadn't been there—if he hadn't failed to report back—they might not have found me."

Logan gave this some thought, but couldn't argue with the logic. "I suppose. And what's Tyler saying about it all? The sleep paralysis and stuff, I mean."

"Tyler doesn't know," Sinead admitted. "He's had enough going on with his recovery. I don't want to worry him. He just sleeps through. When it passes, I don't wake him up."

"You should tell him," Logan said. "You can't run a marriage on secrets and lies. Take it from someone who knows. It doesn't work."

"Aye. I know. It's just... it's been a rough year for him. The car accident. The cancer."

"Getting stuck in a big squirrel costume."

Sinead smirked. "Aye. That, too. We put a safety pin through the zip after he'd wrestled himself into it. Assuming he doesn't roast alive, then I'll talk to him when we get home."

"Will you, though?" Logan asked.

"Yes. Definitely," Sinead said, although it sounded more like a 'probably' to Logan's ears.

"Well, in the meantime, you know where I am."

"I do, sir. And thanks," Sinead said, then she threw an arm forward and grasped at her seatbelt as the BMW came to an abrupt halt in the middle of the road. "What is it? What happened? Did we hit something?" she asked, stretching to see over the bonnet.

"No. Sorry. Just... It's that." Logan indicated a signpost at a junction ahead. It listed various locations, including a ferry terminal, a natural history centre, and the Ardnamurchan Lighthouse.

"Thinking of doing some sightseeing, sir?" Sinead asked.

Logan shook his head and pointed to another sign. This one was smaller, and had been painted by hand onto a wooden board. An arrow pointed in the same direction as the other notices, while the text proclaimed:

WESTERLY WELLNESS RETREAT. ALL WELCOME.

Logan checked the clock on the car's dash, then glanced along the road branching off on the left. "You got a phone signal?" he asked.

"Not a thing, sir, no," Sinead replied. "But I've got a radio. Some rookie constable gave me his to use."

"I think I know the one," Logan said. "Good looking?"

"Eh, not particularly. Just a standard radio, sir," Sinead said, and they shared a smile at the joke.

"Aye, good one," Logan said. "Right, give a call to the station and tell Ben we're going to be later back than expected." He indicated left, then swung the car in that direction. "We're going on a wee detour."

Shona Maguire had just about finished checking in the latest visitor to the Raigmore Hospital Mortuary. The body had been deposited on the trolley in the chilled room next door, and the paperwork had been rattled through, officially logging him in the system.

It was past dinner time now. On her day off. She didn't have to be here. The body, still bagged, could be tucked away in one of the drawers until morning. There was nothing pressing or urgent keeping her here. Nothing forcing her to stay.

But the alternative was to go home. Alone. To a house where she no longer felt safe.

She double-checked the data on her screen, then clicked the button to submit the form, finalising the last of the paperwork.

That done, she swung down off her stool, necked the last few dregs of a *Bombay Bad Boy* flavoured *Pot Noodle* like a Viking quaffing a tankard of ale, then headed to the sink to scrub up.

The water spluttered out at first, cold to the touch, then rapidly becoming hot enough to blister skin. She waited until the steam was rising, then swung the tap a little to the right, mixing in a stream of cold water to bring the temperature back to a tolerable level.

She deployed the soap next—three big pumps from the dispenser, twenty seconds of scrubbing her hands and fingers from every conceivable angle, then into the water they went.

She was well into the process when she raised her head and looked into the mirror fixed to the wall above the sink.

There was a man there. Behind her. A few feet back.

Half-hidden by the steam so she could barely make out his scarred face, his wide, lidless eyes, and the oxygen mask expanding and contracting on his mouth.

He lunged at her. Grabbed for her with withered hands and twisted features. She turned, arms raised, a scream building in her chest.

And then he was gone. Evaporated, like a ghost in the steam.

Shona chastised herself. "Idiot."

She turned back to the sink and finished scrubbing up. Turned off the taps. Dried her hands. Studiously avoided looking in the mirror, for fear of what she might see.

Or what she might remember.

She instructed Alexa to, "Play the mortuary playlist," and waited for the first track—*Axel F* from the *Beverly Hills Cop* soundtrack—to kick in. Then, she got herself gloved up, threw open the double doors to the mortuary like she was a sheriff entering a Wild West saloon, and set to work.

CHAPTER NINE

IF LOGAN and Sinead had thought the road had been rough prior to taking the turn off, they were soon forced to reevaluate. The twenty-mile stretch from Salen, where they'd made the turn, to Kilchoan, which they'd reached just shy of an hour later, must surely have been the inspiration for the world's earliest rollercoasters.

It wound, it twisted, it rose, and it plunged. It tilted at points, so it felt like the car was going to roll sideways off the crumbling tarmac to be dashed on the rocks, flattened in a field, or dumped into the water, depending on which of the three they happened to be passing at the time.

There were points where it was almost too narrow for the car, and stretches where it was wide enough for one-and-a-half vehicles.

Not two, though. Never two. Not at the same time. Not going in opposite directions.

Usually, Logan didn't mind driving. He could switch into a sort of autopilot, letting his hands and feet do all the work and freeing up his brain to concentrate on more pressing issues.

This road, though, didn't allow for autopilot. This road demanded full attention at all times, springing surprises from hairpin bends to kamikaze sheep every few seconds, and never the same thing twice.

Even Taggart pulled his head in and lay down on the seat as the BMW rumbled and bounced through the sharp bends and short straights, driver and passenger alike slowly turning shades of green up front.

"This is a fucking nightmare," Logan had voiced, roughly forty minutes into the drive. "How is this allowed? People shouldn't be driving on this."

Sinead, for fear of projectile vomiting the moment she opened her mouth, said nothing.

They both almost sobbed with relief when, some twelve agonising minutes later, they finally saw another homemade sign indicating their destination lay just two hundred yards ahead.

"Close enough," Logan concluded, immediately swinging the BMW into a lay-by and up onto the grassy verge beside it. "We'll walk from here."

"Aye, be good to stretch our legs," Sinead said, practically falling out of the door.

The ground moved under Logan's feet as he stepped out of the car, lurching like the deck of a ship in a storm.

"Christ," he muttered, leaning on the BMW for support, and wiping the sweat from his brow with the back of his other hand.

There was a smell of cow shit languishing on the breeze. This wasn't doing his stomach any favours, and meant that the big breaths he'd planned to get his nausea under control would probably do just the opposite.

A frantic scurrying from the back window forced him to look up from where he'd been staring at his feet and trying to assure his brain that he was on a solid surface. Taggart was attempting to throw himself out through the gap between the door and the glass, but his legs were too short to give him the launch thrust he needed.

"Right, wait. Out you come," Logan said, shoving the dog back through the window and pulling open the door. "Don't go anywhere," he warned when Taggart jumped out and landed beside him. "Or do. Right now, I don't care."

There was a *hurp* from the other side of the car, and the flavour of the air became even worse. Logan swallowed back a mouthful of saliva that burned his throat all the way down.

"You alright, Detective Constable?"

A hand was thrust into the air. A thumb was raised. "Be right as rain in a minute, sir," Sinead said.

"Good stuff," Logan said, then he suddenly bent double, steadied his hands on his thighs, and vomited onto the dog.

Ten minutes, and one hasty clean-up job later, Logan, Sinead, and a slightly shell-shocked Taggart arrived at the entrance to the Westerly Wellness Retreat.

Or, more accurately, they arrived at the wide metal gate of a field that housed a large marquee with those words emblazoned across the side in a shade of pastel blue.

Several smaller tents had been erected around the main one like orbiting satellites. They were all tipi-style triangles, large enough to accommodate five or six people, as long as none of them had any personal space issues.

The main marquee was roughly thirty feet wide, and maybe forty along the length. Flaps had been lifted on three of the six plastic windows that lined the side facing the gate, and it didn't look as if anyone was inside.

The whole field felt empty, in fact, with not a sound coming from any of the tents, and the sinking sensation Logan felt at the thought that this might have been a wasted trip almost made him chunder again.

The gate wasn't locked, and swung inwards when Logan slid the bolt over. Taggart shot through the gap the moment it was wide enough, and went tearing across the field to check out the closest tent.

"Doesn't look like anyone's home, does it?" Sinead said, clearly sharing the same concerns as him. That drive had been quite an ordeal, if it had all been for nothing. Never mind PTSD over Sinead's abduction, that road would likely haunt both their dreams for months.

"No," Logan admitted. "But you never know. There might be someone about."

He had just stepped through the gate when he heard the *clack* of something behind him that he knew, instinctively, was a weapon.

Pulling Sinead behind him, he turned to find a stout woman with severe hair cradling an over and under shotgun in a way that suggested it wouldn't take much for her to use it.

"You shouldn't be letting your dog run like that," the woman said, and her accent caught Logan off guard far more than the gun had. It was Devon, or Cornwall. Somewhere in that neck of the woods, anyway. Whoever she was, she was a long way from home. "It could worry my sheep."

Logan side-eyed their surroundings, still keeping most of his focus on the gun. "What sheep?" he asked, then he followed the tilt of her head up the hill behind her, to where a handful of microscopic white dots were visible near the distant peak.

"Them sheep."

"They don't look overly concerned at the moment," Logan said. "Though, maybe I could get a better look at them if I had access to the Hubble telescope."

"I could shoot it, you know? The dog. I'd be within my rights. The law's on my side."

"Is that the Protection of Livestock Act, nineteen-fifty-three?" asked Sinead, which drew a lowering of eyebrows from the woman, and a raising of them from Logan. "Because if that's the law you're referring to, then it doesn't apply. There are no sheep in this field."

The woman with the gun sniffed. "I was referring, I'll have you know, to the Scottish Outdoor Access Code, which gives permission for farmers to shoot dogs. I'm a farmer, and that, unless I'm very much mistaken, is a fucking dog."

"If it's attacking livestock," Sinead added.

"Excuse me?"

"It doesn't give you the right to just randomly shoot dogs," Sinead explained. "Only dogs that are attacking livestock." She looked round to where Taggart was joyfully dragging his arse across the grass. "And he clearly isn't."

Logan felt that this was a good time to produce his ID. "Detective Chief Inspector Jack Logan. Police Scotland Major Investigations," he said, hoping this would get some sort of reaction from the gun-toting old crone.

It did not.

"Have you got a licence for that firearm?" he asked, returning the warrant card to his pocket.

"Course I bleedin' do. What do you take me for? One of them gang-bangers, or what haves you?" She patted the gun. "You wouldn't catch Barbara breaking no laws. Not on your life."

"Right," Logan said, making a mental note to have someone check the paperwork later. "Well, Barbara, I wonder—"

"Sorry?" the woman said, interrupting. "Are you talking to me or are you talking to the gun?"

"Why would I be...? Obviously, I'm talking to you."

"I'm not Barbara." She waggled the shotgun, making both detectives tense. "*She's* Barbara."

Logan pinched the bridge of his nose and sighed. He really wasn't in the mood for this. "I see. And your name is?"

"None of your bleedin' business, that's what. I don't need to tell you nothing, I don't. Not on your Nelly. I know my rights, see? Filth or not, you can't go demanding to know nothing of me."

"Filth?" Logan muttered.

"Well, filth, pigs, whatever you want to call yourselves."

"Ideally, neither of those," Logan replied.

"Well, whatever. I don't have to tell you nothin'. Not a bleedin' word, and you can't make me."

"Actually, you do, and we can," Sinead said. "Failing to provide your name, address, date and place of birth, and nationality, when asked, is a criminal offence."

The old woman's eyes narrowed. "Since when?"

"Since you turned up waving a shotgun and threatening to shoot my dog," Logan said. "Until such time as we know for sure that thing's licensed, you're a suspect in a potential criminal investigation. So, how about you stop pissing about and tell us your name? We've no' got all bloody night."

The old woman ran a hand along the back of her shotgun like she was stroking a pet cat, then gave in with a shrug and a grunt. "Fine. If you must know, it's Kathryn."

"Kathryn what?" Logan asked.

"Chegwin. Yes, before you ask, like that smirking little loudmouthed bastard off the telly. Date of birth, twelfth of January, nineteen thirty-eight. You want my bleedin' address? It's there," she said, pointing to a ramshackle old croft house set back from the track a few hundred yards past the end of the field, on the opposite side of the road. "Figure it out yourself. Alright? Alright."

She gestured past them with the end of the gun, to where Taggart was sniffing around the sealed entrance of one of the smaller tents.

"I knew you filth were getting younger and younger, but I didn't realise it applied to your bleedin' dogs, too. That one's barely got its mothers teat out of his mouth, and you've got it sniffing around, looking for clues. Another mindless bleedin' drone of the state. Just what we need. And he won't find nothin', neither."

"Why not?" asked Sinead.

"Well, because there's no bugger there, is there? It's obvious. You can tell just by looking at the place." Kathryn shook her head. "Bunch of weirdo bastards, the lot of them, mind you. God, if I have to listen to any more chanting at all the bleedin' hours, I don't know what I'll do. But I wouldn't like to be on the receiving end of whatever it is, I'll tell you that much for free."

"Chanting?" Logan asked.

"*Chanting*, if you bloody well please!" Kathryn confirmed. "Hippies, they are. Humming and bleedin' hawing, dancing around in their skimpies with their arses hanging out for all the world to see." She rolled her eyes. "And the sex. Oh, Lord Jesus and Mary, the sex. Like fucking rabbits, some of them. In their tents. Two together. Three on one. Swapping around, and all sorts. Orgies. That's what they're up to. *Orgies* of all bleedin' things."

"And you've seen this?" Sinead asked.

"Well, I don't have to see it, do I, dear? Not for want of trying sometimes, mind you. They've had some big strapping lads in there I wouldn't mind getting a right good rogering off. I'd have a right good bleedin' go on some of them, if I had my way, let me tell you. Great big meaty fellas, so's they are. Big, healthy lads."

"Jesus," Logan muttered, pushing that unwelcome mental image away.

"But I hears them, don't I? Hammering away. Pawing and pounding on each other. Moaning, and groaning. '*Yes, yes, yes. Ooh, do it like that! Careful, or you'll have me bleedin' eye out,*' and all sorts. You don't need to see it when you've got it going on in surround sound at all hours of the day and night." She sniffed and shrugged her rounded shoulders. "I mean, give me that over the chanting, right enough. I'll take the shagging over the chanting any day of the week, and that's not a word of a lie."

Logan and Sinead stood in stunned silence for several seconds. Even Taggart, who had been busily exploring the tents, now just sat on the grass like he needed a moment to come to terms with everything he'd just heard.

"But anyway, they're not there at the moment, obviously," Kathryn said. "Any fool could've seen that from the road."

"Do you know where they are?" Logan asked.

"Of course I bleedin' know where they are. It's heading for sunset, isn't it?"

Logan glanced up at the darkening sky. Over on the left, the clouds were being painted in purples and reds. "So?"

"So, they're going to be where they always are at this time. They'll be up at the lighthouse, won't they? Getting up to whatever the fuck it is they get up to up there, the dirty hippie bastards that they are."

"The lighthouse?" Logan asked. He looked off in the direction of the setting sun. "How far away is that?"

"About six miles," Kathryn said. "Though I should warn you, from here on in, the road gets pretty rough..."

CHAPTER TEN

THE CARAVAN WAS... upsetting. That was the best way that Tyler could think to describe it. Even from the outside, there was something depressing about it, like the land it stood on had been afflicted by some low-key witch's curse that just made you feel a bit down in the dumps whenever you got too close.

Down in the dumps, coincidentally, was where he felt the caravan probably belonged. It looked like something from the Seventies, all clunky angles and brown trim. Someone—possibly the owner himself, but it could also have been some random passerby—had scrawled the words, 'The Beacon,' in a particularly dense dirty area, the marks revealing the yellowing paintwork beneath.

He could smell the place from out here, he thought, although that might've been his imagination. Constable Tanaka had warned him about the dead pheasant, and he would've sworn he could smell the thing from half a mile back up the road. Now that he was right outside, it was overpoweringly pungent, and his gag reflex was already slipping out of its tracksuit and running warm-up laps in anticipation of what might happen next.

The DC was immensely grateful, then, that Hamza had volunteered to come with him. And it had only taken some mild to moderate begging on Tyler's part.

"Imagine living in that," he remarked.

"Apparently he didn't," Hamza said. "He... I don't know. Worked there, I suppose. He slept in his tent."

"Probably wise. I wouldn't want to sleep in it, either. In fact, I don't even want to go in it. I'm struggling just looking at it, in fact."

"Aye, well, tough," Hamza replied. "I said I'd come with you, I didn't say I'd do it for you. We're both going in."

Tyler sucked air in through his teeth. "Looks a bit small for that. For the two of us, I mean."

"Right, well you can go in yourself, then."

"Actually, no. No, it'll be fine with the two of us," Tyler said, pulling a U-turn. He indicated the caravan door with a hand gesture. "Do you want to lead the way, or...?"

"Just get in," Hamza said, giving the DC a dunt with his elbow. "Before I leave you here on your own."

Tyler thought about begging some more, but the expression on Hamza's face told him it wasn't going to get him anywhere. So, following a series of deep breaths, he loosened his tie, pulled the neck of his shirt up to cover his mouth and nose, and cautiously entered the caravan.

The floor creaked as it took his weight, the caravan's rusted suspension objecting to his presence. Tyler wholeheartedly agreed with it. He objected to his presence there, too, mostly because his thin cotton shirt was doing nothing whatsoever to block out the smell.

"Oh, God," he muttered, staring in wide-eyed horror at

the maggot-infested pheasant carcass hanging by its feet from the ceiling. "Oh, God. No. No, no, no."

He about-turned, flung himself outside onto the grass, then bent double and swallowed back the urge to vomit.

"Bad?" Hamza asked.

Tyler couldn't yet speak, and his frantic hand movements didn't really help convey anything beyond a general sense of distress.

"It can't be that bad," Hamza said.

He plodded up the steps and disappeared into the caravan.

Then, a few seconds later, he plodded back down again, his face significantly paler than it had been before he'd gone inside.

"Aye, that's grim," he admitted.

"Did you see the—?" Tyler began, then he retched violently, his eyes watering. "The way it was—?"

He bent double again and spat onto the ground, shaking his head like he was trying to drive out the memory of the caravan's interior.

"We need to get the bird out of there," Hamza said.

"I'm not touching it!" Tyler cried, a little more forcefully than he'd intended.

"You've got gloves."

"I don't care if I've got a HAZMAT suit and a pair of fucking tongs, I'm not going near that thing," Tyler insisted.

Hamza tutted. "Right. Well, I suppose I'll do it, will I?"

"Well, I'm not, so..."

Hamza put his hands on his hips, looked back at the caravan for a moment, then returned his attention to Tyler. "I could order you to do it."

"I'll quit," Tyler said. "I mean it, I'd quit. Call one of them Uniforms. Get them to do it."

"Then we'll look like a right pair of arseholes," Hamza pointed out. "Can't even unhook a dead bird from a caravan ceiling. We deal with dead humans all the time!"

"Aye, but I wouldn't want to unhook one of them from a caravan ceiling, either," Tyler retorted. "And most of the time they've no' got maggots crawling out of their—"

He bent over again, made a sound like a blocked drain, then stared at a spot on the grass waiting for the moment to pass.

Hamza scratched his chin, considering the problem. There was an obvious solution, of course. It involved him going in, unhooking the dead bird's feet from the hook, then carrying it outside. It was simple.

And yet...

There really were a *lot* of maggots, and the carcass really did stink.

"Hold on! I've got a bag in the car."

Tyler straightened up, but still appeared a little unsteady on his feet. "What do you mean?"

"Like a bag for life. From Tesco. One of the big heavy ones."

"So?"

"So, we could put that under the bird, then just, like knock it off the hook."

"Knock it off? With what?"

"I don't know. A stick."

Tyler thought this through. "Do I have to be involved?" he asked.

"Yes! I'm not doing it myself!"

"Then I don't like this plan," Tyler replied.

Hamza set off for his car. "Tough. We're doing it. Unless you'd prefer to explain to Logan why you didn't go over the caravan like he told you?"

Tyler groaned. "Fine," he said, searching the line of trees behind the caravan for a decent-sized branch. "But if this goes pear-shaped, I'm running, and I'm not coming back."

The bag was a sizeable sturdy thing with a fold-flat bottom, which made it perfect to sit beneath the hanging pheasant.

In theory.

In reality, the sides kept falling together, closing the top of the bag so that anything falling onto it would slide right off and land on what, despite a lot of evidence to the contrary, Tyler was going to go ahead and call 'the carpet.'

After some experimentation, both detectives reluctantly came to the same conclusion. Someone was going to have to hold the bag open while the other knocked the bird off its hook with the stick.

"I don't mind what one I do," Tyler announced. "As long as I'm not holding the bag. I'll die. I mean it, Hamza, I'll actually die."

"You won't die!" Hamza retorted. "I don't even think you *can* die, given that you're still here after everything that's happened to you."

"This would do it. Holding that bag would finish me off," Tyler insisted, his voice a low, nasal drone now that he'd shut off his nostrils. "You hold it open, I'll knock it in."

Under other circumstances, this might have called for a, "Said the actress to the bishop," type response, but neither man was in the mood. The stakes were too high, the smell was too bad, and this entire exercise had already taken them far longer than anticipated.

Hamza grimaced, squatted, then grasped the handles of the bag and pulled them apart to create the widest possible landing zone for the maggot-infested bird carcass to drop into.

"Ready?" Tyler asked.

"I don't know. Is that under it?"

"I think so, aye," said Tyler from halfway across the caravan. "I can't see from here."

"Then get closer."

"*You* get closer!"

"I am bloody closer! I'm right under the fucking thing! Just... go. Do it. Go."

Tyler raised the metre-long stick he'd found, clutching it right at the end to maintain the maximum possible distance from where the action was. Unfortunately, the stick was quite heavy, and holding it in this way offered him almost no control over it whatsoever. It flailed around above Hamza's head, clunked against the ceiling, then caught the bird a glancing blow that sent half a dozen maggots raining onto the floor below, missing the bag by several inches.

"You need to go left a bit," Tyler said.

"I can... *Get off, you creepy bastard!*" Hamza slapped frantically at his arm. "I can see that, thanks. Be more careful."

He slid the bag a little to the left, covering the maggots that had landed there. Another of the grubs fell from the bird and hit the bottom of the bag with a *thack* that made Tyler drop the stick in fright.

"Christ!" he ejected, covering his head with his arms. He

peeked beneath an elbow, saw that the bird was still hanging there, then quickly tried to cover his overreaction with some reassuring words. "Right, everyone just relax. Calm down."

"I'm perfectly calm," Hamza hissed through gritted teeth. "I'm not the one who threw the stick away. I'm just..." He sighed, shook his head, then sprang upright. "Right, bollocks to this," he announced, snatching up the bag.

He covered the bird with the bag from below, clutched the handles together in one hand at the top, and unhooked the feet with the other.

The DS gave a little cry of triumph as the bird fell into the bag, then he thrust it out to Tyler, who was closer to the door.

"I don't want it!"

"Just get rid of it!" Hamza insisted, forcing it upon him.

After a moment of soul searching, Tyler took the bag by the handle, ran to the door, and launched it with an underarm throw that sent it sailing high into the air.

He and Hamza both watched as the dead bird tumbled out of the bag at the apex of its flight, fell more or less straight down, then landed on the bonnet of Hamza's car with a sound that was both heavy and wet.

"Oh, well," Hamza said, shooting the DC a withering sideways look. "Thanks a fucking bunch."

"I panicked," Tyler admitted.

"You couldn't have just sat it on the ground outside like a normal person?"

"I mean, in hindsight..." Tyler said, then he dusted himself down and fixed the Detective Sergeant with one of his more charming smiles. "Anyway, mission accomplished. Good teamwork there."

"Teamwork my arse," Hamza muttered. He turned his attention to the rest of the caravan, and the conspiracy theory chaos that spread like a rash across its walls. "Now, let's get cataloguing this stuff, or we'll be here all bloody night.

CHAPTER ELEVEN

THE ARDNAMURCHAN LIGHTHOUSE, according to Sinead's local trivia, was the most westerly building in the whole of the United Kingdom. It wasn't quite, as some believed, the westernmost point—that honour belonged to a fairly nondescript area of coastline a few miles to the south—but there wasn't much in it.

And besides, that stretch of jagged rocks wasn't accessible by road, and didn't have a cafe, so who cared about a few feet of difference?

Kathryn Chegwin had been right about the road. It was probably no more twisty and turny than the stretch up until that point had been, but given that the detectives' stomachs and inner ears had already suffered such prolonged abuse on the first part of the drive, it felt much worse.

"Did they no' have straight lines in the old days?" Logan had complained, as they'd rounded the umpteenth up-and-over bend. "This feels like some sort of bloody punishment."

If the road was the punishment, though, then the destination was the reward. The sun was setting as they crested the final hill and saw the lighthouse rising from the shore before them, silhouetted against the swirl of oranges, reds, and purples that burned across the sky.

The lighthouse was under renovation at the moment, according to one of the constables back at Strontian. It was supposed to have been completed months ago, but some sort of industrial dispute had brought it to a standstill. Now, the straight line of its silhouette was broken up by scaffolding and flapping tape.

Still, despite the extra clutter, all thoughts of travel sickness, dead men, and sex cults were soon forgotten as that view wheedled its way into every corner of Logan's headspace, forcing him to look—just look—at the sheer bloody majesty of it.

So enraptured was he, in fact, that he almost missed the next bend, and had to frantically course correct when the BMW's front wheels brushed against the verge at the side of the track, wrenching the wheel in his hands.

"That is pretty stunning," Sinead remarked. She, too, was mesmerised by the sky, and its reflection rippling across the sea, that she didn't seem to notice the car's near miss with the roadside ditch. "It's almost worth the drive up."

Logan nodded. "Aye," he confirmed. "It almost is. What do you think, Taggart?"

From the back seat, the dog *woofed* what Logan took to be his approval.

"Good boy," the DCI said, then he crawled around yet another bend and eased down the accelerator. "Now, let's go find these dirty hippie bastards we've heard so much about."

The dirty hippie bastards in question were not difficult to find. It would've been almost impossible to miss them, in fact, the way they all stood in a line just beyond the off-limits lighthouse, their fingers interlocked as they joined together to face down the setting sun.

It was the chanting that had first drawn the detectives' attention. They were all at it, though none of them seemed to be chanting the same thing, or at the same speed or volume. The effect was like trying to listen to ten different radio stations at once, none of which were playing anything worth listening to.

One man stood apart from the others, facing out to sea. He was giving it laldy on the chanting front. Both his arms were raised above his head, and he was touching various fingers together to form shapes with his hands that presumably meant something to him and his followers, but told Logan nothing aside from the fact that this man was clearly a twat.

The members of the group were all dressed in loose-fitting white cotton garments that looked a size too large for all of them. They swayed, completely out of time with each other, as they each recited their own individual chants.

The leader was dressed similarly, but on a grander scale. He wore a long white robe that was tied around the waist with a length of rope. A gold-coloured satin sash was draped diagonally across his body, making it look like he'd just placed highly in a beauty pageant.

He had the stance and the frame of a young man, and long, flowing brown hair that tumbled over his shoulders and stopped just above the middle of his back. His feet, which were just visible below the hem of his robe, were bare. Presumably, though, he had a pair of shoes he slipped on when he drove the 'Westerly Wellness' minibus that was currently taking up two spaces in the lighthouse car park.

The light at the top of the tower was blinking its warnings out to sea through gaps in the scaffolding. The door at the base was heavily padlocked, though, and warning signs promised both possible death, and likely prosecution for anyone mucking about.

"Your man who found the body would've had some job painting this," Logan remarked. "I take it he didn't know it was under renovation?"

"Presumably not, no,' Sinead said, then she gestured to the chanting crowd on the rocks beyond the tower. "What should we do? Should we wait? I'm not sure how you're meant to handle... whatever this is."

"It's alright, Detective Constable, I know the correct etiquette," Logan assured her, then he stabbed a finger in the direction of the group's leader and bellowed, "Oi. You. Sexy Jesus. A word."

Some of the chanting by the group members faltered. A couple of eyes opened and looked Logan's way.

If the leader had heard, though, he wasn't letting on. He continued with his hand gestures and his gibberish, as the sun ducked further behind the distant horizon. The sea was ablaze with colour now, the Isle of Coll off on the left the only dark spot on the reflected rainbow of the sky.

"Did he just...? Did he just bloody ignore me?" Logan asked Sinead.

"Maybe he didn't hear you, sir."

"Bollocks. He heard me, alright," Logan said, thrusting a hand into the inside pocket of his coat. "I didn't drive ten hours along the Highway to bloody Hell to be ignored by some prick in a dress." He held up his warrant card and set off at a march. "Police. Stop what you're doing right now."

The leader didn't open his eyes or turn, but stopped chanting long enough to respond in a French accent. "We have committed no crime. You have no authority over us," he said, before picking up where he'd left off.

The rest of his group didn't share his confidence, though, and most of them had stopped their cryptic utterings, opened their eyes, and now looked a bit self-conscious about the whole thing.

"I'll be the judge of whether you've committed a crime or not, son," Logan said. He stomped right through the group, scattering them, then stepped in front of the leader, blocking out the fading light from the sun, and casting the younger man into shadow.

'Sexy Jesus,' had been a good call. The man who now opened his eyes to look up at Logan was in his late twenties, with chiselled cheekbones and a close-cropped beard that didn't so much hide his square jaw as emphasise it.

His eyes were a brilliant shade of blue, that seemed to sparkle despite Logan's bulk preventing the dying evening light from reaching them.

Logan had expected the man to be irritated by this interruption, but instead, he just smiled, and Logan—a man for whom 'self-doubt' was something that happened to other people—suddenly couldn't shake the feeling that the other man knew something he didn't.

"My apologies, Detective Chief Inspector Logan," the man in the robe said, his French accent soft and quiet, almost like a purr. "Clearly, this must be more urgent than I thought, for you to interrupt our meditative moment."

Logan frowned. "How did you know...?" he began, before remembering he was still holding up his warrant card. "Oh, right, aye."

"Bonsoir, Monsieur Logan. How may we help you?"

"What's your name, son?"

"Ah, yes. I have the unfair advantage, non? My name is André Douville."

"And you're the leader of this lot, are you?" Logan asked, indicating the rest of the group with a derisory glance.

"We, ah... There is no leader at Westerly Wellness. I am, how you might say, a guide. I am the chaperone. It is my role to lead others by the hand, each on their own journeys."

"Lead them by the hand? So, *literally* a leader, then."

André smirked, showing his polished pearly whites. "As you wish, Monsieur Logan."

"Oh now, please. There's no need for '*Monsieur Logan.*' Let's not stand on formality here," Logan urged. "Call me 'Detective Chief Inspector.'"

The smirk raised higher. André bowed his head in a nod of respect. "As you wish, Detective Chief Inspector. Now, whatever this is, perhaps we can retire to our vehicle, and discuss it over some tea? The acolytes may still be able to channel some solar energy from the last of the sun's rays."

Logan made no attempt to hide his contempt for that sentence. He looked past André to the now mostly scattered line of 'acolytes.' They were a range of ages, from twenties to fifties, he guessed. A pretty even mix of men and women, although the lineup was notably lacking any of the 'strapping big boys' Kathryn Chegwin had been so keen on.

There was nothing strapping about any of this lot. They looked like frightened mice who might throw themselves headfirst off the rocks and into the sea at any moment, rather than get involved in any sort of confrontation with the detectives.

He looked past them, too, to where Sinead stood by the lighthouse itself, watching expectantly to see what Logan was going to do next.

It was at this point that something occurred to the DCI.

He had absolutely no idea why they were there. Not really.

Sure, he'd seen all the 'Westerly Wellness Centre' adverts and the like on the wall in Bernie's caravan, but so what? That wasn't reason enough to deviate from the plan to go pay the local MSP a visit. Not when it meant driving all this way along *that* road at this time of night.

"Detective Chief Inspector?" André pressed, his inscrutable smile still fixed in place. "May I tempt you with that tea?"

"Eh, aye," Logan said. "Don't mind if I do."

"There's a lot of weird shit in here, eh?" asked Tyler, his voice muffled by his jacket sleeves. He had tied them across his face so they covered his mouth and nose, and the body of the jacket itself flapped down his back like Superman's cape, only with greater water-repelling qualities.

Chucking out the dead pheasant may have removed the source of the smell, but the place still stunk to high heaven, and most likely would for the rest of its existence.

The detectives had no idea how many previous owners the caravan had, but it was a safe bet that they'd all been heavy smokers. The inside of the place was painted in a nicotine wash that coloured it in shades of yellow and brown.

"It's like being inside one of them lungs you see in the photos on cigarette packets," Hamza remarked. "Like, stop showing the rotten teeth and show a few pictures of this place. That'd put people off for life."

Someone—presumably Bernie the Beacon—had been

fighting a war against mildew and mould on several different fronts, and was getting roundly humped in every battle. It crept from the corners where the walls met the ceiling, blooming in all directions like a visual representation of the spread of the Black Death.

There were cleaner spots where he'd tried scrubbing it away, mostly around the areas where he'd pinned up his notes and photographs. It hadn't been very effective, though, and several of his handwritten diatribes had been all but consumed by the oozing damp.

"We should have protective gear on for this," Tyler said, unpinning another Polaroid from the wall.

He'd studied them closely to begin with, but was now gathering them up as quickly as possible so they could get the hell out of there and back into the fresh air. They'd taken enough photographs to be able to recreate the scene, if it came to it, and Palmer's team had already swung by earlier to do the same.

"We do have protective gear," Hamza said, waggling his gloved fingers.

"I meant proper protective gear. Like, I don't know, oxygen tanks, say."

"It's no' underwater."

Tyler tutted. "You know what I'm saying. I mean, look at that." He pointed to something that sat on a folding Formica table. It could have been anything—a piece of fruit or a dead rodent, perhaps—but mould had cocooned it, so now it was merely a shapeless furry lump of unknown origin. "I don't want to breathe that in."

"You'd have to take a hell of a big breath to inhale it from all the way over there," Hamza pointed out. He looked from the furry thing on the table to the black stuff on the ceiling and walls. "I get what you're saying, though. We should probably have masks, at least."

"Exactly! Thank you!" He tucked the last of the Polaroids into the evidence bag he was holding and closed over the top. "So, can we go and come back tomorrow when we've got some?"

Hamza sighed. "Aye. Fine."

"Great! And can you tell the boss, so he knows it was your idea?"

"How was it my idea?" Hamza asked.

He turned to face the other detective, and as he did, something tucked beneath the caravan's fold-away sofa bed caught his eye. Lowering his head, he peered into the shadows and saw two matching metal clasps, separated by a handle.

"There's a briefcase or something under there," he remarked.

"Under where?"

"The couch. The sofa bed thing. Look."

He pointed, and Tyler ducked to get a look.

"Oh, aye. So there is. You should get it out."

"Why should *I* get it out? You're closer."

"Aye, but there might be something under there. Like a rat."

"So, again, why should *I* be the one—?"

Hamza stopped talking, and both men turned when a figure appeared in the caravan doorway. He was an older man, painfully thin, and something about him struck Hamza as familiar. He'd seen him before, he was sure of it.

The man stood on the outside step, stared at the detectives for a few confused moments, then ejected a shrill, "Fuck!" and slammed the door shut.

"Oi! Get back here!" Hamza barked.

Tyler rushed to the door, partly to give chase, but mostly through fear of suffocating inside the caravan. He slapped at the area where he knew the catch to be, but found nothing to grab onto.

"There's no handle!" he hissed.

"What? What do you mean?"

"I mean there's no handle! We can't get out!"

"There must be a handle, Tyler!"

"There's not!" the DC insisted. He stepped back. "Here, watch out," he announced, then he threw himself at the door, driving his full weight behind a shoulder-charge.

The door, which had been flimsy when it was new, and was markedly more so after four decades of neglect, flew open at the first touch from Tyler's shoulder.

Unfortunately, this meant that it did nothing to slow his momentum, and he let out a panicky, "Wargh!" as he sailed several feet through the air, crashed heavily onto the ground, then rolled down the embankment into a crop of stinging nettles.

He was on his feet again in an instant—mostly because of the nettles—and through the darkness, he heard the wheezing of the old man running.

"Up there. He's going through the trees," Hamza said, shining his torch in the direction of the sound. It picked out the outline of the scrawny figure just as he plunged beyond the tree line and into the woods.

Both detectives set off in pursuit, Tyler held back by the overwhelming urge to brush himself down and clear away the nettle debris. Pinpricks of pain nipped at his hands, arms, and face. His cape-like jacket had, ironically, fallen off mid-flight, and he could already feel his top lip swelling from one of the nettle stings.

"Hurry up, he's getting away!" Hamza called, and his voice echoed back off the upcoming trees.

"Go! I'm jutht coming!" Tyler replied, and he winced at the lisp. "I mean, *theriously*," he muttered, picking his way back up the slope. "Why doeth thith thit alwayth happen to me?"

Hamza launched himself into the woods, his torchlight dancing across the twisting trunks and grabbing branches. For an old boy, the man they were chasing had an impressive turn of speed. Hamza could no longer hear his puffing and panting, and it was only the snapping of twigs and the rustling of foliage up ahead that told him which way to run.

The face was bothering him. The familiarity of it.

It could've been that he just had one of those faces you often came across in this job—the red nose from too many years of too much bevvy, and the sunken cheeks and glassy-eyed stare that came with it.

His skin had been grey, stretched tight over his bones so you could practically see the ridges and lines of his skull. His hair was so thin and similar in colour to his skin that when he'd first appeared in the doorway, Hamza had thought him bald. It was only when the man had turned to leg it that the DS had spotted the actual bald spot crowning the top of his head, and where there was a bald spot, there had to be hair.

He looked like pretty much any other long-term addict who'd somehow managed to make it into old age, and yet, there was something about him. Something that niggled at Hamza as he crashed through the undergrowth and ducked the whipping branches. He knew him. He was sure of it.

He just couldn't remember from where.

A stitch burned just below his ribcage, and he slowed to a stop, his torch scanning the forest ahead. There was no sound from up ahead now. There hadn't been for thirty seconds or so. Either the old man was even faster than Hamza had thought, or he had stopped somewhere.

Somewhere nearby.

"Ham?" Tyler's voice came from a few dozen yards behind and on the left.

"Here!" Hamza called, waving the torch back in Tyler's direction to guide him.

Hamza waited until he heard Tyler approaching, then turned on the spot, letting the torchlight lick across the woods around him.

"We know you're here," he announced, fighting back his breathlessness to put on his best polis voice. "I'm Detective Sergeant Hamza Khaled. My colleague is Detective Constable Tyler Neish. We just want to talk, that's all. You're not in any trouble."

The only response from the forest was the distant hooting of an owl, and the crashing and wheezing of DC Neish arriving on the scene.

Hamza turned with the torch, then drew back in fright as the light picked out the contours of Tyler's face.

"Bloody hell, mate, what happened to you?" he yelped. "You look like Quasimodo fucked a Muppet."

Tyler dabbed gingerly at the swollen lump of his top lip, then ran his fingers up over a bloated cheek and painfully misshapen eyebrow. "What one?"

Hamza studied the Detective Constable's face in horrified wonder. "I don't know. All of them."

"I thell in nettleth," Tyler explained.

"What?"

Tyler tried again. "I thell in nettleth."

"You fell in nettles? What, when you went flying through the caravan door?"

"Yeth."

"Did you land face first?"

"Yeth, acthually."

Hamza winced. "Does it hurt?"

"I'll give you three guetheth," Tyler croaked, then his nostrils flared. It was quite a big movement, given the current size of them. "Here. Wait. Do you thmell thomething?"

Hamza sniffed the air, then nodded. "Aye," he confirmed. "Smells a bit like..."

His face fell. He turned back in the direction they'd come from. Back in the direction of the caravan. Where there had been only darkness, there was now a suggestion of orange light, dancing somewhere beyond the forest's edge.

"...fire!"

They doubled back, racing together, Tyler just slightly ahead despite his current high levels of physical discomfort. The smoke came to meet them as they drew closer to the caravan, thick, and pungent, and black.

Even before they reached the tree line, they knew. They could see. The flames had already mostly consumed the rickety structure. The Beacon now lived up to its name, burning so brightly in the darkness that even looking at it made the eyes ache.

The detectives both stopped just beyond the trees, when the wall of heat became too much for them to push through.

They stood there together, watching what was left of the structure fall in on itself, as fiery embers danced off into the dark night sky.

"Don't suppose you took any of those evidence bags out with you, did you?" Hamza asked.

Tyler shook his head.

"No, thought not."

"You?"

"Nah," Hamza said.

They watched a while longer, the heat stinging their skin.

"What do you think the botthh ith going to thay?" Tyler lisped.

Hamza blew out his cheeks. "Dunno," he said. "But I can't imagine it's going to be anything nice."

CHAPTER TWELVE

"FOR FUCK'S SAKE!" Logan spat.

He scowled down into the murky depths of the liquid in the cup he'd been given. It was the shape and size of a disposable paper cup, but made from bamboo, apparently. André had seemed very pleased with himself about that.

"What is this? That's not tea," Logan continued.

"It's nettle tea," André said. "Homemade. It's good for urinary tract infections."

"I haven't got a urinary tract infection, though," Logan countered. "Although this tastes like what I'd be pissing if I did."

"It's preventative, oui? Also, it helps with arthritis."

"I haven't got that, either."

"And a range of other things, including blood sugar levels, heart disease, diabetes..."

Logan threw the contents of the cup out through the open door of the minibus, and passed the environmentally friendly container across the aisle to where André sat on the other front-most passenger seat.

The bus was several years old, but it had been well kept. The seats had been reupholstered. At least, Logan assumed the original manufacturer hadn't fitted them with the range of colourful tie-dyed fabrics that currently covered them.

"Thanks anyway," the DCI said, his tongue flicking across his lips like he was trying to get rid of the taste. "But I'm more of a *Tetley's* man myself."

André smiled as he took the cup and set it on the floor at his feet. "It's something of an acquired taste," he said, then he surprised Logan with his next remark. "I knew you were coming."

"Did you now?" Logan asked. "And how did you know that?"

"Ah. Now. There's a question," André said. He shuffled around in the chair like he was settling in for a long story. "I could tell you, but I don't think your mind is open enough to the possibilities."

"To what possibilities?"

"To the possibilities of the Universe. Of the human consciousness."

"Oh. Those possibilities," Logan said. He shook his head. "No, you're right. Not really."

"Do you believe in ghosts, Detective Chief Inspector?"

"No."

André gave a single curt nod. Clearly, this was the response he'd been expecting. "What do you think happens to people when they die?"

"They cut short my day off," Logan said.

André hadn't been expecting that response. He frowned, like he was struggling to translate the reply in his head. "Pardon?"

"Doesn't matter," Logan said. "What's the point you're trying to make here, son?"

"I believe—we at Westerly Wellness believe—that the spirits of the dead are all around us. Some of us—the most fortunate—are selected to be their vessels. The conduits between their world and this one."

"And let me guess, you think you're one of them."

"Think? Non. I know." André sat forward so he was leaning halfway across the aisle. "Do you know what a telephone is, Detective Chief Inspector?"

Logan didn't bother answering that one, and instead just fixed the other man with a flat, unblinking stare, assuming it was a rhetorical question. André just sat there watching him, though, apparently waiting for a response.

"Of course I know what a bloody telephone is."

"And you know how it works, oui?"

"Aye, you talk into one end and it comes out at the other."

"Non. That is what it does, not how it works," André said. "*Écoute.* It works with a diaphragm. There is a coil attached to this diaphragm, and a magnet below. Pressure from the voice flexes the diaphragm, and the magnet generates a current that translates your words into an electrical signal and pings them across the whole world."

Logan blinked slowly. "And?"

"And I am that diaphragm. And that coil. And that magnet."

He sat back and unclasped his hands, but held them close together like he was presenting the detective with an invisible bowl.

"You're saying you're a telephone?"

"In a manner of speaking, yes! The spirits talk through

me. They tell me things. They were the ones who told me you were coming."

Logan sighed, shrugged, then nodded. "Aye. Fine," he said, not wishing to get into any further discussion on that particular matter. "I'm here about Bernie."

"Bernie?" echoed André, sitting back in surprise.

"Oh, so the spirits didn't tell you *why* I was coming, then? Funny that," Logan said. "I believe they call him Bernie—"

"The Beacon. Yes. Everyone knows Bernie. We here at the centre better than most."

"Why's that? He a..." Logan gestured vaguely down in the direction of the lighthouse. "...patient?"

"These people are not ill, Detective Chief Inspector. They are on a path to enlightenment," André explained, and the manner in which he said it suggested it was a stock response he'd been called on to use many times before. "Bernie, on the other hand... Bernie was ill." He tapped the side of his head. "Up here. And probably elsewhere, too, but up here most of all."

A word. Sometimes, that was all it took. Sometimes, if you were lucky, one word gave you the in that you needed.

"What do you mean..." Logan began, leaning closer, "...*was* ill?"

André, to his credit, didn't miss a beat. "I am assuming he is dead, oui? It is a long way for a Detective Chief Inspector of police to travel this late in the evening for any other reason. I assume he is dead, and that you are here to ask me about our feud."

It was Logan who hesitated, but only briefly. "Well worked out. Tell me about your feud. I'd love to hear your side."

"I do not have a 'side,' Detective Chief Inspector. Merely the facts of the matter."

"As you see them."

"As they are," André insisted. "Bernie required help. Mental care. His mind, it did not work rationally. He believed in... improbable things. Impossible things."

"Says the man who talks to ghosts."

André smirked, his pristine white teeth appearing momentarily through a gap in his beard. "Touché. But if you doubt what I believe—"

"I do."

"Then you must doubt also the things Bernie claimed."

"I'm not fully up to date on everything he believed, but aye, the lizard people sent alarm bells ringing," Logan said. "He seemed intrigued by this place, though. He had a lot of cuttings on his wall all about you."

"This does not surprise me," André said. "Since I set up this retreat, Bernie has been... difficult. He believed we were servants of his lizard gods. Doing their bidding, converting the unwary to their clandestine cause. Forging an army, with which to rule."

Logan looked out through the front windscreen of the bus, to where the white robes of Andre's 'acolytes' were just visible in the overspill of light from the lighthouse towering above. They didn't look like an army.

Well, the *Salvation Army*, maybe. Definitely not one capable of enslaving the whole of humanity.

"He tried to lead a campaign against us. He would protest at our gates. Hold signs he had made himself. Scream at the new arrivals, try to scare them away."

"Must've been annoying," Logan said. "Bad for business that, I'd have thought."

André shrugged. "Non. It made no difference. Those who make the journey here have done so because they have come to a decision, Detective Chief Inspector. A decision that they will not be swayed from, no matter who stands against them."

"And what decision is that?"

"To be better than they are," André said. He gestured up and around. "To become one with all this."

"A knackered old minibus?"

There was that smirk again. "With the Universe. That is what we offer here. That is what I give them."

"That's a bold claim," Logan said.

"Fortune favours the bold, Detective Chief Inspector. That is what they say, non?"

"I don't know, I tend not to listen to what *they* say. *They*, from what I can gather, are a shower of interfering arseholes," Logan retorted. "Bernie wasn't the only one with a problem with your place, though, was he?" he asked.

"How do you mean?"

"Well, I mean, close-knit community like this. Older folk, set in their ways, I bet you raised a few eyebrows rocking up with your... I want to say 'cult,' but I'm no' sure that's the right term."

"Ha! It is not. It is a retreat, and a commune. A home for the lost, who wish to be found."

"That sounds a bit culty," Logan said. "If you listen to that back, you'll think, 'Aye, that's a cult I've just described.'"

"I assure you, it is not," André insisted.

"What about your neighbours? What do they make of it?" Logan pressed. "They can't be happy having you on their doorstep."

"We only have one person living nearby, and she is very

accommodating," the other man said. "She comes to visit regularly. Brings baking. Visits the tents to introduce herself to the new arrivals."

Logan grunted. "I bet she bloody does."

"Pardon?"

"Nothing. Forget it." There was a knock at the minibus door, and Logan saw Sinead hovering just beyond the glass. "Aye, in you come," he said.

It took a moment for Sinead to figure out how the door worked, then she slid it aside and popped her head in. "Sorry, sir. Just had Ben on the radio checking in. Had a bit of a problem he wants to discuss with you." She looked back over her shoulder. "Also, the people out here are getting cold. They're asking if they can come in and get their jackets."

"Tell them to become one with somewhere warm for a few minutes. Spain, or something," Logan suggested.

Sinead frowned. "Sir?"

"Doesn't matter. I'll be right out."

He waited until Sinead had retreated, then turned back to the man across the aisle. "I think it's best if we continue this conversation tomorrow, Mr Douville. Down at the station."

"In Strontian? That is not convenient for me, Monsieur. Uh, Detective Chief Inspector, I mean."

"Oh, is it not?" Logan asked, the pitch of his voice climbing. "Oh, well, I'm very sorry. Far be it for me to inconvenience a busy man like yourself. I had no idea, I'm terribly sorry."

André's brow furrowed. "You are being sarcastic, oui?"

"How did you guess?" Logan asked. "One o'clock. At the station in Strontian." He stood up, though the low roof forced him to crouch. "Do *not* make me drive back out here to get you. For both our bloody sakes."

DI Forde sat at one of the mismatched desks in the makeshift Incident Room, talking into the handset of the bulky Airwave radio unit.

"Aye. Sounds like you've had a fun night right enough, Jack," he said. "But here, I'll let them explain themselves."

He looked across both facing desks at the two men sitting opposite. Hamza and Tyler looked mostly shrunken and cowed, with the exception of Tyler's face, much of which was several sizes larger than normal.

The DS and the DC both elbowed each other, each trying to get the other to do the talking.

"Hello? Still there?" Logan asked via the speaker, then his voice grew quieter as he turned away. "I think it's dropped the signal," he said, presumably to Sinead.

"No, we're here, Jack," Ben said, then he extended the handset again.

Hamza drew in a breath, exhaled, then took the offered radio. "Alright, sir? It's Hamza," he announced.

"Aye. I'm familiar with your voice, son," Logan said. "What's happened? What's the big disaster?"

Hamza swallowed. "Well, we were... Tyler and I... The two of us. We were going over the caravan, like you said."

"And?"

"And we were gathering up evidence. And then we spotted a briefcase," Hamza continued. "It was hidden under the couch, or sofa bed, or whatever."

"So far so good," Logan said. "What was in it?"

"The briefcase?" Hamza shifted his gaze sideways to Tyler. The DC was leaning back in his chair, like he was worried the radio might detonate in Hamza's hand. "We, um, we don't know, sir."

"Why not? Couldn't you get it open?"

"We, um, we didn't get a chance, sir."

"How come?"

"Someone... someone turned up at the caravan. A man."

They could practically hear the DCI's ears pricking up over the airwaves. "And?"

"And he ran, sir. So, we gave chase."

"And you caught him," Logan prompted. "Tell me you caught him."

Hamza cleared his throat. Then, to be on the safe side, he cleared it again. Across the table, Ben sat with his arms folded, saying nothing.

"We, eh... No, sir. He got away."

"Jesus..." Logan groaned.

"That's not the half of it, Jack," Ben chipped in, then he nodded at Hamza, urging him to go on.

"What else?" Logan demanded.

"Well, um, you see, sir, while we were away... While we were giving chase..."

Logan's voice suddenly sounded clearer and closer. He'd just brought the radio nearer to his mouth, but both the DS and the DC couldn't help but glance around to check that he wasn't standing in the room beside them.

"Someone set the caravan on fire, sir," Hamza said, just blurting it all out in one big breath.

There was silence from the other end of the line. A deep, dark, drawn-out sort of silence.

Hamza's gaze flitted to the other detectives. Had he

heard? Had the radio lost signal at just that moment? Was he going to have to say it all again?

"On fire?" Logan intoned, just before Hamza opened his mouth again. "What do you mean on fire? Explain 'on fire' to me, Detective Sergeant. How *on fire*?"

"Very on fire, sir," Hamza said. "Like... I'd say completely on fire."

"But you got the evidence out," Logan prompted. "That's what you're going to say next, isn't it, son? You got the evidence out."

"Well, it's... I'd love to..." Hamza looked down at the desktop, composing himself, then rallied. "Sadly not, sir. We felt that giving chase was the priority, so the evidence was still in the caravan."

"The caravan that was on fire?" Logan asked. "The caravan that *I'm guessing* burned down?"

"Uh... aye, sir. Uniform and a couple of local fire volunteers are dealing with it now," Hamza said. "As soon as we get the all-clear, we're going to go and see what we can recover."

"And how much paper do you think you're likely to 'recover' from the burned-out wreckage, do you think? How much of one of the most notoriously flammable substances on Earth do you think you'll be able to salvage?"

"Um... Probably not much, sir," Hamza admitted.

"No. I agree. Probably not much. Probably not much at all." His voice became fainter as he lowered the radio and muttered something that wasn't meant for their ears.

The next voice that emerged from the speaker was Sinead's.

"Uh, hi. The boss is, um... taking a moment," she said as, in the background, they all heard a brief outburst of colourful language. "Can you guys do us a favour? We don't want to drive back on that road tonight, only to have to do it again tomorrow to meet that MSP."

"You're not coming back?" asked Tyler. "But I got uth a double room at a B&B."

There was a pause before Sinead replied. "What's wrong with your voice?"

"Got thtung in the fathe by a load of nettleth," Tyler explained.

They all heard Logan's voice in the background again. "Wait, what did he say?"

"He got stung in the face by a load of nettles," Sinead said.

There was another moment of silence, and then a snort. "Christ, that might be worth driving back to see," Logan said, then the thought of the road brought him to his senses. "Actually, no. No, not even that's worth that drive."

"Will you see if you can find us somewhere? We're still at the lighthouse," Sinead said. "Doesn't have to be fancy, but it needs to take dogs."

"And the closer, the better," Logan added.

"I'll get right on that, *bothh*," Tyler said, mangling the word 'boss' beyond all recognition. He was as eager as ever to win the DCI's approval, and even more so given tonight's cock-up. "I won't let you down."

They didn't recognise the house in the dark. They'd only glimpsed it in passing the first time around, and it wasn't until the elderly woman yanked open the door, revealing herself in a faded full-length nightdress, that Logan realised whose house Tyler had sent them to.

"Bleedin' Nora!" spat Kathryn Chegwin, looking them both up and down. "If I knew it was the filth, I never would've taken that fucking booking."

Logan groaned. "Jesus Christ, Tyler," he muttered, pinching the bridge of his nose, "You have got to be bloody kidding me."

CHAPTER THIRTEEN

THE ROOMS WERE DECENT ENOUGH, although on the small side. At a guess, they had last been decorated in the late nineteen-forties, and while the decor was still relatively fresh-looking, the style very much was not.

The beds had been singles—neither room large enough to accommodate anything larger—but while the mattresses had been thick, solid things that would likely take a team of men to lift, they'd been comfortable, all the same.

Taggart had been made to sleep in the kitchen. *For hygiene purposes*, Kathryn had said, although Logan couldn't help but feel this was *less* hygienic than if the dog had slept in one of the bedrooms. Or literally anywhere else in the house, for that matter.

Still, they were guests, and she was the host, and she made it very clear that under this roof, her word was law.

She had, with some persuasion, allowed Logan to make a phone call from the landline in the morning. Shona had answered on the third ring, and while he would have loved to go over the post-mortem results with her, the way Kathryn hung over him tapping at her watch was enough to put him off the idea.

He arranged to give her a call when he was either back at the station, or somewhere with a phone signal, and said his goodbyes.

"How's she doing?" Sinead asked when Logan returned to the dining room.

The table had space for six people, but only two places had been set for breakfast. Kathryn returned to the kitchen while Logan took his seat and reached for a slice of toast that could best be described as 'well-fired.'

The sizzle and the smell of frying bacon and sausages were making his stomach grumble in anticipation. The toast would've been a poor substitute even without the charcoal coating, but it would help keep the hunger pangs under control until breakfast arrived.

"Aye. Fine," he said, skimming a sliver of butter from the block with the edge of a knife. "Didn't get much chance to talk to her with her majesty lugging in, mind you."

"Any PM results?"

Logan finished spreading his toast and took a bite. "She didn't say. I'm going to call her back somewhere more private."

Sinead nodded and took a slurp from her tea. Black dots swirled around in the milk, Kathryn eschewing the convenience of tea bags in favour of the even greater convenience of simply spooning tea leaves into a cup and then drowning them in boiling water.

"No word from your daughter, I take it?"

Logan shook his head. "No. I mean, I don't know. Maybe, once I get a signal."

"Aye. Probably," Sinead said, though it came out

sounding a little less hopeful than she'd been aiming for. "I'm sure there will be."

A boxy, old-style portable TV stood in the corner of the room, murmuring out the morning news. It was still the national news at this point—the Scottish update would come after—and the presenter was talking about the girl who'd gone missing down south.

Logan watched as it cut to footage of the girl's parents, a well-dressed black couple who'd been doorstepped by a gaggle of journalists. Even on the wee square screen, he could see they were tired. They'd been crying. Of course they had.

"Poor bastards," he remarked, prompting Sinead to turn and follow his gaze.

"Oh. Yeah."

"Grimm."

"It is, aye," Sinead agreed.

"No. Grimm. The fella's name." He indicated the screen, where a caption revealed the identity of an officer addressing the camera at a press conference. "DCI Grimm. But aye. Also grim in the traditional sense."

The segment ended, and the newsreader moved on to a sports round-up just as the kitchen door was nudged open. Kathryn entered backwards, carefully carrying a plate in each hand.

"Here we go. Now we're talking," Logan cheered, unfurling the rolled-up napkin from his side plate and tucking it into the collar of his shirt.

He leaned back in the chair, not wishing to in any way impede the delivery of his breakfast, then stared in confusion at the food that was deposited in front of him.

"What's this?" he asked.

"What does it look like?" Kathryn retorted. "It's porridge."

"But..." Logan's eyes crept to the kitchen door. "There was sausage and bacon. I smelled them."

"Those are for the dog."

"The dog?" Logan frowned. "Wait, so... what are you saying? The dog's getting bacon and sausage, and I'm getting this?"

"Well, that certainly seems to be the case from where I'm standing," Kathryn said.

Logan shot daggers at the kitchen door, then picked up his spoon and plunged it into the bowl of gooey grey mush. He brought it to his lips, blew on it, then stuffed the oats in his mouth and grimaced.

"Christ, that's salty," he grumbled.

"As it should be," Kathryn replied. "None of your sugary rubbish." She tapped Sinead on the shoulder and pointed to her bowl. "Eat. There's nothing of you."

Sinead picked up her spoon and held it over the dish. "I'm not... I don't want to eat too much," she said. "That road makes me a bit... queasy."

"All the more reason to fill up. Better to chuck up the contents of your guts than your guts themselves," Kathryn said. "So, eat. The pair of you. You're not leaving here until you do."

With her ultimatum issued, she pulled out the chair from the head of the table and took a seat, watching them both.

"You're not honestly going to sit there and stare while we eat, are you?" Logan asked.

"Too bleedin' true, I am. You're paying for bed and breakfast, you're getting bed and breakfast. Whether you like it or not."

She nodded at the plates, tapped her wrist where a watch would go, then crossed her arms and sat back, waiting for them to tuck in.

Logan had met enough women like Kathryn over the years to understand how futile it would be to argue. He shoved a spoonful of the salty oat mush into his mouth and filtered the worst of the lumps through his teeth.

Sinead took a different approach, and set about trying to distract Kathryn from the fact she wasn't eating anything.

"We, uh, we met your neighbours last night," she said. "The Westerly Wellness group. They seemed like an interesting bunch."

"They were," Kathryn said. "Slim pickings now, mind."

"Sorry?" Sinead asked. "How do you mean?"

"Well, it used to be stowed out, didn't it? Like bleedin' Woodstock it was, some weeks. Not now, mind. Nothing like it used to be."

Logan forced down the gritty oats. "Business isn't good?" he asked.

"I mean, I don't know what he charges, do I? None of my business, that," Kathryn said. "I'm just saying, he's not getting the numbers he used to. Not as many big, beefy boys around these days."

"What happened, do you think?" Sinead asked.

"I'll tell you what's not happening is you eating your bleedin' breakfast," Kathryn pointed out. "I don't care if it's hot or cold. You're eating it, either way."

Sinead was aware that she was a Detective Constable of police, and that this woman had no authority over her whatsoever. And yet, she found herself scooping up a spoonful of porridge, and gingerly tasting it with the tip of her tongue.

"Bernie happened, didn't he? Him and his bleedin'

protests," the old woman continued. "Right bleedin' nuisance he made of himself. Shouting, and bawling, and talking a load of old shit."

"Your man—André—he said that Bernie didn't affect business," Logan said. "He told me it was as strong as ever."

Kathryn sniffed. "Well, I'm not one to call anyone a fucking liar, but he's a fucking liar if that's what he told you, and you can take that to the bank. Bernie's been a right pain in his arse, and no mistake. And now he's dead, I hear."

"Where did you hear that?" Logan asked.

Kathryn sniffed. "So, it's true then, is it? You never know around here. They're exaggerating bastards, the lot of them. Someone hears you fart at Corran Ferry, and you've shat yourself by Achnalea."

"We haven't formally identified the body yet," Logan said. "But we have reason to believe it could be Bernie, yes."

"Well, I'm not one to point fingers, but I know which way I'd be pointing them if I was," Kathryn said. "Right across the bleedin' road, and that's a fact."

"You think André could have killed Bernie?" Logan asked.

"That's not for me to say," Kathryn said. "But I wouldn't put it past the bugger. Like I say, Bernie's been a right pain in his backside. These last few months especially. If I was him, I'd be dancing a fucking jig now that someone's done the bugger in. And I'll tell you this much for free, if I was you, I'd be having serious words with him."

Before Logan could push her any further, there came a clatter from the kitchen, which was followed a moment later by a burst of excited barking.

Despite her age, Kathryn demonstrated a remarkable turn of speed as she pushed back her chair and jumped to her feet. "My bleedin' sausages!" she cried, then she threw open the door to the kitchen and went racing through.

"What do you mean *your* sausages?" Logan called after her. "I thought they were for the dog?"

He heard a scraping and looked down to find his bowl, which had been almost empty, now practically full once again.

"Come on, sir," Sinead said, smirking as she set her now-empty plate down in front of her again. "Better eat up, or we'll never get out of here."

DI Ben Forde stood in front of the cobbled-together Big Board, holding his breath as he attached a *Post-it note* to the top left corner with the same care and attention he'd shown back in his days on the bomb squad.

When the note was attached, he held both hands an inch or two away, ready to grab the board should the whole thing collapse. Once he was sure it was holding steady, he finally exhaled and stepped back.

He turned with the air of someone who'd just pulled off the single most impressive move in the history of *Jenga* or *Buckaroo,* then nodded to the trio of officers assembled before him.

"Right then," he said, pointing to the single note on the board. "The victim. Bernie. What do we know?"

He, Hamza, and Tyler all turned to PC Suzi Tanaka, who'd been asked to join the meeting. They'd chosen her of the two available local constables because she seemed to be a bit more switched on than her male counterpart, PC Chris Miller.

Also, Constable Miller's looks made the younger officers feel seriously inadequate, so they'd nudged Ben towards approaching PC Tanaka.

"What, is that...? Are you asking me?"

"We are," Ben said.

Constable Tanaka cleared her throat, got to her feet, then opened her mouth to speak. "So..." she began, before a thought struck her. "Do I have to stand up?"

"Only if you want to," Ben told her.

She gave this some further consideration, then sat down again.

"So, Bernie is a well-known local figure," she said. She sounded a little robotic, like she was reading off a cue card.

Ben nodded encouragingly, while Hamza sat with his pen hovering above the notebook he had balanced on his knee.

"Go on," Ben said.

"Um..." PC Tanaka's gaze shifted left and right, like she was looking for the next card. "He's... male. Mid-forties to early sixties, I'd say."

"That's quite a wide range," the DI pointed out.

"Yeah, he's hard to pinpoint. Got one of those faces."

"Last name?" Tyler prompted, trying to help her out. He recognised that look of growing panic. God knew, he'd felt it himself often enough when put on the spot like this.

"Last name. Last name," the constable mumbled. She shrugged. "We just knew him as Bernie the Beacon. Because of, you know, the newsletter thing."

"You don't know his last name?" Hamza said.

"No. Never asked."

Ben frowned. "But I thought there were complaints about him from the health centre, or whatever it is?"

"Westerly Wellness."

"Aye. I thought he'd been spoken to. In an official capacity, I mean."

"Well, I mean... that depends on your definition of 'official capacity,' I suppose," Suzi replied. "We had a word in his ear. Told him to stop playing silly buggers."

"And you didn't take his name?"

"No."

"Or his age?"

"No."

"Or his address?"

"Well, he lives in a tent, doesn't he?" the constable said. She looked around at the shocked faces. Even Tyler, who'd been fully willing her to succeed, was apparently fighting the urge to cringe. "What you've got to understand is that things are a bit different out here. It's a small community. You can't just go wading in. It's a balancing act. You try to keep everyone happy, and not rock the boat too much."

Hamza looked down at his notebook, and the still completely blank page. "So, we don't know anything about him?"

"I wouldn't say that," Constable Tanaka retorted. "We know he believed in space lizards, or whatever it was. We know he didn't get on with... well, most people, really, but he had a particular dislike for politicians, health practitioners, and anyone from an ethnic minority background."

"He was racist?" Hamza asked.

"Oh, very much so. Very much racist. I'd go so far as to say he was *extremely* racist. Not in a screaming in your face sort of way, more in a general, low-level sort of contempt. He was not a big fan of mine, for obvious reasons. First time he saw me, he said I was worse than the Nazis in the Second

World War. Aye, not the Japanese of the time in general, me specifically."

"And what did you say to that?" Ben asked.

The PC took a moment to recall her exact words. "Something like, 'Away an' bile yer heid, ye mad auld bastard,'" she said, her accent becoming a guttural Glaswegian rasp. "Which, I have to say, fairly caught him off guard."

"I can imagine, aye," Ben said, chuckling.

"Most people round here won't necessarily know that about him, of course, seeing as most of them are, well, white. I doubt they'll have seen that side. But he was."

"Noted," Hamza said, tapping his pad. "So, we've got his first name, we've got that he believed some wacky shite about lizards, that he disliked most people, and that he was racist."

"And that he was mid-forties to mid-sixties," Tyler added.

"I said *early* sixties," Suzi corrected. She shifted her weight a little uncomfortably. "Though, he could be mid-sixties, I suppose."

"I'll just put 'adult male,'" Hamza suggested. "It's not a very detailed picture we're building up here."

"That's a point. Do we have any pictures?" Ben wondered. "If we had a photograph, we could maybe put out an appeal for information. See if anyone knows him. From before, I mean."

PC Tanaka sucked in her bottom lip, then shook her head. "Not that I've ever seen, no. I could ask around, though, and see if anyone locally has one. Don't think he was big on getting his photo taken, though. In case, I don't know, goblins got hold of it, or whatever."

"Aye, ask around, will you?" Hamza said. "It'd be

useful if we could get something. None of the Polaroids in the caravan had his face in them. It was mostly just that MSP."

"How would you describe him?" Ben asked the constable. "Bernie. If I asked you to describe him to me, what would you say?"

"Um, five-six, five-seven, white, aged between—"

"No. As a person, I mean. Not the specifics. What was your general impression of him?"

The question took Constable Tanaka aback. Her eyebrows rose halfway up her forehead as she stared ahead at the almost empty Big Board.

"I mean, my first instinct is to say, 'A pain in the arse,' but that's probably not what you're after."

"It's a start, but aye, I was hoping for something a bit more," Ben replied.

"I suppose then... If I had to sum him up... I'd say he seemed troubled," the constable replied.

"Troubled?"

"Aye. Like... I got the impression he wasn't always the way he was. Like maybe something happened to make him that way. A breakdown, or something." Her eyes became alive as she recalled a past encounter. "I remember this one time—not the first time I met him, but soon after—he was walking back from Lochaline. Think he'd been on Mull for a week or two. Anyway, I noticed he was wearing a wedding ring. I mentioned it. Said like, 'Aye aye, Bernie. You got yourself hitched?' and he... He just looked angry. Like, he was furious."

"At you?" asked Ben.

"Not so much, no. At, I don't know, at himself. Or the ring. Or something," the constable clarified. "He just ripped it off and chucked it away. Just chucked it off into the trees and told me to mind my own business.

"Apparently, he spent weeks looking for it after that. I only heard later. No idea if he found it."

"So, he could've been married at some point," Hamza said, making a note of the new information.

"All the more reason to find a photo," Tyler said. "Pump that out on the telly and in the papers, and we might get a hit on him."

"Aye, I agree," Ben said. His upper lip drew back in a sort of sneer of disgust. "But please, for both our sakes, never use the phrase 'pump that out' in my presence again."

"I'll do my best, boss," Tyler chirped. "No promises, though."

For a moment, it looked like Ben was about to issue a further warning, but instead, he shook his head and checked his watch. "Right, I've got a call with Shona Maguire about the PM shortly." He looked around at the other officers. "Anyone else have anything they want to ask or add?"

Hamza raised the rubber end of his pencil as if calling for the teacher's attention. "Just... The Beacon. The newsletter thing he did. Are there any copies still circulating, do you know?"

Try as she might, PC Tanaka couldn't hold back her smile. "Oh, bound to be. We'll have some. It was always a big hit. A lot of people hung onto them." She clicked her fingers. "In fact, Gary at the pub has the full set."

"What pub?" Ben and Tyler asked, both perking up upon hearing the word.

"At the hotel." She took in their blank expressions. "Didn't you... Did you not stay at the hotel last night? The Strontian Hotel?"

"We were in a couple of B&Bs," Hamza told her. "We heard the hotel was shut."

Suzi tapped herself on the side of the head. "Oh. Aye. Course. It's getting redecorated or something. They timed it with the lighthouse being shut to visitors while it gets its renovations. Tourist numbers are down. Bar's open, though. Gary who works there, he's got the full set of Beacons. Proud of it, too, for some reason. I can go over and check with him when he opens up at lunchtime, if you like."

Ben side-eyed the other detectives. "Well, no. No, you've got enough on your plate," he said. "We'll pop over ourselves."

"You sure? I don't mind."

"No, no, it'll help us get to know the place a bit better. Make our faces known." He sat back in his chair, one hand slipping onto his stomach. "And who knows? In the interest of local relations, we may even have to force ourselves to have a wee something to eat..."

CHAPTER FOURTEEN

"SHE'S A STRANGE WOMAN, THAT ONE," Logan remarked, as the BMW dipped and rose, clinging to the lines of the road.

"Aye, she's that, right enough, sir," Sinead agreed. "Some house, too. Was your room full of porcelain dolls in Victorian dresses?"

"Thankfully not, no."

"I barely slept a wink. Kept thinking they were watching me."

Logan grunted. "I wasn't much better. I was convinced she was going to burst into the room and either kill me or ravage me during the night." He shuddered. "And I've not yet decided which one I'd have preferred."

Sinead held her breath as the Beamer banked around a sloping turn before suddenly levelling off again.

"Looked like the Westerly Wellness lot made it back alright," she remarked. "Saw the minibus there when we passed."

"Aye. They were all out doing yoga or whatever the hell

it was when I took the dog out for a walk just after six," Logan said.

Sinead looked pointedly at the DCI's mobile. It sat on the charging pad on the dash, refilling the empty battery. "Any word from... anyone?"

"Maddie, you mean? No. Still nothing. Thought I had a bit of a signal for a while, but it didn't come to anything," Logan replied. "Thought about giving her a ring from the house phone, but it was too early before I went out with the dog, and by the time I got back that old bastard was stalking the halls in her nightdress like some Edwardian ghost."

They sat in silence for a while, before Sinead turned back to him.

"And Shona's fine?"

"Aye. Aye, like I said, she's good." Logan looked ahead again and guided them around another rolling bend. "You're staring, Detective Constable. Why are you staring?"

"Staring, sir? Me? I'm not staring. I'm just... showing an interest."

"You're being a nosy cow, you mean."

"And that, aye," Sinead said. "But you're good? Both of you, I mean? Together?"

Logan nodded. "Yes. If you must know, it is. We are. Good. We're very good." His lips thinned and he gave a half-shrug. "I mean, she's still getting to grips with everything that happened. She's been visiting Olivia. Just... I don't know. Being there for her, I suppose."

"That's good of her," Sinead said. "There a court date set yet?"

"Not yet," Logan said. "Not for her, anyway. With her age, and the lack of any real concrete evidence against her, I reckon she'll walk away with a slap on the wrist."

Sinead nodded. "Tyler and I reckoned the same, yeah. She should be grand." She fixed her gaze on a spot ahead, trying to combat the creeping nausea. "But Shona's fine, though? No... long-term effects of what happened?"

"Eh, no. No. Not that she's mentioned," Logan said. "Why, has she said something to you?"

"No. No, just. You know. Like I said yesterday... What we went through, it was pretty rough. It's still rough, some days worse than others. I know what it's like for me, and I've had more than my fair share of trauma before all this. I'd just... I'd hate to think she was struggling."

Logan side-eyed her. "Aye. Aye, I'd hate to think so, too." He tapped his fingers on the wheel for a while before continuing. "Tell you what, when we're done on this case, you have your talk with Tyler, and I'll have one with Shona."

"Deal," Sinead said. She glanced down at her notepad, but didn't let her gaze linger there for fear the act of reading in the moving car would make her throw up. "So, this MSP then..."

"Don't tell me what party he's with, for God's sake," Logan said before she could go any further. "I don't want to unduly prejudice myself before I meet him."

"Makes sense," Sinead replied. "He's not actually the constituency MSP. He got in on the list vote."

"So, no bugger voted for him, then?" asked Logan, whose grasp of the workings of the Scottish Parliament's electoral system was tenuous at best. Although, to be fair to him, no more or less so than anyone else's, and he was, in this instance, broadly correct.

"Aye. He wouldn't have been named on the ballot paper. Just the party."

"Which I don't want to know."

"Which you don't want to know," Sinead confirmed. "Do you want to know his name, though?"

Logan slowed the car as he realised a rise in the road was about to become a sudden dip on the other side. He wasn't fast enough on the brakes, though, and for a moment he, Sinead, and Taggart all felt weightless, then gravity kicked back in, leaving their stomachs floating somewhere in the air behind them.

"Jesus," Sinead wheezed.

"This bloody road," Logan muttered, then he gave Sinead the nod. "Aye. You'd better give me his name, at least."

"You sure?" Sinead indicated a turning up on the left. "He's just up here, by the way."

Despite there being no other cars on the road, Logan clicked on his indicator. "Aye, I'll need to know his name if I'm going to talk to him."

Sinead shrugged. "Right, well, you asked for it. It's Oberon Finley-Lennox."

"Shut up. It is not!" Logan said, briefly tearing his eyes from the single-track road ahead.

"Honestly. It is."

"That's not an actual person's name. No one is *actually* called that. No one real."

"I hate to tell you, but I'm afraid you're wrong on that one, sir."

Logan tutted. "Great! Well now I know what party he's with, don't I?"

"It might not be the one you're thinking. He might be in... the Greens."

They turned into the driveway of what looked like a Manor House, and almost ploughed straight into the back of a Range Rover Westminster that stood proudly on the cobbles.

"Aye," Logan grumbled, glowering at the car. "The Greens, my arse."

Oberon Finley-Lennox, one of seven Regional MSPs for the Highlands and Islands, was taking breakfast in his study when the detectives arrived. His wife, a woman in her fifties who was wearing a twin set and pearls and a full face of makeup, despite the fact it was barely after ten in the morning, had initially looked like she was going to set the dogs on them when she'd clocked them coming up the path.

Logan had seen or heard nothing to indicate that the family possessed dogs, and yet, he'd never been more sure of anything in his life. Big bastards of things, they'd be, custom-bred to scare off the riff-raff.

It was only once they'd both showed their warrant cards, and she'd had a thorough check of the details, that she relaxed, relented, and ushered them through to where her husband was enjoying his Eggs Benedict over the morning papers.

To the best of Logan's knowledge, he'd never met an 'Oberon' before, and yet, if he'd had to describe one, the description would've matched the man sitting in the leather chair now, blinking in surprise as he smeared the last of a toasted muffin through a sludge of egg yolk and hollandaise sauce.

He had the clear, tanned complexion of someone with plenty of money to spend on self-care and foreign holidays. His hair sat uneasily on his head, like it didn't quite belong there. Not a wig, Logan thought, but maybe implants of some sort. He might be balding, but he was damned if he was going down without a fight.

Like his wife, he seemed overdressed in a light blue shirt, crisply pressed navy blue trousers, and shoes so polished that the detectives could see the underside of the table reflected in them. He had a napkin tucked into his shirt collar, but Logan would put money on him having a tie on underneath it.

He was well presented, and yet he looked a bit like someone was trying hard to polish a turd. The skin may have been tanned and blemish-free, but it was slack and heavy. It made his eyes droop, and folds accumulate below his chin.

His ears gave the impression that they hadn't stopped growing yet, and had no plans to do so in the immediate future. It wasn't just that they stuck out from the side of his head, it was the amount of space they occupied on it. They were so large they gave the impression that the rest of him was attached to *them*, instead of the other way around.

Still, given what genetics had saddled him with, he'd done a decent job of making the best of it.

"Marjorie? Who are these people?" the MSP asked, staring at Logan, but not addressing him. It was a polite enquiry, not a demand, though Logan got the sense that it wouldn't take much for it to become the latter.

"They're with the police, dear," his wife explained, pulling her burgundy cardigan more tightly closed. "They want to ask you some questions."

"Aha. I see," Oberon said, and he forced out a sliver of joviality. "Always a pleasure to greet members of the constabulary."

He dabbed at the corners of his mouth with the napkin, then untucked it to—sure enough—reveal a tie the same shade and colour of his trousers. After wiping his hands on the napkin, he draped it over his breakfast plate, waved vaguely in the direction of the tray it sat on, then shook Logan's hand while his wife withdrew from the study with what was left of the MSP's breakfast.

"You're clearly not the local bobbies though," Oberon remarked, pumping Logan's arm like he was on the campaign trail. His eyes narrowed as he studied the DCI. "Though, I recognise you from somewhere. Have you ever worked private security? You weren't at the party conference, were you?"

"Thankfully not," Logan said.

"Ha! Good lad!" Oberon said, and he gave Logan a hearty slap on the shoulder that might, in other circumstances, have earned him a thick ear. Or a thicker ear, anyway. "Not into politics, then?"

"Not the kind you're thinking of, no," Logan said.

"Then where do I know you from, I wonder?"

Logan knew it was probably from one of his all-too-regular appearances at TV press conferences, but he chose to let the other man continue suffering.

"No idea," he said. "Detective Chief Inspector Jack Logan. Police Scotland Major Investigations. This is my colleague, Detective Constable Sinead Bell."

"Oberon Finley-Lennox. Freedom UK."

Logan squeezed the other man's hand just hard enough to end the handshake, then raised an eyebrow. "Sorry?"

"My party. Freedom UK. I'm sure you've heard of us."

Logan had not. It was hard enough trying to keep track of what the bigger parties were up to—and they were always up to something—without worrying about the smaller groups on the fringe.

"No. It's a new one on me," Logan replied.

"Yes, well, we're growing fast. We've got three MSPs now, myself included. We're a firmly unionist party who believes the UK should be free."

"From what?" Logan asked.

"Just, you know,"—Oberon waved vaguely—"in general."

Logan firmly disagreed with that statement. In his experience, freedom was the opposite of what most of the country needed. Locking them up would be a much better approach.

Of course, it was possible that this viewpoint had been influenced by the sheer number of thieving, pillaging, murderous bastards he'd dealt with over the years, so he didn't bother saying anything.

"So, that's one of your policies, is it? 'Freedom in general.'"

"Yes. More or less," said Oberon, who didn't seem entirely convinced. Like any true politician, he shifted the line of questioning into more comfortable territory. "Some say we're anti-immigration, but we're not. I think that's important. We just think, you know, let's be *sensible* about it. Sure, bring in a few hundred doctors, or scientists, or whatever. Fine. No problem. But we can stack our own supermarket shelves, can't we? We can clean our own toilets, thank you very much!"

Logan suspected—no, Logan *knew*—that the man standing across from him now had never cleaned a toilet in his life. Not one of his own, and certainly not anyone else's.

"Fuck," Logan said. The word came out of nowhere, and caused Oberon to step back like he was afraid he was about to be mugged.

"I'm sorry?"

"Freedom UK," Logan said. "I just realised. Your acronym. It's fuck."

Oberon let out a mirthless little laugh. "We pronounce it *fook.*"

"You can pronounce it however you like. I can guarantee that everyone else will pronounce it as *fuck.*"

"Haha. Yes. Well, they'd be wrong. But, anyway, enjoyable as this is, what brings you to my humble abode?" Oberon asked. He brought up an arm and checked the time on a watch that probably cost half of Logan's yearly salary. "Though, before we get started, I must warn you that I don't have much time. Off to Edinburgh again this morning. Big vote this afternoon. Important political business! I have precisely..." He tilted his head left and right and crinkled his nose. "Mmm, seven, maybe eight minutes, then I'm afraid I really have to set off."

"Right, well, far be it for us to get in the way of the wheels of government. We'll try not to keep you long," Logan said, setting an internal timer for a minimum of fifteen minutes. "I'm sure you heard about all the drama yesterday."

"Drama?" Oberon raised an eyebrow as he looked from Logan to Sinead and back again. "What drama? I wasn't aware of any drama."

"A body was found about fifteen miles from here."

"Oh! Oh, no, I hadn't heard a thing. Oh, how dreadful," the MSP said. He lowered himself onto the edge of his desk, like the news had robbed his legs of their strength. "How utterly dreadful. Local? I mean, tragic either way, obvs, but... Was it somebody local?"

Logan tried not to get too hung up on the 'obvs' and just answered the question.

"Aye. Someone who we believe you know," Logan said. He watched closely for the other man's reaction. But then, he'd been studying Oberon since they'd first set foot in the room.

"Oh no. Who?"

"We believe he was known locally as Bernie the Beacon."

"Oh, that's terrible. Terrible," Oberon said, not skipping a beat. "Oh, such a shame. Bernie. Poor Bernie. He was a real local character."

"Aye, we've been getting that impression," Logan confirmed.

"Oh, that is awful. That poor man," Oberon said, and he wiped the corner of his eye with the back of his hand. It was one of the most transparently fake pretences at grief that Logan had ever had the misfortune to witness. "What happened? Can I ask?"

"We're still waiting on the results of the post-mortem," Logan said. "But it looks like he was burned to death."

"Burned? Good gracious. Oh, that's horrible. Not a nice way to go, I'd imagine," Oberon said, then a frown troubled his brow. "Wait, *was* burned? You mean..."

"We believe there's a possibility that Bernie was murdered, yes."

"Murdered?" Oberon practically shrieked. He stood, head up and shoulders back. "No. No, no. Not round here. That sort of thing simply doesn't happen. You must be mistaken."

"It's possible that it was an accident. We're not ruling anything out at this stage."

"Aha! There we are, then. It'll be an accident. Has to be. No less tragic, of course. Still a terrible loss for..." Oberon's eyebrows dipped. "Did he have a family? Bernie, I mean? I'm not familiar with his background."

Logan chose to ignore the question to pursue his own. "He seemed pretty familiar with yours. Were you aware that Bernie was spying on you?"

"Spying? Bernie? On me?" Oberon asked, each word higher in pitch than the one before it. He gave a laugh that was as false as his grief had been. "Why would he be spying on me? He wasn't freelancing for *Private Eye* was he?"

Logan shook his head. "No," he said. "Pretty sure, they only cover well-known politicians in that, don't they? I don't imagine they'll be troubling you anytime soon."

"Ha!" Oberon pointed at the detective. "Quite the satirist yourself, I see. I'll have to keep an eye on you."

Logan's gaze went to the extended finger and lingered there until the digit was retracted. "Funny," he said. "I was just thinking the same thing."

"What was your relationship with Bernie?" Sinead asked.

"Relationship? I didn't have a relationship. He was just some tra... He was just a homeless."

"'A homeless'? A homeless what?" Logan asked. "You can't just say 'a homeless.'"

"Man. A homeless man, I meant," Oberon said. He was still smiling, but it was clear from the rest of his face that he was finding Logan less amusing by the moment.

"And?" Logan pressed. "You can still have a relationship with a homeless man."

The smile died away completely. "I'm sorry, but I don't think I like what you're implying."

"What am I implying?" Logan asked.

"That I was having some sort of gay relationship with Bernie."

Had 'synchronised shock' been an Olympic event, the looks on Logan and Sinead's faces would have bagged them the gold. Logan half-turned to the DC beside him.

"I wasn't implying that. Were you implying that, Detective Constable?"

"I wasn't implying that, sir," Sinead replied. "I just meant were they friends, enemies, casual acquaintances? That sort of thing."

"That's how I took it, aye," Logan said. "I didn't read anything into that about them being gay lovers."

"If you had, you would've been mistaken, sir," Sinead continued. "Because that was never my intention. I think Mr Finley-Lennox is inferring something that wasn't there."

Logan nodded. "Aye. Aye, that's just what I was thinking." He turned back to Oberon, who he'd kept half an eye on throughout the previous exchange. "I'm not sure if you heard our conversation there."

The MSP tutted. "Of course I heard. I'm three feet away." He held both hands up and brought the smile back out of retirement. It was a smug, slightly lopsided thing that somehow made the world seem like a less happy place. "I apologise for the misunderstanding. It's just that in politics, with the tabloids, you get used to them projecting all sorts of scandal onto you."

"What, even you?" asked Logan.

"Haha. Yes. Quite. Even me."

"Detective Constable, remind me to check up on past tabloid scandals involving Mr Finley-Lennox when we're back in the office, will you?" Logan instructed, not breaking eye contact with the MSP. "Might make for some interesting reading."

"Will do, sir."

"Well, you won't find much," Oberon admitted. "There hasn't been a lot about me, per se. But it happens all the time. In general. One must be on one's guard."

"Aye, I suppose one must," said Logan. "Anyway, getting back to the real world, why do you think Bernie was spying on you?"

"I have absolutely no idea!"

"You seem shocked."

"Yes, well. What can I say? It's been a shocking morning. With the news, and everything." He lowered his head and clasped his hands in front of him, like he was paying his respects at the Cenotaph. "Poor Bernie. Such a sad loss to the community."

"Not to you, though," Logan said.

Oberon raised his head. "I'm sorry?"

"Must be a relief for you," Logan continued. "Given the number of complaints you'd made about him. The restraining order you had against him."

"Oh, that!" Oberon said, trying to dismiss the whole thing with a laugh and a wave of a hand. "That was... I was being silly. Overreacting. That's all I was doing. I can see that now."

"Seemed reasonable to me," said Sinead. "I read the reports. Sounds like he was making a nuisance of himself."

"Yes. Well, yes. Yes, you're right. He was a bit. Thank you. He even approached when I was out with the kids, would you believe? Margaux and Welly were both very alarmed. Welly had to sleep in with us that night."

Logan frowned. "Welly?"

"Yes. Our youngest. Orwellia. We call her Welly."

"I can see why you'd want to shorten it," Logan said.

"I told him at the time. I said... I told him that it wasn't on. Harassing me was one thing, but not when I was out with the children. That's too far." He looked to Sinead for backup. "You'd agree, right?"

"Absolutely," Sinead said. "Bang out of order, that."

"Thank you! Yes. Thank you. Exactly. Hence my complaints, and the... injunction, or whatever it's called. It's one thing to come ranting and raving at me, but not Margaux and Welly. Not the kids."

He checked his watch, and was about to point out that he really had to leave before Logan beat him to the punch.

"What was he ranting and raving about?"

Oberon winced and gave his watch a tap. "I really do have important political business to attend to. I must..." He realised this wasn't carrying any water with the detectives, and sighed. "Just the usual ramblings. Lizard men. People like me. How it was all our fault. How I had blood on my hands. That sort of thing."

"How what was all your fault?" Sinead asked.

Oberon frowned, like he'd never given this any thought before. "Hmm. Do you know, I'm not really sure? It was all just a jumble of nonsense, and very hard to follow."

"Was it something about the world in general, or something specific that had happened to him, do you think?" Logan asked.

"As I say, I don't know."

"I didn't ask what you knew, I asked what you thought. What was your impression?"

The MSP blew out his cheeks, then retrieved his suit jacket and hanger from the back of the study door. "I honestly can't say. Something personal, I suppose, given his passion. But that is a guess, nothing more." He slipped the jacket on, then picked up a lint roller from an antique writing bureau and ran it down his front. "Now, if you'll excuse me, I need to—"

"When did you last see Bernie?" Logan asked.

The sticky lint roller caught the end of Oberon's tie, and the downward stroke almost throttled him.

"Wait," he said, setting the roller down again. "You're not... You don't think I had anything to do with it? With Bernie's death? You don't think I killed him?"

"The thought hadn't crossed my mind," Logan said. "It has now, mind you. I mean, makes sense, when you think of it. Aye. Aye, I could see why you might want him out of the picture. Pain in the arse like that? Scaring your kids? You must've been raging."

"I don't think Mr Finley-Lennox would've killed Bernie, sir," Sinead said.

Oberon clasped his hands together like he was about to drop to his knees in prayer. He shook them in Sinead's direction, so the tips of his fingers were all pointing her way. "Yes! Thank you! Precisely!"

"More likely he'd have paid someone," Sinead concluded.

Logan sniffed as he gave the MSP an appraising once-over. "Aye. Doesn't look the type to get his hands dirty, right enough. Besides, what would the papers say?" He shrugged. "Probably nothing. Or just, 'Who?'"

"This is... No. I'm not having this. This is unacceptable," Oberon said. "I'm not having this in my own house. I'm not being accused of... whatever it is I'm being accused of. I'm not some... some common criminal that you can just push around. I am a duly elected Member of the Scottish Parliament!"

"On the list vote," Logan reminded him.

"That's irrelevant!" Oberon insisted. "Who's your superior? I'm going to have my office contact him to put in a complaint."

"Her," Logan corrected. "It's Detective Superintendent Mitchell, up in Inverness. And I'm sure she'd love another complaint to add to the pile."

"Yes. Well, please do rest assured that she shall be getting one!"

"Oh, I have no doubt that she will," Logan said. He looked around at the office, with its expensive old furniture and grandiose style, then gave the MSP a nod. "Keep your phone on for us," he instructed. "I've got a feeling we'll be talking to each other again very soon."

Taggart bounced around excitedly when the detectives returned to the car, but managed to restrain himself enough to not come bounding into the front and onto their laps. Instead, he stuck his head between the gap in the front seats, and panted happily as Sinead patted his head.

Through the front windscreen, they watched Oberon's Range Rover pull away from the house and go roaring up the road with a turn of speed that skirted defiantly close to the speed limit.

"What do you think?" Sinead asked.

"From a purely personal perspective, I think he's an arsehole," Logan replied.

"And from a professional perspective?"

"I think you're right that he wouldn't have killed Bernie himself." Logan looked up at the house, with its dozen windows, and ivy creeping across the old red bricks. "But he's certainly got the resources to have some other bugger do it for him."

Taggart nudged his arm with his head, then licked his elbow through his coat. Logan begrudgingly reached back and tousled the dog's fur beneath its chin.

"There, you needy bastard. Happy?"

Judging by the way the little dog's tail wagged, he was over the moon.

"Right, you ready to face this road?" asked the DCI, starting the engine.

"Ready as I'll ever be," Sinead said with a groan.

Logan put the car into gear and stole a glance at his mirrors. For a moment, from the corner of his eye, he thought he saw Mrs Finley-Lennox peeking out through the blinds at one of the downstairs windows.

When he looked closer, though, she was gone.

"Right, then," he announced, his gaze lingering there for just a moment. "Let's get a shifty on."

CHAPTER FIFTEEN

BEN WAS HAVING problems of the technical variety. This was not unusual, but given that the technology he was currently attempting to use was so unfamiliar, and the internet speeds so poor, the problems were even worse than usual.

"Hello? Hello?" He tapped the screen of the laptop in an apparently random series of places then, when this achieved precisely nothing, he pecked at the space bar. "Can you hear me? I think there's something wrong with this thing."

"Why would she be able to hear you, boss?" asked Tyler, bending so he leaned over the DI's left shoulder. "You've not started the call."

"What? How do you know?"

Hamza leaned over Ben's right shoulder. "Well, it says 'Start Call' there, doesn't it, sir?"

"What? Where?" Ben peered over his glasses at the button on the screen. "That one?"

"That's the one, boss," Tyler confirmed.

Ben prodded the button and waited.

"It's not touchscreen, sir," Hamza told him. "You need to use the trackpad."

"The trackpad?" Ben squinted at the screen, then down at the keyboard. Then, he repeated his movement several times before asking the obvious question. "What's that?"

"The square bit, boss. There, below the space bar."

"Oh, the swipey bit? Well why didn't you bloody say so?"

Ben shot them both reproachful looks like this was somehow all their fault, then moved a finger across the trackpad. The arrow cursor shot straight to the top of the screen, slid to the far right corner, and stayed there.

"Where's the thingy? I've lost the thingy," he said, eyes hunting the screen for any sign of it.

"It's up there, sir," Hamza said, indicating the top corner. "Would it be easier if I just dialled you in?"

"That definitely sounds easier, boss," Tyler said.

"I'm not going to learn if you keep doing these things for me," Ben said. "You just need to show me how to do it myself."

Hamza had shown him how to do 'these things' for himself. He had shown him this exact thing three times now, and it wasn't getting any easier.

"Maybe we could sit down next week sometime and go through it," Hamza said, before quietly adding an, "again."

"Shona's going to be thinking we're not coming, boss," Tyler pointed out. "We were meant to be dialled in five minutes ago."

Ben sighed and took his hands off the keyboard like he was turning himself in. "Fine. You give it a try. I'm telling you, though, there's something wrong with it. You won't get it to—"

Hamza clicked the button he'd drawn Ben's attention to

earlier, and after a further click to confirm, Shona's face appeared on the screen.

"Aha! There you are!" she said. "I thought you'd stood me up."

"Hello, Shona!" Ben bellowed, loud enough to make the pathologist pull an earbud from her ear in fright.

"You can just talk normally, sir," Hamza told him.

"Aye, there's a microphone, boss. She doesn't have to hear you shouting all the way from Inverness."

"Oh. Right, aye. Sorry about that," Ben said. He was still projecting his voice more than usual, but it was an improvement.

Shona stuffed her earbud back in while her eyes searched the screen. "Jack not there?"

"No, he's still out and about," Ben said. "Not quite sure when he'll be back."

"Ah right. No rest for the wicked!" Shona said. "It's the same here, actually. Pulled an all-nighter with your camper."

"You've been at it all night?" Ben frowned. "You shouldn't have done that. It wasn't especially urgent. You'll be knackered."

"No, I'm wide awake, actually," Shona said, and the way she bounced around in her chair backed this up. "Petrol station at *Tesco* has got this new energy drink in. I stocked up on it. I am, not to put too fine a point on it, buzzing off my tits." Her eyes widened even as she heard the words coming out of her mouth. "By which I mean I'm heavily caffeinated. Anyway, how are you all doing? It's funny seeing you all on the screen like this. The way you're positioned, you look like the video for *Bohemian Rhapsody*."

She fell silent for a moment, sniffed, then clutched her head like it was about to explode.

"Sorry, I'm talking absolute shite. Clearly, I need to get some sleep. You'll be after the post-mortem results?"

"Ideally, yes," Ben said. He leaned a little closer to the screen. "Are you alright?"

"Fine!" Shona chirped. "Just, you know, got carried away. Haven't done an all-nighter in years, so I thought, nothing to do, nowhere to go, why not?"

"You could've gone home," Tyler suggested, which caught the pathologist off guard.

"Um... Home. Yes. God. Yes, I could've done that. That would've made sense, going home. That would've prevented..." She gestured at herself. "...all this going on right now. Sorry."

"You're fine," Ben said. "Maybe just give us the highlights, then go get some rest."

"A fine plan! I agree. Great thinking," Shona said. She winked, fired finger-guns at the camera, then became visibly self-conscious about doing both, and cleared her throat. "Right, so, your man, then. The victim. I don't think he was burned." She shook her head. "I mean, obviously he was burned. But not to death. He was already dead, is what I'm saying. Strangled with some sort of narrow gauge wire. Electrical wire, maybe. Something that cut into his neck."

"So we're definitely looking at murder, then?" Ben asked. He'd been expecting that, of course. They all had. But there was always room for hope.

"I'd say so, yes," Shona confirmed. "No way he could've done that to himself. Did Geoff mention anything about any wire at the scene?"

"No," Ben said.

"There you go, then. Killer must've taken it. Unless it burned up. It could've burned up. Forget I said anything,"

Shona babbled. "Not about him being strangled, about the wire not being there. He was definitely strangled." She tugged at the neck of her scrubs. "Is it hot in here? Or is it just me?"

"I mean..." Ben glanced back at Tyler and Hamza. "It's not hot *here*. Are you sure you're alright, Shona?"

"I'm grand. Just overdid the energy drinks and underdid the sleep. Be right as rain in the morning." She frowned, and looked around at the windowless office. "Wait. It's morning now, isn't it? Ah, shite."

Ben glanced up and to his right at Hamza, who appeared to be sharing many of the DI's current concerns.

"Do you want to maybe just email over the report?" Ben suggested. "And then go and get some rest? I don't want to keep you on this,"—he gestured at the laptop—"contraption if you're not feeling up to it."

"Oh no, I'm fine. I'm grand. Nice to have a bit of company," Shona said. "Your man on the slab there wasn't much for conversation. Not for want of me trying, mind you."

She laughed at that until she snorted, then looked mortified and consulted the clipboard of notes that sat on the desk in front of her.

"Anyway, he was strangled. Well, garrotted with the wire. Then, an accelerant was poured over him—turpentine, Geoff thinks—and he was set alight."

"Turps?" asked Ben. "Like for removing paint? That's an accelerant, aye, but not the easiest to light."

"It was mixed with petroleum jelly," Shona said. "Apparently, that makes it easier. By the time the fire burned out, there wasn't much left of him, which makes it harder to pin down when this happened, of course. A lot of what we'd usually rely on has, you know, melted."

"Can you take an educated guess?" Ben asked.

"Well, going by insect infestation of the remains... the number of animal bites... general decomposition, I'd say we're looking at two to three weeks. Can't really be much more definite than that, I'm afraid. In fact, I can't give you much more than that in general. Stomach contents were all gone."

"Burned up?" asked Tyler.

"Partly. And partly eaten by a scavenging animal of some kind," Shona replied. "Possibly a pine marten."

Tyler grimaced. "Jesus. Sorry I asked."

"I'm going to send him off for imaging to see if there's anything I've missed. Carbonisation like his makes dissection difficult, so there's always a chance the tomography will find more," Shona explained. "What I would say, though, is that he fits the description of the suspected victim. Except, you know, a set-on-fire version of him. Male, about the right height, right age range. Based on what information we have, I'd say it's more likely him than it isn't."

"Right. Well, I suppose that's something," Ben said. "Better to know who we're dealing with, at least, than..."

He fell silent as, on screen, Shona flapped her hands like she was trying to take off, her face suddenly alive with excitement.

"Oh! Sorry for interrupting! I just remembered something," she said.

She reached off-camera and returned with a large, neon-coloured can in one hand, and a small evidence bag in the other. She held up the bag to the camera while she took a big slurp from the can. A trickle of luminous orange liquid dribbled down her chin.

"What are we looking at?" asked Ben, squinting at the out-of-focus contents of the bag.

"It's a ring. Gold," Shona said. "Geoff must've missed it. No wonder, it was sort of fused with the flesh and blackened like the rest of the body."

"Lovely," Tyler remarked.

"It's a wedding ring, I'd say, except it was on the wrong hand. Ring finger on the right hand instead of the left. I'm going to get someone from Geoff's team to come over and collect it, and they can do their stuff on it."

"Any markings? Engravings?" Ben asked.

"Address and phone number of his next of kin?" Hamza added.

"Not sure," Shona admitted. "Probably not that last one, though. It'll need cleaned up before we can get anything like that."

From elsewhere in the station there came a knocking. A swift *rat-a-tat-tat* of someone at the door. Ben nudged Tyler and gave a little jerk of his head. "Better get that, son. There's no one else in."

"On it, boss," said Tyler, who was secretly quite relieved to be getting away from the call. The nitty-gritty of the post-mortem procedure was generally not something he enjoyed digging into.

He left the room with a skip in his step, and pulled the Incident Room door closed behind him.

A moment later, before the conversation could go much further, he opened the door again, and leaned his head around it.

"Eh, I don't know if it's just my imagination," he said. "But I think Jesus might be at the door."

Shona knocked back another swig of her energy drink, then returned to the black rectangle on her screen which had, until just a moment ago, been a window filled with people she knew.

She watched it until she'd finished the can, quietly hoping that the call might resume, and they could pick up where they'd left off.

Besides, if it really *was* the Lord Jesus Christ who was at the door, she'd have quite liked to have said hello.

She added the empty can to the pyramid she was building on the floor by her desk, stood frozen for a few seconds while she waited to see if it would collapse, then she sat back in her chair, rocked it from side to side, and tapped her hands on her legs.

Ben was right, of course. She should go home. She needed to rest.

But she hadn't been home on her own in a long, long time.

And she wasn't about to start now.

CHAPTER SIXTEEN

THE MAN AT THE DOOR, Ben and Hamza both had to admit, did have a certain Christ-like quality about him. He had worked hard to cultivate it, too, not just in his physical appearance and the way he dressed, but in the air of calm and serenity he worked so very hard to project.

"Bonjour. I was told to meet Detective Chief Inspector Logan here," he said, still standing outside while the three detectives stared at him in equal parts confusion and amusement.

"You're French," Tyler told him.

"Oui. Yes. My name is André Douville. I am the chaperone at Westerly Wellness. You know, the retreat?"

"On the wall. In the caravan," Tyler said.

It was André's turn to look confused. "Pardon?"

"Doesn't matter," said Hamza. "We've heard of you, aye."

"You'd best come in," Ben said, stepping aside. "DCI Logan isn't back yet, but if he said to meet him here, I'd imagine he'll be here soon. You can come in and wait."

While André hitched up his long white robe and stepped

inside, Tyler stole a glance at his watch. "Don't forget we're meant to be going to the pub for lu..." he began, then he course corrected. "...for the investigation. To investigate. For the purposes of..." He tapped the watch. "We were going to go there in half an hour."

"Aye, well, I'm sure we can delay it, if necessary," Ben said. Try as he might, though, he was unable to hide his own disappointment. "For a few minutes, anyway. Here, Mr..."

"Douville."

"Take a seat. Would you like a cup of tea or coffee?"

André lifted his nose higher in the air, like he was sniffing out his options. "What kinds of tea do you have?"

Ben pulled a *buggered if I know* face and looked to Tyler and Hamza for assistance.

"Think it was *PG Tips*," Tyler said.

Before André could respond, someone else answered on his behalf.

"Oh, he won't touch any of that shite," Logan said, ducking through the door. "If it's not a squashed lavender chai, an oak leaf espresso, or a bloody... horse shit lozenge, he's no' interested."

The DCI pointed to the two doors that led off from the cramped reception area. "Is one of these the interview room?"

"That's where we've set up the Big Board," Ben said, indicating one of the doors.

Logan nodded, put a hand on André's back, and guided him in the direction of the other one. "Right, then this'll be where we do the interviews. In we go, Mr Douville."

He steered the other man into the room he'd just claimed, vanished in after him, then reappeared half a second later, jabbing a finger at the rest of the team. "And if you bastards even *think* about going for lunch before I'm ready, you're all fired."

Tyler caught up with Sinead near the village centre, where she was giving Taggart his first proper walk of the day. The dog still had wee legs and an inquisitive nose, so even the short trek from the car park to the shops had taken nearly ten minutes, and they were barely halfway there.

"Alright stranger?" he said, jogging up behind her and putting a hand on her back. After a quick glance around to make sure nobody was watching—they were both technically on duty, after all—he leaned in and gave her a quick peck on the cheek.

"Hiya," Sinead said, running a hand down the inside of his arm.

Taggart, who had been devoting every ounce of his attention to a leaf lying on the pavement, suddenly realised that Tyler was there, and sprung at him, his muddy front paws slapping excitedly at the DC's thighs.

"My trousers! Watch my... argh! He does that on purpose. I'm sure of it. I think the boss has got him trained, or something," Tyler said, brushing the mud off his breeks. Or trying to, anyway.

Sinead smirked. "I doubt he'd take the time to..." She thought about it, then nodded. "No, you're probably right. He'll have trained him to do it."

They fell into step. They had both been out of Uniform for a while now—Tyler longer than Sinead—but neither had lost the knack for that synchronised stepping that all Bobbies on the beat developed. They moved in perfect unison, like they were performing some well-rehearsed choreographed dance.

"Anyway, it's just a bit of mud on your trousers," Sinead said. "I've had the same clothes on since yesterday morning. Didn't expect to be away overnight."

"Aye, I thought you were absolutely honking, right enough," Tyler said, which earned him a playful dunt. "There's a shower at the B&B. It's the tiniest shower in the world, though, in the most cramped en suite bathroom I've ever seen. You've got to open the bathroom door to put down the toilet seat."

"Since when do you put down the toilet seat?" Sinead asked.

Tyler laughed. "Aye, well, no. But in *theory,* you would. I haven't tested it."

They continued walking in the direction of the shop. There had been a thin, smirry sort of rain wafting about the place all morning, but it had stopped now, and the air smelt crisp and new. They were far enough from any foliage to limit the number of midges knocking about, too, so the stroll was a pleasant one.

"We were talking to Shona. Video call," Tyler ventured.

"PM results?"

"Aye. Mostly," he said. Then, a few paces further on, he asked, "Have you spoken to her recently?"

"Not really. Just in passing."

"Did she seem, you know, alright?"

"Eh, aye. Fine. Like I say, though, it was just in passing. Why? Did she not seem alright to you?"

Tyler shrugged. "Dunno. Just came across as a bit... manic."

"She's always a bit like that though, isn't she?" Sinead pointed out.

"Well, yeah. But... I dunno." Tyler kicked a stone, and Taggart shot after it, then jerked to a stop when the lead went tight. "She hadn't been home. Stayed in the hospital all night."

"Did she say why?"

"Just for the PM, I think," Tyler said. "But she'd been knocking back the caffeine to stay awake." He watched his legs swinging beneath him for a moment, then asked the question that was troubling him. "You think she's like, traumatised, or something? About everything that happened? Because, she went through a lot."

Sinead hesitated, like she sensed some sort of trap approaching. "I don't know. Maybe."

"Because it would be. It must be. Traumatising. Something like that," Tyler continued. He still hadn't looked at her, and was instead focusing on their synchronised steps. "It must leave a mark. In, like, your brain. Or whatever. It must do damage."

"I... suppose so."

"And, well, she should talk to someone, shouldn't she?" Tyler continued. "If she's still having problems with it. If she's still struggling to process it. She should say. She should come out with it. She shouldn't bottle it up."

Sinead shot him a sideways glance. "Eh, no. No, I suppose she shouldn't."

"Because it could help. It could really help, I think. Telling someone she trusts. Someone who cares for her."

"Like Logan."

"What?" For a moment, Tyler looked hurt. Then, he

remembered the charade. "Oh. Yeah. Shona. Logan. She could tell Logan, yeah. She should. Don't you think?"

Sinead shifted her gaze to the sky. Grey clouds were woven together across much of it, but there were a few patches of blue dotted around here and there. A suggestion of better things to come.

"I suppose... she might just need time," she replied. "Or maybe she just doesn't want to worry him. Maybe he's had enough on himself of late without her adding to the pile."

"But that's what marriage is about," Tyler said, then he flinched. "Not that... not that they're married yet. But who knows? Maybe one day. But they're in a relationship, and that's..." He stopped walking, sighed, and finally turned to face her. "Whenever she wants to talk. Whatever she wants to tell him. He'll be there. I know he will. And he'll understand. Whatever it is, he'll understand."

Sinead searched his face and saw nothing but raw, honest sincerity there. She stretched forward and kissed him on the lips this time, and without bothering to check if the others were around to see.

"I know he will," she whispered, resting her forehead against his. "Always."

They stood like that for a while, then Taggart's insistent pulling on the lead dragged them apart.

"And, you know, if *you* ever need to talk to *me* about anything, that's fine, too," Tyler said.

Sinead laughed at that. "Nah, you're alright!"

"Yeah." Tyler grinned, as he slipped an arm around his wife's waist. "Probably best not. I'm not much good at that sort of thing."

"Oh, I don't know," Sinead replied. "Maybe you're better at it than I give you credit for."

The set-up that Logan cobbled together in the interview room wasn't exactly the traditional one. There was one chair —a moulded plastic number with metal legs and a hole low down in the back whose only possible purpose could be to show the top of your arse to the person sitting behind you.

Logan had selflessly given the chair to André, which had left him free to pace around the weirdo hippie bastard like this was some sort of military interrogation session that might turn to waterboarding at any moment.

André, to his credit, did not seem remotely concerned about the giant, surly-looking man padding in circles around him, and so far, none of Logan's questions had caused him any distress, not even the blunt, out of nowhere, "Why did you kill him?" that could usually be relied on to put interviewees onto the back foot.

He hadn't killed him, he claimed. He hadn't heard from him in weeks. Hadn't seen him in over a month. Bernie's death was truly tragic, but it was hee-haw to do with him.

"So, tell me about the last time you saw him, then," Logan said, stopping in front of the man in the chair just long enough to ask the question, then setting off on another lap around him.

"He tied himself to the gate," André said, and he appeared amused by the memory. "Arms out. Like this," he continued, then he spread his arms wide and briefly became a living image of Christ on the cross. "Bound to the fence rail."

"Why?"

"To stop new arrivals. We had acolytes arriving for initiation. They come and go all the time, but that day happened to be a day when there were four arriving at once, and he thought he could put them off, I think."

Logan stopped in front of him again. "How would he know you had four new people arriving that day?" he wondered. "Was that public knowledge?"

"Non. I... I do not know. I never gave it much thought," André admitted. "We just used the other gate."

"And what, he just packed up and went home, did he?"

"Ha! Chance would be a fine thing. Bernie was no quitter. He shouted. A lot. He told the new arrivals that they were being tricked, that I was stealing their money, and that, like all doctors, I was a charlatan."

Logan stopped pacing. "Doctors?"

"Oui. I am a doctor."

Logan looked the younger man up and down. "Of what?"

"Of alternative and holistic medicine."

"Right," Logan said. He took a moment to process this. "So, you're not an actual doctor, then?"

"That depends on your definition of—"

"Are you licensed to practise medicine?"

André seemed amused by this notion, like the detective's interpretation of the word was naive and childish.

"What is 'licensed' really, huh?" he asked. "Who gives some group or body the right to say, 'Yes, you can do this, you can not'?"

"The government, I'd imagine," Logan said.

"Exactly. And do you think the government has your best interests at heart? Hmm? Or do you think they wish to continue taking bribes from pharmaceutical companies, knowing all the while that sunlight and nature can cure all ailments? Do you think they wish you to know this? Non.

They do not. They wish it to be kept secret, so they can profit at our expense."

He crossed one leg over the other, then rested both hands on top of the uppermost knee. Judging by the look on his face, he felt like the argument had just been well and truly won.

Logan sucked in his bottom lip, then spat it out. "Right, so *not* a doctor, then."

"You have your definition, Detective Chief Inspector, and I have mine," André said. "Bernie considered me a doctor."

"Bernie thought the world was a box and run by lizard people. I wouldn't be taking his word as gospel on anything," Logan said. "Speaking of which, what is with the whole Jesus thing by the way? Is that part of the shtick?"

"Stick?" André frowned. "Apologies. I do not understand the question. What about a stick?"

Logan sighed. "Doesn't matter. So, Bernie was shouting, calling you a fraud—can't think why—then what?"

"Then... he stopped. I do not know. He left."

"Just untied himself and walked off?"

"Non. He was picked up."

"In a car?"

"A van. Small. Like a car, but with... a van back. You know?"

Logan nodded. "Aye. Did you recognise it?"

"Non. It went west. Towards the lighthouse, I think. I did not watch for long."

"Did you get any details? Registration? Can you give us a description, at least?"

"White. Small. Dirty. Rust above the wheels. I did not get number, no. I was just happy to see him go."

"I bet you were," Logan said. He began pacing again, this time talking as he walked. "You told me yesterday that Bernie didn't affect your business. That this grudge he had wasn't a problem."

"Oui. That is correct."

"And yet, a little birdie tells me that numbers are right down," Logan continued. "By the sounds of it, Bernie's antics have had a real impact on the number of new cult members coming through your door, or... tent flaps, or whatever."

André uncrossed his legs, then crossed them again the other way. He adjusted his robe, sniffed, then shrugged. Throughout it all, he didn't once stop smiling. "Attendance ebbs and flows, just like everything else. The Universe fluctuates. Seasons come and go. The tides rise and fall. It is the way of all things. Even here and now, in this room, there are changes going on, so subtle, that we do not see them. But they are happening. A wall may creak as it contracts. A window groans as the sun heats the glass. If I shout at the sky, would you blame me for the sunset, Detective Chief Inspector?"

Logan rubbed his temples, nursing the headache he could feel starting to build there. "No. Because that would be mental," he said. "But shaking your fist at the sky isn't the same as telling people they're being ripped off, is it? There's fuck all the sun can do, but people can always choose to take their business elsewhere. And by the sounds of it, that's exactly what's been happening."

"That is incorrect."

"My arse it's incorrect," Logan barked. "He was messing with your business. He was costing you money, and nothing you could do was going to make him stop. You couldn't reason with a man like that. No one could. Not the police, not the community. Hell, probably not even himself. There's only one way you stop someone like that. And that's permanently."

André's smile became a chuckle, then a laugh that he tried and failed to conceal behind his beard. This did nothing to endear him to the detective towering over him.

"Something funny?"

"Non. Oui. It is... It is just the ludicrousness of this. Of accusing moi, me, of something like this."

"And why's that amusing?" Logan wondered.

"I detest violence in all its forms, Detective Chief Inspector. I have dedicated my life to healing others. Helping them. Even Bernie himself, in fact."

Logan's eyes narrowed. "Oh? In what way?"

"I mentioned the last time I had seen Bernie was a month ago. But I had heard from him just a few weeks back. Two, maybe three. He telephoned me."

"He phoned you? Out here?" Logan said, looking highly doubtful. "How? There's no bloody signal. And, from what we can gather, he didn't have a phone."

"I have satellite telephone for the retreat. Bernie was not calling from here. He was calling from a number in Glasgow. I assumed it was a new enquiry about attending the centre, but when I answered there was nothing. No reply. Nothing, so I hang up."

"How did you know it was Bernie, then?"

"He called back. Three, perhaps four times. On the last time, that is when he spoke to me. He sounded different then. Smaller. Does that make sense? Sounding smaller? Not quieter, exactly, just like he had been shrunken down. Like he was a tiny person."

"What, you mean like he was squeaky? Like a mouse?" Logan asked. "Had he been on the Helium or something?"

"Non. Non, not squeaky. Just... like he had no fight in him. Like his strength—like his *soul* was smaller, not his physical form. Like his energy had been compressed."

"Oh, like his energy had been compressed. Gotcha. Why didn't you say that to start with?" Logan replied. "What did he say?"

"He said sorry, would you believe?"

"Sorry? Bernie, the man who had been calling you a fraud and leading a relentless one-man campaign to shut you down, called you up to say sorry?"

"Oui. And he said he would no longer be bothering me. He was calling a truce between us."

"That's convenient for you. You making friends like that, right before someone murders him," Logan said, not buying a word of it. "Well, I suppose that's you in the clear then."

"You do not believe me, I understand," André said. "But I am telling the truth. He called me, apologised, and then he asked me for my help."

"What sort of help? To do what?"

The man in the chair ran a hand down his beard, stroking it as he sized the detective up. "You are sceptical about the spirit realm, oui? About the possibilities to commune with those who have passed to the other side?"

"If by 'sceptical' you mean I think it's a load of absolute horse shite, then aye, that's a pretty accurate summing up."

"Oui. Well, Bernie, for all his faults and prejudices, was more open-minded. He called me asking if anyone had a message for him. From beyond the veil, so to speak. I am a spiritual medium, you see?"

"Aye. You mentioned. You're a magic telephone. Very good," Logan said.

"You may not believe me, but Bernie did. And he was hoping to hear from someone."

"Someone dead?"

"Oui."

"Did he say who?"

André shook his head. "Non. He gave me nothing to work with. He merely asked if there was anyone from the other side who wished to talk to him. He said he wanted to know if what he was going to do was right."

"What was he going to do?"

"He would not say. But the spirits believed—"

"I'm going to stop you there," Logan said, cutting him short. "I've got zero interest in any bloody *ghost gossip* you claim to have heard. If Bernie didn't say it, I don't care."

André got to his feet. The smile he put on was a patronising, infuriating thing that made Logan's fingers curl into fists.

"I get it, Detective Chief Inspector. You do not like to dwell on things you cannot comprehend. You like to think that you are in control. You ignore or ridicule what you do not understand, rather than face up to the possibility that the world is a place filled with magic and wonder."

"Aye. That's a fairly accurate description, son. Well done. Very insightful. Sit down."

"Ah, non. Apologies, Detective Chief Inspector Logan, but I have other appointments to attend to."

"Other appointments? I don't care what other appointments you've got. They're cancelled."

André laughed. "You are a funny man, monsieur. But I am not under arrest. This is not an official interview. This is just a conversation, oui? Two little motes of stardust briefly crossing paths, neither one bound to the other. I am free to leave at any time, I think."

Logan felt his back teeth grinding together. He swallowed, forcing down a big wad of anger that was threatening to burst out of him. "I'd appreciate it if you stayed a little longer, Mr Douville."

"Ah. Were it only possible. Alas, my other appointments are too pressing." He turned away—turned his back on the DCI—without anything in any way resembling permission.

Fortunately, for his sake, he turned back just a second later.

"You may not believe that the dead can talk to us, Detective Chief Inspector. But Bernie did. And he was hoping to hear from someone. Someone who had been very close to him, I think." He started to turn again, then stopped. "I think grief does funny things to people. It affects them in different ways. Some become cold. Angry. They bury themselves in their work, and distance themselves from others for fear of losing someone else, and feeling that pain again."

His eyes flicked up and down, giving Logan a very pointed once over.

"Others, they do the opposite. They throw themselves into life with a new *joie de vivre*. They embrace those they love. They hold them tight, and they live every last moment." André interlocked his fingers in a relaxed clasp, and let them fall to his waist. "Bernie lost someone, but he chose neither of these paths. He became something else, I think."

"A nutter, you mean?"

"Lost, I think. Lost in a fantasy world of his own creation."

The words 'pot' and 'kettle' had rarely been more appropriate, Logan thought, but he resisted the temptation to say so, and went for a more subtle approach.

"Was that what happened to you? Did you get 'lost,' Mr Douville?"

André's smile widened. "Quite the opposite, Detective Chief Inspector. Moi? I was found."

"Well, lucky you," Logan remarked.

"Oui. Most fortunate," André agreed. He inhaled through his nose, held it like he was wringing every last drop of oxygen from it, then blew whatever was left out through his mouth. "But I would like to help you, Detective Chief Inspector Logan. I may be able to talk to someone who can provide some information for your case."

"And who would that be?"

"It is best that I do not make any promises. Let me come back later. Perhaps... around six? Then... we will see what happens."

"How about you just give me their details, and I'll talk to them myself?"

"Aha. Non. Non, Detective Chief Inspector," André said, and his voice was a sing-song of barely contained amusement. "I'm afraid he will only talk to me."

"Is it Bernie?"

"Pardon?"

"Is it Bernie?" Logan asked again. The look on his face suggested it had bloody well better not be, but André was apparently oblivious to the signals.

"Ah, well worked out! Oui. I am hoping to—"

Logan, who had already been towering above the man in the robes, grew taller. He positively swelled, in fact, until he appeared to fill the room.

"A word of advice, son," he said. "If you come back here and try telling me some magic bloody woo-woo about ghosts talking to you, I'm going to arrest you for wasting police time. Is that clear?"

"I would have thought that you would appreciate all the help you could—"

"Is. That. Clear?"

André finally took the hint and conceded with a nod. "Very well, Detective Chief Inspector. Should Bernie contact me from beyond the veil, I shall keep his secrets to myself."

"Good. I appreciate that," Logan said. He waved a hand to dismiss the other man, before remembering a question that Ben had wanted him to ask. "Oh, one final thing. Bernie. Did he wear any jewellery?"

"Ah... oui. A ring, I think. A wedding band, perhaps, but on the other hand."

Logan nodded. "See?" he said. "Turns out you can be helpful, after all."

CHAPTER SEVENTEEN

LOGAN STOOD in the station car park, glowering at the back of the Westerly Wellness minibus as it chugged its way back out west.

A scrabbling of paws on gravel indicated the arrival of Taggart. He pulled desperately on the lead, eyes bulging and tongue flopping around, as he tried to race to greet his master.

"Alright, alright, steady," Sinead protested. The dog wasn't strong enough to pull her along, but he was plenty strong enough to throttle himself on his collar, so she picked up the pace and jogged the last few steps.

Logan squatted down to greet the dog, who instantly became a squirming, thrashing tangle of limbs and tail, rolling onto his back, then onto his front, then springing up on his hind legs, before going through the whole routine all over again a second later.

"Aye, I see you, you needy wee bastard," Logan said, patting various bits of the dog's torso as they were presented to him. "Calm down."

"That the son of God away, then, boss?" asked Tyler, strolling over to join them.

"Aye. For now, anyway," Logan said. "He's going to come back, though."

"*Classic* Jesus," Tyler remarked, and he smiled like he was quite pleased with himself for the comment.

"Get anything useful from him?" Sinead asked Logan, both of them ignoring Tyler completely.

"Maybe. Not sure yet. He reckoned—"

"Actually, boss, I'm going to stop you there," Tyler said, taking his life in his hands. Fortunately, he had the perfect reason for cutting the DCI short. "Why don't you tell us all over lunch at the pub?"

Logan stood up—and up, and up—until he was dwarfing the younger officer, and glaring straight down at him. "Do you know something, Detective Constable?" he intoned. "That might just be the best idea you've ever had."

If the pub lunch wasn't the best idea Tyler had ever had, it was certainly up there near the top of the list. The Bothy Bar was attached to the front of the Strontian Hotel, with a view that went on forever along Loch Sunart and to the ragged lines of the mountains beyond.

The better view was offered from the restaurant area, but the presence of Taggart meant the detectives were restricted to the bar. There were fewer windows in there, but the crackling log fire more than made up for it.

Besides, the restaurant was too pretty and too light for Logan's liking. It wasn't the sort of place he felt comfortable in. Give him the bar, though, with its wood-panelled walls and cardboard beer mats, and he was right at home.

They'd found a table big enough for the five of them that was far enough from anyone else to allow them to talk more or less freely, but close enough to the fire that they still got the benefit. It may have only been September, but the relentless drizzle and the wind whipping along the loch meant the heat from the flames was very welcome.

Although, it quickly became unwelcome for Hamza and Tyler, when the sight of the flames reminded Logan of the bone he had to pick with them.

"Oh, and great job with the caravan, by the way," he said, slowly clapping hands the size of goalies' gloves. "Seriously. Really impressive work there."

"Aye, eh, sorry about that, boss," Tyler hummed.

"Not our finest moment," Hamza hawed.

"You can say that again. Every shred of bloody evidence up in flames."

"We got photos, though," Tyler said. "Aye, before the fire. And after, actually. And some during because, you know, it was pretty impressive to see it when it was all..." Some internal alarm bell rang when he spotted the look on Logan's face, and the sentence fell away. "But, eh, aye. Not ideal."

"What about the guy you saw?" Logan asked them. "The guy you chased?"

"You mean the old boy, boss?" Tyler asked.

Logan's forehead became a series of parallel letter V's. "What do you mean 'old boy'? How old are we talking?"

Tyler and Hamza swapped glances, neither of them keen to volunteer the information. "I'd, eh, I'd say he was knocking on, sir."

Logan's head snapped in Hamza's direction. "Knocking

on? Knocking on what? Sixty? Seventy? Death's door? What exactly was he knocking on, Detective Sergeant?"

Hamza swallowed. He looked to Tyler for help, but the DC now seemed to be absolutely transfixed by a beer mat and was refusing to meet his eye. "I'd say, about... sixty-five, sir."

"Sixty-five?!" Logan cried, loudly enough to draw looks from the handful of other punters in the bar. "You chased a sixty-five-year-old man on foot, and you let him get away?"

"There were trees, boss," Tyler ventured.

"Well, unless he was George of the fucking Jungle, son, I don't really see how that makes a whole lot of difference."

"Hamza reckoned he recognised him," Ben offered, throwing the lads a lifeline. "Didn't you, Hamza?"

"Um, aye," Hamza said.

"Oh?" Logan sat up a little. "From where?"

"I can't... I can't quite place him at the moment, sir."

"Oh, for fu—" Logan caught himself in time, and lowered his voice before he earned them any further dirty looks from the other customers. "So, you didn't recognise him, then? If you recognised him, you'd know who he was. That's how recognising someone works. What you did is you saw the guy, and you thought, 'He looks familiar,' which doesn't really do a lot to help us, does it?"

"No, sir," Hamza admitted. "I'm sure it'll come to me, though."

"Aye, well, I bloody hope so," Logan grunted. "What about the briefcase you found? Anything salvageable in that?"

A look flew across the table between Hamza and Tyler. It did not go unnoticed.

"What?" Logan asked. "What now?"

"It was gone, boss," Tyler said.

"What, burned up?"

"No. No, like, *gone* gone. Like it wasn't there."

"Someone must've taken it," Hamza said. "When we were out chasing the, eh..."

"Pensioner," Logan said, finishing the sentence for him.

"Not quite, boss. I think you need to be sixty-seven to get your pension nowadays, don't you?" Tyler said, then he wilted under the heat of Logan's glare, and nodded. "Aye, boss. While we were chasing the pensioner."

Logan leaned back in his chair and tapped a fingernail on the table, eyeballing both detectives. "Well, that is marvellous. That is fucking marvellous. I don't suppose you got a photograph of the contents of that briefcase, did you? When you were snapping away at everything else?"

Hamza straightened in his chair. "Eh, no. We didn't, sir. But Palmer's team was in before us. Maybe they did."

"Aye!" Tyler said, grasping this sliver of hope with both hands. "They might have looked inside. Want me to phone them?"

He produced his mobile, clocked the message on-screen alerting him to the fact that he had no signal, then returned the phone to his pocket.

"I'll have to do it from the station," he said. "I'll get on it as soon as we're back."

"Are we doing starters and mains, or just mains?" Ben asked.

He spoke the words loudly and forcefully, making it clear that the 'burning caravan' part of the conversation was over, and the much more pressing part where they ordered food had now begun.

Ben studied the menu through his glasses, which were balanced near the end of his nose. "Because I'm easy."

"Have whatever you want," Logan said, turning his attention to the menu and scanning quickly through the available options.

"Aye, but I'm not going to be the only one to order a starter if no other bugger is having one," the DI replied. "Then you'd all have to sit and watch me eating it. Which would be fine, but you'd all be dipping into it and helping yourselves."

"Well, don't have a starter then."

"Aye, but I was fancying the haggis and goat's cheese."

"I'd quite like a starter, boss," Tyler said.

This news pleased Ben immensely, judging by the smile that lit up his face. "Right. Good man. There's a lad who can make a decision. I'll have a starter, then. Haggis and goat's cheese."

"We might as well all get starters, in that case," Hamza suggested. He looked around the table. "Unless... does anyone not want a starter?"

"I could eat a starter," Sinead said.

Ben nodded his approval. "Good. Right. So, that's four starters. What about yourself, Jack? You having a starter?"

"If you give me a bloody minute to look, I'll tell you!" Logan said. "I'm still reading the menu."

"We're not asking you to decide what you're having, just if you're having a—"

"Fine! I'll have a bloody starter!" Logan told him. "We can all have starters. Starters for everyone. Happy?"

Ben nodded to confirm that he was, then turned his attention back to the menu.

There was silence while they all read through the list of dishes that were on offer.

It didn't last for long.

"And what about puddings?" Ben wondered. He turned the menu over, then looked around at the others. "Is it just me, or is anyone else fancying a wee pudding?"

Once the food was ordered—starters and mains for everyone, and they'd decide on the dessert options once they saw how hungry they still were at the end—the conversation began in earnest.

It wasn't all business. Not right away. To Tyler and Hamza's relief, it didn't loop straight back to the whole 'burning caravan' situation, either.

Instead, Logan and Sinead talked about their trip the previous day—about the road, and the vomiting, and the encounter with the inimitable Kathryn Chegwin, who they all agreed sounded like an absolute belter.

"So, what, like they're all shagging each other?" asked Tyler, his eyes wide. "In the tents? They're all at it with each other?"

"Apparently so, aye," Logan confirmed.

"Like everyone? Like everyone *all the time*?"

"I don't know the details, son. I've no' been watching them, but so the old woman claimed, aye."

"Do not even think about suggesting you go in undercover," Sinead warned, which earned a laugh from the others.

"I mean, I wouldn't want to, obviously, but sometimes you've got to take one for the team," Tyler replied. "It's a hell of a job, but I suppose someone's got to do it."

"I can just imagine your face if old Cheggers turned up at your tent with her shotgun," Sinead said, smirking at the thought. "Not sure you'd be up for taking that one for the team."

Tyler shuddered. He might not have met the woman, but their description of her had been vivid enough that he felt like he had.

"Aye. Maybe best getting someone else for that job, now that I think about it."

The drinks arrived—all non-alcoholic—and Logan waited until the barman had left before continuing with the recap.

He told them about the 'acolytes' gathered at the lighthouse, about his conversation with André Douville, and the contradictions that had arisen when talking to Kathryn Chegwin later.

"So, he's saying that having a random nutter ranting and raving at his gate didn't affect business, but she's saying that it did?" Ben said, checking he had it all straight.

"Aye. He told us Bernie's protests had no impact. The neighbour disagreed," Logan confirmed. "I asked him about it today and he doubled down. Admitted that attendance wasn't what it was, but denied it was anything to do with Bernie. He reckons it was just the bloody... I don't know. The whims of the Universe, or some shite."

"You think Bernie was costing him money?"

"I do. When I pressed him on it, he said he and Bernie had kissed and made up," Logan said, then he remembered that Tyler was sitting at the table. "No' literally. Metaphorically. He said Bernie phoned him up two or three weeks back and asked for his help."

"His help? After going out of his way to badmouth him

and screw him over?" Sinead asked. "Doesn't sound likely. What sort of help was he looking for?"

"Some magic ghost nonsense," Logan said. "He's claiming that Bernie wanted him to contact someone who'd died. Wouldn't say who."

"And did he?" asked Ben. "Contact them, I mean."

Logan tutted. "Of course he bloody didn't! He might look like Jesus, but there the similarities end. He's a conman selling woo-woo to the gullible. He's no more in touch with the dead than I am."

"Are we treating André as a suspect?" Sinead asked.

"I don't see how we couldn't," Logan replied. "He's certainly got the motive. Stronger than the MSP, even. Though, I'm not ruling that bastard out, either."

The starters arrived before Logan could explain further. They all leaned back from the table as their plates were placed in front of them, and all *oohed* and *aahed* at the sights and smells being presented.

Taggart emerged from under the table, already working on the puppy dog eyes and the tilt of the head that he hoped would earn him a share of everyone's grub.

"This looks lovely," Ben told the waitress—a young lassie who couldn't have been long out of school, but who had developed a quite astonishing knack for balancing plates all the way up her forearms.

"Well, I hope you enjoy it," she said, addressing the table at large once she'd given them all their food. "If you need anything else, just give me a wave."

Ben raised a hand. "Eh. Sorry. Is Gary around?"

Logan looked across the table at the DI. "Gary?" he asked, but Ben waved him into silence.

"Not yet. He should be here soon, though. Want me to get him to come over when he's in?"

"Please. That would be great," Ben said, then he picked up his knife and fork, and the waitress took her cue to leave.

"Who's Gary?" Logan asked.

"Apparently, he's got the full back catalogue of Bernie's newsletter," Ben explained. "Thought it might be worth us having a look through. See if there are any patterns, or what have you. Help build a picture."

"Makes sense," Logan agreed. He pronged a garlic mushroom with his fork, and dipped it into the accompanying garlic mayo. "I want us digging into that MSP, too. There's something no' right there."

"In what way, boss?" Tyler asked through a mouthful of food.

"He tried to hide the fact that he had the restraining order on Bernie. Played dumb about Bernie spying on him, until I reminded him of the multiple complaints he'd made."

"Plus," Sinead added, "he just doesn't like him."

Logan chewed thoughtfully, then shrugged. "Plus, I just don't like him," he admitted. "I mean, who calls their child 'Orwellia,' for Christ's sake? And, aye, he's the sort that gets on my tits, right enough. He's got a big flash car, a big flash house, big angry dog, and—"

Sinead frowned. "Dog? I didn't see a dog?"

"Aye, but come on, you know they've got one," Logan said. "A big scary thing for scaring off the riff-raff. It was probably away getting its bloody nails done when we were there, but they've got one. Mark my words."

There was a *clank* as Hamza dropped his fork. "Dog. A big scary dog," he said, staring straight ahead.

Tyler stopped chewing, his mouth crammed to the brim.

His eyes shifted in the direction that Hamza was looking. "Where?"

"What? No. Not here. Up the road. That house we went to a few months back. The decapitation case. The dog that chased you."

Tyler forced down a swallow, started to choke, and took a swig of *Irn Bru* to clear the blockage. "Oh. That. Aye. I still have nightmares about that big bastard. Bit my arse. What about it?"

"That was it. That was the place."

"What place?" Logan asked. "What are you on about, son?"

"That's where I know him from," Hamza said, a little breathlessly. "That's where I know the old guy at the caravan from! He was in the house with Dinky, the loan shark guy."

"The dwarf!" Tyler said.

"Aye. Shite. What did he call himself?" Hamza muttered, setting down his knife. "It wasn't a real name, it was something..." He clicked his fingers. "Ally Bally! That was it."

"Like the song?" asked Ben.

"Exactly. He sang it."

"I remember you telling us about him," Logan said. "Did you no' say he was an absolute wreck of a human being?"

"Oh, he was, sir, aye," Hamza confirmed. "Absolute state."

"And yet," Logan intoned, eyeballing him and Tyler across the table. "He managed to outrun you both."

"Eh..." Hamza began, but there was nothing else forthcoming.

"Still, at least we've got a lead on him now," Ben said,

stepping into the firing line. "We can arrange to go and pay him a visit.

"Yeah! We can go pull him in!" Tyler said. He pointed down at his plate. "But... after lunch though, right?"

"Oh aye, after lunch," Ben confirmed. "And we've still to decide on that pudding..."

The front door was thrown open so suddenly that it *banged* against the wall, drawing the attention of everyone in the pub. A man in his forties stumbled in, red-faced and breathless.

"Help! I need help!" he cried.

Hamza and Sinead were first on their feet. "You OK, sir?" Sinead asked. "What's the problem?"

"We're with the police," Hamza said, and the newcomer's face lit up with relief.

"Seriously? The police? Oh, brilliant! Brilliant! Quick. Come quick."

He hurried out of the bar again. At the table, the other detectives reluctantly set down their cutlery, got to their feet, and joined Hamza and Sinead in following the man outside.

They all stopped when they saw the road. Or, more accurately, when they saw what was *on* the road.

"Sheep," Tyler muttered. "That's a lot of sheep."

And it was. Dozens of them. Hundreds, perhaps, cluttering the whole area and blocking the road.

"They're everywhere," the man who'd come running in announced, just in case the detectives were unable to see that for themselves. "My dog got off the lead and chased them down the hill. I don't know what to do!"

"DS Khaled. DC Neish. Now's your chance to make amends for past failures," Logan said, patting both men on their shoulders. "Get those sheep off the road and back onto the hill. Though, maybe try and no' set them on fire, eh?"

He ushered Ben and Sinead back into the pub, leaving the other two detectives to deal with the wayward flock. He was feeling quite pleased with himself, too, though that passed quickly when he saw the table, and the small dog standing on it, his face buried in a plate of black pudding.

"Oh," Logan spat. "You dirty, thieving wee bastard!"

CHAPTER EIGHTEEN

ONCE THE SHEEP situation was resolved, and the dog had been repeatedly informed that he was an arsehole, the team returned to the Strontian station to divvy up the workload.

After some debate, a couple of complaints, and a bit of reorganisation, they finally came up with a plan that everyone was happy with.

They were taking two cars—Hamza and Ben in one, Logan and Tyler in the other. The first car would go to the station in Fort William, where the detectives would access HOLMES 2, the secure computer system that, theoretically at least, gave them full access to past and ongoing police investigations across the UK.

Considering that DI Forde's experience with the software was both minimal and disastrous, it was an odd choice to send him to accompany Hamza on this particular mission, but he'd insisted, and Logan didn't have the inclination nor the energy to overrule him.

The second car would continue up the road past

Letterfinlay, where Logan and Tyler would pay a visit to the house owned by the loan shark, Dinky. If they were lucky, the man known as Ally Bally would be there.

Sinead, for her part, was staying behind in Strontian and would be roping in the two local Uniforms to help her go through the seventy-odd issues of The Beacon newsletter, which Gary at the pub had begrudgingly provided them with after some persuasion.

It was, of course, highly unlikely that the newsletters would turn up anything relevant to the case, but there was always a possibility that something of interest might turn up in the stack of fading, photocopied pages.

There had been some debate over who would assume responsibility for Taggart. Despite the multiple tellings-off the dog had received, he'd looked pretty pleased with himself since he'd wolfed down everyone's starters, and Sinead eventually decided that, for the animal's safety, it was better that he stayed behind with her.

After everyone had said their goodbyes, she and the dog stood watching the rest of the team make their way to their respective cars. Logan was taking the BMW, naturally, and had sent Tyler to the village shop to grab some plastic carrier bags and cleaning supplies so any vomit-based emergencies could be quickly attended to.

Ben was content to let Hamza drive, so he could sit back and take in the scenery. In fact, they were going to take a longer route around, heading up past the Corran Ferry terminal, until they met the Mallaig road half an hour or so further on. He packed a flask of tea and some biscuits for the trip, and was already talking about stopping to get some photos up at the head of the loch.

"Aye, well, you pair just enjoy your wee day out," Logan

told them, as he pulled open the door to his SUV. "I'll be sat here listening to this arsehole the whole way."

"How come we've not got biscuits, boss?" asked Tyler, opening the passenger door.

"Who says I don't?" Logan replied, sliding into his seat. "But good luck finding them."

Sinead waved, and Taggart wagged his tail as they watched the cars pull away. Tyler blew her a kiss and she smiled back at him, but then the BMW and Hamza's Audi turned onto the main road and she lost sight of them as they headed off east on their separate quests.

"Looks like it's just you and me, pup," she said, looking down at the dog. Taggart tilted his head, and one of his ears perked up. "What do you think, get to work or go for a walk first?"

Taggart leapt up onto his hind legs so his front paws were on one of Sinead's knees. His tail swished furiously from side to side, like a windscreen wiper trying to fend off a downpour.

Sinead patted his head and laughed. "Aye, it's funny," she told him. "I thought you might say that."

It was an hour and a half later, and Tyler had still not been sick. He'd come close on the short ferry trip, and had got out of the car to go hang over the side for the duration of the three-minute crossing.

The boot of the BMW—a sizeable space—was crammed so full that Logan could barely see out of the back window. He still couldn't quite believe what it had been crammed *with*, but Tyler had practically begged to bring the item in question along, and Logan hadn't had the energy to argue.

Nor had he complained about the brief, blessed silence that had been afforded to him while Tyler was out on the deck of the ferry. He had taken the opportunity to check his messages, which had come through in a succession of rapid-fire *pings* when his phone had picked up a signal again.

There were a few from Shona, mostly asking if he was around and whether he had a signal yet, plus one where she'd sent a link to a new rumoured Katsu Curry-flavoured *Pot Noodle.* That one had included five exclamation marks and an emoji of someone's head exploding.

He'd been reading through them when another batch of messages came through. These were mostly voicemail notifications, but there was one in there that made his heart soar.

'She's nice. I like her. x'

That one was from Maddie. It didn't say much, but it said everything. It said there was a route, however long and winding it may be, to forgiveness. That there was a chance for them. For him. Even after everything.

He hurriedly tapped out a reply.

'Sorry, had no signal. Aye, yours seems alright, too. For a guy with two last names.'

He sent it, and was just going back in to reply to the latest message from Shona, when the passenger door had opened and Tyler had clambered back in and the ferry approached the jetty.

That had been an hour ago. There had been no more messages received since. Or none that could have been heard over DC Neish's constant wittering, anyway.

"Pretty sure it's up this way, boss," Tyler said, with a degree of confidence that felt misplaced, given that he'd made the same statement three other times already. "I recognise that hill."

"You recognised those trees last time, and then you recognised that big rock, and you were wrong both those times," Logan reminded him.

"Aye, but this is different," Tyler insisted. "The track takes a right just up this hill."

He sat in silence while Logan steered the BMW up the rugged, rocky incline.

"Yeah, I meant left," he said. "It goes left, and then it goes right. Or left again. I can't remember. I'm sure it's up this way, though."

"How sure are we talking?"

"Like, ninety percent," Tyler said. The track came to an abrupt end at a wall of trees, and the DC quietly cleared his throat. "Maybe closer to seventy."

Logan sighed and crunched the BMW into reverse. "Hasn't anyone ever told you you're a liability, son?" he asked. "Because if not, I feel I've been remiss in my duties as your superior—"

"Wait!" Tyler cried. He prodded a finger against the side window, to where a ramshackle old house was just visible through gaps in the branches. "Trees are thicker. That's all. More leaves. That's it there, though. I'm positive that's the place, boss. That's where Dinky lives."

Logan grunted, then shut off the engine. "Aye, well. No' before bloody time," Logan said, throwing open his door and stepping down from the car.

"You'll want to go canny, boss," Tyler said, lowering his voice into a whisper. "You really don't want to get on the wrong side of his dog." He turned to look at the bulky item that filled the boot of the car. "That's why I brought this."

"I think you imagined things, son," Logan said. He looked over in the direction of the house, then back at Tyler, who still hadn't opened his door. "I don't see any dog."

And that was when the howling started.

Hamza approached the front door of the Fort William Police Station, caught sight of the figure standing on the other side of the reception desk, then briskly about-turned.

"Oh, great," he muttered.

"What's up?" asked Ben, marching up the path behind him.

"That old dragon's back," Hamza said. "Behind the front desk."

"Is she? Is she, indeed?" asked Ben, fighting back a grin. "I heard a wee rumour that she might be back, right enough."

"Where did you hear that? Some sort of ancient prophesy about the end times?"

"Ha! Aye, something like that," Ben said, pulling open the door.

He stood up straight as he approached the desk, his smile battling through his attempts to hold it in until it lit up his whole face. Behind the glass, Moira Corson sniffed once and blinked twice, but otherwise didn't react in the slightest.

"Moira. Good to see you back with us," Ben said, stopping across the counter from the receptionist. "You're looking well."

"Well, looks can be deceiving," Moira replied. "Especially at your age, with your eyes."

"True. True," Ben agreed. "Still, you're up and about."

"I was up and about when you saw me last week, too," she retorted.

Ben shot a wary glance back at Hamza, and was relieved to see that the DS was still hovering just out of earshot.

"You'll have forms for us to fill in, I'm sure," Ben said, and he practically clapped his hands as two small bundles of paper were slid towards him through the gap at the bottom of the glass.

He picked up one of the piles and rifled through the pages, listening closely.

"Are these thicker?" he asked. "They feel thicker."

For a moment, Moira almost looked impressed. It didn't last. "There's an extra page," she said. "Visitor ethnicity."

"Why's that been added?" asked Hamza, stepping in closer.

"Do I make the rules?" Moira snapped, sharply enough to stop Hamza in his tracks.

"I, um, I don't know," the DS admitted. "Do you?"

Moira eyeballed him until he looked like he might fold in on himself, then shifted her attention back to Ben. "Is he serious?

"Tell you what, son. Why don't I fill in both forms?" Ben suggested. "I'm sure Mrs Corson here will find that acceptable."

There was a *clack* as Moira sat a ballpoint pen down on the counter beside the paperwork.

And then, there was a second *clack*, as she placed another one alongside it.

"Everyone fills out their own forms," she instructed. "Or they don't get in."

Ben chuckled, picked up both pens, and handed one to Hamza.

"And to think," he told Moira, fishing his glasses out of his shirt pocket. "I actually missed you..."

Logan stood in front of his car, listening to the sound of barking growing steadily louder. He turned at the sound of the BMW's boot being shut, and found himself face to face with Dinny the Drink-Driving Squirrel.

"Jesus Christ, son," he sighed. "Like I told you back at the station, I think that's maybe overkill."

"You've no' seen it, boss," Tyler said, raising his voice to be heard from inside the mascot costume. "It's a monster. It's probably evolved since last time, too."

"Evolved?"

Tyler shambled out from behind the car, praying that the thick padding of the outfit would offer protection from the jaws of the oncoming beast. "Aye, it'll have two heads or something by now. Or teeth on its paws."

"I'm sure it's not that bad. I'm sure it's just a dog," Logan replied.

"Aye, well, you weren't here when it nearly bit my whole arse off, boss. I mean it, you should get in the car," Tyler insisted. "It doesn't sound happy."

He had a point. Logan couldn't see the dog yet, beyond a vague impression of speeding movement beyond the trees, but the sounds it was making were big, and powerful, and very, *very* angry.

It was the sort of barking that existed only in horror movies, or TV dramas about the rabies virus running out of control. Each bark was followed by a frenzied series of growls and snarls, like the dog was so enraged by the sounds coming out of its own mouth that it was trying to eat them.

Not the sharpest pup in the litter, then.

"Eh, boss. I mean it," Tyler said, feeling his way along the car. "It's a beast of a thing. It's like a shark with legs. It'll go right for your throat. If you're lucky. If you're unlucky, it'll go for somewhere else. At least the throat would be quick, unlike—" The giant squirrel head turned sharply, and Tyler's muffled voiced rose in both pitch and volume. "Shit, shit, here it comes!"

Logan turned and saw the thing come exploding out from within the trees. Technically, it was running, he knew, and yet it seemed to be flying a couple of feet above the ground, its big furious bounds so powerful that its feet didn't appear to touch the ground.

It was a mongrel. Not in the same way that Taggart was, though. This thing wasn't a random mish-mash of mismatched bits and pieces, it was a carefully orchestrated living nightmare. If Dr Frankenstein had turned his back on monster-making and gone into animal husbandry, this thing would be his *pièce de résistance.*

It was part Rottweiler, part German Shepherd, part Hellhound, and almost certainly had a wee bit of werewolf ancestry a couple of generations back.

And it was running at Logan very quickly indeed.

He had two options, he knew. Three, if you counted shitting himself, but he'd ruled that one out. The two he'd been left with were familiar to anyone who'd done his job and walked in his shoes. It was the choice that all polis everywhere were faced with all the time.

Fight or flight.

Stand his ground, or run for his life.

He could get in the car. He could shut the dog outside.

Its claws would make a mess of the paintwork, though, and there was no saying it couldn't bite right through the metal.

And it could *definitely* bite through foam padding and fake fur, regardless of what Tyler had managed to tell himself.

Standing his ground in the face of this wild beast was dangerous, though.

Standing his ground was *madness*, in fact.

"Boss, hurry! Get in, I'll hold him off."

The snarling missile streaked towards them, its barking so frenzied now that its eyes were threatening to pop right out of their sockets. It had seen Tyler, but had clearly decided that the best course of action was to completely ignore him.

An animal after Logan's own heart.

Actually, given the look on the fucking thing's face, and the size of its teeth, it might literally have been after his heart. But, there was no backing down now. No chickening out. Showing fear would only make the situation worse.

Which, considering how bad it was already shaping up to be, didn't bear thinking about.

Logan stood tall, his feet planted. He stared the dog down as it chewed up the ground between them, its jaws slavering and snapping. The fur on the back of its neck was standing so tall it looked like someone had given the animal a Mohican.

It was ten feet away now. Eight. Five.

Tyler's nerve went. He pulled open the back door of the car, and tried to climb in, but the cumbersome suit meant he ended up wedged in the doorway with his big furry backside presented like a delicious banquet.

"Shite, shite, not my arse! Not my arse!" he wailed from beneath the headpiece, twisting to give himself a view of the approaching beast.

But his arse remained untroubled. The dog was fixated on Logan. Its hind legs kicked, propelling it into the air as it launched its attack on the DCI.

There was a hand movement. It was fast, but through the fogged-up plastic lenses of Dinny the Drink-Driving Squirrel, it looked slow, deliberate, and calculated.

There was a yelp as Logan's enormous hand clamped around the dog's throat, jerking it to a stop in mid-flight. This was followed by a second louder yelp a moment later when the animal was slammed, back-first, onto the ground and pinned there.

"Get *down*!" he bellowed, staring into the dog's bulbous, bloodshot eyes. He grabbed its collar to give him a better hold as it wriggled and thrashed beneath him, "And you can cut that shite out right now," he warned it.

With his free hand, he fished in his pocket and produced a small handful of dog treats. He held them out to the mutt, his hand flat so his fingers were safely out of reach of its teeth, then nodded approvingly as it scoffed them down.

"There. See? Was there any need to throw a paddy like that? It's not a problem."

He let the dog sniff at his hand for a moment, then fished out some more of the treats. This time, though, rather than let the mutt devour them all at once, he let it have just one, which was gobbled down so quickly that it was practically inhaled.

"Right, you want more? Stop being an arsehole," Logan

told the animal, his voice a kindly sing-song designed to calm and soothe the beast.

He unhooked the hand that had been pinning the dog down by the collar, and ran the back of his fingers in circles on its chest, ready to grab again should the aggression return. It turned its head, but rather than locking on his throat, its eyes went to the treats.

Logan held out another. Then, when the dog went to lunge, he pulled it away. "Gently," he said, then he held it out again. This time, the dog slowly brought its muzzle closer, pincered the treat between its front teeth, and carefully withdrew before swallowing.

"Good boy," Logan said.

He stood and stared off in the direction of the house, pointedly ignoring the dog. It got up, looked around for a while like it wasn't quite sure what was going on, then it sat at his feet and—gently—accepted another treat.

"You can come out now, Tyler," he said.

Still wedged half inside the car, Dinny the Drink-Driving Squirrel shook his head. "Nah, boss. It's a trick."

"What do you mean?" Logan asked.

"It's lulling me into a false sense of security. It'll have my leg off if I make a move. Best if I wait here."

"Except I need you to ID this *Ally Bally* character if he's here," Logan reminded him. "So, come on. Out. It's not going to hurt you."

Tyler's groaning echoed around inside the headpiece of the costume.

"Right. OK. Fine. I'm coming out," he announced.

He started to wriggle backwards out of the car.

The dog growled, showing its teeth.

Tyler stopped moving again.

"See? It hates me."

"Maybe if you weren't dressed as a giant bloody rodent he'd be less wary of you. Anyway, pretty much everyone hates you to begin with, son," Logan told him. "But, that'll all change once he gets to know you, and—just like the rest of us —he'll come to begrudgingly tolerate your existence. Now, come on, out of the car before your man in there does a runner."

Tyler groaned and pushed the head of the costume off, revealing a face that was bright red and slicked with sweat. "I get compensation from work if this thing attacks me, don't I?"

"Aye," Logan confirmed. He shrugged. "Or Sinead will. It really depends on the severity of the attack."

"You're not helping, boss!" Tyler wailed. Then, with a deep breath, he pushed himself backwards out of the SUV.

Down on the ground, the dog rose onto all four legs, its head lowering and hackles rising.

"Sit!" Logan boomed, and Tyler's legs gave out from under him, plonking him onto the ground. "No' you, for fu... The dog, Tyler. I meant the dog."

Tyler's cheeks reddened. "Eh. Aye. I knew that, boss," he replied. Then, trying to salvage some tiny shred of dignity, he dragged himself to his feet using one of the car's door handles, and dusted himself down.

He stared at the dog.

The dog stared at him.

"Don't show it you're scared," Logan said.

"How'm I meant to do that?!"

"Well, maybe stop crying for one thing," Logan suggested. "And don't stand there covering your crotch like someone's about to take a free kick."

"I'm not crying, boss. It's the wind. I wasn't expecting the wind. It's made my eyes water," Tyler insisted.

He cautiously removed his cartoonishly oversized hands from where they'd been cupping his groin, but kept them close by in case the dog should make its move. It seemed content just to growl suspiciously at him for the moment, though, and when Logan fed it another treat it quickly lost interest in him altogether.

"See? It's just a dog. Nothing to worry about," Logan said. "Do you want to pat it?"

"Do I fuck!" Tyler ejected. "I mean... No thanks, boss. I'll pass."

"Right. Fair enough," Logan grunted. He turned in the direction of the house, and the dog turned with him. "Now, let's go see if any bugger's at home."

"Do you, eh, do you want to help me out of this outfit first?" Tyler asked, indicating the zip at the back.

Logan sucked in his bottom lip, spat it out, then shook his head. "No," he said. "No' really."

CHAPTER NINETEEN

THERE WASN'T enough table space in the Strontian station for Sinead's current needs, so she sat cross-legged on the floor, ten piles of paper spread out in a semi-circle in front of her, all within stretching reach.

After his bumper lunch and the subsequent walk, Taggart had found a corner of the room to lie down in, and was now snoring softly, his legs occasionally twitching as he dreamed some doggy dream.

Splitting the newsletters up into years had seemed like a decent method of breaking the daunting mass of paper into more manageable bite-sized chunks. Doing so also came with the unexpected side effect of giving her an insight into Bernie's production schedules over the years.

He'd started slowly—two issues in the first year, each just a single sheet of A4, printed on one side.

The next year, he'd gone bigger. Four issues, each still just a single sheet, but now double-sided. The print on the reverse was upside down, so you had to flip the paper vertically rather than horizontally when you were turning the page. Sinead wasn't sure if this was a deliberate style decision, or an error on Bernie's part. The fact he had done it four times suggested the former, but then again, he hadn't done it again in the eight years since, so it may have been an accident.

The next two years were bumper ones, with eight and twelve issues respectively. These ranged in page length from two to six, and were fixed together with three or four staples down one side to form a sort of spine.

That had been the peak of his production, and it had fallen away to just a handful of issues each year.

Until this year. This year, he'd put out seven—more than the past two years combined, and there were still a few months left until the year was out. Something had driven him to throw himself into the newsletter with renewed enthusiasm and vigour.

But what?

"Hiya."

Sinead looked up from the piles of paper to find the male PC leaning against the doorframe. He smiled at her, and her heart missed a beat.

Just not in a good way.

"You alright down there?" he asked, padding into the room.

He didn't move like PC Jason Hall had. Not exactly. But there were enough similarities—the swing of the arms, the little smirk on his face—that brought him to mind, all the same.

"I'm fine, Constable..."

"Just call me Chris. Chris Miller."

He was dressed for the outdoors, with his high-vis jacket and cap still on. The closer he came, the larger he loomed, and Sinead suddenly felt very vulnerable sitting down there on the floor. She looked over to the corner, but Taggart was still fast asleep. Not that the dog would be able to do much, anyway. Maybe in a year or two, but not yet.

She glanced at the floor around her, searching for a weapon. She almost felt bad about it. The constable had done nothing wrong—nothing to warrant getting a baton to the knee, certainly—and yet her instincts were screaming at her to defend herself. To protect herself. To fight back before he landed the first blow.

But, short of the newsletters, there was nothing within reach, and she wasn't sure that a paper cut would be enough to dissuade him from whatever he was planning to do.

"I hear you had a sheep incident," the PC said, that smile still fixed on his face.

"Eh, aye," Sinead said. She kept an eye on him as she clambered to her feet. Her legs tingled as the blood flow returned. "They were all over the road outside the hotel."

"That's a pretty regular occurrence round here. They get everywhere. Same with cows. Not so much pigs, you don't really get a lot of pigs around here." He looked ahead at the far wall, his eyes darting left and right. "I don't think I've ever even seen a pig. A real pig, I mean. Have you ever seen a pig?"

"Eh... aye," Sinead said.

"Alright. Good. Glad one of us has," Chris replied. He indicated the paperwork spread out on the floor. "Busy?"

"Um, yes, actually," Sinead said. She had backed up against the desk, and a hand was now exploring the desktop in search of a weapon of some kind. Something blunt and heavy, ideally, but she'd take sharp and pointy if she had to. "So... I should probably get on."

"Want a hand?"

Sinead shook her head. "It's fine. I'm fine. No. Thanks."

Chris's smile faded. Sinead's fingers locked around the handle of a hole punch.

"Oh," the constable said. "It's just... well, it's pissing down, and Suzi's put the kettle on. We thought we might be able to make ourselves useful. It's a lot of reading."

They both looked over at the door as Constable Tanaka stuck her head around the frame. "Tea or coffee? Who's having what?" she asked, then she held up a pack of *Tunnock's Snowballs* to seal the deal. "And I'm assuming I'm just emptying these onto a plate and throwing away the box?"

"Sounds good to me!" Chris said. He turned back to Sinead, his smile returning. With Suzi there, the smile seemed different. Not sinister at all. "So, you want some help?"

Sinead looked from one constable to the other, then down at the bundles of paper on the floor. "Aye," she said, her heart rate starting to drop back down from triple digits. "Why not?"

Hamza and Ben hadn't been given a full Incident Room to use during their visit, and had instead been shunted into a small side office that overlooked the building site at the back of the Fort William station.

The large *Tesco* superstore that had been promised for out the front of the building had long-since been cancelled, although the road sign on the approach to the junction outside still insisted it was there somewhere.

Once that project had been called off, the land had been earmarked as the site for the new local hospital—a state-of-the-art jewel in the crown of the Highland NHS, which had similarly failed to materialise. It was *definitely* coming, the powers that be insisted, there was just no saying if it was coming this year, this decade, or indeed, this century.

The land out the back had seen some serious development in the past few months, though. What had been a big patch of waste ground between the polis station and the medical centre was now home to houses and blocks of flats, all at various stages of construction.

They'd sprung up quickly. Looked quite nice, too.

Ben sat at a seat by the window, watching a couple of guys strolling around on the scaffolding of one of the taller blocks of flats. One of them was clearly the gaffer. You could tell by the way he pointed at things and gave instructions, rather than doing any of the actual work himself.

"What a lazy bastard," Ben mumbled, then he turned away from the window, took a sip of his tea, and indicated the computer Hamza was typing away at. "You got that thing going yet?"

"Eh, aye. Well, yes and no. I'm into HOLMES, but it's slow."

"It's always slow."

"Aye, but it's even slower than usual. Might be a network problem."

Ben took another swig of his tea, swallowed, then set the mug down. "I could go and ask Moira if she knows what's going on." He caught Hamza's puzzled look, and quickly corrected. "Ask at reception, I mean. If anyone should know, then it's—"

"Got it," Hamza announced. "It's kicking in now. Must've just been congestion, or something."

"Oh. Good. Aye," Ben said, relaxing back into his chair and trying not to hide his disappointment. "Must've been that, right enough."

He picked up his mug again, and nursed it in his hands as he watched Hamza tapping away at the keyboard.

"How you doing, son?" he asked, which drew a confused look from Hamza.

"Eh, just getting set up."

"No, I mean... in general. How are you doing?" Ben said. "You seemed a bit... down for a while there."

Hamza gave a little nod. "You were talking to DCI Logan."

Ben tried very hard to look innocent, but made a bit of a meal of it. "I mean, he may have mentioned that you were feeling a bit... out of sorts."

"I was," Hamza confirmed. "But I'm fine now. I was feeling a bit... I don't know. Useless. Like the stuff we do—that I was doing—didn't matter."

"It matters, son," Ben assured him.

"Oh, I know. I know. We found Sinead. We got Shona back," Hamza replied. "We might not win them all, but we win some. And that counts for something."

Ben raised his mug in toast. "Couldn't have put it better myself," he said, then he nodded at the computer. "Now, what's the plan?"

"Right, so, here's what I'm thinking," the DS declared. "We want background on André Douville and his weird cult thing, same on..." He checked his notes. "...Oberon Finley-Lennox, that MSP."

"Yes to both of those," Ben said. He pointed to the

screen. "Maybe go through missing persons around the time that Bernie turned up. See if there's anything that'll give us a better idea of who he actually is."

"Aye, good call, sir," Hamza said.

Ben slapped his thighs, then stood up. "Right, well, that'll keep you busy for a while. No point in me sitting here twiddling my thumbs, is there?"

Hamza raised his eyebrows. "Um, no. Suppose not. What will you do?"

Ben put his hands on his lower back and stretched. "Och, I think I'll just get a few steps in." He tapped the centre of his chest. "Doctor's orders for the old ticker. You be alright here on your own?"

"I'm sure I'll cope, sir. You go get... your steps in. The heart needs what the heart needs."

Ben's eyes narrowed a fraction as he tried to suss out if there was any meaning behind the Detective Sergeant's response. Hamza had already turned his attention back to the computer now, though, and was giving nothing away.

"Aye, son," Ben agreed. He blew into his hand and sniffed it, then fished a packet of *Polos* out of his pocket. "I suppose it does, at that."

Ben stood patiently on the other side of the glass, waiting for Moira Corson to look up from the form she was in the process of filling out. He had no idea what the form was, but given the level of concentration she was displaying towards it, he could only assume it was somehow connected to lasting peace in the Middle East.

He cleared his throat for a second time, and gave another tap on the glass.

"I can see you, Detective Inspector. I know you're there," Moira said, not looking up. "But unless this is a work-related enquiry, I have nothing to say. Some of us still take our jobs seriously. I know that's hard to believe in this day and age, but there we are."

"Eh, aye. Well, maybe it is work-related," Ben said.

Moira sighed, placed a finger on the paperwork to mark her place, then looked up. "Is it?"

Ben smiled, shrugged, and shook his head all at once. "Well, I mean, no, not exactly, but—"

"Then please move along, Detective Inspector," Moira said, lowering her head again. "I need to get this paperwork completed in the next seven minutes."

Ben frowned. "Seven minutes? Why, what'll happen if you don't?"

"Nothing."

"Nothing?"

"That's what I said. Nothing," Moira confirmed. "But that's when I'm due my afternoon break."

Without looking, she reached under the desk, then placed a pristine copy of *Love It!* magazine on the counter between them and slid it through the gap at the bottom of the glass. "Maybe you could go stick the kettle on."

Ben grinned as he picked up the magazine. He rolled it up, then tapped it against the counter. "Aye," he said, practically skipping towards the door that would take him back to the rest of the station. "I'm sure I can manage that."

CHAPTER TWENTY

DINKY PULLED open the door on the third knock, shot a positively filthy look upwards, and spat out the first few words of a sentence demanding to know what the caller thought they were playing at.

It was at this point that he realised he was not looking at a face, as he had expected, and had instead fixed his glare on the chest of a substantially larger than anticipated man.

He took a step back to give him a better angle, rallied quickly, and launched into his tirade with renewed enthusiasm.

"What the hell's with all the knocking? Didn't you see the sign?" the little man demanded. "No cold callers. And what have you done to my dog?"

"We've done nothing to your dog," Logan assured him.

"Then how come it's just standing there and not trying to chew your nuts off? You must've done something to him!"

Logan wasn't sure what the correct term was for describing someone of Dinky's stature. There had been a training course that had touched on it at some point, he was sure. But then, there had been training courses that had touched on a lot of things over the years, most of which he'd forgotten or ignored.

This had been one of the important ones, though. The polis had been coming under heavy fire for alleged institutional racism, and mandatory training had been brought in as a matter of urgency.

It had been possibly the most patronising hour of Logan's career, and he was pretty sure the content of the training itself was the most racist thing about it. Logan had asked the higher-ups if they genuinely believed that a forty-five minute training session—fifteen minutes at the end were spent filling out the feedback forms—was going to combat institutional racial bias.

"Fingers crossed!" they'd said. And without a hint of irony, either.

The session had been eighty percent about how to appropriately engage with people of other races and cultures, ten percent about those of other sexual and gender identities, and then a bit at the end that covered—and Logan remembered the quote verbatim—'any other oddities we might meet out there.'

They had touched on little people then—not literally, it wasn't *that* inappropriate a workshop—but all Logan could remember was that 'midgets' was unacceptable.

Still, as he'd voiced during the training session, shortly before being threatened with eviction, he'd found that the most effective way of dealing with anyone from any sort of minority group was to 'treat them like a fucking human being,' and not get bogged down by any of the other stuff.

"Are you Dinky?" he asked.

"What's that meant to mean?" the man in the doorway asked. "You taking the piss?"

Logan sighed. It was a long, drawn-out thing, designed to highlight the fact that he had no intentions of taking any shit. "Your name. Is it Dinky?"

Dinky appeared a bit disappointed by the lack of reaction, then shrugged and nodded. "Aye. Who's asking?"

Logan produced his warrant card. "Detective Chief Inspector Jack Logan."

"What, from the police?" Dinky asked. He looked from Logan to Tyler, who was standing several feet back, warily watching the still perfectly behaved dog. "Are you two both police?"

"We are," Logan confirmed, returning the ID to his coat pocket.

"Why's he dressed like a big squirrel?"

"He was worried the dog might attack him," Logan explained.

Dinky looked from Logan to Tyler and back again. "And... what? He thought dressing as a fucking huge squirrel was going to somehow make that less likely?"

"I've given up trying to fathom how his mind works," Logan said. "Mind if we ask you a few questions?"

Dinky rubbed his stubby fingers across his chin, then drummed them on his bottom teeth like he was playing the xylophone. "Why?" he asked, after some consideration. "What am I meant to have done?"

"We're not here to accuse you of anything, sir," Logan said. "We're trying to find a friend of yours."

"I've got loads of friends. Just head into town on a Friday or Saturday night and chuck a stone, and you'll hit a friend of mine," Dinky said, his chest puffing up with pride. "Except don't, because I don't want my pals being pelted with stones."

"One specific friend," Logan said. "We believe he goes by the name *Ally Bally*."

"Ally Bally?" Dinky stuck out his bottom lip and shook his head. "Never heard of him."

"Aye, you have," Tyler said, chipping in from the back.

"How the fuck would you know?" Dinky spat, lunging his top half forward like he was angling for a fight. "How would you know who I know and who I don't know? Eh? You big squirrely bastard."

"I just..." Tyler tore his eyes from the dog just long enough to reply. "I know you know him. He was here a few months back."

Dinky sniffed and backed down. "Well, he's not here now. I've not seen him in months," he claimed. "But, if I do ever see him, you'll be the first to know. Alright? Now, off you fuck. This is private property."

While Dinky was talking, the dog's ears had pricked up. It turned its head to the right, and Tyler followed the direction of its gaze. There, fifty yards from the house, a wiry, grey-haired man was legging it through the trees.

"Boss!"

Logan turned and looked in the direction Tyler was now pointing. "Well, what are you bloody standing around here for?" he snapped. "Get after the bastard!"

"Right, boss! On it, boss!" Tyler cried.

An oversized squirrel mascot costume was not the ideal outfit with which to initiate an on-foot pursuit, but Tyler made the best of it. He launched himself across the overgrown garden, dodging the big dauds of dog shite, tried to vault the fence, but tumbled over it and did a clumsy forward roll on the other side.

"On it!" he cried again, then he clambered to his big furry feet, and set off in pursuit.

Back at the house, Logan, Dinky, and Dinky's now docile dog all watched him go racing after the old man. As they disappeared into the trees, Logan turned and glowered down at the man inside the house.

"Oh," Dinky said. "You mean *that* Ally Bally?"

Ben stood by the kettle in the staff canteen, waiting for the water to come to the boil. The magazine that Moira had given him sat on a table for two, face down so he wouldn't be tempted to read the front-page headlines. That had become their 'thing'. He wasn't sure how, exactly, but it had. It didn't feel right to even skim them without her there.

Not that she'd appreciate him waiting, of course. She'd probably read the magazine cover to cover already, scouring it for some fresh tidbits of misery and misfortune to cackle over.

But, still. He was saving it. It was their thing.

The TV was on in the corner. A uniformed constable sat clutching a plastic tub, eyes glued to the screen as she blew on her spoon and slurped down what smelled like vegetable soup. The news was on, showing the wee lassie who'd gone missing down in the north of England.

She was a pretty wee thing in her photo. Dark skin, big bright eyes, and a smile that was nothing but mischief from ear to ear. What was she? Nine? Ten? He'd heard it mentioned, but hadn't been paying too much attention.

The case was getting a lot of coverage. Rich parents, Ben guessed. Maybe a small town. Always easier to get the press interested if the parents were wealthy upstanding members of the community. Had she been from a council estate, she'd be lucky to get a half-inch mention in the local paper.

"Terrible this, isn't it?" the constable volunteered between *slurps*. "Such a shame."

"Aye."

"Parents must be climbing the walls."

"Must be," Ben agreed. "Did it say what they do? The parents? For a living, I mean."

"Doctors, I think. He is, anyway. Specialist of some sort. Not sure about her."

Ben nodded, his suspicions confirmed. He turned back to the kettle and half-listened to the report as he rummaged around for the tea bags.

The girl—Jameelah— had been nabbed on her way home from school. That was the theory, anyway. Nobody had come forward to say they'd seen her being taken, but her bag had been found on a quiet stretch of leafy suburban road on her usual route home, her phone still inside.

On-screen, the SIO was telling a reporter that they'd ruled out the possibility of her having run away. He was an imposing figure, his face ravaged by some sort of injury that hadn't healed well. The way he was talking to the journalist reminded Ben a lot of Logan. Like he was just tolerating the interviewer's existence for the sake of the missing girl.

"That tea not made yet?"

Ben turned from the TV just as Moira made her way across the canteen. She still wasn't as sprightly as she'd been before the stroke, but she was showing vast improvement.

There was a bit of a lean and a hint of a limp, but you had to be looking for it to notice.

The *clack* of a Tupperware lid being closed signalled the imminent departure of the constable at the table. She hurriedly gathered up her things, regularly shooting glances at Moira like she was trying to keep track of the older woman's location.

Once she'd collected everything, she sidled for the door, picked up the pace for the final few steps, then went hurrying off.

"Was it something I said, do you think?" Moira asked.

"I'm sure it's just coincidence," Ben told her.

"It absolutely is not!" Moira insisted. She looked annoyed by the suggestion, and Ben got the impression she was quite pleased with the effect her arrival had on the PC.

She took a seat at the table for two, then tapped the back cover of the magazine. "Now hurry up with that tea, so we can look at this."

Ben's eyes went to the publication on the table. "Haven't you already read it?"

"Of course I haven't read it! Why would I have read it?" Moira asked, her nostrils flaring in disgust, outrage, or possibly both. She sniffed loudly. "No bloody point reading it on my own, is there?" she asked. "It's our thing."

Ben paused with the kettle halfway to the first cup. "Do you know, I've never thought of it like that before," he said, then he looked back over his shoulder and smiled. "But aye, I suppose it is."

When Tyler had moved out of Uniform and into plain clothes, he'd been led to believe that there was a lot less running involved. This, in his experience, had not turned out to be the case.

He seemed to spend a lot of his time running. He ran after things—fleeing suspects, stray sheep, that sort of thing. He ran away from things, too—dogs, mostly, although also that steam train that one time.

It was getting to the stage that he thought he should probably just wear trainers to work. Ideally quite a cheap pair, too, given that much of his running took place through mud and wet bracken.

He'd hoped that after his big operation, running duties might be passed on to someone else. Hamza, maybe. He was a handful of years older, but he still had a turn of speed about him when he wanted to.

But no. Sergeants didn't run, apparently. Not unless it was absolutely necessary, and even then, not without complaining about it.

No, Tyler knew his place. He was the youngest, he was the fittest, and he was at the bottom of the ladder. If there was running to be done, and he was anywhere in the vicinity, he was the bugger that was going to end up doing it.

Like here. Now. Today.

Running was not in any way unusual. Running while dressed as Dinny the Drink-Driving Squirrel, on the other hand, was not something he had ever expected to be called on to do.

In a way, he was grateful for the outfit. The trees would otherwise have been unforgiving as he huffed and puffed his way between them. Their spindly branches were like tiny claws, pricking and scratching at him, but failing to do any damage through the thick padding of the suit.

The midges were more of a problem. They gathered in clouds, shimmering in the air with the anticipation of his arrival, then swarming his head as he crashed through them. He swiped and swatted at them like King Kong battling the bi-planes, but the hungry wee bastards weren't taking the hint, and he could feel lumps and bumps forming on his face and neck as he closed in on the surprisingly sprightly old geezer up ahead.

Even without the suit slowing him down, Tyler would've said that Ally Bally was fast. Much faster than his frame suggested should be possible. He seemed to have some sort of sixth sense, too, that steered him through the gaps in the trees and let him avoid the branches.

They hit a clearing for a moment, and Ally Bally almost tripped when he looked back to find the costumed Tyler lumbering furiously up the hillside behind him.

"No' this again!" the old man cried. He waved a hand, like his pursuer was a stain he could just wipe out of existence. "Fuck off, you big squirrel!"

From somewhere behind—though not nearly far enough behind for Tyler's liking—came the sound of a big dog barking. The same big dog that had tried to tear Logan's throat out a few minutes earlier. The same big dog that had taken a bite at Tyler's arse some months before then.

He could hear it racing through the trees, bounding through the bracken, closing in fast.

"Fuck, fuck, fuck!" Tyler found some untapped reserve of speed and hurried on. "Are you chasing him or are you chasing me?" he called back over his shoulder. "Are you chasing him or me?!"

The dog, perhaps unsurprisingly, didn't offer any sort of clarification, and Tyler found himself caught up in a personal first, both running after *and* away from something at the same time.

"Bloody dogs!" he sobbed. Then, he choked on a cloud of midges, hissed as a thin branch sprung back and whipped him across the cheek, and threw himself into the chase.

CHAPTER TWENTY-ONE

DINKY'S HOUSE WAS, not to put too fine a point on it, an absolute fucking state. A large, moth-eaten, sideways-slumping couch had been converted into some sort of makeshift paperwork storage unit, and was teetering with glossy magazines, old newspapers, and stacks of paper covered in notes both printed and handwritten.

The couch also held several empty cans of *Special Brew* lager, half a sandwich, and a banana that had presumably been purchased with the best intentions some weeks previously, but never consumed.

The rest of the living room was not much better. In many ways, it was actually worse. At least the mess on the couch had some sense of organisation to it. Ignoring the beer cans and the rotting food, the couch was more of a clutter than a mess. The items there at least appeared to serve some purpose, even if that purpose was only to see who could build the biggest tower.

Everywhere else, though, was mess. Proper mess. Discarded clothes lay strewn on the floor. Several small shoes

—none of them matching—were scattered around like they were part of a footwear-based scavenger hunt that no one would ever want to win.

There was a dog bed in the corner with what looked like a king-sized duvet lining the inside. The corner of the duvet had been chewed to pieces, and long white fibres of stuffing had drifted across the room like the first snow of winter, only significantly more flammable.

Posters of statuesque supermodels adorned the walls, alongside a picture of a red Ferrari that had been printed on a box canvas just a little smaller than the living room window. The window itself was hidden behind a pair of thick red curtains. They looked like heavy big buggers, and Logan couldn't imagine they'd be easy for a man of Dinky's diminutive stature to open and shut.

And then, there was the smell. Or rather, the *smells*. The room was a symphony of them—wet dog, rotting fruit, old paper, and damp walls, all accompanied by a marijuana top note and a throbbing bass of cheap booze.

"Sit down. You're making the place look untidy," Dinky instructed, hopping up onto an armchair so large he was in danger of being lost down the back of the cushions.

"I'm pretty sure it's the place that's making the place look untidy, son. No' me," Logan replied. "You had a party recently?"

"Always," Dinky said. "It's party central, this place, like I told your pal last time he was here."

"You remember DS Khaled, then," Logan said. "Good."

"Why's that good?" Dinky asked. He produced a small metal pipe from down the side of the armchair, lit it with a disposable lighter, then took a long draw from it.

"Means your brain's not totally addled," Logan said. He sniffed the air, then eyeballed the pipe. "Is that cannabis?"

"It's medicinal."

"You'll have a prescription, then?"

Dinky removed the pipe from his mouth and used it to gesture at the DCI. "You're not a very good detective, are you? If I have this prescribed, why would I still have the prescription? They don't give you it back to use the next time."

Logan chose not to get into it. From somewhere outside, he heard the barking of Dinky's dog getting fainter and further away, and felt a flicker of concern for the welfare of DC Neish.

It faded quickly—not because he didn't care about the younger officer, but because he knew something that Tyler didn't.

He knew that, despite plenty of evidence to the contrary, the lad could handle himself.

"You still not caught your killer yet?"

"Sorry?" Logan asked.

"Your pal who was here last time. He was investigating a murder." Dinky sucked on his pipe. "You still not got someone for that?"

"We did," Logan said. "I'm not here about that. We're here for Ally Bally."

"Why?" Dinky asked, his eyes narrowing. "What's he done?"

"That's still to be determined," Logan said. "We're investigating the death of a man we only know at the moment as Bernie."

Dinky choked on his next lungful of smoke. He whipped the pipe from his mouth, then spent several seconds hacking and coughing and wheezing, his eyes bulging like they were about to pop.

"Fuck off!" he gasped, when he could finally get a breath. "Bernie's dead?"

"You knew him?"

"Prick owed me eight hundred quid!" Dinky cried. "Jesus Christ, why does this keep happening to me? The last guy owed me money, too. Never fucking saw that again, did I?"

"You'd loaned him money?"

"You deaf, or something? You not hear me way up there? Yes, he owed me money. He owed me eight hundred quid."

"Since when?"

"Since he fucking borrowed it," Dinky snapped back.

Logan bit his tongue and swallowed down his rising temper. "Which was...?"

"I don't know. Three weeks. A month. Something like that. *Bastard!*" He flopped like a fish as he dismounted the armchair, then scurried past Logan, heading for the couch. "Wait till I check my paperwork."

"You've got paperwork?"

"Course I've got paperwork. I'm a businessman. Businessmen have paperwork."

Logan watched him clamber up onto the arm of the couch. The teetering piles of paper wobbled dangerously, but Dinky remained unconcerned. Stretching for the top of the closest pile, he pulled down three or four sheets, rifled through them, then gave a nod of satisfaction.

"Here we are," he said, then his face scrunched up in rage. "It's fucking nine hundred! Nine ton, up in smoke. Just like that."

Logan took his hands from his coat pockets and crossed

them in front of himself. "Interesting choice of words there, Dinky."

Standing on the couch, the little man was close to the height of the average adult. This still made him substantially shorter than Logan, though, and he looked up at the detective with a look that might have been genuine confusion, but could equally have been an act.

"What words are they, then?"

"That your money's 'up in smoke.' Bernie's body was set on fire."

Dinky's jaw dropped. "I didn't know that. That's just..." He pulled himself together. "Aye, bad choice of words, but he's fuck all to do with me. Guy owes me eight hundred quid."

"Nine hundred," Logan corrected.

"Fuck!" Dinky spat. "Guy owes me nine hundred quid. Why am I going to kill him? What benefit would that possibly bring me?"

"Maybe he wasn't paying you back."

Dinky laughed at that. It would've been a big, booming laugh for a full-sized man, so from someone of his size, it was something quite exceptional. He threw back his head, and the laughter filled the room and shook the towers of papers where they stood.

"Aye. No. I don't think so," he said, once the hilarity had come to an end. "He might've been a headcase, but he wasn't daft. Not after last time."

Logan raised an eyebrow. "Last time? What do you mean?"

Dinky shrugged, a sly smile curving one corner of his mouth. "Let's just say, he's borrowed money off me a few times before, and that on one of those occasions he 'forgot' to pay it back on the agreed timetable."

"What did you do?" Logan asked. He expected Dinky to act coy about it, and at most to give some vague hint of what had transpired without getting into the details.

Coy, however, did not seem to be in the man's vocabulary.

"Let's just say that during discussions, one of his wrists got broken," he said, practically rubbing his hands together with glee.

"Are you confessing to a crime here, Dinky?"

Realisation darted across the other man's face, and he gave a sad little shake of his head. "Of course not. It was an accident, obviously. Nothing for you lot to get involved in. Real shame. But, on the upside, we've had a long and successful business relationship since, with clarity and understanding on both sides. He was one of my best customers."

He got down from the couch and presented Logan with a handwritten sheet of paper.

"What's this?" The DCI asked, squinting at the indecipherable series of swirls and squiggles.

"Loan agreement. As you can see, he wasn't due to start paying me back until next week. I had no beef with Bernie, pal. In fact, I'm pretty much the last person who wanted him dead. So, if it's a murderer you're looking for, you're barking up the wrong tree."

The dog was closing in. Tyler could no longer just hear it, he would swear he could feel it, too. The vibrations of its paws hitting the ground. The warm swirl of its breath on the back of his legs, even through the mascot outfit.

He could sense its hunger, too. Its hatred, and its rage. Its desire to sink its teeth into Tyler's juicy flesh, and rip it from his bones.

It was going to eat him alive. He was sure of it. No doubt in his head. This four-legged torpedo—this furry land shark—was closing in on him. Any second now, it would make the leap. There would be pain. He'd fall. And then, squirrel suit or no squirrel suit, his world would be nothing but sharp teeth, dog breath, and a growing number of open wounds.

Why hadn't be brought the dog treats? He could've thrown them. They might have bought him a second or two to climb a tree. He could've waited there for Logan to come find him. Or, if it really came to it, lived there indefinitely.

But oh no, he'd gone racing off without a thought, determined to catch the fleeing suspect, and desperate to impress the boss.

He stumbled as that realisation hit him, and almost tripped. God. It was pathetic, really. He was going to die—he was going to be eaten alive, in fact—just to win Logan's approval. Just to get a pat on the head, or a nod of acknowledgement.

Is that really what it had come to? Is that how far he'd sunk?

"Bollocks to that," he said, the words wheezing out between pained breaths.

Tyler stopped running. He turned and saw the dog thirty yards behind, but closing fast. He raised a hand like he was directing traffic.

"Stop!"

The dog did not stop.

"Sit!"

The dog did not sit. If anything, it ran faster.

Tyler tried to summon more confidence, but the fast-approaching hellhound was making that a challenge. He thrust his hand out further, raised his voice, and bellowed a, "Stay!"

But the dog, to his disappointment, did not stay. And now, there was no time for it to stop, or sit, or do very much of anything. It was almost on him now.

It was almost the end.

"OK, bad plan," Tyler whispered. Then, he jammed his arms straight down at his sides, stood tall, shut his eyes, and waited for the end.

There was a gust of wind as the dog raced straight past him. He opened first one eye, and then the other, and turned to follow the sound of barking.

Just a handful of seconds later, he heard a yelp from through the trees up ahead, and the pitiful protests of an out of breath old man.

"Argh! No! Down! Fucking quit that! Stop humping ma leg!"

"Oh, thank God for that," Tyler muttered. Then, after a couple of steadying breaths, he set off to round up the suspect.

CHAPTER TWENTY-TWO

HAMZA WAS LEAVING the office when he almost collided with Ben coming the other way.

"Aha, there you are. Everything alright, sir?" the Detective Sergeant asked.

"It's grand. Aye," Ben said, all smiles. "Why d'you ask?"

"It's just..." Hamza looked along the corridor behind him. "You've been a while."

"I've no' been that long, have I?" Ben checked his watch, then let out a low whistle. "Oh. Wait. No, I have. Time flies, eh? Do we have something?"

Hamza nodded. "Maybe, aye." He stepped back and motioned for the door, indicating for the older man to take the lead. "Best if we talk in here."

Inside the office, Hamza rolled a second chair over to the computer, then sat on the seat he'd been using. Ben took the hint and sat beside him, then peered at the screen while he searched his pockets for his glasses.

"What am I looking at?" the DI asked, still patting himself down.

"Andrew Dorlin."

Ben squinted, and a balding, slightly overweight man came into a vague sort of focus. "Who's Andrew Dorlin when he's at home?"

"Well, he looks less like Jesus in this picture, right enough," Hamza said. "That's André Douville. That's the guy who runs the..."

"Sex cult?"

"Wellness retreat thing, aye," Hamza confirmed.

Ben gave up looking for his glasses and sat back in the chair. "He's not French?"

"He's not, no. He's from Buckie. And those long flowing locks of his are as fake as his accent, going by this photo," Hamza continued. "Which, I'm not sure if you can tell without your specs, is a mugshot."

"He's got a record?"

"He does. Did two years for insurance fraud back in twenty-thirteen. Before that, he'd had cautions for disturbing the peace, and was charged with assaulting a police officer, though that was later dropped."

"Not the Christ-like know-it-all he'd like us to believe, then?"

"Definitely not," Hamza confirmed. "He worked in an office before serving time. There's a note on his record about complaints of sexual harassment from some of his female colleagues, but nothing ever went anywhere. After he was free, he pretty much vanished off the face of the Earth for a while, from what I can tell."

"Then came back with a new name and a half-decent wig, and set himself up in the Messiah business," Ben concluded.

"Pretty much that exactly, sir, aye," Hamza confirmed.

"This is good work," Ben said. "Print that off, will you?"

"Already done it," Hamza said. He clicked the mouse a couple of times and Ben watched one blurry screen be replaced with another. "Oberon Finley-Lennox is a bit less interesting. Private education up at Gordonstoun."

"That's where Prince Charles went, I think," said Ben, offering up the only bit of information he had on the school.

"Aye, I think so," Hamza replied. "Not at the same time, though, obviously. And I think I remember hearing that Charlie hated it. Mr Finley-Lennox seems to have thrived. He was a prefect, in all the clubs—drama, debating, sailing, you name it."

"He comes from money, then?"

"He does, aye. Formed Freedom UK in the wake of Brexit. Everyone wrote him off as just another right-leaning Farage-wannabe trying to capitalise on the anti-EU sentiment. He wasn't expected to get a seat. Bit of a shock result, really, although he had a good PR team working for him, and he did a big push for the Christian vote."

"No record, I take it?"

"Squeaky clean. Not so much as a parking ticket."

Ben picked up a pen and tapped it idly against the edge of the desk. "He married?"

"Since he was nineteen."

"You checked out the wife?"

"Aye. No record for her, either. She's a member of Freedom UK, but doesn't seem to have much, if any, involvement besides smiling and waving in a couple of pictures."

Ben twisted from side to side in the swivel chair, contemplating all this new information. "Missing persons throw anything up?"

Hamza shook his head. "Not really got anything to go on.

We don't even have a picture of Bernie to compare, and the date range for his arrival in the area is too broad to sift through. The name 'Bernie' brought up a few hits, but nothing that's unresolved, unless he's a hundred and twenty years old, in which case there's one possibility. Pretty sure that's not going to be him, though."

"Unlikely, aye," Ben agreed. He set down the pen and sat forward. "So, our French psychic is the big headline. We're going to want to take a closer look at him."

"You thinking we bring him in for a more formal interview?" Hamza asked.

Ben shook his head. "Not that, no. Not yet," he said. "I was thinking we might try something a wee bit more sneaky."

"Undercover? In a magic sex cult?" Constable Dave Davidson switched his phone from one hand to the other, like he couldn't believe what the ear on that side was telling him. "You want me to go undercover in a magic sex cult?"

The voice of Detective Inspector Ben Forde spoke from the telephone's handset. "It's not magic."

"But it *is* a sex cult?" Dave asked.

"If you think it's too dangerous, I'm sure we can find someone else," Ben said.

"Dangerous? No, I'm not worried about it being dangerous!" Dave said. "I'm in."

"Are you sure?" Ben asked. "You've never done anything like this before."

"I don't care. I'm in," Dave insisted. He realised he might be coming across as a little *too* enthusiastic, and dialled it down a notch. "If me putting myself at risk like this is what it takes to help crack this case, then I'll do it. I'll take my chances."

"Well, if you're sure..."

"I've never been more sure of anything in my life," Dave replied. "Do they have a pool, do you know? It doesn't matter if they don't, I was just wondering."

"No. It's in tents."

Dave's smile almost split his face in two. "Oh, I bet it is! But I can handle it! Is there a pool, though?"

"I mean... everyone stays in tents. Like a campsite."

"Oh. Right. Sorry, I thought you said..." Dave shook his head. "Doesn't matter."

"I'll have to run it by Mitchell, of course," Ben said. "Are you sure we wouldn't be taking you away from anything important?"

Dave sat up straighter in his wheelchair and looked around at the banks of monitors that currently displayed footage from the city's network of CCTV cameras. "Nothing they can't dingy off onto some other poor bugger."

"Good. Right. Leave it with me. We'll be in touch," Ben said.

They said their goodbyes, and Dave had barely hung up the phone when his fingers flew to the keyboard of his computer. He tabbed to a browser, typed the words, 'back, sack, and crack waxing Inverness' into the search bar, then sighed happily as he hit Enter.

CHAPTER TWENTY-THREE

WHILE LOGAN HAD his reservations about sitting down anywhere in Dinky's house, Ally Bally had no such qualms. He'd flopped down onto the couch after Tyler had led him into the living room. It was apparently not the first time he'd done this, as while the stacks of paperwork wobbled precariously, not a single sheet fell.

The bottom of the old man's trousers were hanging in rags from where the dog had ripped at them, but he had otherwise escaped unharmed.

Despite dozens of tiny scratches on his face, a few hundred thousand midge bites, and the fact that he was still stuck inside what was now a seriously dishevelled squirrel costume, Tyler looked pleased with himself when he brought Ally Bally in.

Too pleased with himself, Logan thought. The bastard was up to something.

That was a concern for another time, though. For now, he turned his attention to the old man on the couch.

"You must be Ally Bally."

At the mention of his name, Ally Bally grinned to reveal more gums than teeth, and launched into a slurred rendition of the nursery rhyme.

"Ally Bally, Ally Bally Bee, sitting on—"

"Aye, we get it," Logan said, cutting him off. He shot a sideways look at Tyler. "This the guy from the caravan?"

"It is, boss," Tyler confirmed.

"This?" Logan asked again, gesturing to the drink and drug-addled wreck of a man jammed between the towers of newspapers and magazines. "This is the man who evaded capture?"

"He's faster than he looks, boss," Tyler said. He was holding eye contact, Logan noted. Not so much as a blink. "We did our best, given the circumstances, but we were on unfamiliar territory, and—"

"Alright, alright, fine," Logan said, dismissing the rest of the explanation. He turned back to Ally Bally. "Nippy old bugger then, are you?"

"I used to be a sprinter," Ally Bally said, his eyes wide like he was staring back into the past. "I used to run roond and roond. Roond, and roond, and roond. Whoosh. You know? Just like... whoosh, so I was. Wasn't I, Dinky?"

"The fuck should I know?" Dinky asked. "You've just been an old jakey bastard for as long as I've known you."

Ally Bally's smile widened and became a dry, rasping laugh that made Logan crave a throat lozenge.

"He's good, isn't he? Wee Dinky," the old man said to the detectives. "He's a good wee guy."

"Well, I suppose that's what we're here to find out," Logan said. "See, we've got reason to believe that you were at a caravan owned by Bernie the Beacon."

"Was that yesterday?" Ally Bally asked.

Logan nodded. "Aye."

The old man's sun-ravaged brow furrowed into a series of deep grooves, like he was struggling to hold onto some thought. "Aye. No. That wasn't us. We weren't there. Were we, Dinky?"

"No," Dinky confirmed. "We weren't there."

"Except you were," Tyler said, addressing the man on the couch. "Because I saw you."

"He says he saw me, Dinky."

"Well, he couldn't have."

Ally Bally shook his head. "You couldn't have seen me."

"Aye, but I did. You opened the caravan door, and you saw me there."

"Naw. I'd have minded seeing you, cos you're a big squirrel," Ally Bally reasoned.

"I wasn't wearing this at the time," Tyler said. "You opened the door, saw me and my colleague, and ran away."

"Is that the Indian man?" Ally Bally asked. He winced. "Because, like, I didn't see him either. Did I, Dinky?"

Dinky groaned, looked up at the ceiling, and asked the gods for a strength that apparently didn't come.

"Right, fine. We were there," he announced. "We were at the caravan yesterday."

"You said we weren't," Ally Bally told him.

"You fucking know we were!"

Ally Bally folded his skinny arms. He looked genuinely hurt. "You shouldn't make me confused like that, Dinky. It's no' funny." He shifted his gaze to the detectives. "Were we there, or were we no'?"

"You were there," Logan told him.

This seemed to please the older man. "I thought we were there, right enough. That's what I was wondering. 'Cause wee Dinky said that we weren't. I thought..." He raised his hands and mimed his head exploding, complete with accompanying sound effects. "Know what I mean?"

"Tell you what, from now on just you tell us what you think happened," Logan told him. "Forget about what Dinky said, alright?"

Ally Bally frowned. It was quite a slow process, like the signals had to stop for a rest somewhere between his brain and his facial muscles. "What Dinky said about what?" He looked across to the little man in the armchair. "Did you say something there, Dinky?"

Dinky slapped a stubby hand on his forehead, whispered, "Fucking hell," and then completely gave up. "Fine. You want the truth? Like I say, aye, we were at the caravan yesterday. Alright? No crime in that."

"Except the arson," Logan said. "Pretty sure that qualifies as a crime."

"Arson?" Dinky's features squished together like his face was made of rubber. "What do you mean?"

"Thought you said we were telling the truth here, Dinky," Logan continued. "The caravan. You burned it down."

"What? No, we didn't. Ally Bally, tell him. Did we burn down the caravan?"

The old man bit his top lip with his one good bottom tooth, and thought this over. "What caravan?" he eventually asked. "Did you get a caravan, Dinky? That's pure magic, wee man! Can I get a shot?"

"No, the... Jesus. You're getting worse, do you know that?" Dinky said, then he raised his eyes to Logan again. "We went there looking for Bernie. That's all. We didn't set fire to anything."

"Why were you looking for him?" Logan asked. "I thought he wasn't due a payment yet."

"He isn't. Wasn't. But he would have been soon," Dinky explained. "Hadn't heard from him in a while, and considering what he bought with the money I loaned him, I wanted to make sure he hadn't done a runner."

"What did he buy?" Tyler asked.

"A van. Knackered old thing off Craigslist. Said he didn't want to hitchhike up the road anymore. Said he was worried someone might do him in."

"Someone specific?"

Dinky shrugged and pulled a face at the Detective Constable. "The fuck should I know? I'm not his mum. I've already got one useless headcase to take care of. But, I think he just meant in general. Because people are bastards."

Logan shared that sentiment so offered no argument. Instead, he focused on the big headline reveal. "He bought a van?"

"Aye. Sent me a link to the listing."

"You still have that?" Logan asked.

"Maybe. What's it worth?"

"It's worth me not calling the drug squad in here and having them turn this place upside down," Logan countered.

Dinky tutted. "Right, fine. Aye. I'll find it," he said, taking out his phone.

Logan continued the questioning while Dinky scrolled through his old messages.

"So, you went to visit him yesterday. Then what?"

"Then Ally Bally clocked a bunch of people already in there, and legged it back to the car."

Both detectives looked down at the old man on the couch in horror. "He doesn't drive, does he?" Tyler asked.

"Fuck no. I wouldn't trust him to ride a bike. I do, though."

"Oh. Right," the DC said. His gaze flitted from the top of Dinky's head to the tips of his toes. "Do you have, like, a special wee car?"

Dinky frowned. "What do you mean? Like a dodgem?"

"He's no' *Noddy*, son," Logan said. "It'll be a specially adapted vehicle, I'd have thought. Right?"

"Right. Exactly," Dinky said.

Tyler wanted to ask more. 'Specially adapted' could mean almost anything. It could even mean that they'd taken a standard-sized vehicle and shrunk it. Obviously not with a shrink ray or anything—he knew that much—but just by building the parts smaller and slotting them all together.

He decided, though, that it was probably best if he kept his mouth shut on the matter, or face the prospect of repeating his diversity training.

"So, he ran back to the car, you drove off," Logan said. "That's what you're claiming?"

"That's what happened."

"Nothing in there you've forgotten to mention?"

Dinky shook his head. "Nothing."

"Except that briefcase," Ally Bally said. He beamed proudly, and winked at the dwarf in the armchair. "Who's the one whose brain's all spangled now, Dinky, eh? And he says I'm the one wi' a bad memory."

Logan and Tyler both peered down at Dinky, saying nothing. The little man gritted his teeth and shot a look at Ally Bally that said he was in for a hiding later, then ejected a sigh of frustration.

"Alright, I may have had a wee peek in when they two clowns were off chasing that numptie fuck," he announced.

"And I may—*may*—have acquired a briefcase, which I intended to hold onto as security until my money was repaid."

"You took the briefcase," Tyler said. "Boss, he took the briefcase!"

"Aye, I heard him, Detective Constable. I'm going to choose to ignore the legalities of taking an item that doesn't belong to you, Dinky. I'm sure you'll be relieved to hear that," Logan said. "But I'm sure it won't come as any surprise when I say that my doing so hinges entirely on you handing it over."

"That's my collateral," Dinky protested. "I need to be compensated for him being dead somehow, don't I?"

Logan made a show of giving this some thought. "Eh, no. No, you don't," he concluded. "So, get up off your arse, get us the briefcase, and send us that link to the van he was buying."

He bent over, bringing his face closer to the little man in the chair, and glaring at him like some vengeful ancient god. "Or, would you rather we did this the hard way?"

Tyler didn't turn back. Not even when the dog started growling as he and Logan trudged away from the house. He'd already told it in no uncertain terms to, "Fuck off, mate!" while it was humping and ripping at the fallen Ally Bally, and it had, to his surprise, done as it was told.

Neither detective said a word until they were back in the car. Tyler had been carrying the briefcase, and now that he'd managed to shed the squirrel outfit, he set the case on his knees with the handle facing him. It was an old-style boxy thing with a coating of artificial black leather. There were combination locks on both clasps, Dinky didn't know the combination, and hadn't yet got around to forcing the case open, so they were none the wiser as to what was inside.

It felt reasonably heavy, though. When Tyler shook it, he thought it sounded like paperwork. But, when Logan pointed out that for all they knew the briefcase might contain an explosive device, he'd given up trying to figure out what was inside, and had cautiously lowered the case to his side.

"What now, boss?" he asked, warily eyeing the thing's worn leather patina. "Should we... Do we open it?"

"We don't know the code, and I don't really want to force it until we know what's in there. It's probably just paperwork, but I don't want to go buggering about with the locks until we know for sure.

Tyler exhaled, clearly relieved. "Aye, that sounds like a good plan. I'd rather not get blown to bits, if I can avoid it."

Logan gazed ahead, deep in thought, watching the movements of the trees. They were exposed this high on the hillside, and the wind creaked the thick branches as it blew along the neighbouring Loch Lochy—so named because... Well, presumably because someone was a lazy bastard.

"You fancy a wee run up the road to Inverness?" he asked.

Tyler glanced out across the loch at the darkening sky. It was well past dinner time now, and Strontian—and Sinead—felt like a very long way away. "What for, boss?"

Logan tapped the top of the briefcase. "I've got an idea," he said.

He put the car into reverse, eased his foot down on the accelerator, and was thrown forward on his seat when Tyler reapplied the handbrake.

"What the hell are you doing?" he demanded.

Tyler swallowed, but didn't look away from the DCI's glare. "What's the idea, boss?"

"Excuse me?"

"You asked me what I thought about a run up the road to Inverness. I asked you why, and you said you had an idea," Tyler said, the words coming out in a sort of rapid-fire where each flowed into the next. "That doesn't help me make a decision. If you really want my opinion, you need to tell me why we're going." He swallowed again as everything he'd said replayed in his head. "Boss."

"I don't really want your opinion," Logan told him. He turned to look out the back windscreen, but Tyler wasn't done.

"Aye, well, I want to give it," the DC persevered. "I deserve the information, boss. I'm a valuable member of this team. I've nearly died, like, eight times doing stuff for you. Doing stuff to *impress you*. I at least deserve to know why I'm doing them."

Logan grunted, then disengaged the handbrake and started to reverse. Tyler reached for the controls once more, but Logan slapped his hand away.

"Touch that again and I'll break your fingers," he warned. Then, once he'd turned the car so it was facing back down the hill, he put his foot on the brakes and turned to the man beside him. "I want to take the case to Shona so she can X-ray it," he said. "I also, on a personal level, could do with picking up some more clothes, since I think we're going to be down there a few days yet at least, and there's no' exactly an abundance of places to buy pants."

"Actually, that wee shop sells pants, boss," Tyler said. "They sell everything."

"Great! Do they sell medical-grade X-ray machines, too?"

"Not unless they keep them through the back," Tyler admitted.

"Right. So, I'd like, if it's alright with you, to go to Inverness, get the case checked out, probably spend the night, given the time, then drive back down the road with supplies first thing tomorrow morning.

"If you'd prefer, I can drop you back in the Fort and you can go back to Strontian with Hamza and Ben, assuming they've no' left yet. Your choice, son. Far be it from me to make it for you. You are, after all, a valuable member of this team."

Tyler's eyes narrowed a fraction. "Was that sarcasm, boss?"

"Which bit?"

"Any of it."

Logan shrugged. "Some bits more so than others, maybe, but by and large no. You're right, Tyler. If I'm dragging you hundreds of miles up and down the country, you've got a right to know."

"I do?" Tyler asked, unable to keep the surprise from his voice. He cleared his throat and nodded. "I mean, aye. I do. Too right I do."

"Don't push it, son," Logan warned. "You coming to Inverness or not?"

"Aye. Aye, I'll come, boss. Could do with getting Sinead and me some more clothes, too, and I should check in with Harris and Jan."

"Right. Good. It's agreed, then," Logan said. He indicated the car's controls. "May I?"

"Fire on, boss."

"You're not going to have a hissy fit and suddenly swerve us off the road?"

"No plans for now, boss, but I'll keep you posted."

"Right. Good." Logan started to pull away, then stopped again. He let out a sigh so faint it was almost non-existent, then turned to the Detective Constable. "What you said. About trying to impress me. You don't have to, son. There's no need."

Tyler's eyes and mouth formed three little *O's* of surprise. "Oh. Eh, cheers, boss."

"I've long since given up on the prospect of that ever happening," Logan clarified. Then, fighting back a grin, he patted Tyler on the leg, and started off down the bumpy, uneven track.

CHAPTER TWENTY-FOUR

LOGAN AND TYLER were north of Fort Augustus on the main A82 road to Inverness when the phone rang and a Fort William number flashed up on the car's internal display.

Tyler, who had been scouring the surface of Loch Ness through the breaks in the trees like he always did when he wasn't behind the wheel on this stretch of road, looked to Logan for approval, then tapped the icon that answered the call.

"DCI Jack Logan."

"Jack. Hello. Can you hear me?" asked Ben. His voice was muffled, yet was echoing at the same time in a way that was quite unpleasant to listen to. These were, Logan knew, the telltale signs of a conference call.

"Aye, I can hear you."

Ben became quieter still as he turned away to talk to someone else. "He can hear me."

"Aye, I heard him say that," Hamza confirmed.

"Jack, it's Ben. Ben Forde," the DI continued, his voice echoing as a loud crackle from the speakers.

Logan rolled his eyes. He could picture him now, leaning in far too close to the pyramid-shaped gadget on the desk, raising his voice to make himself heard.

"You're coming in loud and clear," Logan told him. "We're on Loch Ness side, though, so signal might dip in and out. We're headed back up the road. We're going to swing in and see Shona."

"Good idea," Ben said. "She seemed to be in a hell of a state earlier."

Logan tore his eyes from the road and let them linger on the stereo system for a moment. "What? How do you mean?"

"Just... Did nobody say?" Ben asked.

"Say what?"

"She just seemed a bit..." Ben's voice went quieter again as he turned to Hamza. "What would you say?"

"A bit manic, maybe, sir," Hamza said.

"Bit highly strung, boss," Tyler added. "She'd pulled an all-nighter for the PM."

"Is that Tyler?" Ben asked, his voice becoming a high volume crackle again. "Is Tyler with you?"

"Aye, he's here. What do you mean 'manic'? How highly-strung are we talking?" Logan asked, not yet ready to change the subject. "Was she... Was something wrong?"

"I don't know about *wrong*, Jack, no. I don't think there was anything wrong, exactly. She'd been on the energy drinks all night. Probably just a bit jittery. You can always ask her yourself when you see her."

Logan looked down at the screen again, then shot a sideways glance at Tyler.

"I don't think it's anything major, boss," the younger detective assured him. "Probably just buzzing from the caffeine."

"Aye. Probably," Logan conceded, trying not to show his concern.

The trip back up the road was *mostly* for the reasons he'd told Tyler, but partly it was to surprise her with a visit. It wasn't exactly a big romantic gesture, but then big romantic gestures weren't really his forte. Hopefully, it would put a smile on her face, at least.

"I've got Sinead on the call, too," Ben boomed from the speakers. "Have we got Sinead?"

"I'm here, sir," Sinead said.

"Can everyone hear her OK?" Ben asked. He turned to Hamza. "Can they hear her OK?"

"You'd have to ask them, sir," Hamza replied.

"I did ask them, but they didn't say anything."

"You didn't exactly give us a chance," Logan pointed out. "Aye, we can hear Sinead. We can hear everyone."

"Can everyone hear us?" Tyler asked.

Ben's voice once again became quieter. "Can everyone hear them?"

"We can hear you," Sinead said, and though he didn't say anything, a smile lit up Tyler's face at his wife's reply.

"Right, everyone can hear everyone else. That's a solid start," Logan said, guiding the car around a Z-shaped series of bends in the road, before picking up speed on the straight that followed. "What's happening?"

"Thought we'd do a quick catch-up call," Ben explained. "A few things have come up, and I've set something in motion that I probably should've discussed with you first."

"What have you done?" Logan asked, his fingers tightening on the wheel as he tensed.

"I'm putting Constable Dave Davidson into Westerly Wellness. André Douville's place."

"Is he sick?" Tyler asked, which earned him a disparaging look and a shake of the head from Logan.

"*Is he sick?*" the DCI muttered. "Undercover, son."

"Oh. Aye. Aye, that makes more sense," Tyler said, then he frowned and turned his attention back to the screen. "Wait, he's getting to go to the sex cult? How does he get to go to the sex cult?"

Sinead loudly cleared her throat, and Tyler hurriedly moved to cover his tracks.

"I meant why isn't it someone from CID, obviously. Not me. I wouldn't be interested in that sort of thing."

"Dave just felt like the right man for the job," Ben said. "Besides, you can see most of these buggers in CID coming a mile off. They've practically got the word 'polis' stamped on their heads. Whereas, with Dave, sometimes even I forget he's on the force, even if he's sat there in uniform."

Both occupants of the BMW nodded their agreement at that. There was something about Dave Davidson that made him an unlikely police officer, and it was nothing to do with his wheelchair.

It wasn't so much that he didn't respect authority, more that he didn't really notice it. He didn't bow and scrape to superior officers, but he didn't act the big man around anyone, either. It was like he considered everyone to be on an equal footing, and no more worthy of respect or scorn than the next man.

Some officers saw the uniform as a licence to throw their weight around. An excuse for a power trip. Dave, on the other hand, saw it as a thing he had to wear for work, and he was probably a far better officer because of that.

Even if that same attitude sometimes made the others forget he was an officer at all.

"Eh... OK," Logan said. "Did you just fancy giving him a wee holiday, or...?"

Ben gave way to Hamza then, who went over everything they'd found on the man currently calling himself André Douville. Logan sat in silence, eyes fixed on the road ahead, his jaw tightening as the man's criminal history was read out, and all his deceptions uncovered.

"So, he's not even French?" Tyler asked once Hamza had finished.

"No," Ben confirmed. "And he doesn't look like Jesus, either. Even those big blue sparkly eyes of his are contacts. He's a bloody charlatan."

"We should haul the bastard in by the beard and hammer the bloody truth out of him," Logan said.

"I think we'll all pretend we didn't hear that, Jack, and stick with my plan for the moment," Ben said. "Besides, I think Dave's excited to get stuck in."

Tyler snorted. "I bet he bloody is."

Once Hamza had given a potted history of the MSP, Oberon Finley-Lennox, Sinead took her turn at going over what she'd found. Right now, that wasn't much. Even with the help of the two constables, wading through the densely packed, often nonsensical newsletters was a slow process.

There were no smoking guns in any of the issues they'd gone through yet—nothing that pointed to any one individual who might be Bernie's killer. A few trends were starting to emerge, though, which Sinead felt were worthy of note.

"He didn't like doctors," she said. "Well, medical professionals in general, but doctors especially. He repeatedly claimed that they're all running tests on us."

"Well, they are, aren't they?" asked Tyler. "That's sort of their job."

"Aye, but not for our own benefit. For the government. Who are lizards."

"Obviously," Hamza said.

"He reckoned they were using us like lab rats to test new drugs, implants, mind control techniques... That sort of thing."

"So he's proper mental, then?" Tyler said. He looked from the stereo to Logan and back again. "Is that a pretty accurate summary?"

"Well, I'm not sure it'd stand up as a medical diagnosis," Sinead told him. "But aye, that's definitely the impression his newsletter gives off. There's top tips on preventing radio signals getting inside your head, one of which involves removing all your teeth with pliers."

Tyler instinctively rubbed his hand across his mouth at the thought of this, but said nothing. Logan shot a glance at the screen where the number was still being displayed.

"He didn't do that to himself. The body still had teeth."

"No, he said it's only necessary if you have metal fillings. He says he didn't, so there was no need," Sinead explained. "If you don't have fillings, you just have to rub bacon fat on your temples and the back of your neck."

"I thought they all used tinfoil?" said Ben. "The conspiracy theory nutters, I mean."

"That's for the amateurs, sir. So the newsletter says," Sinead explained. "Apparently, bacon fat is where it's at."

"Here, that'd be quite a good advertising slogan," Tyler said. "*Bacon fat is where it's at!*"

Logan side-eyed him. "Who's advertising bacon fat?" he asked.

Tyler shifted in his seat. "Well... No. But, I'm just saying... If they were."

There was a moment of silence in which everyone came to the same decision to ignore everything that Tyler had just said.

"Anyway, that's about all we've got for now," Sinead continued.

"Nothing about the MSP or the wellness centre?" Logan asked.

"Nothing specific, sir, no. But we'll keep looking."

Logan steered the BMW around a couple of twists in the road. They were going quite fast, so Tyler was forced to grip the handle above the door and stare straight ahead at some imagined spot on the horizon to stop his nausea from rising too far to contain.

As luck would have it, there was a queue of traffic waiting to make the turn into Urquhart Castle around the next bend, and Logan cursed below his breath as he brought the car to a stop.

"Bloody tourists, eh, boss?" Tyler said, trying hard to hide his relief.

"Aye, you can say that again," Logan replied in a series of irritated grunts.

Sinead announced that her update was over, so Logan took his turn as they inched forward in the queue.

"We've got the briefcase that was in Bernie's caravan," he announced, drawing sounds of surprise and celebration from the speaker system. "While Ally Bally had Tyler and Hamza running around like a pair of Muppets, Dinky snuck in and took it. Someone find out their real names, by the way, I'm no' going to keep calling them that."

"Will do, sir," Hamza said.

"So, this Dinky character..." Ben began. "Presumably, he also set the caravan on fire, then?"

"He says he didn't."

"Well, he's hardly going to just own up to it, is he?" Ben replied.

"I actually think he might've," Logan said. "Don't ask me why, but my hunch is that he didn't do it."

"We actually got a report through about the fire," Hamza said.

Ben's voice became quieter again as he turned to the DS. "Did we? When? I didn't see it."

"It came in when you were out, sir," Hamza said. "Looks like the same accelerant was used on the caravan as on the body. A turpentine, petroleum jelly mix."

"We used to use that in my army days, when we were out in the wilds," Ben said. "We'd mix up a jar or two, and take it with us. You could use it on cuts, to keep insects at bay, and it was one of the best firestarters around. Smear it on a bit of kindling, and away you went. Wouldn't blow out, no matter what the wind was doing."

"Still no' exactly common, I'd have thought," Logan remarked. "Hell of a coincidence if it's not the same person responsible for both fires."

"It's not uncommon among campers and the like," Ben said. "But aye, that'd be a bit of a stretch, right enough."

The road on the right cleared enough to let three of the queuing cars turn into the castle car park, freeing the traffic behind them to continue on up the road towards Inverness.

"So, what are we saying, boss?" Tyler asked, though it wasn't immediately clear which boss he was addressing. "The killer was there? At the caravan? Watching us?"

"Probably, aye," Logan confirmed. "When you two went blundering off, he must've seen his chance. Waited for Dinky to leave, then set the place alight."

"So, presumably there was something in there that might have identified him," said Sinead.

"Aye," Logan said. He shot Tyler an accusing look. "Though fat lot of good that does us now."

Tyler flashed a nervous smile. "Still, least we got the briefcase."

"You had a chance to open it yet?" Ben asked.

Logan explained that they hadn't, and his slight concerns that, even if they were able to work out the combinations for the locks, the case might explode in their faces the moment they opened it.

"Hence the visit to Shona," he said. "Since she's the only one I know with easy access to an X-ray machine."

"Oh, you old charmer, sir," Sinead said, and there was a general sense from the speakers of the others trying not to laugh.

"Less of the 'old,' please, Detective Constable," Logan warned. "Oh, and there's one other thing. Bernie borrowed money off Dinky to buy a van."

"A van?" asked Ben. "What sort of van?"

"We don't know. Bernie had sent Dinky a link to it on Craigslist, which Dinky has given us. But the listing has expired, or something. It's no' there."

Hamza's voice became louder again as he came closer to the microphone of the speakerphone. "Fire it over to me, sir, and I can take a look. Might be able to find it on the Wayback Machine."

"What the hell's a Wayback Machine?" Ben asked. "When did we get one of them?"

"It's a website, sir," Hamza told him. "Like an archive of webpages. If we can't get it there, I might be able to get it from Craigslist."

"Good. Aye. That'd be very handy," Logan said. "Tyler'll send it over to you."

"Aye, but not until we get to Inverness," the DC said. He caught the inquisitive look from Logan. "Can't text when I'm in a moving car. Makes me sick."

Logan tutted. "Of course it does." He sighed.

They were heading through the village of Drumnadrochit now, and another mobile reception blackspot was looming, so Logan moved to wrap up the call.

"Right, everyone keep at it. We'll be stopping up here overnight, then heading back in the morning," he said. "What about Dave? Are we bringing him back with us?"

"Dave?" Ben chuckled. "You must be joking," he said. "The bugger's so keen he'll have already passed you on the way down the road!"

CHAPTER TWENTY-FIVE

LOGAN'S PLAN TO surprise Shona by turning up out of the blue was dealt a bit of a blow when he realised he had absolutely no idea where she was. If she'd pulled an all-nighter, there was a good chance she was at home sleeping the effects of that off. Then again, she might've already done that, and be back at the hospital now to start another late shift.

Or, unhappily, she could be literally anywhere else in the Inverness area, and potentially beyond.

The hospital was closest. After dropping Tyler off at home, he decided to start there, not least because they had flowers for sale at the shop in the foyer, and given his lack of recent phone communication, he felt it best not to turn up empty-handed.

The lights were on when he arrived at her office, but there was no sign of her through the glass. Further lights were visible beneath the double doors of the mortuary, suggesting she was in there somewhere, hard at work.

Either that, or they'd brought former pathologist Albert

Rickett back out of his enforced retirement. Even with the current state of NHS Highland staffing levels, he thought that was probably unlikely, given the old bastard's current whereabouts.

"Hello?" Logan called, easing open the outer door and stepping into the office. Music was playing from the smartspeaker that sat on one of the shelves—an acoustic cover version of what Logan guessed was a recent chart hit. And by 'recent' he meant 'from some point within the last fifteen years.'

There were no sounds of dismemberment echoing out from within the mortuary. No sawing, or drilling, or cracking of bones. No anything, in fact. If it wasn't for the music, the place would've been—fittingly enough—as quiet as the grave.

Still, best not to go through and disturb her. For all he knew, she'd be elbows deep in some poor bugger, and while he was no stranger to corpses and gore, he didn't tend to seek them out.

He crossed to the counter which doubled as a desk, sat down the rather disappointing bouquet of Dutch Freesias, then jumped back in fright when Shona reared up from the other side, all wild hair and wide eyes, gasping like she'd just surfaced from an undersea dive.

She windmilled frantically, screamed sharply, then fell backwards off her stool and landed on the floor with a thud that rattled the glass beakers and test tubes on the shelves.

"Jesus. You alright?" Logan asked, hurrying around to where Shona lay flat on her back on the carpet tiles. "What happened?"

"I fell off," Shona wheezed. "Just then."

"Aye, no. I saw that. Bloody impressive it was, too, with the waving arms and everything." He extended a hand, gave

Shona a moment to grab on, then helped her back to her feet. "Were you sleeping, or something?"

"What? No. No, of course I wasn't sleeping. I was just resting my eyes." She yawned and stretched. "And, you know, my brain."

She caught her reflection in the glass of the door, and pawed at her hair in a hopeless attempt to flatten it down, straighten it out, or otherwise stop it looking like it had recently played home to a family of slovenly birds.

"You alright?" Logan asked.

"Me? Fine!" Shona replied, a little too forcefully. "What? Yeah. Fine. Right as rain. Why?"

"You seem..." Logan gestured at her, not quite finding the right word. "Different."

"Nope. Still me," she insisted, then she pinched her cheek and pulled it, as if trying to prove it wasn't a mask. "See?"

She threw her arms around him and pressed her head against his chest before he could ask anything more. Or perhaps just to hide her face because she knew that he would.

"You seem stressed," he said.

Not quite a question then, but close enough.

"Oh, you know me. Work, work, work," Shona said. Her eyes fell on the perfect excuse to change the subject. "Flowers! You brought flowers? Jack Logan, I'll make a romantic of you yet."

"I just got them in the shop in the foyer," Logan explained. "They were discounted since they're wilting a bit."

"OK, so maybe not one of the all-time *great* romantics,

but still," Shona said. She withdrew her arms and picked up the bouquet. "They're lovely. Thanks."

Logan cleared his throat and nodded, finding himself on unfamiliar territory. "Aye, well, I've been a bit... shite on the phone front the last couple of days."

"You had no signal."

"Well, aye. I had no signal," he said. "But, still."

Shona shrugged. "You're not to blame for the lack of network coverage, Jack."

"True." Logan looked from her to the flowers. "Sod it, I'll take them back, then."

She laughed and whipped the bouquet away before he could reach for it. "Not a chance," she said, giving the flowers a sniff. "That you all done, then? Mystery solved and back up the road?"

Logan explained he was just there for the night, and failed to spot the disappointment behind her smile. She looked around for another excuse to switch subjects, and spotted the briefcase he had set on the floor by his feet when Shona had fallen.

"This a new look for you?" she teased. "Nineteen-eighties corporate banker. It's a bold style choice, I'll give you that."

"Eh, actually, no. I'm hoping it's something you can help me with."

"You need to open it? I've got a vertebrae chisel that should do the job."

Something about the combination of the words 'vertebrae' and 'chisel' momentarily stopped the detective in his tracks.

"Or is it a code?" Shona asked, picking up the case by the

handle. "We could try one each. We could make it a race! Last one to get it open buys dinner."

"Actually, I was concerned it might be explosive," Logan said.

Shona's smile remained fixed in place, but her gaze crept slowly down to the briefcase she was holding in what she now realised was quite a cavalier manner.

"Like... a bomb?" she whispered, then she swallowed as if trying to clear something that had become stuck in her throat. "You brought me a bomb?"

Logan took the case from her. "It's probably not a bomb," he said. Then, when he realised this didn't have quite the desired calming effect, he went bolder. "It's almost certainly not a bomb. The chances of it being a bomb are minuscule. But, I thought maybe we could X-ray it to check. Just to be on the safe side."

"On the safe side for who?" Shona squeaked. "I didn't have a bomb here five minutes ago."

"Potential bomb. It's highly doubtful that it's going to explode." He stole a glance at the door to the post-mortem room. "Anyway, you'll be behind a lead screen, won't you?"

"*We'll* be behind a lead screen," Shona replied, grabbing him by the front of the shirt. "If I'm getting blown to tiny little bits, then so are you."

As expected, the briefcase did not contain a bomb. Going by the X-ray image, it didn't contain very much of anything, in fact, besides some paperwork and—potentially more interestingly—a small bundle of Polaroids.

Once they were sure it wasn't going to explode, they

perched on the stools by the worktop out in the office, and worked their way through the combinations. This was partly because Logan really didn't want to know what a vertebrae chisel looked like, but mostly so he could enjoy the closeness of the woman beside him.

"Have you spoken to Maddie yet?" Shona asked, fiddling her way through the rightmost digit on the rotating lock. The dials were stiff, and the fact they were both wearing gloves so as to minimise contamination wasn't making the job any easier.

"How do you mean?" Logan asked.

Shona paused, mid-turn. Her eyes darted around like she was searching for a flaw in the question she'd just asked. "I mean... have you spoken to Maddie yet?"

"Aye. No. I mean... Do you mean *spoke* to her, spoke to her?"

"What's the alternative meaning?" Shona wondered. "*Not spoke* to her, spoke to her?"

"We texted," Logan said.

Shona, who had briefly resumed working through the combinations, stopped again. "You texted?"

"Aye. Well, she texted me."

"*She texted you?!*"

"I replied!" Logan said, suddenly defensive. "I mean, it was a few hours after she sent it, but I replied."

"Oof!"

"What? What do you mean, 'Oof'? What's 'Oof'?" he asked.

"She reached out to you, and you took hours to reply."

"I had no signal!" Logan protested. "You said yourself, I can't be blamed for lack of network coverage."

Shona sucked air in through her teeth and shook her head. "In this instance, you can."

"What was I meant to do? Drive to somewhere with mobile reception?" Logan cried. His eyes flitted left and right, his brow furrowing. "I mean... That doesn't sound entirely unreasonable, now that I say it out loud. Shite!" He slapped his forehead and ran a hand down his face. "I should've driven to somewhere with a mobile reception."

"And...?"

Logan sighed. "And I should have called her. I shouldn't have waited for her to text me."

"Good. You're learning," Shona told him. "I'm done with this, by the way."

Logan blinked. "You're what? You're done with this?"

She smirked. "The case. My side. It's double-oh-nine." She adopted a passable Sean Connery accent. "Licence to scald."

Logan blinked for the second time in five seconds. "Eh?"

"Double-oh-seven is licence to kill, double-oh-eight will be, like, licence to generally maim, and nine will be exclusively licensed to cause scalding," Shona said. "I mean, if I was in charge of the franchise that's how it would work, anyway."

"Have you... have you actually thought about this?" Logan asked. "Before now, I mean?"

"Erm..." Shona looked away for a moment, then locked eyes with him again. "No," she said, quite unconvincingly. "Why would I spend hours doing something like that?" She tapped his side of the case. "Come on, chop-chop."

"It's not double-oh-nine on my side," he replied, turning the dial.

"Oh well, looks like dinner's on you, then," Shona

announced, hopping down from the stool. She yawned, ran a hand back through her unkempt hair, and went plodding over to the kettle. "But I think we'll have some coffee, while we're waiting."

Over two-hundred-and-thirty rotations later, the second of the briefcase's clasps sprung open, and Logan let out a sigh of relief.

"We did it!" Shona cheered, raising her half-empty coffee cup aloft. "We cracked the case!"

Logan opened the lid to reveal two large brown envelopes, neither one sealed at the end.

"This is exciting, isn't it?" Shona whispered, bouncing her stool closer. "It's like being a detective."

"I am a detective," Logan reminded her.

"I know, but like a *proper* detective," Shona said. "Like Sherlock Holmes. Or Batman."

"Don't get me started on Sherlock bloody Holmes," Logan warned. "The arsehole," he added, then he turned his attention back to the case and the envelopes contained within it.

The topmost envelope was the thicker of the two, and as good a place as any to start. He prised the flap open and looked inside, then tipped the contents onto the worktop before them.

A dozen or more Polaroids slid out, face down on the worktop. He picked one at random and flipped it over. It wasn't the best picture. It was a little out of focus, and taken from behind a tree.

It showed a familiar Range Rover parked up in a lay-by at

the side of a road. The driver—Oberon Finley-Lennox—wasn't in the front seat. From this angle, he didn't seem to be inside the vehicle at all, in fact, although the way the sun was catching the back passenger side window made it difficult to be sure.

The next photo showed the car driving up to the spot, and this time Oberon was clearly visible behind the wheel. There was another car there, too. A much smaller, less ostentatious one. A Ford of some kind, Logan thought, though the framing of the photograph cropped out many of the identifying features.

Shona turned over the next picture. The Range Rover again. The driver's door was open, and Oberon was out of the car, standing beside it. He was smiling—a big, broad, happy grin that made him look five years younger than the man Logan had met earlier that day.

"Who's he?" Shona asked.

"He's an MSP."

"Tory?"

Logan shook his head. "Freedom UK."

Shona snorted. "Please tell me they abbreviate that on the campaign posters."

"It's pronounced 'fook,' apparently," Logan replied.

"Haha! No, it isn't," Shona scoffed.

She turned over another photo. In this one, Oberon was not alone. They regarded it in silence for several seconds.

"Maybe she's his daughter," Shona proposed.

Logan turned over the next picture. "Fuck. I hope not," he remarked.

"Yeah, that would be inappropriate behaviour, right enough," Shona concurred.

This picture had been taken up close through the back

window of the parked Range Rover. The seats had been folded flat, and a blanket had been spread out in the bed-sized space that this had created.

The blanket was not the only thing that had been spread, either. The young blonde-haired woman who had popped up in the previous photo now lay on her back with Oberon on top of her. Neither one was fully naked, but they were well on the way, and the MSP's big hairy bare arse took up about a third of the image.

"She's noticed him," Logan said.

"I mean, sure, it'd be hard not to, what with him grinding away on top of her like that," Shona said. "Not the sort of thing that's easy to remain oblivious to at the best of times, never mind crammed in the back of a car, roomy as that particular model may be."

"No, I mean she's noticed the camera," Logan said, indicating the face of the woman in the photo. He'd thought her wide eyes and shocked expression had been related to the goings-on inside the car, but then he'd noticed that she was looking straight down the lens.

They turned over the other photos in quick succession, hunting for the next part of the story that was unfolding before them. It seemed, however, that this was the last image in the sequence.

Most of the others were quite damning in terms of Oberon Finley-Lennox's reputation and relationship, but that final one was damning in a whole different sense.

The woman, whoever she was, had spotted the photographer—presumably Bernie—at the window. From the look on her face, she was a half-second away from screaming. And not in a good way.

If she knew Bernie was there, then so did Oberon.

He would know that if those pictures were shared, then his dirty little secret would get out. Given his party's big push on Christian values, he would've known that the publication of these photos would've destroyed him. His career and his marriage would be in ruins.

What would a man like him do to ensure those things didn't come to pass? How far would a man like him go to protect everything he'd built?

"That's motive, isn't it?" Shona said, catching his thoughts. "Those photos prove that Shagger there had a motive to kill him."

"Certainly looks that way."

"What's in the other envelope?" Shona asked, fully invested now.

Logan took out his phone and snapped off a few photographs of the Polaroids spread out on the worktop. Once they'd finished here, he'd send copies of everything to the shared inbox so the rest of the team had the most up-to-date information to hand.

Pictures taken, he returned the photographs to the first envelope, then took the second from the briefcase.

This time, when he reached inside, he produced five sheets of A4 paper, all photocopies of the same handwritten letter. Logan squinted at the top copy, then passed it across to Shona to read.

"What are you giving it to me for?" she asked.

"You're a doctor. Sort of," Logan explained.

"So?"

"So, you lot have all got bloody awful handwriting. You'll have a better chance of reading that than me."

"I've got lovely handwriting," Shona objected.

"Aye? Well, maybe try using it next time you write something," Logan suggested. "Instead of that scrawl you usually use."

She gave him a dunt with her elbow, then turned her attention to the sheet of paper clutched between her gloved fingers.

"Can you read it?" Logan asked.

"Hold your horses, man, I've just looked at it," she said, then she went back to studying the page. "I mean, it's definitely in English, so that's a start. It's shocking writing, though. It's like he wrote it while drunk. And on horseback."

"Can you make out anything?"

Shona angled the paper away a little, then brought it closer. "'*We are surrounded by great...'* Something," she read. "Deceivers, maybe? '*We are surrounded by great deceivers. Hunted...'* or possibly '*haunted... by devils in four skins.*'"

"Devils in foreskins?" Logan asked. "What the hell does that mean?"

"No, not foreskins like on your..." She glanced at Logan's crotch, looked momentarily mortified, then blundered on through. "Not like on a *man's lad.* Like the number four. Devils in four-space-skins."

Logan gave this some thought, then confessed that he was still none the wiser.

"Ah, wait. It's about lizards. Apparently, lizards have four skins. Again, not... foreskins. Four, the number."

"Do they?" Logan asked.

"Does who what?"

"Do lizards have four skins?"

Shona frowned. "How should I know? I'm just reading the letter."

"Aye, but you're, you know, a medical professional," Logan reasoned.

"Of human beings. Anyway, shut up and let me read," Shona said. He started to say something, but she placed a finger on his lips to silence him. "'*I have tried to share the truth. I have...*' Jesus, what's that? Attempted? Attempted. '*I have attempted to open your eyes to the lies and the deceit,*' spelled wrong, '*of the lizard men who dwell both below and above. But again and again I am...*'" She screwed up her eyes and peered closer. "Jesus, now you're asking. '*Routinely derided,*' maybe, but that's a guess from context."

"He's using a lot of words to not really say much, isn't he?" Logan remarked, but Shona shushed him again.

"'*None are so blind as those who refuse to see, and you are wilful in your ignorance. And so, I take leave of my...*' He's scribbled out a few things here. '*And so, I take leave of my responsibility to you. I leave you to the lizards and the liars, and turn at last to my own needs. The guilty shall be met with righteous punishment. An eye for an eye, a tooth for a tooth, a life for a life.*'" Shona tutted and shook her head. "You're right. I feel he could've written this in one carefully planned sentence."

Logan frowned. "What, is that it?"

"No, there's more, but the writing gets even worse. Hang on." She studied the page in silence for a few moments. Logan picked up one of the other copies, scanned down the page himself, then concluded it was best left to Shona.

He'd just returned his copy to the pile when the pathologist started reading again.

"'*I take my leave of you. They will come for me, for what I am about to do. They will hunt me with their dogs and their...*' God. I don't... '*Birds,*' maybe. '*With their dogs and their birds.*'"

"Who will?" Logan asked.

Shona shrugged. "I don't know. It's not a play. He hasn't put a list of characters at the start. Just 'they,' I think. Whichever individual or organisation that have trained dogs and birds to hunt nutters."

"We've got dogs. The polis, I mean. Not so much the birds, though."

"Last bit. Here we go," Shona said, looking down at the page again. "'*I am, and forever shall be, guided by the light. I stand tall. Proud. Erect...*' Sounds like he's getting a bit saucy there. '*...before all who have done me wrong. This is my end, and the end shall be as the beginning. A life for a life. A soul for a soul. Death is coming. Slowly.*'"

Shona turned the page over, saw that side was blank, then handed it to Logan.

"So, you know, make of that what you will," she said.

Logan rubbed a hand across his mouth as he contemplated the contents of the letter. "Suicide note?" he pondered, though he didn't sound convinced. "He's talking about his end, and about death, and..." He shook his head. "No. It wasn't that. He was saying something more than that."

"Oh, he was definitely saying more," Shona agreed. "Christ knows what, though."

After taking some more pictures, Logan returned the photocopies to the envelope, and placed it back in the briefcase with the pack of photos. "Maybe I should head back down the road," he said. "Talk to the MSP."

"What? No!" Shona spluttered, her eyes widening in panic. She forced a smile, shook her head, then hurriedly tried to explain her outburst. "I mean... it's a long drive. You've been out and about all day, and it's getting late. You should stay here tonight. Well, not here in this office. But... we could go to yours."

Logan watched the way the lines in her face moved, and how her hands wrung themselves together. "You alright?" he asked.

"I'm grand!" She grabbed his thigh and shook it playfully. "Just worried about you, you big eejit. You don't really want to go driving down that road again tonight, do you? Ferry will be off, so you'll have to go the long road. And you'd have to go get Tyler..."

"Shite. Aye. Didn't think about that. Another three hours in the car with that bugger."

"At least!" Shona said. She scoffed at the very suggestion, then shook her head quite forcefully. "No, you're staying here tonight, and that's settled! And besides, you owe me dinner for taking fecking ages to open your side of the case."

"Wait. The case," Logan said. "That reminds me..."

He picked it up and checked out the digits on the dials. More often than not with combination locks like these, both codes would be the same. They didn't have to be, of course, but it was human nature for people to give themselves one less thing to have to remember, so nine times out of ten the numbers on both sides would match.

When they didn't, there was usually a reason for it.

He made a note of the digits - two-four-one on the left, then zero-zero-nine on the right.

"Two-four-one," Shona said, watching him write. "Isn't that like a formation, or something?"

"A what?"

"Like a football formation, or whatever you call it? Two-four-one. You know, like five-five-two, or three-one-four, or whatever?"

"Exactly how many players do you think are in a football team?" Logan asked.

"God, how should I know? It's an awful game. I want to say, like... fifteen."

"Well, none of those numbers add up to fifteen," Logan said. "And anyway, it's eleven."

"Well, I'm more into the Gaelic football, if I'm honest," Shona said. "Though, even then, I'm largely indifferent to the whole thing." She looked down at the numbers in his notepad again. "So, not that, then. Two-four-one. What about, like, a supermarket deal? Like, a two for one deal?"

"What would the double-oh-nine be, then?" Logan asked, then he jumped in before Shona could respond with her Sean Connery impression. "Apart from being licensed to scald, I mean."

"Oh! Oh! I've got it!" the pathologist said, jumping down from her stool. "Two-four-one-oh-oh-nine—"

"Twenty-fourth of October, two-thousand-and-nine," Logan finished. "It's a date."

Shona tutted. "Like, I had it a second before you said it. I want that on record. You might've said it first, but I figured it out before you."

"You did," Logan said, failing to mention the fact that he'd been leaning towards the date theory since she'd first opened the lock on her side and his had failed to match it.

"But what's it a date for?" Shona wondered, taking out her phone. She tapped the numbers into a search, and hummed quietly while she waited for the results to come up. "Right, here we are, so..." She flicked her finger across the screen, scrolling the page. "...absolutely nothing whatsoever happened on that date. Like, literally nothing except a new episode of 'Harry Hill's TV Burp.' I can show you a clip of that, if you like?"

"It'd be safer all round if you didn't," Logan warned. "More likely to be a date of personal significance, anyway, rather than some big event."

Shona nodded. "Or it might be something else entirely. Like a phone number. Or... part of a phone number."

Logan closed the briefcase and got down off the stool. "I mean, it's not impossible," he conceded. "But I'm pretty confident on the date thing."

"Speaking of which," Shona said, patting him on the chest. "I believe you were taking me to dinner."

She caught sight of her reflection in the glass panels of the door again, and had another bash at smoothing down her hair. Then, when she realised it was an impossible task, she shrugged and left it to its own devices.

"Probably best if we don't go anywhere too fancy," she suggested. "And somewhere without too many people. Or, if there are people, ideally they'll all be blind or partially sighted." She bent her head forward and gave herself a sniff. "But without the enhanced sense of smell they're supposed to have."

Logan smiled, picked up the briefcase, then held a hand out. She took it in both of hers and clung to his arm like it was a life ring on the surface of a dark unending ocean.

"I think," the DCI began. "I know just the very place..."

CHAPTER TWENTY-SIX

IT WAS after nine o'clock when Dave Davidson pulled up at the gate of the field that housed Westerly Wellness, his car's tyres practically glowing red with heat.

He had long since mastered getting himself out of the car and getting his chair out of the backseat by using the open doors for support.

Unfolding the wheelchair was always the most fiddly part, and given his current excitement levels, it proved even more difficult than normal to expand the chair to its correct size.

Once he'd finally achieved that, he flopped down onto it, shut and locked the car doors, then wheeled himself across the grass towards the gate.

Inside the field, someone who appeared to be Jesus of Nazareth was heading to meet him, an old-fashioned oil lamp held before him to drive away the oncoming darkness.

Dave reached the gate, and fought the urge to rub his hands together with glee when he spotted three women wandering from the main marquee to a smaller satellite tent over on the right. They were dressed in the same long white robes as the man making his way towards him, but their shoulders were bare and, frankly, they just wore them better than the guy did.

Based on DI Forde's description—"He's a dead ringer for Jesus"—then this had to be André Douville, the man who would ultimately decide if Dave was being granted access to the retreat. Dave had called on the way down the road, and been told that they usually didn't accept new arrivals out of the blue so late in the evening, but André had eventually agreed to meet him to discuss it in person.

"Good evening, mon ami," said Douville.

To the untrained ear, the accent would've sounded fine. To Dave, it was so bad that it bordered on parody.

He had spent some time in France in his late teens and very early twenties, and had picked up a fair bit of the language during his travels. This tube, on the other hand, seemed to have based his studies on the BBC wartime sitcom, *'Allo 'Allo,* and specifically the character of the undercover British police officer.

Dave did not fail to spot the irony.

"You are the gentleman I spoke to on the telephone, yes?"

"Aye, that's me," Dave confirmed. He held up his mobile and waggled it. "Impressed you get a signal out here. I lost mine miles back."

"We use satellite here. Expensive, but necessary, oui?"

"Ah, oui. Nous devons continuer à faire fonctionner les affaires, non?"

André stopped a few feet from the other side of the fence, looked briefly taken aback, then laughed and nodded. "Oui. C'est vrai," he said with a laugh, suggesting a deeper understanding of the language than Dave had expected.

Although, to be fair, it might have been a lucky guess. "I see you are in a wheelchair," he said, conveniently switching both subject and language.

"Well spotted," Dave said.

"Do you mind me enquiring... Was it an illness of some kind?" André asked, then he held up a hand to silence Dave before he could reply. He closed his eyes and tilted his head, as if listening to whispers on the breeze. "Ah. Non. An accident. You had an accident, oui? In traffic. A vehicle, I think."

"That's right," Dave confirmed.

"And... oh! It was terrible. So much noise. So much... so much *violence*. And pain. So much pain and suffering."

"Well, it wasn't exactly a picnic, I'll give you," Dave said. He saw an opportunity. "And, eh, that's why I'm here, actually. Sorry for landing myself on you out of the blue, but I've heard you work wonders."

"You thought I could help you to walk again?"

Dave laughed. "I mean, I wouldn't say no to that, if you're offering, but I was more thinking in terms of pain relief. I'm sick of taking the drugs they give you, you know? You've got no idea what's in them, and I'm not even sure the doctors know themselves, half the time. I reckon nature can provide all we need. Far better than chemicals can, anyway."

"Ah, bon. I share your sentiments exactly," the man on the other side of the fence said. "But, I'm afraid we have set arrival and check-in times. There are processes and procedures we must adhere to for the safety of our other guests. You understand, oui?"

"Please," Dave said, and there was a begging note to his voice. "I can do all that tomorrow. I just... I just need..." His voice cracked. Inside his head, he awarded himself an imaginary Academy Award for Best Actor. "I just need help to stop the pain."

The light grew brighter around him as André brought the lamp closer. It danced off the fake Frenchman's shimmering blue eyes as they examined the man in the wheelchair.

"Very well. Très bien," André said, opening the gate. "Though, I should warn you, there is an additional fee for last-minute bookings like this. Is this likely to pose a problem?"

"My employer's covering the cost, so it's not going to be a problem at all," Dave said, wheeling himself through the opening before the other man could change his mind. He glanced at the yurt that the three women had been heading for. "So, do we choose our own tents, or...?"

"Ah. Non. Your accommodation will be assigned," André replied. The gate creaked as he pushed it, then rang out an ominous *clang* when it closed. "And I think I know just where to put you."

Sinead sat cross-legged on the floor, peering down at the piles of newsletters spread out before her. She and the two constables had taken a short break to eat a couple of hours ago—microwave meals secured from the shop up the road—and had been hard at it ever since.

She'd noticed them both yawning a couple of times each in the last ten minutes. This wasn't really any sort of testament to her observational skills, though, as neither of them had exactly been subtle about it.

When Constable Suzi Tanaka yawned for a third time and threw in an exaggerated stretch, she decided to call time.

"You two should go," she said, leaning back. "You've been a big help. Thanks."

Constable Tanaka feigned a look of surprise at the suggestion, but her colleague, PC Chris Miller, bounced to his feet like he'd been poised waiting for Sinead to utter those very words.

"Aye, long day," he said, catching one of his ankles and pulling the foot up behind him to stretch his cramping thigh muscles. "We should definitely go home."

"You packing up for the night, too, yeah?" asked Suzi, getting to her feet and shaking the feeling back into them. "This can wait until morning."

"Hmm?" asked Sinead, whose eyes had already begun to drift back to the topmost newsletter on the closest pile. "Oh. Yeah. Yeah, I'll pack up shortly. Just going to finish this one first."

Suzi shot a look to Chris, who gave a firm yet subtle shake of his head. "You, eh... You sure you don't want us to stay a bit longer?"

"Haha! No!" Chris laughed. "Of course she doesn't!"

"Thanks, but I'm fine," Sinead said.

"She's fine!" Chris echoed. "She doesn't need us getting in the road. Especially when, you know, I'm back in at five tomorrow morning. Which is..." He looked at his watch, but it was late, and his brain was having none of it. "...just a few hours from now."

"Yes, it's all good. You've been a big help. Thanks," Sinead told them. "But, I've got it from here. Honestly. I'm almost done myself, then I'm going to head to the B&B." She glanced over to the corner, where Taggart lay on his back with his legs in the air, fast asleep. "They do take dogs, yeah?"

"Yeah, course," Chris said, keen to get going. "If they say anything, just tell them he's a police dog, and that we said it's fine."

Sinead gave him a thumbs up, then got up and followed the constables to the front door.

"And you're sure you're alright?" asked Suzi. "You know how to lock up?"

"Do I use the big key you told me about three times already?"

Suzi smiled. "Yeah. That's the one. You've got this!"

"We know she's got it," Chris said, practically dragging the other constable out of the station. "What we need to get is some sleep!"

Sinead waved them both off, then closed the door behind them. She returned to the room with the stacks of newsletters all laid out on the floor, and Taggart's tail gave a happy little flick, despite the fact he still appeared to be asleep.

She found herself yawning, and took a moment to click on the kettle that stood on a cluttered tabletop in the corner. Her hand hovered over a half-empty coffee jar, contemplating her choices. The jolt of caffeine would buy her another hour or so, though she'd probably pay for it by not sleeping when she got to bed.

Besides, for all she knew, she was already taking the piss a bit by bringing Taggart back to the B&B. Best not push her luck further by rocking up at the house after midnight.

She took a teabag from an open carton, dropped it into her mug, then wandered back to the piles of paper while she waited for the kettle to boil.

The stack that Suzi had been working through was closest. She stopped beside it, squatted down, and looked over the topmost sheet. It was from five years back, and much of it was dedicated to the proposed new hospital up the road in Fort William, which was apparently going to be a front for either a cloning lab or a series of gas chambers, depending on which paragraph you paid most attention to.

An article on page two listed all the people in the mainstream media who were under the direct hypnotic control of the UK Royal Family. The list included a few big-name news presenters and political correspondents, but also—more surprisingly—former *Really Wild Show* presenter, Michaela Strachan.

Apparently, for reasons best known to themselves, the royals had stuffed Michaela Strachan with explosives which, upon their command, would detonate, killing her and everyone within a fifty-feet radius.

Quite what Michaela Strachan had done to deserve such a fate wasn't clear, but there it was in black and white.

Well, blue and white. The ink used for this edition was a couple of steps down from navy on the colour spectrum, unlike most of the others.

Not all the others, though. She'd seen other editions with blue print, too. Three or four of them.

The water in the kettle roiled and rolled as the temperature climbed. Sinead took the blue-printed sheet and set it in a pile by itself, then went through the rest of Suzi's bundle until she found a second issue printed with the same colour of ink.

By the time the water reached boiling point and the kettle's switch clicked off, Sinead had gathered ten issues of the newsletter, all of them printed in blue. They stretched right back to the beginning, so some were written by hand, while others had been typed. They were all photocopies of an original document, though, so getting them done in colour would've been more expensive than the standard black on white.

Which meant it was a deliberate choice. There was some purpose to it. A meaning.

But what?

She laid the sheets out side by side on the floor. Spread out like that, the evolution of the publication was plain to see. The leftmost edition was written in messy but well-intentioned block capitals on a sheet of lined paper, with the title and date written at the top slightly larger than the rest of the text.

The next issue wasn't much different, just double-sided. Two further along to the right, Bernie had clearly discovered desktop publishing software, although he hadn't actually invested any time in learning to use it other than to create a logo of sorts. 'The Beacon' stood at the top of the page in an ornately cursive script. He'd drawn a picture of a lighthouse next to it, and some lines that were intended to suggest it was illuminating the title.

The rest of the text was, like the handwritten editions before, done in one big solid block that flowed all the way from the left of the page to the right, before dropping down onto the line below. The words were more or less a stream of consciousness, jumping from one subject to the next, and often switching conspiracy theories mid-sentence.

The world was flat, but it was also hollow. The world was all a simulation, but aliens walked among us. Anyone in power was a lizard, but also a robot.

And *Springwatch* presenter, Michaela Strachan, was still a ticking time bomb of death.

By the later editions, he'd discovered columns and subheadings. At first glance, this made those issues easier to read, but once you drilled down into the content, the whole thing was as indecipherably batshit crazy as before.

She stood and let her gaze wander across the pages. Aside from the ink colour and the rambling content, they had nothing obviously in common. Nothing that...

"Wait," Sinead said, and Taggart rolled over onto his front like she'd spoken his name.

Kneeling, she checked the first few issues. The date. The date was the same. A quick scan across the rest of the line confirmed that the publication dates matched on all of them. They'd all been put out on the same day, and were all one year apart.

Grabbing a few sheets from one of the other piles, she checked the dates on those. Those dates didn't match the blue-printed editions, and they didn't match each other, either. There seemed to be no pattern to when those other issues had been published, just the ones in blue.

Behind her, Taggart growled.

Still crouching, Sinead turned to find the little dog lying flat on the floor, the fur on his collar rising as his eyes went to the window, and the darkness that lay beyond it.

"What's the matter?" Sinead asked.

She reached out and patted the dog, and the growling abated. His eyes, however, remained locked on the darkened glass, and the moment Sinead lifted her hand away, the scruff of Taggart's neck began to rise again.

And then, she heard it, too—the scuff of a footstep on the gravel outside.

She froze solid, her outsides becoming a statue of ice, while her insides churned, and whirled, and spun. Taggart, either sensing her distress or terrified himself, commando-crawled closer to her on his belly, and pressed his shoulder against her ankle.

"It's OK. It's nothing. Don't worry," she said, though she couldn't say if she was talking to the dog or to herself.

Without moving from her spot, she tried to look outside, but with the station lights on the window had become a mirror that reflected a view of the ceiling tiles and showed nothing of the darkened world beyond.

Her heart was a hummingbird in her chest, fifty beats per second, *badabadabadabadabum*.

Taggart's ears twitched, and his growl crept further back into his throat. First his eyes, then his head shifted, like he was following the progress of someone as they made their way around the side of the building towards the...

The door. Had she locked the door? She'd closed it, yes, but locked it?

She cursed herself below her breath, not daring to make too much noise. Could she get to the door in the next few seconds? Without being seen? Without being caught?

She tried to logic away her fear—it was probably nothing, and even if there was someone there, so what? That didn't mean they meant her any harm.

But try as she might, her body wasn't listening. Her adrenal glands had drowned out all sense of reason, and now she was back in that farmhouse, back in that room, back on that bed with the monsters closing in from the shadows around her.

There was a knock on the door out front, and Taggart let out three high-pitched barks and the start of a howl, then rolled onto his back and pawed at the air like he was going to get in trouble.

She should move. She knew that. She should get up off the floor, go to the front, see who was there.

But she couldn't. Try as she might, fight as much as she liked, her legs were not for budging.

Another knock, louder this time. Sinead took her phone from her pocket. No signal. Of course.

The landline was out front. The radio, too.

She was alone in a strange place, with somebody hammering on the door.

"Come on. Get it together," she hissed, curving her hands into tight fists until her fingernails dug into her palms. "Grow up."

But growing up wasn't the problem. Sinead of five years ago would've had no problem marching over to the door and pulling it open.

Sinead of six months ago would've thought nothing of confronting the late-night caller, or of giving him a mouthful about sneaking around in the dark.

But that Sinead hadn't been on that bed, in that room. That Sinead hadn't gone through what she had.

That Sinead was an idiot.

There was another knock, and this time the door creaked open. Sinead's breath caught at the back of her throat. Even Taggart had frozen now, his eyes bulging with the stress of it all, his big tongue licking furtively across his lips.

Whoever had been out there wasn't out there any longer. They were inside. In here. With her.

"Hello? Is anyone here?" a man's voice called. Older, she thought, and some vague sense of familiarity made her rising heartbeat level off. "I was passing, and I... I saw the light on. I was hoping to talk to someone."

Sinead gritted her teeth and forced her legs to move

against their will. She stood, inhaled through her nose until her lungs were full, then tried to remember how to walk as she headed through to greet the late arrival.

He had been turning as if to leave when she emerged from the room at the back of the station, and jumped with fright when she said his name.

"Mr Finley-Lennox?" she said, recognising the politician, even from behind.

Oberon turned, looked momentarily surprised, and then a smile spread slowly across his face. "Aha! I was beginning to think the place had been deserted," he said.

"Almost," Sinead said. "We were about to pack up."

"We?" Oberon's gaze flitted past her to the room she'd come from. "Is there someone else here?"

Sinead had left the door open, so the MSP had a decent view of the inside from where he was standing. There was no point in lying to him.

"The others are going to be back in a moment," she said. "Would you like to wait a few minutes, or is there something I can help you with?"

"Uh..." He looked her up and down. "Actually, I think you'll do just fine," he said, then he closed the station door with a *click*. "You see, I'm afraid I have a confession to make."

CHAPTER TWENTY-SEVEN

THERE WAS something inherently amusing about a chip shop smoked sausage. The shape played a big part in that, obviously. The size helped. What really made Shona laugh, though, was the way it waggled about if you held it by one end, as she'd demonstrated three times now, in the past two minutes.

They'd swung by the Hilton Chip Shop on the way back to his place. Logan had gone traditional—fish supper, lots of salt and vinegar, couple of pickled onions on the side. Add a wee squirt of salad cream for dipping, and you had Heaven on a plate. Or, in this case, in a cardboard box that was rapidly being disintegrated by hot grease.

Shona finished *boinging* her jumbo-sized smoked sausage around like it was some sort of large mammal sex aid, and took a bite off the end that drew an involuntary wince from the man on the couch beside her.

"I'm not actually that keen on the taste," she said as she chewed. "I just can't resist when I see one, though."

"I was going to say you're such a child," Logan told her.

"But I'd have some serious welfare concerns about any child I saw waggling one of those big bastards around like you've been."

"Can I have one of your chips?" Shona asked, helping herself without waiting for his approval.

"You could've had chips," Logan reminded her. "I asked if you wanted chips."

"I don't," Shona said.

"Well, you're holding a chip now," Logan pointed out. "It's there in your hand, see?"

"Yeah, but I don't want it," Shona said. She tossed the chip in her mouth. It was hotter than she'd been ready for, and she had to keep it moving with her tongue as she spoke so it didn't get a chance to burn her. "I'm just eating it out of spite."

Logan looked down at the contents of her Styrofoam tray. Ignoring the big bite she'd taken out of the end, the tray contained one large, curved smoked sausage, and two pickled eggs that couldn't possibly have rolled into their current position by accident.

"You mean you didn't leave off the chips for the aesthetics?" he asked.

Shona looked down at her tray and frowned. "How d'you mean?"

"Well..." Logan gestured at her food. "Look at it."

"What about it?"

"You've done that deliberately."

She looked up at him, shook her head, then studied the tray again. "Done what? What do you mean? Is this supposed to look like something? Because if so, whatever it is, I don't see it."

Picking up the sausage, Shona took another big bite off the end.

"You must just have a dirty mind," she told him as she chewed. "Which, you know, I might be interested in hearing some more about."

Logan picked up his fish, dunked it in the salad cream, then took a bite. He chewed and swallowed before replying. "Actually, I wanted to talk to you about something."

"Shit. Are you pregnant?" Shona asked.

"No."

"Am I pregnant? Or... wait. You're not dumping me, are you?"

"What?" Logan shook his head. "No. No, nothing like..." He sighed. "It was just something that Maddie said. And then I was talking to Sinead, and she told me I should... That we should talk. About it."

Shona stole another chip from his box. "About what?"

"About... I don't know. About what happened."

"When?"

"With..." Logan shuffled around on the couch, which was suddenly lumpier and far less comfortable than it had previously seemed. "During the last big case. When you were..."

"Oh. *That.*" She waved her big sausage and made a sound like a deflating balloon. "Yeah, I'm fine. Nothing to worry about on that front. Like, at all. At *all.*"

"You sure?"

She made the same *pfffft* sound again and rolled her eyes. "I'm sure as *shoite,*" she said, really playing up her Irish accent. "I don't even give it a second thought. Or a first thought, even. There's not a thought about it in my head. What are we even talking about again?"

She laughed, but it was so paper-thin he needed none of his detective skills to see through it.

"Is that why you didn't go home?" he asked. "Because I wasn't around?"

"What? Haha, no! Get you all full of yourself, ye big eejit!"

"It was your first night alone, wasn't it? Since I got out of hospital," Logan realised. "Either you've been here, or I've been at yours every night since then. Mostly here."

He reached out for her hand, but she pulled it away. "It's not that," she insisted, her paper smile still fastened in place. "I just... I wanted to get ahead with the PM. That's all."

"You can talk to me."

"I am talking to you now. Look." She pointed to her mouth. "See my lips moving and hear the sound coming out? I am grand on the talking front."

"Aye, but—"

"Jack." She barked out his name, the smile falling away like a switch had been flicked off. "Can we just... Can we just not talk about it? Not right now?"

She fell sideways against him, and he put an arm around her shoulder, holding her in close. "OK. If that's what you want," Logan said. "But—"

"*Psssht!*" She put a finger to her lips. "Not tonight, alright? Just... just not tonight. Let's just be normal."

Logan plucked one of his chips from his box and dunked it in the sauce. "Do you do normal? If so, you've hidden that well."

Shona smiled. "OK, maybe not *normal*, exactly. But normal for us."

"Normal for us is me getting a phone call at the worst possible time, and—"

His phone rang, and he felt Shona tense up against him. Logan looked at the mobile that lay on the coffee table between the briefcase and Shona's laptop bag. The screen was lit up, but he couldn't make out the name on it.

"You should get it," Shona said, after they'd sat staring at it for a while. With some effort, she detached herself from him. "It might be important."

Logan sighed, set aside his fish supper, then leaned over and picked up the phone. "It's just Tyler," he said.

"It might be important," Shona reiterated.

Logan grunted. "Did you no' hear what I said? It's just Tyler."

Shona let out the first few notes of a laugh, then took a bite out of a pickled egg and nodded to the phone. "Quick, before he hangs up."

With a sigh, Logan answered the ringing phone. "Tyler. What is it?"

"Alright, boss?" came the reply, chirpy as ever. "How's it going?"

"It was going fine," Logan said. "What's happening?"

"Just got Harris to bed. Thought I'd check in to see what's happening in the morning."

Logan tutted. "And you couldn't have texted?"

There was a moment of silence from the other end. Logan heard Tyler take a breath, and could almost picture him puffing himself up.

Good on the lad.

"I could've, boss, but I decided not to," he replied. "Because I think you've missed something."

Logan frowned. "What do you mean? Missed what?"

"Well, I've just been in the shared inbox looking at the

photos and stuff you sent," Tyler continued. "And in one of them, you can see a computer screen."

"And?"

"And the X-ray of the briefcase is on there."

Logan pinched the bridge of his nose and sighed. "Get to the point, son."

"I think there's something else in the case, boss. Something you didn't take a picture of."

Logan frowned, then indicated Shona's laptop. "Can you get the X-ray we took tonight on there?"

"Mm-hm," Shona said through a mouthful of vinegar-infused boiled egg. She took her bag from the table, slipped out the laptop, and Logan watched her fingers dance across the keys like revellers at a rave.

"We're looking now," Logan said into the phone.

Shona said something, but her full mouth turned it into an incomprehensible mush of vowels and consonants. Logan got the gist from the way she presented the screen to him, though.

It showed the X-ray they'd taken a couple of hours ago, the boxy outline of the briefcase clear to see, along with the photocopied letters, the bundle of photographs, and the outlines of the envelopes containing both.

"I'm not seeing..." the DCI began, but then he stopped when Shona tapped a spot on the screen.

It wasn't obvious. Not right away. Whatever it was had been well-hidden in the image by the photographs on top of it, but there was definitely something else there. Something thicker than the other items in the case. A notebook, maybe, or...

No. Best not to get his hopes up.

"You spotted it yet, boss? Middle right. Looks a bit like—"

"Aye, I see it," Logan confirmed. "Good spot, son. We were looking for bombs, and clearly not paying enough attention to the details."

He heard Tyler puffing up again, this time with pride. "Cheers, boss. I was just looking through it, you know, and I thought, 'Oh-ho! What's this?' and then—"

"Aye, very good, son. Don't tell me anymore, though, I'm waiting for the TV adaptation," Logan said, cutting the story short. He switched the phone to speaker mode, then set it on the couch beside. "Hold on, we're having a look."

He got up, retrieved a pair of rubber gloves from the pocket of his coat which he'd dumped over the back of an armchair, then returned to the couch and sat forward to give himself easy access to the briefcase on the table.

They'd turned just one number on each dial of the lock to secure it again, so it took just a second to get the lid open. Shona cleared the food out of the way as he removed the two envelopes and set them down on the coffee table beside the case.

"I can't see any pockets," he announced, running his hand along the inner lining.

"Must be something, boss," Tyler replied, his voice echoing from the phone's loudspeaker.

Logan picked up the case and turned it over in his hands. There was a sound like something sliding, and then a faint *clunk* as it came to a stop.

"It must be stitched into the lining," Shona said. "Can't believe we didn't see that."

"Right, then!" Logan bounced to his feet and headed for the kitchen.

"Where're you going?" Shona asked.

"To get a pair of scissors. I want to see what's hidden in there."

Reaching into her bag, Shona produced a small leather pouch with a zip running around three of the four sides. She opened it to reveal an assortment of worrying looking implements, then presented Logan with a scalpel.

"Some of the tools they give me are proper shite," she explained. "So I bring my own from home."

Logan stared at the offered scalpel, took it, then stared at it some more before replying. "I'm not going to dwell too much on that for the moment," he told her.

He perched on the front of the couch again, opened the briefcase, and ran his fingers over the lining again, more firmly this time.

"There," he announced, as he brushed against something stowed beneath the silky fabric. He traced the outline, and felt a surge of excitement.

It couldn't be, though. It couldn't.

He was never that lucky.

He shot a sideways glance to Shona.

Well, *almost* never.

"Right, then," he said, adjusting his grip on the scalpel. "Let's see what we've got."

CHAPTER TWENTY-EIGHT

WHETHER BY ACCIDENT OR DESIGN, Oberon Finley-Wallace was blocking the door. This was not something Sinead would necessarily have noted a few months back. She'd have noticed, yes, but she wouldn't have particularly cared. It wouldn't have bothered her. It wouldn't have made her feel uneasy. Not like it did now.

He was quite a large man. Imposing, in his own way.

When she'd last seen him, he'd been heading out the door, his shirt crisp and immaculate, his trousers pressed with matching creases down the front.

He still wore the same clothes, but now they were rumpled and creased, his tie hanging slackly, his top button undone. One side of his shirt had come completely untucked at the front, and he'd made no attempt to tuck it back in.

The MSP was swaying slightly, though Sinead couldn't tell if he was drunk, exhausted, or some combination of the two. His hand movements were quick. Anxious. Fidgety.

He was smiling, and yet he was very much not. Sinead didn't know the man beyond the few minutes spent in his company that morning, but she'd put money on the fact that he was one wrong word away from bursting into tears.

"Are you alright, Mr Finley-Lennox?" she asked.

He shook his head and sniffed, then took a step closer. She took a step back, subconsciously maintaining the distance between them.

"Not really. It's been a bit of a day," Oberon replied. He was fighting to keep the emotion from his voice, resulting in the words coming out as a low, flat monotone. "Shocker of a day, really. And... I'm not even supposed to be here, I'm supposed to be in Edinburgh. But, well, I had to come back, and then I saw the lights were on, and..." He looked past her to the empty room beyond. "Are you sure there's nobody else here?"

"Well, there's the dog," Sinead said, really hoping that Taggart remained out of sight so that the MSP's imagination could come up with an animal far larger and more aggressive. "And, as I say, my colleagues will be back any minute. So, if you'd prefer to wait..."

"No!" Oberon cried, and the suddenness of it made Sinead jump back. "Sorry, sorry. I just... I need to get this off my chest. It's... I just... I need to tell you what I've done."

"OK." Sinead indicated a hard plastic chair tucked in beside the room's only desk. "Would you like to take a seat?"

Oberon shook his head and bounced from foot to foot. "No. No, can't sit down. Don't want to sit down. Just need to... I just need to get it out. I need to say it. Now."

He was on edge. Tense. His fingers, which had been dancing and fidgeting, now curled into fists in time with his breathing, like he was in the early stages of giving birth. In, out. In, out.

"Go ahead," Sinead urged. "I'm listening."

The MSP's head bobbed rapidly up and down in a series of fast tiny nods that continued for several seconds. "OK. OK. Yes, yes, right. Yes, I just... I just need to say it."

He inhaled deeply and suddenly, as if he was about to start shouting. When he did speak, though, it was in that same flat monotone as before.

"I... You see... I've done something. That I shouldn't. Have done." He repeated himself, but this time without the pauses, "I've done something that I shouldn't have done."

He was still in front of the door, still blocking the way out. A rivulet of sweat trickled the length of Sinead's spine. Her head felt light, her limbs heavy, just like they'd been in that farmhouse.

Just like they'd been on that bed with that bastard hanging over her, his hands working at the clasp of her belt.

"What have you done?" she asked, her lungs barely providing enough breath to form the words.

"It was silly. I... It was a silly mistake," Oberon said.

He stepped closer again, and when Sinead retreated she bumped against the corner of the desk and a knot of pain throbbed at the impact point on her thigh.

"Could you... Could you stay there?" she asked. It should've been an order, but it came out as a request. As a plea, almost.

"What?" Oberon looked down at his own feet. "Why?"

"Just... I'd feel more comfortable if you just stayed where you are," Sinead explained.

Why was she explaining? She shouldn't be explaining, but the words had come out on their own.

"I'm not going to hurt you!" Oberon laughed. It was a harsh, braying, two-note laugh that only made Sinead's heart beat faster. "I'm not going to attack you, for God's sake.

You're a woman! I love women!" He blew out his cheeks. "I mean, that's really the crux of it, isn't it? I love women. Too much, one might argue."

"Stay where you are," Sinead said. This time, it was an order, though there wasn't the force behind it that there should have been.

"Oh, don't be so silly. I'm a bloody MSP, for God's sake. I'm not a thug off the street." He moved closer, as if proving a point. "See? It's fine. I'm not going to do anything to you. I just... God. This isn't..." He pointed to the side of his head. "I'd rehearsed this, you know? Gone over and over it during the drive up the road. I had it all worked out, but then, I don't know. It's not easy."

He began to pace back and forth in front of the door. Sinead watched every step, anticipating each movement, bracing herself for what might come next.

"It could ruin me. I mean... if it gets out. It could destroy me. My career. My family. My whole reputation, everything I've worked so hard for, it could all go. I could lose it all."

"Mr Finley-Lennox, I think—"

His words came out as a roar. His legs kicked, propelling himself closer until he was within striking distance. "Will you just shut up and *listen*? I'm trying to say something. I'm trying to tell you what I've done, and you just keep talking!"

Sinead tried to draw back, but he grabbed her by the shoulders, pinning her arms to her sides. His face was all bunched up in fury, and the smell of expensive whisky suddenly filled her nostrils and nipped at her eyes.

"That's what you do, isn't it? You talk, and you talk, and you whisper sweet little nothings in our ears. A little flash of cleavage. A short skirt. A couple of cheeky remarks and you've got us eating out of the palm of your bloody hands, don't you?"

The moment he'd grabbed her—the moment his hands had clamped down—something inside Sinead had shut itself down. Tucked itself away. Hid, out of sight.

She may not have been drugged this time, but fear was having the same effect. She wanted to shrug him off, to push him away, to fight back, but her body refused. She felt like a bystander, watching helplessly on, unable to do a thing to stop whatever was about to happen.

"You want my confession? Here's my confession. The nanny. Margaux and Orwellia's nanny. I fucked her. Alright? More than once." He exhaled with such force that the air between them became thick with the smell of his breath. "There. I said it. It wasn't my fault, though, she was bloody parading around the place, giggling and teasing me. She *made* me. She was the one who wanted it, not me. She's the one to blame! But you lot, you'll use that against me, won't you? Because Bernie knew. Bernie had photos. And you'll make it look like I did it, like I killed him!"

The raised voice brought Taggart sauntering through from the back room. When the little dog saw the stranger pinning Sinead in place he exploded into a frenzy of barking and launched himself at Oberon's ankles.

"What the hell is...? Get off," the MSP warned, swiping at the little dog with his foot. "Ow! Cut that out, you little shit!"

He swung a leg more forcefully. Sinead felt the impact vibrate through him and into her as his foot made contact with Taggart's ribcage.

She heard the dog cry out in fright and in pain, then the *thud* and a second yelp as he hit the wall.

That part of Sinead that had been asleep was roused by the sight of the dog collapsing to the floor. The old her—the real her, the her from before—flicked open her eyes, dragged herself to her feet, and dusted herself down.

She raised a knee that immediately found its target. Or, to be more specific, both its targets. She caught a wrist before the MSP had a chance to bend double, yanked it hard, and then twisted it up his back. With a strangled cry, he lost his balance and she stuck with him all the way to the floor, the knee that had devastated his bollocks now pressing into the back of his thigh.

"Ow! Ow! Jesus, stop! Stop!"

"Don't you ever hurt our dog again," she hissed in his ear. "And next time you put your hands on me, I'll break them off and stick them up your arse. You got that?"

From across the room there came the sound of a throat being cleared. Sinead looked up to find Ben and Hamza standing in the doorway, staring down in wide-eyed wonder.

"Um... everything alright here, Detective Constable?" Ben asked.

"Aye, sir," Sinead said, and she smiled because it was true. "Everything's just peachy."

CHAPTER TWENTY-NINE

LOGAN AND SHONA stared at the document in the lining of the case, not quite able to believe it was real. There were lucky breaks, and there were lucky breaks, and then there was this.

They had been staring at it for almost a full thirty seconds before Tyler piped up from Logan's phone. "Hello? Still there, boss? Have I been cut off?"

"What? No. Sorry, still here," Logan said.

"Good stuff. Thought maybe I'd accidentally hung up with my cheek again. They really should come up with a way of stopping that. It must happen to people all the time."

"Just you, son," Logan said. He reached into the briefcase, and carefully took out the stiff-backed little burgundy book that had been hidden away inside it. "It's a passport. We've got a passport."

"Wow. Seriously, boss? Whose passport is it?"

Logan opened the book and flicked through pages until he found the page with the identifying information. A man stared blankly ahead from the photograph in the corner, face limp and devoid of all emotion other than perhaps the faintest hint of embarrassment.

So pretty standard for a passport photograph, really.

In the picture, he looked to be in his late twenties, although the passport had expired almost ten years previously, so that would fit with Bernie's estimated age. The date of birth put him as forty-eight. He was born in December, so would have been forty-nine in just a few months.

"It says his name is Alan Rigg," Logan said.

"Alan Rigg?" Tyler replied. "So, it's not the victim's, then?"

"Well, I didn't think his name was *actually* Bernie the Beacon," Logan said. "So, for all we know, this is him. I'll send a copy to the inbox in a minute, and we can run the photo by Uniform in the local area, see if they recognise him."

His phone buzzed, and a landline number Logan didn't recognise came up on his screen. The phone, clever bugger of a thing that it was, told him that the area code belonged to Strontian.

"Hang on, this might be Ben," he said. "I'll call you back."

He prodded the screen, ending one call and answering the other. Ben was in mid-conversation with someone when the call connected.

"Aye, well, I don't care if your balls are sore. You brought that on your— Hello?"

"Ben. Aye. I'm here. What's going on?" Logan asked.

"Oh, all sorts, Jack," the DI replied. "Hang on, I'll go somewhere private. We've got Mr Finley-Lennox here with us. Sinead had a bit of a run-in with him."

"What do you mean?" Logan asked, leaning closer to the phone.

"Nothing she couldn't handle. He came in here shouting the odds. Got a bit grabby."

"Jesus," Shona said. "Is she OK?"

"I'm fine," Sinead called from the background.

"Which is more than I can say for Mr Finley-Lennox's groin," Ben concluded. "Hang on..."

Logan and Shona listened to muffled footsteps, a door opening and closing again, then Ben's voice returned, a little more hushed than before.

"Right. Aye. So, we've got him on a drink-driving charge at the moment. He's three times the limit, and he drove here from Edinburgh. Half-bottle of whisky in the car. Says he came here to confess."

"To the murder?"

"Sadly not, no. To shagging the nanny. I think he thought his whole house of cards was going to come falling down around his ears, and wanted to get ahead of it in some way," Ben explained. "Backfired pretty spectacularly, I'd say."

"Aye, sounds like it," Logan agreed.

"Also, he kicked the dog."

"He did what?" Logan asked.

"What a dick!" Shona spat.

"Aye. Really stuck the boot in, Sinead says."

Logan slowly rolled his head around on his shoulders until the bones in his neck went *crick*. "Right. Well, should another opportunity to hoof Mr Finley-Lennox squarely in the Billy Bollocks present itself, you have my full permission to take it."

"It was a knee, actually, but noted."

"Is he alright?" Logan asked.

"He's moaning about the handcuffs and he's not a big fan of the testicle trauma, but—"

"The dog, I meant," Logan said. "Is he alright? He's not... He's not hurt or anything, is he?"

"Doesn't seem to be, no," Ben said, and it was impossible not to hear the note of amusement in his voice. "Why, you're not actually concerned about him, are you, Jack? You're not saying you actually like him, are you? Surely that can't be what I'm hearing, can it?"

"I'm just thinking of the vet's bill, that's all," Logan said.

"Sure you are," Ben said. "Got a couple of bits of news to share with you, too."

"Aye, same here," Logan told him, eyeing the passport. "You go first."

"That link you gave us to the van on Craigslist? Hamza got stuck in and managed to get the listing back. Somehow. Don't ask me. Anyway, he found a photo. The van's a bit of a shitheap of a thing. Listed for five hundred quid. Lot of rust. Wheel arches are nearly eaten through. I'd be surprised if it was road legal, although the ad says it is."

"Sounds like the van that supposedly picked Bernie up from Westerly Wellness," Logan said. "Did the ad show the plate?"

"No, that's blurred out. But we got the seller details. He's local, so we're going to pay him a visit in the morning. See what we can find out."

"Keep me posted," Logan said.

"Also, hang on, Sinead wants to tell you something she found. Something about a date. One sec..."

The line went muffled again. They heard the creak of a door, and a distant-sounding muttering that sounded like Ben. It was followed by an even more distant-sounding muttering that didn't, then the phone was handed over, the door was closed, and Sinead's voice came more clearly.

"Hiya, sir. Just a quick one, really. I was looking through Bernie's newsletters, and something jumped out at me. A date. Most of the issues were published at random times, but there was always one published on the same date every year."

Logan looked over to the open briefcase, and the dials of the twin locks. "Twenty-fourth of October, by any chance?"

There was a moment of silence from the other end. The sound of thunder being stolen.

"Eh, yeah. That's it. How did you know that, sir?"

"Lucky guess," Logan told her. "I'll explain later. I'm going to send a photo of a passport to the shared inbox."

"What? Bernie's?"

"The name on it is Alan Rigg," Logan explained. "But might still be him. I want you to run it by those two Uniforms down there. Or, better still, show it to the politician and see if he recognises Bernie from the photo. Might as well get some use out of the bastard."

"Send it over and I'll ask him," Sinead said.

"We've also got photos of him at it with the nanny. Well, I assume it's the nanny, anyway. I'll send those over, too, and you can use them to beat him with."

"Will do."

"And... you're OK?" Logan asked. "He didn't... He wasn't..."

"I took care of it, sir," Sinead replied. "It was touch and go for a bit, but I should never have let it get that far. My fault."

"Bollocks it's your fault," Shona chimed in.

"Aye, what she said," Logan agreed.

"Thanks. Either way, I'm fine," Sinead said, then she

neatly steered the conversation away from that particular topic. "Where did you get this stuff, sir? The passport and the photos, I mean?"

"Passport, photos, and a handwritten note from Bernie himself, no less," Logan said. "It was in the briefcase we got from the loan shark. The one he'd nicked from Bernie's caravan."

"And you don't think he's a suspect, sir? Bernie did owe him money."

"I don't know. Maybe. Not really feeling it, though," Logan said. "Mind you, they've had their run-ins before. Bernie failed to pay back a previous loan on time, and earned himself a broken wrist in the process."

"Definitely sounds suss, sir," Sinead said.

"Wait, wait. What?" Shona interrupted. "Who told you he broke his wrist?"

"Dinky," Logan said.

Shona shook her head. "I have no idea who or what that is."

"Little fella," Logan said, like that would be enough to explain everything. "He's like a... a dwarf."

"He's a loan shark dwarf?" Shona asked.

"Aye."

"He's a little person with a big stash of money? What, is he a leprechaun or something?" Shona asked, then she waved away her own question before Logan could answer. "Forget it. So, he told you that Bernie... what, exactly?"

"Broke his wrist?"

"Bernie broke the little fella's wrist, or...?"

"Other way around."

Shona sat back, blinked several times in a row, then

hunched over her laptop and started prodding furiously at the touchpad.

Sinead, who had been listening to the whole exchange, asked the question that had just come to Logan's mind, too.

"Eh, is everything alright?"

"Uh... let me get back to you on that," Logan told her, watching Shona scroll through a series of thumbnail images on her computer screen. "We're just... I don't know what we're doing."

"Aha! There. See?" Shona cried, double-tapping the touchpad. The small image grew in size to fill the whole screen. It was an X-ray that showed an arm from the elbow down to the tips of the fingers. "No damage. Not on that one, and not on the other one, either."

"What?" Logan joined her in perching at the front of the couch. "What are you saying?"

"These wrists have never been broken. Not a break, not a hairline fracture, nothing."

"Jesus," Logan muttered. "So..."

"So, either your money lender's lying," Shona said, indicating the X-ray. "Or that body doesn't belong to who we think it does."

"Teeth," Logan said.

Shona frowned. "Teeth?"

"His teeth. Did he have any fillings?"

"Um... His teeth were pretty badly damaged in the fire, but three, I think," Shona said, her eyes darting back and forth like she was consulting a report inside her head. "I'll have to double-check. Definitely at least two, though. Why?"

Logan stood up. He didn't intend to, but his legs hoisted him aloft all on their own.

"It's not him. The body. That's not Bernie," he said.

Sinead's voice crackled from the mobile. "Well then, that begs the obvious question, sir."

Logan nodded and looked down at the passport. "Who the bloody hell is it?"

Three minutes later, Sinead stormed into the makeshift interview room and thrust her phone into Oberon Finley-Lennox's face so suddenly he gave a shriek of fright and covered his head with his hands.

"I'm sorry! I said I'm sorry!" he cried.

"Oh grow up, I'm not going to hurt you," Sinead said. Behind her, Taggart gave a low, menacing growl.

"But he might," Hamza pointed out.

"Look at the screen," Sinead instructed. "Look at it."

Slowly, like a tortoise emerging from its shell, Oberon removed his arms from his head enough to let him look at Sinead's mobile, and at the blank, expressionless face of the man in the photograph.

"Do you recognise this man?" Sinead asked.

Oberon eyed her cautiously, like he was trying to figure out what she was up to. "Yes. Of course," he said. "I mean, he's younger here, obviously, but that's him. That's Bernie." He tore his eyes from the screen, then looked between the three detectives who were now assembled there in the room with him. "I mean... it is, isn't it? Or isn't it?"

"You tell us." Sinead moved the phone closer, and the MSP retreated further into his seat. "It's not a trick. It's not a test. It's just a question. Is this Bernie the Beacon?"

"Well, yes! Obviously!"

"Thank you," Sinead said, lowering the phone and turning away.

"You're welcome. But, I don't understand what—"

Sinead turned back. The look on her face snapped the politician's mouth shut. "Do not speak to me unless I tell you to. Understood?"

For a moment, it looked like Oberon might be about to burst into tears, but then he nodded and lowered his head, cowed by her words and the manner in which she'd said them.

"Good," Sinead said. She turned to Ben and Hamza. "Now, would one of you two mind charging Mr Finley-Lennox for me?"

With a final look back over her shoulder, she fixed the MSP with a stare and a sneer.

"I've got better things to do with my time."

And with that, she swept out of the room, with a starry-eyed Taggart trotting along behind her.

CHAPTER THIRTY

DAVE DAVIDSON'S night had not been what he was hoping for. He had spent it lying on a thin mat in a stuffy tent that he shared with one other human occupant, and eight-hundred-thousand hungry midges.

He wouldn't have minded so much if the other human occupant had been of the female persuasion, but Frank was a big lad with a loud snore and restless legs, who had come to Westerly Wellness to help get his digestive problems and chronic flatulence under control.

It had not been effective thus far.

The night had crept by slowly, with Dave made sleepless by insect bites, flailing feet, and repeated exposure to gasses he felt were either banned under the Geneva Convention, or bloody well should be.

Morning, on the other hand, had pounced suddenly the moment he'd finally managed to nod off. The light of it shone through the tent, peeling his eyes open, and then forcing them closed again.

"Fucking fuck!" he muttered. "Fucking, fucking, fuckityfuck!"

It was shortly after this burst of swearing that Dave sensed the empty space beside him where, for several agonising hours, a lumbering great oaf of a man had been. He forced his eyes open again, raised his head to check, and discovered Frank's rucksack not just empty, but neatly rolled and stashed in the corner. Or whatever the equivalent to a corner was in a tent as round as this one.

The yurt was a decent size—big enough for Dave to bring his wheelchair inside—which had made the other occupant's habit of moving endlessly closer in his sleep even more infuriating.

Dave thumbed the sleep from his eyes, stretched, and yawned. It was then that he heard the music—a soft and gentle lilting tune that may well have soothed him back to sleep were it not for the fact that he was desperate for a pee.

He unzipped his sleeping bag and several dozen midges flew out, full to the gunnels after the feast of their lives. They circled around inside the tent for a few seconds, then flew straight for his face and started devouring him again, prompting a fresh outburst of swearing and some frantic scratching that finally brought their reign of terror to an end.

With some effort, he clambered back into his chair, pulled aside the tent flap, rolled himself out into a crisp, bright morning, and came eye to arsehole with a man he instinctively knew was his bunkmate.

He wasn't sure how he knew, exactly. He had never seen Frank from this angle. He hadn't seen many people from this angle, in fact, and none of those he had were men.

Frank lay on his back, gripping his bare feet to better spread his legs. His robe was hitched up above his waist, so that his bare backside was fully exposed to the morning sun.

And, to his dismay, to Dave himself.

"Jesus!" the constable hissed, turning away from Frank's winking anus.

This, it transpired, was a mistake, as his gaze instantly fell on the arse of another man he had not yet been formally introduced to. This one lay parallel to Frank, but several feet away on Dave's right, so the view—mercifully—wasn't quite as straight-on and clinical.

However, the other fella—a man in his late fifties, was making eye contact with Dave and smiling, which somehow made the whole thing seem even more sordid. Worse still, this man sported what looked like an impressively powerful erection, although nobody but Dave seemed remotely bothered about this.

Instinctively, Dave turned away again. His gaze swept across half a dozen gaping arses—mostly men's, but a couple of women's, too—all aiming past him and upwards to where the sun was climbing up the sky.

"The fuck...?" Dave mumbled. It was a thought that had been building since he'd first rolled out of the tent, but which was only now finally finding its voice.

"Ah! Good morning, mon ami. Would you like to join us?"

Dave turned sharply to his left, grateful to have something to focus on that wasn't in danger of showing him what a group of total strangers had eaten for lunch the day before. André was pacing between the rows, his hands clasped lightly in front of his body, his robe swishing across the dew-dampened grass.

"What, flashing my ringpiece to the world?" Dave asked. "Nah, you're alright."

"Perineum sunning is an ancient Taoist practice," André

told him. He smiled benevolently down at a middle-aged woman with stretch marks on the back of her legs. "Excellent, Sandra. Wider, if you can."

With some effort, Sandra obligingly hoisted her legs further apart, and grinned hopefully, clearly seeking her coach's approval.

André kissed his fingers like a proud chef, then continued strolling and returned his attention to Dave. "The perineum—or 'Hui Yin'— is the gate of life and death. It is a gateway where energy enters and exits the body."

Dave's gaze flitted across the exposed rumps and raised legs. "You mean... the arse?"

André smiled, as if fondly recalling a joke. "Yes. If you like. It has many health benefits. It prevents the leakage of chi—or life force energy—from the body. I'm sure you can appreciate how important this is to physical, mental, and spiritual health, oui?"

"Oh, aye. Vital, all that," Dave muttered, copping another accidental eyeful of Frank's lightly crisping anus. Having spent the night breathing in what came out of the bloody thing, he couldn't shake the feeling that he was staring down the barrel of a loaded weapon.

"Just thirty seconds of sunshine—or prana—on the Hui Yin is the equivalent of a full day on the rest of the body. It regulates the circadian rhythms, increases your personal magnetism and auric field, and grounds you to the very Earth herself."

"That all sounds very important," Dave lied.

"And, as Tony is so ably demonstrating, it provides a boost to the libido, too."

Against his better judgement, Dave followed André's outstretched finger until he found himself eye to eye with the erection bearer once more. Tony smiled. Dave, for reasons he would later come to question, saluted.

"Right. Aye." Dave turned back to André and nodded. He felt like he nodded for quite a long time, in fact. He was working on the basis that the longer he nodded, the further back he could push the inevitable question he knew was coming his way again.

But, alas, nobody could keep nodding forever.

"Would you care to join us?"

Dave swallowed. "What, like..." He indicated the literal group of arseholes before him. "With this?"

"Oui."

Dave shifted in his wheelchair. "Am I no' better starting off slow? Like, with a massage, or something? Maybe just, like, some muesli and a singsong?"

"Aha. Non. This is how we start the day here. This is how we energise every morning."

"Come on, Dave," Frank urged, raising his head to look at the constable through his widely spread legs. "You'll love it."

"Yeah, come on, Dave!" urged Tony, his erection flapping as he spoke, like the tail of an excited dog. "It's seriously life-changing."

There was agreement from all corners of the field. Dave looked around at the smiling faces and arses, then glanced over at the road to judge how likely it was that he was going to be seen.

An old woman leaned against the fence a few hundred yards away, eating a banana and watching the show, but otherwise, there wasn't another living soul in sight.

"Ah, what the hell?" Dave said, sliding out of his chair. "In for a penny..."

CHAPTER THIRTY-ONE

SHE HADN'T WANTED him to leave. She hadn't said as much—she wouldn't—but she'd been desperate for him to stay in Inverness. To stay with her. To not leave her alone, not again.

But he couldn't stay, of course. He wanted to. He did.

But he *needed* to go. To get on. To unravel the mystery that had been niggling away at him all night since Sinead had got back to him to confirm that Bernie the Beacon and Alan Rigg were the same man.

When they'd uncovered that passport, he'd thought they'd identified their victim. Now, though, he wasn't sure what to think. It was highly unlikely that the remains in the mortuary were those of Bernie, Alan, or whatever you wanted to call him.

So, whose were they? And where was Bernie?

The accelerant used to burn both the body and the caravan was not an unusual mixture for wild campers to carry with them. Wild campers like Bernie himself.

But, a bit of reading had confirmed, the mixture of

turpentine and petroleum jelly was also popular among those living off-grid, particularly in the US. People who had shunned the rest of the world, and formed their own little retreats out of the way, miles from anywhere.

Retreats like Westerly Wellness, perhaps.

Logan and Shona had said their goodbyes, then he'd dropped her at the hospital. She was going to dig out Alan Rigg's medical and dental records and definitively rule out that the remains were his.

After picking up Tyler, the detectives had set off on the long drive back down the road. Logan had filled the younger officer in on everything that had come up the night before. Tyler nodded, looked thoughtful, and made appropriate noises at the important parts, before eventually admitting that Sinead had told him everything when she'd called him late the night before.

"She, eh, she had a bit of a run-in with that politician guy," Tyler said, and this time it was Logan's turn to act ignorant.

"Did she?" Logan asked, feigning ignorance. "How did that go?"

"Eh, alright for her, not so great for him," Tyler said. He was fiddling with his hands, and Logan knew something else was coming. "We, eh, we had a good long chat."

"Good," Logan said. "About...?"

"About what happened. You know. In that farmhouse. She said she wanted to do it face to face, but I think after last night, she just needed to say it, you know? Get it out. I think keeping it in was doing way more harm than good."

Logan thought back to the conversation he'd had with Sinead here in this car just a couple of days before.

And to the conversation Shona had talked her way out of having just last night.

"Aye. You need to share that stuff," he said. He side-eyed Tyler, who was gazing out of the window. They were passing Loch Ness again, this time in the opposite direction. The sun was shining. It was, to the casual observer, going to be a good day. "She going to be alright?"

Tyler half-turned. He nodded, but there was no certainty to it. "I mean... I hope so, boss. We're going to keep talking. I think maybe... I think maybe she'll need more help than I can give, though. Like... I think there's some stuff that might be hard to talk to me about. I mean, I'll listen, obviously, just... I don't know. There might be some stuff she doesn't want me to hear."

"Aye, well. We'll all support her, son," Logan said. "Both of you. Whatever you need."

"Cheers, boss," Tyler said.

He looked out of the side window again, and Logan made a point of failing to notice the way the younger detective ran the back of his hand across his eyes, or how he took a moment to steady his breathing before clearing his throat.

"But anyway, boss," Tyler said, bright and chipper once more. "What's on the agenda for today?"

"I was thinking we might solve this bloody murder," Logan replied. "You in?"

"I'm well up for that, boss, aye. You know me when it comes to solving murders."

"Well-meaning but largely ineffectual?" Logan guessed, earning a laugh from the other man.

"That's me to a tee, boss. Bumbling along, cheering everyone else on!"

Logan's eyebrows twitched downwards. Something about the DC's reply had struck a nerve.

"That's not you, son," he said. "Don't sell yourself short. Selling yourself short is my job. Yesterday, when we left Dinky's, you gave me some backchat. You became a lippy wee bastard."

Tyler adjusted his seatbelt and wriggled in his seat. "Aye. Sorry about that, boss, I was just having a bit of—"

"Shut up, Tyler, I'm not finished," Logan snapped.

"Sorry, boss."

Logan sighed. "What I'm trying to say—ironically, I suppose, given that I just told you to shut up—is that you need to do that more."

Tyler frowned. "Do what?"

"Put me in my place. Tell *me* to shut the fuck up occasionally."

Tyler laughed, then it quickly crumbled away into a look of sheer terror. "What? I can't say that, boss."

"Aye, you can."

"But... you'd kill me."

"I wouldn't. Well, I might. But take the chance every once in a while. I said you're well-meaning but largely ineffectual. And that's fine. I'm going to keep doing that," Logan said. He tore his eyes from the road long enough to shoot the DC a warning look. "But don't you ever agree with me, because it's not true. You are a damn good officer, Tyler. A bit... unconventional sometimes, and a massive pain in the arse, but a damn good officer. If I had to build the team from scratch all over again—if I had to start with an empty Incident Room and fill it with people I wanted working alongside me—you'd be right there on the list."

Tyler cleared his throat for the second time in as many minutes. "Oh," he said. "Eh... cheers, boss."

"Or, you know, on the back-up list, anyway," Logan said, his supply of sincerity all-but depleted. "In case any of the main ones dropped out."

"Still, that's pretty good!" Tyler said. "And you'd probably be on my list, too, boss, if I was in charge. You know, for making tea, and that?"

Logan smirked. "I'd be honoured, son. Although, I would gob in it."

"That's fair," Tyler said. "Am I right in thinking that if I try and tell anyone about this conversation, you'll deny it?"

"No. God, no, I wouldn't deny it," Logan said. "But I would have you fired and maybe, depending on my mood at the time, crucified."

"That sounds reasonable enough, boss," Tyler agreed. He watched the sunlight dappling the waves of Loch Ness, then looked out at the road ahead of them. "So, are me and you going to go solve this murder or what?"

"Aye, let's me and you do that," Logan confirmed, pushing his foot down on the accelerator as they rounded a bend onto a long straight. "Just, you know, mostly me."

CHAPTER THIRTY-TWO

THE STATION WAS a hub of activity when Logan and Tyler returned to it. Or as much a hub of activity as a building that size could really be. There was just the one landline, so Hamza had been left in charge of that, and had been making calls all morning, asking questions and following up leads, which Sinead then pulled together on her homemade Big Board.

Ben had spent the morning interviewing and then subsequently charging Oberon Finley-Lennox for driving while under the influence. They left the assaulting a police officer charge hanging over him for the moment, making it clear that it wasn't off the table. People tended to be more willing to cooperate if they thought their situation could take a sudden turn for the worse.

Following the interview, and with space at a premium, Oberon was told to go and sit in the store cupboard at the back of the station while they decided what to do with him. Many moons ago, the cupboard had been a holding cell for prisoners, but storage space had been a far more necessary resource, and so it had been hastily converted. It still served its purpose in its former role, though, if and when the need arose.

Like last night, for example, when the MSP had been detained, given a thin rollaway mattress to sleep on, and a bucket in the corner in case he needed a late-night trip to the toilet after the detectives had left for the night.

He had been back in there for an hour now, and had spent approximately half of that with his arms folded in indignation, and the other half sobbing quietly into his hands.

When the door finally opened, he raised his head and physically flinched at the sight of DCI Logan looming there in silhouette, like some kind of fairytale giant.

"You," Logan said, beckoning him with a crooked finger. "Out. Now."

Oberon hesitated, but only for a moment. Everything about the detective's demeanour told him that it was not in his best interests to disobey, and he emerged from the cupboard looking suitably cowed and crestfallen.

"Look, I just... I want to explain," he began, but Logan silenced him with a look. At least, Oberon thought it was a look, yet it landed with the impact of a punch to the face.

"You are free to go, Mr Finley-Lennox."

Oberon's gaze flitted to the front door of the station. From the look of him, he could barely believe his luck. "I can... I can go? I'm free?"

"Yes," Logan confirmed. He let the smile spread across the bastard's face just far enough. "You'll be contacted about a court date soon. And we're keeping your car."

Oberon's face seemed to change texture, like the fat

below his skin had all melted at the same time. "You're what? You can't do that."

"We can. And we are," Logan said. "We'll hold it until you can arrange for someone else to pick it up."

"That's... fine. My wife will come get it."

Logan sucked air in through his teeth. "I wouldn't be so sure of that. See, we spoke to your wife. Told her everything. She wants us to send her the photos."

"Because she doesn't believe you! She has faith in me," Oberon said, although it wasn't quite clear who he was trying to kid.

"Because she wants to give them to the press, I believe," Logan corrected. "She did not sound like a happy woman, Mr Finley-Lennox. She did not sound happy at all."

Oberon swallowed and smoothed down the front of his crumpled shirt. "Fine. I'll... I'll... I can call a taxi."

"If you've got a signal, aye," Logan said. "Our phone is in use. Important polis business."

"Well... no. Of course, I don't have a signal. Nobody has a signal!" Oberon protested.

"Ah well, I'm sure you'll figure it out. I hear it's a lovely walk," Logan said. He opened the front door and stood aside, clearing the way for the MSP to leave.

"It's miles! I can't be expected to—"

"Do us both a favour, Mr Finley-Lennox," Logan said. He wasn't smiling, exactly, but he wasn't *not* smiling, either. "Get the *Freedom UK* out of this station."

The not-quite-smile became a fully-fledged grin then. It showed too many teeth, and drew a little *cheep* of fear from the politician.

"You'll be hearing from my solicitor," Oberon squeaked, scuttling through the open door.

"Aye, well, maybe let him know you're facing six months and an unlimited fine. He might want to prioritise that," Logan said.

Then, before the other man could reply, he closed the door, turned back to the audience of detectives who'd been pretending not to be watching and listening to the entire exchange, and graciously accepted their applause.

Even Taggart, who had been lying under what passed for the reception desk, thumped his tail against the floor in approval.

"Do you know?" Logan began, shrugging off his coat. "I thoroughly enjoyed that."

"I think we all did, sir," Hamza said.

"It was his face I enjoyed the most," Sinead said. "The way it sort of collapsed when you mentioned his wife taking the photos to the papers."

There was some general agreement that this had indeed been a particularly good bit.

"Right. Anyway. We got an update or what?" the DCI asked, getting them back on track.

"Big Board's all ready," Sinead informed him.

"Good. Let's go over that, then." He pointed to DC Neish. "Tyler, go make tea," he said, then he turned and headed for what currently served as the Incident Room.

"How about you make your own tea, you big arsehole?"

Logan stopped.

Three gasps of shock rang out in the silence. Three pairs of eyes deftly darted in the DC's direction.

Under the table, Taggart lay very still, sensing the change of pressure in the room that suggested an oncoming storm.

Despite all this, Tyler stood his ground.

To start with, anyway. That soon changed once Logan turned on the spot to face him.

"Was that... Was that too far?" he asked, his voice a dry croak.

"What do you think, son?" Logan intoned.

Tyler swallowed. "I think... I think maybe I'll go make the tea, boss."

"I think that's a very wise decision," the DCI agreed.

Tyler rallied slightly. "But, just so we're clear, I'm only doing it because *I* want to. Not because you said."

"You tell yourself whatever you need to tell yourself, Detective Constable," Logan replied. "Everyone else, Incident Room. Now. Let's get this thing wrapped up."

"Right you are, Jack," Ben said, following along behind. "By the way, has anyone heard from Dave this morning?"

It was a common complaint, Dave Davidson was assured. That much sun, on an area that had previously seen so little? A touch of sunburn was always going to be a danger. But the discomfort would pass. The main thing was that he had opened himself up to a life-changing experience—literally—and his *Hui Yin* would never be the same again.

In hindsight, he quite liked his old *Hui Yin*, he thought. The *Hui Yin* whose itchiness wasn't driving him up the wall, and which didn't elicit a little yelp of pain every time he broke wind.

The accident that had left him wheelchair bound had robbed him of his strength below the waist, but not of all sensation. Previously, this was something he'd been happy about. Today, not so much.

It wasn't something he'd generally given much thought to over the years, his arse, but he was regretting that now. He felt he hadn't appreciated it properly. It had just sort of been there, steadfastly doing its duties, day in, day out, never complaining too much.

It had certainly never flaked before. Of all the medical complaints he had ever suffered from—and there had been plenty—a flaky arsehole had never been one that had so much as crossed his mind.

Fifteen minutes flat on his back in a field had put paid to that. Now, the flakiness of the region in question was pretty much the only thing he could think about.

He was not the first Westerly Wellness 'acolyte' this had happened to, and he almost certainly wouldn't be the last. It was so common, in fact, that André had created a special ointment designed to help alleviate the discomfort.

"A couple of dabs, and you shall be right as rain, oui?" he'd promised, as he'd handed Dave the tub.

Not one to do things by halves, Dave had elected to scoop out half the tub's contents, and smear the greenish-white gunk liberally over the affected area.

The relief was instantaneous.

And then, a moment later, it wasn't.

"Shit. Shit, shit, fuck, ow!" he hissed, scratching furiously at his sun-ravaged anus.

"Everything alright?" André called from just outside the tent.

"It stings. It's fucking... Ow! Jesus! What is this stuff?" Dave asked.

"It is made from nettle leaves," André replied.

"Fucking *nettles*?!" Dave yelped. "Why?!"

"It should not sting if you just dab." There was a moment

of silence from beyond the tent flaps. "You *did* just dab, like I instructed, oui?"

Dave stared at the half-empty tub in horror. "Erm…" he began. "Define 'dab.'"

Logan and the others sat back, tea in hand, while Sinead went over everything they'd pulled together in the past twenty-four hours.

There were now two main threads to the investigation—the identity of the body, and the whereabouts of Alan Rigg, aka Bernie the Beacon. One of those threads was far more developed than the other, although neither seemed to be nearing any sort of resolution.

"We've gone through Alan Rigg's history. No criminal record. No social media presence. Lots coming up on Google, but nothing so far that looks like it's referring to him. It's quite a common name, it seems," Sinead explained.

"If he's been hiding out here for a decade or more, it's hardly surprising he's no' all over the internet," Logan said. "Have we been able to track down any family?"

"We have, sir," Sinead confirmed. "His wife. She lives in Leeds. They both did, apparently, until he had what she describes as, 'a total fucking breakdown,' and upped and left. They're technically still married, though she says she hasn't seen or heard from him since."

"And she never reported him missing?" asked Ben, helping himself to a Rich Tea from a plate of biscuits that Tyler had brought in with the tea—entirely of his own free will, the DC had stressed.

"She did about ten years ago, but nothing was done,"

Sinead continued. "He'd basically told her he was leaving and wasn't coming back, so it wasn't seen as a priority and was never really followed up on."

"What prompted the breakdown, do we know?" Logan asked.

It was Hamza who fielded that question. "She didn't say, sir. No history of mental illness though, from what I can gather from his records. To be honest, his wife wasn't very forthcoming. I got the impression that she's moved on and didn't like having it all dredged up again. I didn't get a whole lot out of her. Thought it best to end it there and try again later." He shot a hopeful look in Sinead's direction. "I thought maybe someone else might have more luck..."

"I can follow up after this," Sinead confirmed, and the DS gave her a double thumbs-up in appreciation.

"Nice one, ta."

"Any other family?" Ben asked.

"The last his wife knew, his mother was still alive, but she's got no idea where she's living these days. We're trying to track her down, but it could take time."

"OK. Fine. Right, moving on. We been out to see the seller of that van yet?" Logan asked.

Ben told him that they hadn't, but it was on the agenda. Hamza had done a quick scroll through the lad's social media profiles and ran a check on his background. He had a handful of cautions for various minor but annoying offences, and a couple of charges for supplying Class B drugs. He lived over the water in Ballachulish, and was well known to the handful of Bobbies based in the station at Glen Coe.

"I can see him being difficult," Ben said. "Might have to slap him about a bit to get answers out of him. Metaphorically, I mean."

"I'll go," Logan announced. "You stay here."

Ben, who did not relish the thought of driving all that way, was quick to take up the offer.

"Deal," he said. "I'm sure if anyone can charm the truth out of him, it's you."

"I *am* a charming individual," Logan agreed.

"You want company, boss?" Tyler asked.

"Aye, but no' yours," Logan replied. "I've had quite enough of that for the moment. Stay here. Work the phones. Mind you, there's only one, isn't there? So, Hamza, you do that. Tyler, get out there and knock doors. Ask around. See if anyone else is missing. I want to know whose body it is we found."

"Right you are, boss," Tyler said. "I can do that."

"So, who's going with you, Jack?" Ben asked. "You've given us all jobs to do here, so who are you taking?"

Logan whistled softly. There was a flurry of movement from the reception area and Taggart came bounding in so quickly he wasn't able to stop in time to avoid colliding with the legs of the easel that currently supported the Big Board. It was only some quick reactions from Sinead that saved the whole thing from toppling over.

"Thought I'd get this idiot out from under your feet," Logan said. He sniffed. It was quite a complicated sniff. It was a sniff that said he really didn't want to take the dog with him, but—out of the goodness of his heart—he was taking one for the team on this occasion.

At least, he thought that was what the sniff said. But Ben, who had known the DCI longer than most people, saw right through it.

"That's very thoughtful of you, Jack," the DI said, suppressing a grin. "You might want to take a ball."

"I'm getting him out of your hair, that's all. I won't be *playing* with the bugger," Logan said. He looked down at the dog, who stared adoringly back at him, his tail thumping against the floor. "But, I suppose, if there happens to be a ball handy..."

CHAPTER THIRTY-THREE

THE SELLER of the van was one Leon Robinson, and he was, as Ben had predicted, a right wee dick.

He lived in a council house on Ballachulish's Croft Road, his overgrown garden, rusted metal fence, and scabby front door all working hard to bring down the overall tone of an otherwise lovely residential street.

The curtains were shut in three of the four windows, with only the smallest—the bathroom, judging by the dimpled glass—remaining uncovered.

What may, judging by the state of it, have been the world's oldest satellite dish sagged sadly from one wall, and Logan was sure he'd heard it rattling and creaking when he'd thumped on the front door.

It took several minutes of knocking and hammering to rouse the house's occupant, so when an irate, semi-naked twenty-something eventually pulled the door open, he made it three whole words into his angry outburst before Logan barked at him to shut up.

Leon, not fancying his chances with the ogre-like figure

on his front step, tried to close the door, but he was a scrawny wee runt of a lad, and Logan pushed it open again with the flat of one hand.

"I wouldn't do that if I were you, Mr Robinson," the DCI warned. He produced his ID and let the other man peel open his eyelids far enough to let him read the details. As he read, Leon took on the appearance and demeanour of a startled rabbit, albeit without the ears.

"What do you want?" Leon asked. "I haven't done nothing."

"Mind if I come in, Mr Robinson?"

"No. Yes. I mean..." Leon swallowed. "What's the right one? For you not coming in? It's just..." He looked back over his shoulder. "It's a mess."

"You surprise me, son. From the outside, I expected it to be a palace in there," Logan said. "I don't mind a bit of mess, though."

"No, I... it's not... I don't have to let you in," Leon said. He stood tall, but only for a moment. "Or do I? I should have a solicitor. I'm allowed a phone call. Can I make a phone call?"

"You're not under arrest, Mr Robinson," Logan told him. "There's a matter I think you might be able to help me out with. I just want to ask you a few questions, that's all."

"Oh! Right! So..." Leon stuck out his bottom lip and furrowed his brow, his brain working hard to process his options. "...no, then."

The pause that followed was a half-second longer than was comfortable. Logan needed that extra moment to swallow down his rising temper.

"I'm sorry?" he asked. His tone was light—joking, almost

—like he was assuming this was just some funny misunderstanding they'd laugh about in a minute.

Leon scratched his bare chest. He really was painfully skinny. Had Logan been so inclined, he could've counted every one of the wee nyaff's ribs. "I said no. I don't want to talk to you. You can't make me. I know my rights, so kindly—"

Logan sniffed the air. It was loud and theatrical, and cut short the younger man's reply. "Is that... is that cannabis I smell?"

Leon went all rabbity again. He didn't just swallow this time, he *gulped*. "What? No. What? Where? I don't smell anything."

"I do. Strong, too," Logan said. He jabbed a thumb back in the direction of his BMW. "Maybe I should get the dog out. He'd be able to confirm."

"Dog?! What, no!" Leon said, and from the look on his face, he was picturing a very different canine to the one currently curled up on the backseat of the car. A larger one, probably. With sharper teeth.

"This conversation can go one of two ways, Mr Robinson," Logan said, still managing to keep things light despite his growing urge to hoist the lad aloft by his face. "You, me, and the dog can all discuss this aroma of illegal narcotics that seems to be wafting out of your front door, or you can tell me about the van you recently sold to a gentleman over in Ardnamurchan."

This time, it was Leon who took a little longer to reply than was natural. "What van?" he asked.

Logan rocked on his heels as he eyeballed the lad in the doorway, then he shrugged and turned away. "Right. I'll get the dog."

"Wait! No! OK, OK! The van. Yes. What about it? What do you want to know?"

Logan about-turned, already fishing in his pocket for his notebook. "Everything, Mr Robinson," he said. "I want you to tell me *everything*."

Eleanor Rigg had been just as standoffish with Sinead as she had been when Hamza had called. Possibly even more so, in fact, given that she'd made it very clear she didn't want any further contact regarding the whereabouts of her estranged husband.

And yet, here they were again, calling her up, ignoring her wishes. She had a good mind to complain, she'd said.

And then, something had changed. The more Sinead talked—the more she empathised with the woman on the other end of the line—the less abrasive Eleanor became. And the less abrasive she became, the more she started to open up.

Five minutes after being urged to piss off and leave Eleanor alone, Sinead was chatting away to her like they'd been friends for years.

Eleanor and Alan—she referred to him exclusively by that name, and had never known him as anything else—had married quite young. They'd met at university where she was studying English Literature and he was doing Art History.

The wedding had taken place shortly after they'd both graduated. And it had been good. For a long time, it had been great. They'd travelled for a while, then they'd found an old fixer-upper of a house for sale in the north of England, less than an hour from where Eleanor's parents lived.

It was much further to Alan's mum's farmhouse down in

the southwest, and he'd been reluctant to leave her alone, as his dad had died a few years earlier. But she was a fiercely independent woman, and she had plans to move out of the old family home, anyway, so Alan had eventually made peace with it.

It had taken a few years of long days and hard work, but together they'd turned it into a home. There had been disagreements along the way, but never an argument. Not one, in all those years.

"Do you mind me asking what changed?" Sinead asked.

"Well... Lucy."

Sinead scribbled the name in her pad. "Lucy?"

There was silence from the other end of the line. Sinead pressed the handset to her ear. She could still hear Eleanor breathing, so the line hadn't dropped.

"You still there, Mrs Rigg?"

"Our daughter." The words were thin and fragile, like they'd been forced through a narrow gap.

"Lucy is your daughter?"

Another silence. This time, Sinead let it run its course.

"You don't know, do you?" Eleanor asked.

"We don't know a whole lot at the moment, no," Sinead admitted. "That's why we were hoping you might—"

"I thought... after everything on TV. I thought this must be connected to... Oh, God. You don't know."

"Know what, Mrs Rigg? What don't we know?"

"Please, just... Give me a minute," Eleanor replied, and it was clear from her voice that she was fighting a losing battle against tears.

While Sinead waited for the other woman to compose herself, she took out her phone, checked she was still connected to the station's Wi-Fi, then tapped the name 'Lucy

Rigg' into Google. A scroll through showed various social media profiles and an Etsy store, but nothing of any obvious interest.

"Lucy died. Eleven years ago," Eleanor said, battling through the pain that sentence brought with it. "She had an aggressive form of cancer, and she died. She was ten years old."

"Oh. Oh, I'm so sorry, I didn't..."

"She was a daddy's girl, was Lucy. And Alan, he... God, he adored her. When we lost her... I lost him, too. He became... different. Angry. I don't know. You could say paranoid, I suppose."

"In what way?" Sinead probed.

"He blamed her doctor. That's why I thought you were phoning, see? He said the doctor had been testing stuff on her. Like he had killed her on purpose."

Across the room, Hamza stood up suddenly, then had to scramble to grab his laptop that had been balanced on his knees. "Holy shit!" he cried, then he remembered Sinead was on the phone and winced in apology.

Sinead shot him a questioning smile, and he hurried over to where she was sitting, turning his laptop screen so she could see it. A photograph of a sombre-looking black man in a long white coat took up a chunk of a webpage. The caption below gave his name as Dr Ekon Oboko.

Something about him was familiar, Sinead felt, like she'd met him, or...

"When I saw the stuff on the TV. On the news. I thought... it couldn't be a coincidence. It just... it couldn't."

The TV. God. The TV. That's where she knew him from. That's where she'd seen him. He'd been at the press conference. He and his wife together. They'd made the appeal.

"She's the same age as Lucy was when we lost her," Eleanor said, her voice breaking into a sob. "Alan's taken her, hasn't he? Alan's taken Dr Oboko's little girl!"

Logan was traipsing through a field, watching Taggart go sniffing excitedly through the undergrowth, when the call came through. It was another conference call, and he could hear at least three voices all trying to talk to him at the same time.

"Right, right, one at a time, for Christ's sake," he said. "What's happened?"

He heard Sinead say, "You go," then Hamza's voice came on.

"I've been digging a bit deeper into Alan Rigg's record, sir," he said. "Got CID in Inverness to do a full report in HOLMES. Turns out, he's got an outstanding warrant."

"For what?"

"For assaulting the doctor who was treating his daughter before she died."

Logan stopped walking. The ground beneath him was wet and muddy, but since moving north from Glasgow he had long since given up hope of keeping his boots clean.

"Go on," he said, sensing there was much more to come.

"He blamed the doctor for his daughter's death. Said it was deliberate. Said he had been doing tests on her, and that's what had killed her, not the cancer."

"And?" Logan urged.

Sinead took over, clearly sharing the DCI's impatience.

"The doctor is the father of that girl that's missing down south, sir. Jameelah Oboko. She's been all over the news."

"I've seen her, aye," Logan confirmed, the hair on the back of his neck standing on end.

"She's the same age as Alan Rigg's daughter was when she died," the Detective Constable continued. "Alan Rigg—Bernie—his wife thinks he's behind it. She thinks that he's taken the girl as revenge."

"Jesus," Logan muttered.

"You get anywhere on the van, Jack?" That was Ben, jumping into the gap in the conversation. "Because, if it can help us find the bugger..."

"Aye. I got the reg. Going to text it through. I wouldn't waste your time with the DVLA, though. Let's just say the seller wasn't exactly doing things above board when it came to paperwork. I've told him to expect a visit from Uniform to follow up on that."

"ANPR cameras might get a hit," Ben suggested.

"Aye, hopefully," Logan agreed. "Run it and we'll see. I'm heading back now. Should be there in about an hour. Log this with the team running the investigation in England, will you? They should know."

"Will do, sir," Hamza confirmed.

Logan whistled, drawing Taggart's attention. The dog came bounding back to him, tail spinning in circles so it looked like it was propelling him across the grass.

"And get me a number for the DCI leading the case down there," Logan said, as Taggart skidded to a stop beside him. "I think it's time that he and I had a little chat."

CHAPTER THIRTY-FOUR

TYLER OPENED the front door to Strontian Police Station, wiped his feet on the mat, then announced his presence by proclaiming, "Well, that was a complete waste of time."

He entered their improvised Incident Room, hung his jacket on the back of the door, then had a sniff of his armpits.

"Warm out there," he said. "Especially when you're walking miles going door to door. Why can't people just live closer together?"

He realised then that nobody was listening to him. Sinead was adding reams of information to the Big Board, Hamza sat typing away on his laptop, while Ben was talking on the phone.

"Did I miss something?" Tyler asked. "Has something happened?"

The door behind him was thrown open, and he had to dart out of its path to avoid being splattered against the wall.

Taggart ran into the room first, his whole body *thrumming* with excitement, his tail swinging so wildly he was walloping himself with it over and over again.

Logan came through a moment later, his coat off, and his sleeves rolled up like he meant business. Either that, or he, too, was feeling the heat.

"Alright, boss?" Tyler looked from the DCI to the other detectives. "I think something's happening."

"Where the hell have you been?" Logan demanded.

Tyler blinked. "I was... You told me to do door-to-door."

"Oh. Aye. Anything?"

"Total waste of time, boss. Half of them thought I was a Jehovah's Witness." His brow furrowed, like he was being haunted by a troubling memory. "And one older woman said I was late, then started taking her kit off. I think... I think she might've thought I was a prostitute."

"That's a fine bit of deduction there, son," Logan told him.

Hamza looked up from the laptop. "Well, while you've been hooring and touring it around out there, some of us have been making real progress."

"Aye?" Tyler gave a self-deprecating laugh. "Maybe you should send me away to do pointless stuff more often. Clearly, I'm a jinx."

Logan fixed him with a solemn look of reproach. Tyler shrunk for a moment, nodded, then turned back to Hamza.

"I mean... go fuck yourself." He winked up at Logan, but it was clear from the DCI's face that his retort hadn't quite hit the mark. "Go fuck yourself, *Sergeant*?" He shook his head and shrugged. "I'll be honest, I'm not sure I'm going to get the hang of this, boss."

"You can work on it," Logan instructed. He started to close the door, then stopped when the two uniformed constables arrived in the reception area, and beckoned them both inside.

"Morning, all," said Constable Tanaka. "We were out by Sanna beach."

PC Miller interjected. "Aye, not for... We weren't surfing or anything. We were on a call-out, she means."

"What? Aye. We were at a call out. Came as quickly as we could."

"Fine. I don't care. You're here now, so find a spot," Logan urged, then he shut the door behind them.

Tyler took a seat next to Hamza, who was still staring at him in shock. "What the hell was that about?" asked the DS.

"What was what about?"

"You telling me to go fuck myself."

"Oh, *that!*" Tyler replied in a whisper. "Just... the boss told me to have a bit more confidence in my own abilities. To be my own cheerleader, sort of thing. I mean, he didn't use those words, exactly, but that was the general gist of it."

Hamza considered this. "And how does, 'Go fuck yourself, Sergeant,' help on that front?"

"Well, I mean..." Tyler began, but the rest of the sentence eluded him. Instead, he indicated Sinead and the Big Board with a nod. "What's happening?" he asked. "Looks major."

"It is," Hamza confirmed, but before he could go any further, Sinead turned from the board and, for the benefit of the constables, detective, and otherwise, she provided a quick recap that brought everyone in the room up to date on the death of Alan Rigg's daughter, the missing Jameelah Oboko, and the very real possibility that those two things were connected.

And the information didn't stop there.

"Got an ANPR ping on the vehicle already," she said, and Logan's ears practically pricked up.

"We have? Where?"

"M6, just south of Penrith. Headed north," Sinead said. She anticipated the next question, too. "Four days ago. The day Jameelah was taken."

"Well, that all-but confirms it, then," Logan said. "Bernie—Alan, I mean—he must've taken the girl."

"We've got the search still running for the plate," Hamza said. "If it's been picked up anywhere else, we should know in a couple of hours. And we've got eyes peeled for it all over the country. The team down south are going to put out Alan's name and photograph, as well as the reg and description of the van in a new appeal. If he's still driving it, we'll get him."

"I just hope we're not too late," Ben said. He shook his head. "That poor girl."

At the back of the room, Constable Miller and Constable Tanaka swapped looks. They both tilted their heads, each encouraging the other to be the one to interrupt, until Suzi got fed up with this and just blurted it out.

"Oh, for God's sake. Sorry to interrupt, and everything, but... van?"

The detectives all turned her way. Even Taggart looked up at her, although he was mostly just following the crowd.

"Uh, yes," Sinead confirmed. "We believe Bernie—Alan—was driving a van."

The constables swapped glances again. "White van? Shitheap of a thing? Rust on the wheel arches?"

"Aye," Logan said. "Like that. Why?"

Now that the hard work of interrupting the briefing had been done, Constable Miller swooped in to steal all the glory. "Our call-out to Sanna Bay, it was for an abandoned vehicle.

Down an embankment at the side of the track, hidden by bushes."

Logan pointed to Hamza and clicked his fingers. The DS took his cue and read out the number plate of Alan Rigg's recently acquired vehicle.

"Aye. That's it," Constable Tanaka confirmed.

"Should you not check your notepad?" asked PC Miller.

"I don't need to check my notepad, Chris, I can remember things that happened in the very recent past," Suzi replied. "And that's the right reg."

It was only when she turned away from her colleague that she realised everyone else in the room was now on their feet and staring at her.

"The van? You saw the van?" Logan asked.

"Yes."

"You've seen *this* van? The van we're after? The van we've got half the bloody polis in the country out hunting for?"

Constable Tanaka shifted her weight from foot to foot. "Well, I mean, we didn't know you were looking for it until now."

"I was going to say something about it earlier," PC Miller interjected.

"What? No you weren't!" his partner protested.

"Right, right, shut up!" Logan barked. "Hamza, map."

Hamza's fingers danced across his computer keyboard, then he turned the screen to reveal a Google Map of the area.

"Where is it?"

"Just south of Sanna Bay," Constable Tanaka said. "A bit before you get to... I don't know how to pronounce it. Portu-airk. *Portu-airik*. Something like that."

"On the map. Point!" Logan told her.

"Oh, sorry. It's..." Her finger circled above the screen as she tried to pinpoint the location. "There. Wait, no, that's miles away. There."

Logan bent and studied the map. The area she had pointed to was more or less due north of Westerly Wellness. Two or three miles if you didn't mind getting your feet wet, but far longer by road. It wasn't all that far away from the MSP's house, either, although in almost the opposite direction.

"What's around there?" Logan asked.

"Not a lot, really. Nice bit of shoreline," Constable Miller said. "Couple of houses. There's a dog that knocks about. Collie, I think. Friendly enough."

Logan shot the officer a disparaging look, and addressed his partner, instead. "We need to either get out there, or phone those houses. See if they've seen Bernie, or a girl. For all we know, he's holed up in one of them."

"We did that already," Constable Tanaka said. "Everyone came out to see what the fuss was about, and we asked if anyone had seen anything unusual. Anyone leaving the van, or whatever. Nobody saw anything."

"What about the van itself?" asked Ben. "I'm assuming you checked inside?"

"Yeah. Doors weren't locked," the constable confirmed. "No sign of anyone inside. Though, there was a blanket in the back. We thought maybe for a dog, but..."

Logan turned away and jabbed a finger at no one detective in particular. "Get Palmer out there. Helicopter the bastard down if necessary. I want him to comb that van from bumper to bumper. I want to know if the girl was in there, when, and what condition she was in."

"On it, sir," Hamza announced, reaching across the desk for the phone.

"So, eh, do you want us to cancel the recovery vehicle?" asked PC Miller.

Logan almost managed to stop himself rolling his eyes. "Yes, son. Cancel the bloody recovery vehicle."

"It's just... if he's already on the way, we'll still have to pay the call-out charge, so I wasn't sure..." The ferocity of Logan's glare killed the words dead in his throat. "I'll cancel the recovery vehicle," he announced, then he gestured to DS Khaled. "But I'll have to wait until he's off the phone."

"You could go use the phone in the shop," Constable Tanaka suggested. "We sometimes do that if this one isn't working," she told the detectives. "Which happens a fair bit."

"Just get it done!" Logan ordered, and Constable Miller hurriedly scarpered out of the room.

Sinead, meanwhile, was bending over the desk, studying the map on the screen. Hamza had dropped a marker pin on the spot that Suzi had pointed to, and a quick zoom in on the area revealed nothing much of interest.

"There's nothing else there?" she asked. "Just those few houses?"

"Yeah, that's it," the PC confirmed. "Most of the people who go out that way are walkers. It's the start of a pretty popular trek along the shore. Bit strenuous for my liking, but the tourists like it."

"Right, well, we need to focus the search around where the van was found," Logan instructed. "I want extra manpower brought in for this. Area's far too big for us to cover with just us lot, so—"

"This walk," said Tyler, raising his voice to be heard above the DCI's barked orders. "Where does it go?"

For a moment, Logan looked like he might unhinge his jaws and bite Tyler's head clean off his shoulders, but then he snapped his head in Suzi's direction.

"Eh, just by the shore, like I say."

"Up or down?" Tyler asked.

"He means north or south?" Sinead translated.

"South," Constable Tanaka said. She drew a squiggly line with her finger on the screen. "Sort of along here and down there, I think. As I say, I've never done it. But I think it ends at—"

"The lighthouse," said Sinead, her gaze racing ahead of the wandering finger. "It ends at the lighthouse?"

"Yeah. Round about there."

Sinead and Logan locked eyes, and both spoke at the same time.

"It's locked up."

"There's nobody there."

"It's bloody perfect."

"Mind filling us in here, Jack?" Ben asked.

Logan grabbed for his coat. "The lighthouse is covered in scaffolding. It's meant to be having work done, but there's some sort of industrial dispute going on. So it's locked, and it's empty, and it's walking distance from where he dumped his van."

"God. Aye. Aye, it's perfect. He's got to be there, surely?"

"I want a helicopter," Logan barked.

Hamza hung up the phone, announced that Palmer's team had been notified about the car, then immediately started dialling again just as a breathless PC Miller sidled back into the room.

"Chopper could take a while to get here, Jack," Ben

pointed out. "Even if it's available, we're talking over an hour, maybe two."

Logan wheeled around to face the two Uniforms, who both drew back like vampires caught out by the sun.

"You two, how long to drive out there with the foot down and the sirens on?"

Constable Miller blew out his cheeks. He was lightly sweating from his sprint to and from the shop. "An hour and twenty, maybe."

"Nah, less than that," PC Tanaka said. "An hour and ten."

"No way you're doing it in an hour and ten. I've never done it in less than an hour and twenty."

"That's because you drive like you're a hundred years old."

Logan ejected a guttural, animalistic sound that silenced them both. "You two take lead. Full sirens until we're close enough that the bastard might hear us, then cut them," he instructed. "Tyler, Sinead, you're with me. Hamza, keep working on that helicopter. I want it here on standby if we need to get the girl to hospital."

Hamza gave a thumbs up and pointed to the phone earpiece to indicate that he was listening to someone on the other end.

Logan clapped his hands and ushered the Uniforms out of the room, then practically shoved Sinead and Tyler out after them.

"Be careful, Jack," Ben urged. "Keep us posted, best you can."

Logan acknowledged the DI's concern with a nod, then pulled on his coat and went striding across the car park after the others.

Tyler was up front in the passenger seat of the BMW, with Sinead sitting directly behind him. When Logan climbed in and shut the door, Taggart let out an excited *woof* from the back.

"How the...?" Logan asked, turning to look over his shoulder. "How did the bloody dog get in?"

"Don't know, sir. He just sort of appeared."

Logan muttered something, then fired up the engine. Across the car park, the polis 4x4 roared into life, its sirens breaking into a piercing scream.

"Are you going to throw up on this road?" Logan asked, turning to the DC sitting beside him.

"Hopefully not, boss," Tyler replied.

Logan glowered. "Let's try that again, son. Are you going to throw up on this road?"

"Eh... no, boss. I'm not."

"That's more like it," Logan said, then he gave a blast of his horn to encourage the other vehicle to move.

As soon as it had, he floored the accelerator, and the BMW went tearing out of the car park in a cloud of fumes and gravel.

CHAPTER THIRTY-FIVE

IT WAS FIFTY MINUTES LATER, and Tyler had been true to his word. But only just. Every hump in the road, every sudden twist and bend, had elicited a noise, or a flinch, or a gasped, "Fuck!"

They had gone tearing up the road far faster than Logan and Sinead had done it a couple of days before, the sirens of their escort forcing any oncoming traffic to divert into laybys in order to let them past.

The speed, while helping them get there sooner, was doing Tyler's stomach no favours, at all. Or, for that matter, anyone else's.

"Why did they do this?!" Tyler wailed, after a particularly twisted chicane that had forced him to swallow down something that had been pretty damn adamant about coming up. "Why would anyone build a road like this on purp—?"

The rest of the sentence was cut off by a *hwurk*, a, "Jesus Christ!" and a clamped hand across his mouth.

The other detectives had offered words of support for the first twenty minutes of the journey, albeit in their own very different styles. Now, though, they were both so focused on not throwing up themselves that they frankly didn't have time for Tyler's shit, so nobody offered a response.

"How far now?" Logan asked, stealing a glance in his rearview mirror at a decidedly green-looking Sinead in the back.

Her side window was open, and Taggart sat in her lap, letting the fast-moving air ruffle his ears and flap his tongue around. He, unlike every other bugger in the car, was having a thoroughly lovely time.

"Not sure," Sinead said. It was safer to speak in short, staccato sentences, she and the DCI had both found. It limited the opportunity for anything to... escape. "Can't be far," she offered, although she knew this was probably just wishful thinking.

The polis car flung itself around a bend up ahead, and was lost out of sight behind a stack of hay bales bound and rolled in purple plastic. Tyler hissed and braced himself for the turn, then let out a cry of fright when they took the corner to find the 4x4 stopped in the road just ahead of them.

"Brakes, brakes, brakes!" he howled, despite the fact that the BMW's tyres were already screeching, leaving four slug trails of melted rubber on the road behind them.

There was a thump from the back, and quite an annoyed sounding yelp from Taggart.

"He's fine!" Sinead announced, as the car jerked to a halt just inches from the vehicle in front.

It was only then, once the initial panic of the emergency stop was over, that they realised the reason they had been forced to stop.

Sheep. Scores of them. Hundreds, maybe. They flocked

across the road and onto the embankments on either side, penned in by the fences of the fields.

Logan blasted his horn and leaned out of the window. "Get them shifted!"

Constable Tanaka leaned out of the driver's side window of the 4x4 and called back. "Not sure I can, sir. There's loads of them."

"I can see there's fu—" Logan began, then he decided that actions spoke louder than words. Throwing himself out of the car, he charged the sheep, clapping his hands to scare them away.

It worked. To an extent. The sheep moved away, though not as quickly as he would've liked, and not in any of the directions he'd have chosen.

The problem was the fences of the fields on either side. They were too high for the animals to jump over, and they formed a narrow passageway which allowed them only two directions of travel—towards the cars, or away from them. Given the sheer mass of the flock, and its relatively lumbering pace, it could take hours to clear the buggers. Hours that they or Jameelah Oboko may not have.

"What do we do, boss?" asked Tyler, stumbling up behind him. He was a deathly shade of white, but looked relieved to be back on solid ground.

Logan looked down and around at the impassable mass of sheep. He looked over to where Constables Tanaka and Miller were vaguely trying to shepherd them out of the way, well aware that they were fighting a losing battle.

And then, he looked ahead, along the road, to where the top of a white marquee tent was just visible over the crest of a hill.

"Taggart, no!"

Sinead made a grab for the dog, but he was too fast. He launched himself towards the sheep, barking and yipping his hairy wee head off. Tyler tried to catch him, but the dog dodged the grasping hands and vanished between the legs of the closest sheep.

The world erupted into a chaos of bleated cries and stamping hooves. The sheep, which had been forming one big knot on the road, now started shooting off in all directions like sparks from a Catherine Wheel. This did not make it easier to drive past them. Quite the opposite, in fact. Penned in by the fences, they rebounded back and forth across the road, making what was already an impassable obstacle markedly more so.

"Sinead, you two, catch that wee bastard," Logan instructed. "Tyler, you're with me."

"What are we going to do, boss?" the DC asked again.

"Run, Tyler," Logan said. "We're going to run."

Logan shrugged off his coat and tossed it onto the bonnet of the BMW. With a grunt, he vaulted the fence on the left. Then, without bothering to check if Tyler was following, he set his sights on the top of the tent, and he ran.

Constable Dave Davidson was facing down a bowl of something that looked like semi-digested twigs, with a level of enthusiasm usually reserved for people who've just been diagnosed with a terminal illness.

André Douville sat cross-legged on the floor beside him, egging him on, and assuring him that the plate full of misery was, "Really good stuff," as well as being meat, gluten, and dairy-free.

"And there's definitely no bacon rolls, or chips, or anything?" Dave asked, prodding something that he was convinced was a stick insect with the prong of a fork. To his relief, it didn't get up and walk away. Although, if it had, it would've been one less thing in the bowl to worry about.

"It's nutritious," André continued. He gestured around at his small army of acolytes, who were half-heartedly getting stuck into their portions. "And look, the others enjoy it."

Dave felt that this was a generous description of how the others appeared to feel about their lunch. If any of them were genuinely enjoying the food (another generous description, he thought), then they hadn't bothered to let their faces know.

It had been quite a day so far, and it wasn't even half done. Between the sunburn and the nettle cream, his arse was red raw and felt like it was hanging in tatters. That was the main issue he had with the day so far, although the food was rapidly gaining ground.

He was just going to suggest he drive to the shop to pick up some frozen pizzas, when the flap of the dining tent flew open, and a wheezing, red-faced DCI Logan stumbled in.

"Oh, thank fuck for that!" both men ejected at precisely the same moment, but before either of them could say any more, André Douville rose from where he'd been sitting cross-legged on the floor, and held up a spoon like it was some magical trinket.

"Halt! You have entered a sacred eating space," he proclaimed, and half a dozen of his weirdo punters all raised their own cutlery in what was presumably a show of support. "This is a protected area, and I will not—"

"I suggest you shut your mouth, Mr Dorlin," Logan told him, and the mention of his real name made the charlatan physically flinch. "Unless you want me to let slip about your convictions for fraud, and all those sexual harassment complaints you've got on your record."

The man masquerading as André Douville lowered his spoon. His gaze flitted around the tent to where his acolytes all sat on rugs, half-heartedly munching through their own stick piles.

"I... I don't know what you're talking about," he said, although the shake of his voice told Logan otherwise. It told a few of his more switched-on acolytes the same, as they turned, frowning, to face their leader.

"Aye, you do, Andrew," Logan said. "You spoken to Bernie yet, by the way? He contacted you from beyond the grave, has he?"

André saw his opportunity to impress the shower of gullible bastards gathered around him. "He has, actually. Yes. He told me that—"

"I'm going to stop you there. He's no' deid," Logan said.

The man in the Jesus robes blinked. "What?"

"Bernie the Beacon. He isn't dead, Andrew. So fuck knows who you've been chatting to, but it's no' him." Logan clicked his fingers at Dave to draw his attention, then pointed to André's head. "Wig," he announced, and Dave immediately grasped his meaning.

He also grasped the hair of the man beside him, and pulled it off with *shrrrik* of Velcro that left André's bald head exposed for all the world to see.

Gasps went around the tent. Cutlery *clanked* into bowls of inedible not-quite-food.

"You're a liar and a conman, Mr Dorlin," Logan said. "I suggest you give these good people their money back." He beckoned to Dave. "You, with me."

Dave twirled the wig around on his fingertip, then launched it across the room. It landed in the lap of a female acolyte, who leapt to her feet, screaming, like she'd just been attacked by a rabid rat.

"Thought you'd never ask!" Dave laughed, wheeling himself across the uneven tent floor.

He stopped just before following Logan out through the flap, and looked back over his shoulder at what was now quite a disgruntled looking group of individuals.

"Oh, and by the way, sunning your arsehole?" he announced. "That's not normal!"

He followed Logan out through the flap, and was met by a confused look from the DCI.

"Don't ask," he said, shifting uncomfortably in his chair. He nodded when he saw DC Neish bent over outside, desperately trying to catch his breath. "Alright, Tyler?"

"Grand, aye. I'm... He's just... *Jesus*. He's just got longer legs."

"Your car, Constable," Logan said.

"What about it?"

Logan held out a hand for the keys. "We're going to need to borrow it."

Dave considered the outstretched hand as he reached into his pocket.

"I've got a better idea," he said. He produced the keys and twirled them around his finger. "You point the way, and leave the driving to me."

They had just skidded left out of the field when Dave slammed on the anchors and they stopped just short of running over an elderly woman standing in the middle of the road. Kathryn Chegwin squinted in through the front windscreen, eyeing the men suspiciously, with her shotgun draped across her forearm.

"Christ, what does she want?" Logan muttered. He wound down the window—a manual process that he found quite awkward, given his size in comparison to the interior of Dave's Peugeot 208—and leaned his head out. "Out of the bloody road you!"

"Oh, it's you," Kathryn said. "I thought I heard some commotion, right enough. Thought, *'Oh ho, what's this now?'* I thought. 'Who's this lot, playing silly buggers?' I should've known you'd be behind it."

"Just move!" Logan barked. "Get out of the way, we're in a hurry here!"

"Alright, alright, keep your fucking hair on," Kathryn grumbled, shuffling out of the car's path.

Dave started to power the Peugeot forward, but a shout from Logan made him brake hard again. The DCI's window was level with the woman now standing on the embankment. He pointed to the shotgun, then made a beckoning motion with a finger. "Give me that."

"I beg your bloody pardon!" Kathryn said with a gasp. "I ain't handing Barbara here over to no one. No way, no how. Not on your fucking Nelly!"

"Barbara?" Tyler mumbled from the back seat. "Who calls a gun Barbara?"

Logan wasn't taking no for an answer. He wound down his window the rest of the way, and fixed the old woman with his most polis-like glare. "I'm confiscating that firearm. Hand it over, or I'll place you under arrest."

Kathryn wrestled with her options for a moment, then thrust the shotgun through the open window, barrels first.

"Jesus! Point it the other way!" Logan snapped.

"Then it'll be pointing at me, won't it? And you can get that idea right out of your fucking head, right now. You want it, take it. Go on."

Logan grabbed the shotgun by the barrels, yanked it from the old woman's grip, then passed it back to a jittery Tyler.

"Thanks. You can have it back later," Logan said. He reached forward to tap the dashboard to indicate that Dave should drive on, but the constable was one step ahead, and both detectives were thrown back into their seats as he accelerated them up the incline and past Kathryn Chegwin's cottage.

"How quickly can you get us to the lighthouse?" Logan asked, clutching the handle above the door so tightly the plastic groaned in complaint.

"Dunno," Dave admitted. He grinned, and dropped down a gear. "But let's find out."

The answer to Logan's question, it turned out, was somewhere between 'very fast' and 'too fast,' and both detectives arrived at the lighthouse as changed men. And, in Tyler's case, with some light Post Traumatic Stress Disorder.

There was one other car in the car park. A woman in her thirties was playing down at a rock pool with two kids under five. They all looked up when the Peugeot came screeching to a halt, then turned their attention back to the pool they were prodding around in.

"Tyler, get that lot out of here," Logan instructed. "I

want them in their car and on the road in the next two minutes."

"On it, boss," Tyler said, throwing open the door and all-but falling out of the vehicle.

He wasted a moment savouring the feeling of standing still, then he set off on a lumbering, shaky-legged run down towards the rocks.

"You alright getting into the cafe there?" Logan asked Dave, who responded with a nod. "Good. Check in with them, see if they've seen anyone going in or out of the lighthouse since it was shut."

"What about you? Where are you going?" Dave asked.

Logan reached into the back and took the shotgun from where Tyler had propped it up in one of the rear footwells. His gaze went to the tower of the lighthouse, standing proud against the sky.

"There," he said. "I'm going there."

CHAPTER THIRTY-SIX

LOGAN PACED AROUND the building at the base of the lighthouse, peeking in the windows and searching the gloom inside for any signs of movement.

Nothing.

The builders were using the room for storage, it seemed, and while it was possible that Bernie and the girl were tucked away in there somewhere, it would've been a big risk. There were a lot of windows, and not a lot of hiding places, so staying hidden would've taken effort.

Much better to keep her somewhere that nobody could just wander up to and have a peek inside.

His gaze, once again, crept upwards to the tower of the lighthouse itself.

The door at the base was locked. Logan put a shoulder to it, but it was a half-hearted attempt. The door was thick and heavy. No way that bloody thing was shifting without a battering ram, or...

He considered the shotgun he was carrying, shrugged, and took aim at the lock. Jamming the butt of the gun against his shoulder, he gritted his teeth, screwed his eyes half-shut, and—

"Boss!" Tyler's voice called to him from across the car park. The DC ran ahead of Dave Davidson, holding up something that glinted in the midday sun. "Keys, boss! I've got keys!"

Once he was close enough, he tossed the bunch to Logan, who snatched them from the air. There were a dozen or more keys on the ring, of all shapes, sizes, and makes. Logan picked the most likely candidate, then thrust the shotgun into Tyler's arms just as the DC stumbled to a stop.

"What am I meant to do with this?" Tyler asked, fumbling with the weapon.

"Just hang onto it," Logan instructed, trying the first key. It didn't fit, so he moved on to the next.

"Why'd you even take it, boss?"

"I don't know," Logan admitted. "Seemed like a good idea at the time."

He tried another key that didn't fit the lock, and pressed on again. The sound of an engine drew his attention for a moment, and he gave a satisfied little grunt when the woman and her kids pulled out of the car park.

"Maybe I should go put it back in the car," Tyler suggested. He was holding the gun like it was a deadly snake that might wrap itself around his throat at any moment. "I don't want to accidentally shoot anyone."

"Well, then don't point it at anyone, or pull the trigger," Logan suggested, then a triumphant, "Aha!" followed the click of the key turning in the lock. "Right, wait here. Eyes and ears peeled. If I shout, you come running."

"With or without the gun?"

"With."

Tyler bit his lip. "Should I be running with a gun? Is that not asking for trouble?"

"Just bloody..." Logan sighed, shook his head, then tried again. "Just come if I shout," he said, then he edged open the door and stepped into the base of the lighthouse.

Had he been going for stealth, then that was right out the window, thanks to the shrill creaking of the door's hinges, aged by the rain and the salty sea air.

It was a long way to the top, but anyone up there would know someone was coming, so Logan decided it was best to get ahead of the situation and announce his presence.

"Mr Rigg. It's Detective Chief Inspector Jack Logan of Police Scotland Major Investigations Team," he shouted, his voice booming up the steps and echoing around inside the narrow stone tube. "I must warn you that I have armed officers standing by with me, ready to move in."

He shot a look back over his shoulder to where Tyler was holding the shotgun like it was smeared in human excrement, and hoped that Bernie—if he was up there—didn't call his bluff.

"I'm coming up, Mr Rigg. Stay calm, and do not be alarmed."

"Be careful, boss," Tyler whispered.

Logan eyed the gun once again, briefly considered taking it with him, then decided against it. "Aye, you too."

The climb started well enough. The first few steps of the spiral staircase passed uneventfully. The next thirty to forty were harder going.

By the time he'd passed a hundred or so, Logan's thighs and calves were burning, his breath squeaked in and out like a chronic asthmatic in the grip of a panic attack, and the sweat was coming off him in buckets.

"Christ Almighty," he wheezed. Between the exertion and the spiral effect, his head was spinning, and there was still plenty of climb left to do.

He spent a few seconds getting his breathing under control, then called up again. "Mr Rigg? Bernie. Can you hear me? I need you to respond if you can hear me."

Only the echo of his own voice answered him. He swore quietly but passionately, then set off again, his big feet slapping on each step as he heaved himself onwards and upwards.

A few steps from the top, the staircase became a steep ladder that led up to the lamp that crowned the tower's top.

Logan could hear nothing but the wind swirling around outside, rattling the panes of glass in their frames.

Well, that and his own body fighting for oxygen and, if he listened closely enough, praying for a swift and merciful death.

Even before he'd popped his head up through the hatch, he knew there was nobody up there. And, sure enough, when he dragged his gasping, sweating carcass up those final few steps, he found the circular lamp area empty.

Well, almost. A small pile of empty beer cans, *Coke* bottles, sandwich wrappers, and crisp bags had been pushed to one side. A couple of the bottles were filled with an amber liquid. Piss, presumably. Someone had been here, and they'd dug in for the long haul.

He felt the bottle, and could detect just a lingering hint of warmth in the plastic. Recent, then. Within the last hour, maybe.

A door led out onto a circular balcony that ran around the top of the lighthouse. Logan stepped out and was accosted by the wind. He hadn't noticed it down at ground level, but up here, fully exposed, it blew in off the water and rose up from the jagged shoreline below, dragging waves so they crashed against the rocks.

"Where are you, you bastard?" Logan said, but the words were snatched from his lips even as they formed in the air.

He looked back at the debris stashed on the other side of the glass. He'd been here recently, and for a while, too. And now, he wasn't. Just before they'd arrived, he'd left.

Hell of a coincidence.

Logan gazed out at the islands nestled on the horizon, shafts of sunlight cutting through the clouds like the fingers of God. On another day, at another time, he could stand up there for hours, just savouring that view.

Not today, though. Not now.

He had just turned away when he caught a glimpse of movement down beside the big red foghorn that stood on the shore. It was attached to the top of a white stone box about the size of a large shed, and for a moment, Logan had thought he'd seen something darting out of sight around the front, where it faced the water.

Keeping watch for any other sign of movement, he reached into his pocket and took out his phone to call Tyler, then cursed when he saw the 'No Signal' warning.

Feeling for the door, he backed up as far as he could go while keeping the foghorn in sight. Then, when he couldn't watch it any longer, he all-but jumped down the ladder and launched himself down the spiralling staircase towards the ground far below.

Tyler almost dropped the shotgun when Logan came barrelling out through the door of the lighthouse, panting and red of face.

"Alright, boss?" he asked, but the question bounced off Logan's broad back as the DCI set off around the lighthouse building in an unsteady, lumbering jog.

Tyler followed Logan as he slowed, then went creeping over to the foghorn building and pressed himself in against the side. The DCI beckoned for the younger officer to follow, but placed a finger to his lips, urging him to keep quiet.

Here, so close to the water, the sound of the wind had been replaced by the thunder of the waves on the rocks as the tide raged against the shore.

Logan inched his way to the front of the building, hidden by the shadow of the foghorn on the roof. He peeked around the corner, and saw a glass and metal frontage with its windows obscured by newspaper on the inside. A hand-written sign taped to the front announced that the building was currently off-limits to visitors.

This did not, Logan decided, apply to him.

"Mr Rigg, this is the police. We're coming in," he announced. Then, without waiting for a response, he pulled the door open and found an empty room. A museum of some sort, by the looks of it. But no Bernie the Beacon. No Jameelah Oboko.

"Boss!"

The urgency in Tyler's voice spun Logan around. There, half-hidden by a jagged outcrop along the shore, a bearded man in tattered clothing was dragging a hooded female figure along by the arm.

"Shite!" Logan spat, then he and Tyler both set off running again.

Bernie saw them coming, and searched frantically for a way to escape. Finding no safe passage between the rocks, he pushed Jameelah towards the edge, keeping a hold of her as she stumbled closer to the drop into the crashing water below.

"Stay where you are!" Bernie roared, eyeballing the approaching detectives.

Momentum carried Logan on a few paces before he managed to stop. A second or two later, Tyler thudded against his back, muttered an apology, then stepped forward so they were standing side by side.

Spotting the gun, Bernie tucked himself in behind Jameelah. She was alive, and apparently unhurt. She wasn't making any sound, though. None that they could hear above the waves, at least.

"Let her go, Alan," Logan said. "It is Alan, isn't it? We know all about you, Mr Rigg. We know why you're doing this."

"You have *no idea* why I'm doing this!" the other man seethed. He pointed to Tyler. "Unload the shotgun and throw it to me."

Tyler looked down at the gun he was holding. "What?"

Alan Rigg gave the girl a shake, drawing a scream that sounded hoarse and exhausted. "Unload the fucking shotgun and throw it to me!"

"I don't know how to unload it!" Tyler yelped. Then, in a panic, he hurled the gun into the water and held his hands up like he was surrendering. "I threw it in the sea!"

"Why'd you throw it in the sea? I didn't tell you to throw it in the fucking sea!" Alan screeched.

"I don't know, I just panicked!" Tyler said.

This wasn't entirely true. Better for the weapon to be

underwater than in enemy hands. At least, that was the excuse he planned to give Logan should it come up in conversation later.

"You'd better start doing as I say, or it's this little bitch who'll end up in the sea!" Alan warned, and he gave her another shake that almost sent her tumbling over the edge.

Bernie the Beacon, Alan Rigg, call him what you liked, was not much to write home about physically. He was probably average height, but with a scrawny build and weathered features. His hair and beard were greying and unkempt.

His clothes were little more than rags, and he wore plastic carrier bags inside his tatty boots to keep his feet dry. Logan knew that last part because he could see the tops of the bag taped to the man's trousers, just below his knees.

The outer appearance matched what Logan knew of the man's mind. It was not a stretch of the imagination to think that this was someone who believed he was being tormented by lizard people, or tested on by shady government agencies. This was a man who had side-stepped out of both society and reality some time ago, and currently had no intentions of stepping back into either.

This was a dangerous man with nothing left to lose.

"We know what happened to your daughter, Alan," Logan told him.

"Shut up."

"I'm sorry for your loss."

"Shut up!"

"But none of that is Jameelah's fault," Logan continued. "None of what happened is down to her."

"He killed my little girl! Why should he get to keep his?! How is that fair?"

"Fair? It's not. God. No, nothing's fair about any of this,

Alan," Logan replied. "Nothing's fair about losing a child. Nothing's fair about losing any loved one. But... your daughter?"

He shook his head, and risked a tiny step closer. They were maybe twenty feet apart. No chance either Logan or Tyler could rush in fast enough to catch her before she fell.

"I've got a daughter. She's older now. Married. But the thought of something happening to her? The thought of losing her? No. No, that would not feel fair," he agreed. "But just because something isn't fair, doesn't mean it's some other bugger's fault, Alan."

"It was his fault. It was all his fault!" Alan spat. His eyes searched the sky, like they were being watched. "And them! His fault, and theirs!"

"We spoke to your wife, Alan. She told us what happened. To Lucy. How she got sick. How you did everything you could."

"They *made* her sick!"

"They didn't, Alan," Logan said. "Nobody made her sick. Not on purpose. It was just... It was tragic, and it was unfair, and I can't imagine how terrible it must've been. But it was nobody's fault. And it certainly wasn't Jameelah's. Hurting her, killing her..." Logan shook his head. "What would she say, Alan? What would Lucy say if she knew what you were doing?"

The words came out of him like some sort of primal roar. "Don't you say that! Don't you say her name! You didn't know her! You don't know!"

"You're right, I don't know her. But you did. You do. So tell me, is this the legacy she'd want?" Logan pressed. He chanced another step forward. Alan's eyes darted to the detective's feet, but he said nothing. "Is this how Lucy would choose to be remembered, if she could? As the catalyst for an innocent girl's death? I bet she never hurt a fly in her life, did she?"

Alan's head shook. A tear cut through the grime on one cheek. "No. She was... she was kind. She was kind, and she was funny, and she was beautiful." He sniffed like he could draw his grief back into him. His face darkened. "And she's gone. He took her. My little girl, he took her away. So I'm going to take his away. I'm going to kill his daughter, like he killed mine."

"But I don't think you are, Alan," Logan told him. Another step. Closer. "I think, if you were going to do that, you'd have done it by now. I think you know that you shouldn't. That you can't. That you *won't* do it. You know Jameelah has done nothing to you, Alan. You know how disappointed Lucy would be in you if you destroyed her memory like this. That's why you haven't hurt her yet. And that's why you won't do it now."

He chanced three steps in a row. Tyler hadn't moved, and so was several paces back now. Alan Rigg was no longer looking Logan in the eye and was fixated on his feet, instead. He hadn't objected to the detective coming closer, but then he was still safely out of reach. Still too far away.

There was no way Logan would reach Jameelah in time if Alan decided to give her a push. No way he could stop her smashing onto the rocks and tumbling into the foaming water below. One shove, and she was gone.

"Let me take her, Alan. We can talk. Man to man, father to father. This is not a complete disaster yet, Alan. There are a lot of happy endings still available to us here."

Alan flinched, like he'd been struck. "It is. It's too late. I already did it. I already killed him."

Logan nodded, just once. "The man in the tent. Who was he?"

"He was me," Alan said, his movements were becoming jerky, his voice a hiss barely audible above the wind and the waves. "And I'm him. Or was going to be. Because, you'd figure it out. Someone. Maybe not you. But someone would figure out what had happened. Why I'd done it. But, if I was dead, then I was dead, and you wouldn't look for me. So I found someone in Glasgow that nobody would miss, and I swapped. Me for him. Him for me. He would be me, and I would be him. You see?"

"Not really," Logan admitted. "You're saying the man in the tent we found. The body. You brought someone up here, and you killed them so we'd think it was you?"

"And now I'm him. I'm nobody," Alan concluded. "I can go sit on the street like him. People will pass me by and not even notice. Not even look. They won't see me sitting there. They won't know what I've done, or why I've done it."

"Except, now we do know, Alan," Logan pointed out. "We know everything, so you can't disappear anymore. You can't run away and pretend you didn't do this. All you can do is try to fix what you still can. Do what's right, Alan. For Lucy's sake. Don't be someone else, be you. Be her dad."

For a moment—but just that, and no longer—it looked like he was buying it. It looked like he might let the girl go.

And then, as if a switch had been flicked, his expression changed. His grip tightened, and his eyes blazed with fury.

"You're them, aren't you? You're like the rest of them. You're fucking lizards, both of you!"

Jameelah cried out in fright as he shoved her right to the edge. Her foot slipped, and her hands, which were bound in front of her, grasped at Alan's ragged clothing, searching for something to hold onto.

"Alan, don't do this!" Logan barked. "Please. Let's keep talking. Let's—"

"Shut up! Stop talking! I don't listen to lizards! I don't let lizards tell me what to do!"

Tyler stepped forward before Logan could respond. "Wait, you're right! You're right!" he cried. Logan and Alan Rigg both turned to him, eyes narrowed. Tyler swallowed, and shuffled past the DCI, hands still raised in surrender. "We're lizards. Under this."

Alan's mouth fell open, then snapped shut again, his jaw clenching until the veins on the side of his head looked like they might go pop.

"I knew it," he whispered. "They said it was in my head, but I knew it."

"I can prove it," Tyler said. "I can show you."

"What the fuck do you think you're doing?" Logan whispered, but Tyler took another half-step onwards, leaving him behind.

"You can feel the scales. Under my skin," he said, pulling up his shirt sleeve to reveal the underside of his bare forearm. "You can feel them for yourself. I'll give you my phone. You can take pictures. You can finally prove it. You can finally prove you've been right all this time."

Alan was focused on nothing else now but Tyler's arm. His face twitched, like each individual muscle was alive and engaged in some sort of complicated dance that none of them had thought to rehearse.

"What does it... What's it like?" he asked. "What does it feel like?"

"It's... I can't really explain. It feels normal to us," Tyler said. He moved closer. Twelve feet now. Ten. "But you can feel it. See what you think. And we'll tell you everything."

Alan's lips moved, repeating that last word in silence.

"Anything you want to know, we'll tell you. About the Earth. About the government. About the Royal Family. Everything we've done, we'll tell you."

Nine feet.

Eight.

The intrigue and uncertainty that had started to fog over Alan's gaze lifted in the blink of an eye. His head snapped up, meeting Tyler's gaze. His lips drew back, becoming a snarl.

"You're lying!" he hissed.

And with that, he pushed.

CHAPTER THIRTY-SEVEN

TYLER SPRANG FORWARDS, grabbing for the girl's outstretched arms. His fingers brushed against her, nails scraping white lines up the dark skin of her forearm, and then he found purchase on the rope around her wrists just as she plunged over the edge towards the rocks below.

"Shit, shit, shit!" Tyler cried, her momentum pulling him, dragging him over. He held on, looking down at her, and at the thunderous waves swirling and crashing impatiently below.

The world lurched. His centre of balance shifted inexorably forward. There was nothing he could do but go down with her, take the fall, take the hits, try to be alive enough at the bottom to keep her head above water. To keep her from drowning in the—

A hand caught him by the back of the trousers, jerking him away from the edge and setting his recovery from his testicular cancer operation back by at least a fortnight.

"I've got you, son," Logan announced, planting his feet and becoming something solid and immovable. "Hold on."

Anchored by the DCI, Tyler threw out his other hand and grabbed Jameelah's arm. She had gone limp soon after falling, and while this made her a dead weight, at least she wasn't wriggling around in his grip.

"Got her!" Tyler announced.

With a grunt, Logan pulled, dragging both of them back up onto solid ground.

"Cheers, boss. Don't think I've ever been more grateful to have my bollocks jammed up my own arse," Tyler wheezed. He lay the motionless Jameelah down on the ground, and started working at the string holding the hood in place.

"You got her?" Logan asked, already turning to where Alan Rigg was clambering up the steep embankment towards the lighthouse.

"Got her, boss. Go!"

Logan charged. That was the best description for it. It wasn't a run. It wasn't a dash. It was the charge of the fucking Light Brigade. He wasn't a man giving chase, he was an oncoming storm.

He reached the embankment, dug his hands into the soil and the grass, and kicked upwards, scrambling and heaving his way towards the top.

As he grabbed for the top, a boot came down, a plastic bag crinkling inside it. Pain ignited in Logan's hand, then in his cheek when a dropped rock cracked him just below his eye socket.

His fingers lost their grip. He spat out a string of obscenities as he slid down the embankment, and Alan Rigg—Bernie the Beacon—disappeared from sight.

Constable Dave Davidson was sitting back in his car, twiddling his thumbs and minding his own business, when he saw the straggly-haired man come racing up from the shore like the devil himself was at his heels.

Dave wasn't entirely sure that this was the suspect they'd come to apprehend, but he felt that, given the state of him, the speed at which he was running, and the rictus of terror on his face, there was at least a good chance.

That was why he disengaged the handbrake and lurched the Peugeot into reverse, just as the man who was now running through the car park entered the space directly behind the car. There was a solid-sounding *thunk*, and quite a high-pitched cry. Something broke, and not something, Dave thought, that could be fixed at a garage.

Sure enough, the cry of shock became a squeal of pain. Dave checked his wing mirror, and watched as the man who had been running very quickly away from the scene now hopped quite slowly, both arms thrown out for balance, and one leg flapping unpleasantly.

He managed half a dozen good hops, but gravity was a fickle mistress, and on the seventh hop, he lost his balance, toppled to the ground, and lay there screaming at the top of his lungs.

Dave faced front in time to see Logan come clambering up the embankment, his shirt stained brown with mud, his face red with rage and exertion.

Winding down his window, the constable stuck his head out, then jabbed a thumb in the direction of the screaming man behind the car.

"Is that the guy?" he called. Then, when Logan nodded, he let out a sigh of relief. "Well, thank fuck for that."

It was a little less than ten minutes later when they heard the first *thrumming* of the rotor blades. The sound coincided almost to the second with the wailing of sirens from somewhere out east.

The helicopter, unsurprisingly, arrived first. It roared overhead, downdraught sending dust and debris swirling across the car park. Then, once the pilot concluded that there was no safe landing spot available, it pulled up and weaved a figure of eight that took it in to land in a field a little way back along the road.

By the time it had touched down, the polis 4x4 was howling to a stop, the piercing chirps of its siren grinding Logan's teeth together.

"Shut that bloody thing off," he instructed. Then, he sighed with relief when the Uniforms obeyed and cut the siren dead.

One racket was replaced almost immediately by another, though, when his BMW pulled in off the road with Taggart barking excitedly from the partially open back window.

"It's a puppy."

Logan looked down at Jameelah, who was standing in close beside him like she was trying to make herself invisible to the still-downed Alan Rigg. The man formerly known as Bernie the Beacon was having his injuries tended to by Tyler and Dave. Logan almost felt for the bastard. Murderer and kidnapper he may be, but did anyone deserve those two handling their medical care?

Actually, aye. Aye, he did.

Jameelah was a striking wee lassie, with eyes so big and wide she looked like she'd stepped out of a Japanese cartoon.

Her frizzy hair was matted and tangled, and she pulled and fiddled nervously with it, like she was trying to bring it back to life.

Her wrists were raw where the rope had been, her clothes were dirty, and she'd already gone through a big bottle of water and two whole scones, but she didn't seem badly hurt. Not on the outside, anyway. Mentally, there was no saying what lay ahead for the girl.

"That's Taggart," Logan said. "You want to go see him?"

Jameelah wiped her eyes on the blanket Logan had secured for her from the wee cafe and shop. She nodded, so Logan took her hand and led her over to where Taggart was currently throttling himself trying to squeeze through the window.

"Alright, sir?" Sinead asked. She looked over to where Tyler and Dave were poking at the prisoner, then smiled at Jameelah and gave a little wave. "Hiya. I'm Sinead."

"No time for that, Detective Constable," Logan said. "We've got a dog to play with."

Jameelah reached up to pat the daft mutt, then yelped and drew back her hand when Taggart's tongue flopped across her fingers.

"He licked me!" she said, half shocked, half delighted. "He licked my hand!"

"That means he likes you," Logan told her. "You want to sit in there with him?"

Jameelah laughed. It was a small and nervous thing, but given everything she'd been through, it chimed like a miracle. "Can I?" she asked.

Sinead quietly cleared her throat. "Forensic evidence, sir," she said, shooting a deliberate look at the girl.

Logan winced. She had a point. Taggart would no doubt

compromise a lot of the forensic evidence on the girl's clothes. They didn't know for sure yet what had happened to her. Aye, they had his confession, but that might not be the whole of it. Whatever the bastard had done to her—whatever evil he had inflicted—Logan was determined he was going to pay for it all.

"Tell you what," he said, giving the girl's hand a squeeze. "He's a bit too excited right now. We'll get you back to the station in the police car, get you cleaned up and let your mum and dad know you're safe, then you can play with him for as long as you like, OK?"

Taggart gave a *woof* to indicate he was happy with this plan, which drew another nervous giggle from Jameelah. "OK," she said. She let herself be escorted to the police vehicle, and she didn't once take her eyes off the dog with his big flapping tongue.

"You got them, then," Sinead said, once Logan had returned to the BMW.

"Aye. Thanks in a big part to Tyler," Logan said.

"Oh, I find that very hard to believe, sir," Sinead replied.

"Aye. I probably imagined it," Logan agreed.

They stood watching Tyler and Dave either tending to or tormenting Alan Rigg. It was hard to tell from there. Either way, he didn't seem to be particularly enjoying it.

"He'll need the hospital," Logan said.

"Will we take him in the helicopter?"

Logan started to nod, then shook his head. "Actually, no. Fuck him. We'll let Dave drive him along that road, and put Tyler in the back with him. That'll teach the bastard."

Sinead chuckled. "You're a cruel man, sir."

"I have my moments," Logan confessed. "I want you to go in the helicopter with Jameelah. Get her to hospital in

Fort William. She'll need checking over." He side-eyed her. "Thoroughly. We don't know what happened."

Sinead's laughter was now notable by its absence. "Got it, sir," she said.

"Tell her the dog's going to be waiting to play with her when she's done."

The DC nodded. "Will do." She started for the 4x4, then turned so she was walking backwards. "What about you, sir? You heading back to Strontian?"

"I am," Logan confirmed. He looked over to the sobbing Alan Rigg, then up at the lighthouse standing tall above them all. "There's just something I have to do first."

She was waiting for him by the door when he arrived, dressed in a stern black frock with sensible shoes and a coat in case it should rain. She looked smaller than before. Less intimidating. Although, that may just have been the lack of shotgun.

Alan had known they were coming. He'd left with just minutes to spare.

Out here, the sirens carried for miles. Long enough for her to drive the sheep out of the field. To funnel them between the fences, blocking the way.

She'd been standing in the road when they'd got to Dave's car. She'd delayed them, just for one more moment. Just to buy him some extra time.

It had to be her who had warned him. It could *only* have been her. Logan had figured that out, but there was something he didn't know.

"Why?" he asked.

"Why? I'll tell you why. Because it's a fucking travesty what they did to that little girl of his. It's a bloody outrage, and no mistake. Poor little precious lamb that she was."

"Your granddaughter," Logan said.

It was a deductive leap into the abyss, but also the only way this made sense. Why would this woman help a relative stranger and local headcase in his attempt to murder a child? How would she get mixed up in such a plot? What would she possibly have to gain?

Besides, someone had helped tie both the then Bernie the Beacon's arms to the Westerly Wellness gate. Someone had picked him up after his protest and driven him 'out towards the lighthouse.'

Or, to put it another way, out towards Kathryn Chegwin's house.

It was a stretch, yes. But there was very little he'd been more certain of in his life.

There wasn't much reaction to the statement from the woman on the front step, aside from a slight thinning of the lips and a rolling back of the shoulders. Nothing to confirm Logan's suspicions, but no denials, either.

"Alan's your son, isn't he?" Logan pressed. "That's why he came here. His ex-wife mentioned that you were going to move when they first started living together. You moved here. That's what brought him up this way. You. And you've been plotting together this whole time. Pretending not to know each other. Pretending that you weren't mother and son. And for what? So you could steal a wee girl? So you could kill her?"

"It weren't nothing personal. Not on the little 'un. Weren't her fault. It was her father who needed punishing. It was him who couldn't be let to get away with what he'd done.

That weren't right. Not one bit of it. And we weren't going to kill her, neither. Of course not. We were just going to give him a scare, is all. Maybe get him to confess to what he'd done."

"She almost died," Logan said. "He tried to throw her into the bloody water."

Kathryn gave a shake of her head. Firm. Adamant. "No. You're wrong."

"I assure you I am not," Logan said. "And what about the body? The homeless guy?"

"I don't know anything about that," the woman insisted.

"Who did that? You or Alan?"

"Neither. I don't know what you're on about. That weren't us."

"You burned a man alive!" Logan roared.

Kathryn roared right back. "He wasn't alive! He was already..."

Her voice dried up as she realised what she'd said. She started to say something else, to take it back, to change her tune.

But then, with a sniff, she smoothed down her coat, and picked up a small suitcase that sat on the step beside her.

She locked the door. Checked it. Placed a hand on the old wood and kept it pressed there for a moment, like she was calming some skittish animal.

"Right, then," she said. She fixed her gaze ahead at the BMW standing at the end of her path. "No use in us standing around here all day. Let's get off before the rain comes in."

Logan looked up at the mostly blue sky. The earlier cloud had all but burned away.

"You think it's going to rain?" he asked, escorting the woman up the path towards the waiting car.

"It's never far away," Kathryn said.

Logan motioned to Taggart to stay where he was in the back. "No," he said, opening the front passenger door for Kathryn. "No, I don't suppose it is."

CHAPTER THIRTY-EIGHT

THINGS FELL into place quite quickly over the next few hours. The team had two confessions to work with, plus a statement from Jameelah. Add in Logan and Tyler's own eyewitness accounts, and a successful prosecution was looking like a certainty.

There hadn't been a lot of forensic evidence to salvage from the girl. There had been no sexual assault. Logan had felt a tingling at the back of his eyeballs when he'd been given that news, but had gritted his teeth and given just a single nod of relieved acknowledgement.

Her parents had arrived at Fort William in a remarkably short space of time, the team down south having sorted a helicopter to bring them straight up.

DCI Grimm, the SIO on Jameelah's case, had accompanied them. His facial scars had been noticeable during his telly appearances, but they were considerably more prominent in the flesh, and Tyler had let out an involuntary, "Fuck!" at the sight of him, before scurrying off and trying to make himself look busy.

"Detective Chief Inspector," Logan said, dipping his head in acknowledgement of the other man.

DCI Grimm mirrored the gesture. "Detective Chief Inspector."

And that was the end of that conversation.

There would, no doubt, be some wrangling in the coming days about where Alan and his mother were to be prosecuted, but that was a worry for another time. For now, all that mattered was that the girl was safe in the arms of her parents.

They hugged each other. They sobbed. They laughed. They shivered and shook, their bodies reacting to the joy, and the relief, and the terror, and the dread that was all wrapped up in knots around them.

Jameelah had spent the hour before the helicopter's arrival out in the car park, throwing a tennis ball for the dog. Taggart, who Dave Davidson had always insisted was 'thick as mince,' had failed to grasp the point of the game, and it had been Jameelah herself who had done much of the fetching, with the dog trotting happily along at her heels.

Still, they'd both seemed to enjoy themselves. Despite what she'd been through, playing with the dog seemed to melt Jameelah's worries away.

And now, as Logan stood there, watching the girl with her parents and thinking of all the things she was going to have to face in the days and weeks to come, he knew what he had to do.

"Excuse me for a moment," he told Grimm, then he headed through to the canteen, where Ben and Hamza were getting stuck into bacon rolls from *JJ's* while Taggart sat staring hopefully up at them both.

"Alright, Jack?" Ben said, hurriedly swallowing. He shot

a guilty look at what was left of his roll. "We just... We didn't think you'd be ready for anything yet."

"We can go back and get you something later," Hamza added.

Logan reprimanded them by telling them they were a pair of selfish bastards, then scooped Taggart up into his arms. The dog panted happily, but didn't break eye contact with the bacon butties.

"Everything OK, sir?" Hamza asked.

Logan gave the dog's head a pat, then ruffled the fur beneath its chin.

"Aye, son," he said, then he turned to the door. "Everything's going to be just fine."

Shona Maguire plucked one of Logan's chips from his tray and dunked it in the tomato sauce. She tossed it in her mouth, then chewed and swallowed before speaking.

"And she said no?"

"Aye. Bloody cheek," Logan said. "Said thanks, but no thanks. She's got a cat. And she said she thought he looked a bit daft."

He threw a chip onto the floor, where Taggart instantly devoured it.

"So, you're stuck with him, then?"

"Looks like it, aye," Logan said. "Can't keep dragging the bugger around with me, though. I'll need to figure something out."

Shona smiled and pilfered another chip. "Well, you're pretty good at that sort of thing."

Logan frowned. "Looking after dugs?"

"Figuring stuff out," Shona said.

"Oh. Aye," Logan said. "Because I was going to say, I'm shite at looking after dugs."

"You're not the best, no," Shona agreed. "But figuring stuff out? You're top ten, easy. You're up there at the top of the league."

And he was, he supposed.

There were a couple of things he'd struggled with, but the interviews with Alan Rigg and Kathryn Chegwin—her maiden name, it turned out, which she'd gone back to a few years after her husband's death—had helped clarify.

The plan had been to burn the victim inside the caravan, destroying any clues to Alan's past and giving the police a body that they'd think was his. The victim, though, had other ideas, and when he'd figured out what Alan had in store for him, he'd done a runner, forcing Alan to kill him out in the open. He'd built the tent around him, planted the ring and the caravan key in the hope it would be used to identify him, then set the body alight.

Of course, at that point, he discovered that he was locked out of the caravan. He also needed the door to remain intact so the police could figure out that the key fit the lock.

Once he'd realised this, he had also concluded that he couldn't let himself be seen by anyone, or the police would know that the body wasn't his. So, he'd slunk off, planning to come back and take care of the caravan later, once he was believed to be dead.

He'd watched from the trees as Hamza and Tyler had gone inside, and thought he was too late. But, when Ally Bally and Dinky had turned up and the detectives had run off, he'd seen his chance. He hadn't seen Dinky leave with the briefcase. As far as he'd known, the fire had covered his tracks.

"How is she doing?" Shona asked. "The girl, I mean."

Logan leaned an arm across the back of the couch and blew out his cheeks. "Good question. She says she's fine, but... I don't know. What do you think?"

Shona looked down at the tray of chips, picked out a couple, and gave one to the dog. "I don't know," she said.

"No, I know. But... If you were to put yourself in her shoes. How do you think she'll be holding up? After everything she went through. Being taken and held like that."

"I mean... God. I don't know," Shona said. Her voice sounded younger. Smaller, maybe. "I suppose... she'll be scared. About... everything. Or, not everything, but anything. Random stuff. For a while. Even when she knows it's stupid. She'll probably panic a lot. Overthink stuff. See things that aren't there sometimes. Jump at her own shadow."

Logan said nothing. Just listened for once. Shona was still fixated on the tray of chips. Even more so than Taggart, which was saying something.

"She'll probably doubt herself. She'll wonder if she was to blame somehow. She'll know she wasn't, of course. Deep down. But she'll have doubts. She'll think... if she'd done things differently. If she'd been quicker. If she'd been stronger." Shona ground the heels of her hands into her eyes and sniffed. "She'll need help. She might not say it. She might never say it. But she will. She'll need help, and she'll need support, and patience and understanding."

She smiled faintly, and met Logan's eye for a moment. "I suppose... I suppose that's what I think."

"She'll get it," Logan promised. "All of it. That's a promise."

Shona placed her hand on his much larger one, and their fingers locked together.

"I'm sure she appreciates that more than she can say."

"And I suppose... if she was really worried being at home..." His eyes darted around the room. "...she could always move in here."

Shona pulled a concerned face. "Sure, that's a bit creepy, she's not even twelve. Not sure her parents would—"

He kissed her, his fingers brushing back her hair, his hand warm against her cheek.

When it broke off, they rested their foreheads against one another, and Shona's voice cracked as she offered her response.

"Oh, go on, then."

Logan leaned back, eyes widening as he looked at her in surprise. Shona winced.

"Was I not supposed to say yes to that?" she asked. "Was that like one of those, 'I'll make a nice offer and hope she turns it down,' sort of things?"

"What? No. No. I just... I mean, I didn't expect you to say..." He shook his head, like he was annoyed at himself. "So, is this happening? Are we... shacking up together?"

"Such a romantic turn of phrase. You're like a poet," Shona said. "But, like, a really shite one." She shrugged, playing down her keenness. "I mean, if you want the company, or whatever, I could come and crash here. Or not. Or just, you know, whatever."

Logan smirked. "Such a romantic turn of phrase," he said, then he reached for another chip and found the tray empty.

Down on the floor, Taggart licked his chops and pointedly refused to make eye contact.

Logan had just begun to call the dog a thieving wee bastard, when his phone rang.

And then, a moment later, Shona's rang, too.

They both checked their screens. They both sighed.

"It's the office," they said, almost simultaneously.

Shona sprang to her feet, headed for the door, and pointed to her mobile. "I'll go take it in your bedroom." She stopped to think about this. "Or... I mean... our bedroom?"

"I said you could stay here, I didn't say you were getting to share my room," Logan replied.

He watched her laugh at that, and felt a surge of something that couldn't quite be explained in words.

Taggart jumped up onto the spot on the couch where she'd been, sniffed around, then flopped down against Logan's side. He stroked the dog's head as he answered the call.

"Benjamin. To what do I owe the pleasure?" he asked. He listened for a while, then once DI Forde had finished, he nodded. "Right, then," he said. He glanced through to his bedroom.

Their bedroom.

"We're on our way."

HAVE YOU TRIED...?

Northwind: A Robert Hoon Thriller

Discover a (slightly) softer side of Logan's old sparring partner, Bob Hoon, in the first in a series of new thrillers.

Made in the USA
Coppell, TX
15 December 2021

68721543R00225